PHANTASMA

KAYLIE SMITH

FOREVER

NEW YORK BOSTON

Forever
Hachette Book Group
1290 Avenue of the Americas, New York, NY 10104
read-forever.com

@readforeverpub

Originally published by Second Sky in 2024. An imprint of Storyfire Ltd., Carmelite House, 50 Victoria Embankment, London EC4Y0DZ, United Kingdom

First Grand Central Publishing Edition: September 2024

Forever is an imprint of Grand Central Publishing. The Forever name and logo are registered trademarks of Hachette Book Group, Inc.

The publisher is not responsible for websites (or their content) that are not owned by the publisher.

Forever books may be purchased in bulk for business, educational, or promotional use. For information, please contact your local bookseller or the Hachette Book Group Special Markets Department at special.markets@hbgusa.com.

Library of Congress Cataloging-in-Publication Data has been applied for.

ISBN: 978-1-5387-6925-6 (trade paperback)

Printed in the United States of America

LSC-H

Printing 6, 2024

*To those who've had to claw their way out of the dark and still
choose to be a light in this world—
I'm proud of you.*

CONTENT AND TRIGGER WARNINGS

This work contains explicit sexual content and scenes with elements of horror, as well as in-depth depictions of obsessive-compulsive tendencies, such as intrusive thoughts and compulsive tics. An in-depth list of content is available at the author's website:

www.KaylieSmithBooks.com

HIERARCHY OF PARANORMAL BEINGS

KING OF THE DEVILS
|
PRINCE OF THE DEVILS
|
DEVILS
|
DEMONS
OFFSPRING OF A DEVIL & ANOTHER
PARANORMAL BEING
|
WRAITHS
OFFSPRING OF A DEMON & ANOTHER PARANORMAL BEING

OTHER IMMORTAL PARANORMAL BEINGS

VAMPIRES
SHAPESHIFTERS
FAMILIARS
GHOSTS

MORTAL PARANORMAL BEINGS

NECROMANCERS
SEERS
WITCHES
SPECTERS

CLASSIFICATIONS OF GHOSTS

PHANTOMS
MOST CORPOREAL AND POWERFUL TYPE OF GHOST

POLTERGEISTS
TYPE OF GHOST ABLE TO POSSESS THE CORPOREAL VESSEL OF
ANOTHER BEING

APPARITIONS
MOST COMMON TYPE OF GHOST, COMPLETELY NON-CORPOREAL,
AND IF LEFT LINGERING ON ANY CORPOREAL PLANE TOO LONG
WITHOUT CROSSING OVER CAN DETERIORATE INTO A GHOUL

GHOULS
AN APPARITION THAT HAS DETERIORATED INTO A
NUMB, MINDLESS ENTITY

"What a phantasmagoria the mind is and meeting-place of dissemblables!"

—Virginia Woolf, *Orlando*

Prologue
Wicked

The Devil had a wicked mouth and a voice as smooth as bourbon.

"What is your decision?" he pressed as he trailed the tip of his index finger down one side of her throat, his lips mere centimeters from her racing pulse on the other.

"You tricked me," she whispered.

He laughed in response, his breath caressing her feverish skin.

He was so close that she could barely think.

Any coherent response to his question eluded her as another shot of adrenaline rushed through her veins, but the events leading up to this moment were burned into her mind with vivid clarity.

Three Nights Until Phantasma

1

MIDNIGHT SPELL

Moonlight glinted off the gilded locket clasped around the corpse's cold neck.

Ophelia Grimm unfastened her mother's heart-shaped necklace with fervor before stepping clear of the spell circle and reaching beneath her loose, umber curls to secure the familiar bauble around her own throat. A shiver ran down her spine when the chilled metal settled against her skin, and her flesh prickled beneath it.

Ophelia sank to her knees on the left of her mother's pale corpse, her sister, Genevieve, watching a few feet away in rapt silence. Tightening her grip around the silver blade in her hand, Ophelia pressed its sharp tip into the soft, ivory flesh of her inner arm. The slice was deep but precise, drawing enough blood that it dripped and pooled onto the ground before her and dyed the delicate white material of her nightgown a macabre shade of vermilion. The scent of iron and salt was pungent.

Ophelia let the blade clatter to the floor, and Genevieve flinched like a spooked hare. Ophelia ignored her sister's cringing as she struck a match, relishing the *hiss* of the igniting fire in the dead quiet of Grimm Manor. She reached toward the nearest candle and waited for its wick to flare to life, tapping the side of the waxy pillar while she counted each touch silently in her head.

One, two, three.

When the candle finally lit, Ophelia nudged it into place within the spell circle, and the rest of the pillars around Tessie

Grimm's lifeless body instantly ignited. The Grimm sisters' shadows stretched all the way up to the ceiling as the velvet curtains billowed violently.

It had been Ophelia that awoke, sweat-soaked in the middle of this balmy New Orleans night, to find their mother lying stiff on the cream chambray rug. There had been no horrified screams or signs of panic or foul play. No signs of any peril at all. Just her mother sprawled out on the ground as if the woman had decided to retire for the night on the floor of the living room instead of a bed. If the foreign, crackling feeling of magic had not alerted her that something was very wrong, she might not have found her mother until the sun rose. And by then, it would have been too late.

Ophelia had been vaguely aware of her sister padding down the creaky stairs after her, but had been too busy scouring her memories to warn Genevieve of the gruesome scene below. Ophelia flipped through her recollection for confirmation that she had knocked on her headboard enough times and tapped her knuckles in the correct pattern on her wall before she went to sleep. But she knew she had. Her compulsions were routine at this point. This was not her fault. It couldn't be. She'd done everything perfectly.

For a moment, she'd considered leaving the corpse as it was and going back to bed, convinced it would disappear in the morning just as all her mind's conjurings did. It wasn't until Genevieve's blistering sob and the pulse of power in the air that she sprang into action. She'd snapped at Genevieve to find a box of matches, and had dashed through Grimm Manor to their mother's study, ransacking the room for the seven black candles she needed to perform the spell before the window of opportunity closed forever.

Ophelia was now the eldest Grimm. A dead mother made her much more than an orphan.

Hurry, your time is running out, the Shadow Voice that haunted her every waking thought whispered inside her mind. *If you miss your window, there will be consequences.*

Ophelia pushed the voice away as she dipped two fingers into her own blood—careful not to reach past the circle of candles lest she break it and screw up the one thing she had been training for her entire life. This was it. The eleventh hour. Whatever she decided to do next would change her irrevocably. She could refuse to finish the spell and stay as she was, the only version of herself that she'd ever known. Or she could pay the price of continuing her family's legacy.

"You don't have to do it, Ophie," Genevieve whispered in the dark. Almost pleaded.

But Ophelia couldn't be the one who ended her family's magic. As much as this ritual would change the makeup of her very being, not going through with it would change her in a way that would break her spirit. The need to be good, to do well by everyone who had ever expected anything of her, was nestled deep inside her bones. Inextricable from her soul.

Closing her eyes, Ophelia whispered the words of the spell she had recited every night like an unholy prayer since she had learned to speak. The heat of the flames intensified as she finished whispering the incantation, the balmy air making her entire body flush while she concentrated on the power crackling over her skin. A charred, bitter fragrance burned her nose. The scent of magic.

When the last word dripped from her lips, each of the black candles extinguished one by one. Wisps of obsidian smoke rose around the circle as she reached beneath the collar of her unbuttoned nightgown and drew a crimson sigil right over her heart with her blood-dipped fingers.

Then they waited. Ophelia with anticipation. Genevieve with apprehension.

The temperature in the manor dropped ten degrees and the silence became heavy, the darkness too still. Ophelia suddenly felt eyes on her, gazes burning into her skin from every side. Eyes of those she could not see. Yet.

They waited in the dark for what felt like an agonizing amount of time. The midnight bells of the grand clock in the foyer had not yet tolled, but Ophelia thought surely the spell should have worked by now. Maybe she did it wrong, maybe she didn't say the words correctly, or clear enough. Maybe she was a complete and utter failure—

A scream erupted from her throat as fire suddenly seared through her bones and over every inch of her skin. She fell forward, onto her hands, spine cracking and popping into an unnatural arch, mewls of pain breaking free from her lips as her mother's magic flooded her system. She pressed her forehead to the ground, the pool of blood coating her face as her voice grew hoarse from her shrieks. Genevieve strode over to lay a hand on her back in comfort, unable to do anything but watch.

When it was finally over, Ophelia slumped to the floor, where she stayed for another long minute, trying to catch her breath. Eventually, she was able to stand and, taking a deep breath, she whispered a demand to the dark. The one that would seal her fate forever.

Genevieve's mouth fell open in awe as the dark answered Ophelia's request, the candles reigniting with the hushed command. This time, the flames were a silvery blue. Grimm Blue.

Ophelia caught a glimpse of her reflection flickering in the window. Her dark hair and wispy nightgown were caked in blood. Crimson was smeared across her razor-sharp cheekbones and dripping over the bridge of her delicately pointed nose—a startling contrast against her porcelain skin. That wasn't what caught her attention, however. Not when the gaze staring back at her was no longer her own. Her irises no longer the bright, warm cerulean of her childhood. The color Genevieve's still were. Instead, they had changed to a haunting, icy hue, almost bleached of their pigment entirely. It was the same chilling color that their mother's had been, the same as their grandmother's in the oil portrait that hung in the foyer. The same as every Grimm woman who had accepted her magic before them.

The same color as the hazy, glowing outlines of the Apparitions she could now see lurking in the shadows of the room.

Grimm Blue.

A venomous pride shot through her, but the wave of grief and fear that chased it almost buckled her knees. Part of her had hoped the magic wouldn't transfer, that their mother wasn't truly gone from this corporeal plane even though the cold corpse at her feet clearly told a different story. The other part of her, the one that successfully completed the spell and unleashed the magic now flowing through her veins, was satisfied.

A flickering reflection in the glass caught her eye. A curious Apparition with a wispy smile gazed back at her, knowingly, before blinking out of sight.

"Fucking Hell, Ophie," Genevieve whispered, shaking Ophelia out of her trance. "Are you alright?"

Ophelia said nothing as she reached up to smooth her finger over the locket at her throat, tapping it as she felt the first prick of tears in her eyes.

One, two, three.

Ophelia let out a strangled curse on the last tap and stumbled back a step, looking down at the necklace in disbelief. She held her breath as she waited for confirmation that she hadn't imagined it.

A moment later, the locket pulsed again, syncopating to the thrum within her own chest.

A heartbeat.

Two Nights Until Phantasma

2

FAREWELLS

Very few things were considered unusual when you came from a family of prolific Necromancers. Every day of Ophelia's childhood had consisted of corpses being dragged in and out of Grimm Manor, trips to the cemetery, listening to her mother complain about yet another possible Demon-inflicted virus sweeping through New Orleans, or spending hours reciting lessons on each type of paranormal being she might one day encounter. Shapeshifters, Vampires, Witches.

But waking up to Ghosts lurking in her bedroom and hallways the morning after she had found her mother's lifeless body was strange even by her standards. She wasn't sure if she would ever get used to the pale blue beings popping in and out of sight around her. For their part, the Ghosts mostly ignored her, passing through Grimm Manor and around the streets of New Orleans like aimless will-o'-the-wisps as she and Genevieve attended to the practicalities of their mother's death. If she paid them no attention, most gave her the same courtesy. Some, however, seemed to enjoy making her squirm. When she accidentally caught the gazes of those, they refused to look away. Watching her every move. Beckoning for her to talk to them.

The two of them had been up since dawn. Or rather, they had been out of bed since dawn. Ophelia had spent the morning preparing her mother to be taken by the city coroner while Genevieve collected everything they'd need to get a death certificate and release an obituary in the *New Orleans Post*. Now, it was only an hour before dusk, and she and Genevieve were about a block from the coroner's office to say one last goodbye. Unlike other mortals, Necromancers didn't bother with traditions such as funerals or wakes. They said their goodbyes to the corporeal forms of their loved ones and then waited until the opportunity to reach them in the afterlife presented itself. Having any sort of grand ceremony felt too final when they had such a connection to the dead.

Ophelia wondered if the solemn tension that clung to the humidity in the air was only in her mind, or if the city somehow felt the grave loss of one of its own. If it knew that she would never be able to fill Tessie Grimm's shoes and it was grieving.

The new weight of magic sitting in her core churned her stomach. It would only be a matter of time until she felt the urge to expel it in some way. Too much energy left to build up without release would corrode her internally.

"Are you alright?" Genevieve murmured at her side.

"I'm fine," Ophelia lied.

Instead of calling her bluff, Genevieve graciously moved on. "Have I ever told you how much I hate living in a city so humid?"

"Almost constantly."

"It always destroys my curls," Genevieve griped as if Ophelia hadn't spoken. "Hell must be less humid than this."

Ophelia snorted. "You know what they say. Come to Hell— we may have Devils and Demons, but at least your hair won't get frizzy."

Genevieve wrinkled her nose. "Ugh, don't mention *them*. That's just asking for one to show up."

That wasn't how it worked, of course. Unless you actually stumbled upon a Devil, or they stumbled upon you, individual Devils could only be summoned if you invoked the right words or names—as was the case for many paranormal beings. Which she was almost positive Genevieve knew, but, then again, her sister hadn't received the same brand of education as Ophelia. And even if Genevieve had, Ophelia was certain her sister wouldn't have had any desire to retain it. Genevieve almost always changed the subject at the mention of Devils or other such beings. Meanwhile, of all her mother's lessons growing up, Ophelia found the ones about the Nine Circles of Hell particularly enthralling. More than the hours and hours of lectures about how to reanimate corpses to do your bidding, how to talk to the dead, and how to avoid being possessed... the tales of the territories of Hell had always been Ophelia's macabre fascination of choice.

Probably because, unlike her own reality, there was the possibility of something fantastical promised with a place like Hell. Handsome Devils, and Wraiths and Demons, that might sweep you into their magical, dangerous world. Like one of the dark romance novels she'd read in Grimm Manor's library when she couldn't sleep. And maybe danger shouldn't be as appealing to Ophelia as it was, but most of her life had been spent sequestered within the dusty walls of Grimm Manor and she craved something to make her heart race. Something other than the unfamiliar magic now thrumming in her veins.

Of course, as with the magic, Ophelia was quickly learning that the idea of something was only pleasurable when it stayed an idea. A distant daydream. Having any sort of power was as foreign to Ophelia as the prospect of adventure or romance. And she wasn't sure it was settling well in her core. Watching her mother deal with the dead had never disturbed her, but the idea of manipulating such a fragile thing as life itself made her almost wish she had discovered her mother's tragic fate after the midnight deadline and not received her magic at all.

If you aren't home before dark, you and Genevieve will die, the

Shadow Voice whispered, unfurling like smoke in her mind as it awakened at her anxiousness.

For as long as she could remember, the voice had been there, in the darkest corners of her mind, telling her to walk through certain doorways or her entire family would perish. Making her knock incessantly on doors to buy a moment of silence with her own thoughts. Harping on at her to commit the most gruesome crimes on the most vulnerable beings. When she was younger, she had worried she was possessed. She had packed all her bags and made it a mile up the road to spare her family of her evil before her mother found her and explained that the Shadow Voice wasn't actually real. It was just a fixture of her mind. One she would have to live with forever.

The sun will set soon, the Shadow Voice pressed on. *Tick, tock. Tick, tock. Tick, tock.*

She pushed the voice away, shifting her focus to the morgue finally coming into view ahead of them. Genevieve hooked her arm in the crook of Ophelia's elbow, searching for comfort as they marched into the quaint building, sending the tinkle of a bell through the small front sitting area.

"Hello, dears," the familiar man greeted them. Their town was small enough that the man acted as both coroner and funeral director, not to mention whatever other odd, macabre job might come up. He was older, maybe sixty or so, with salt-and-pepper hair and a white mustache that desperately needed a trim. "This way."

They followed the coroner out of the waiting room and down a hall to the very back of the building. He held open the door for them as he waved them into a large room filled with coffins.

"I hate this," Genevieve whispered.

Ophelia gave the room a quick scan, eyes snagging on the single open casket to their right. She swallowed thickly as she approached, nearly choking on her dread as she peered down at the woman inside.

The simple cream dress their mother had been wearing the night before was long gone, now replaced with an intricate black chiffon gown that made their mother's already fair complexion look even more pallid. Their mother had been the one to originally pick this dress in case her spirit decided to stick around—Tessie Grimm was adamant about not spending eternity as a Ghost in a corset—but seeing the dress on display in the coffin now, Ophelia thought it might have been the wrong decision.

"*Shit.* This just makes her look..." Genevieve wrinkled her small, pointed nose as she stepped up by Ophelia's side to look into the coffin herself. "Ghostly. I told you we should have gone with the purple one."

Ophelia sighed, tapping her knuckles—*one, two, three*—on the side of the casket to soothe her mind. She agreed about the dress, but it was much too late now. Besides, the window in which their mother's spirit could return was long closed anyway. Souls that decided not to immediately cross to the Other Side came back within hours of their death. Which meant this would be their final goodbye. The dress they picked hardly seemed to matter.

Ophelia knew she ought to be happy their mother's soul had been at peace enough to pass over, a sentiment she repeated to herself during the grueling process of threading a needle through her mother's delicate eyelids before the coroner had collected the body from the house this morning—an old Necromancer's trick to ensure the soul could rest peacefully without being disturbed by any unwanted resurrections. Still, there was something nagging at the back of her mind, telling her that this goodbye was not forever. It's why she had yet to shed a single tear.

"If you could just sign here, Miss Grimm," the coroner prompted, shaking her out of her thoughts as he tapped the back of her hand gently with a pen.

Ophelia grabbed the pen from him, tapping the back of her hand twice more before scribbling her name on the bottom of the parchment he had placed atop the closed side of the casket. The coroner gave her an odd look as he observed the tic, but only nodded in thanks as he tucked the pen back into his jacket pocket with a soft pat.

"And you're both sure you don't wish for an autopsy?" he pressed. "I know all the signs point to a heart attack, but she was awfully young for her heart to give out without—"

"You aren't cutting open our mother," Genevieve inserted, firm. "It's bad enough Ophelia already sewed her—"

Ophelia elbowed her sister in the gut. Sewing a corpse's eyes shut with Demon-blessed thread was a well-kept secret in the Necromancy community. Otherwise normal mortals might start taking up the practice themselves, and render a Necromancer's ability to reanimate or have someone else possess them null and void. Which meant their mother would not have been able to profit off those wanting to resurrect their dead loved ones for one grotesque reason or another. Not that most people had the stomach for such a task anyway—Genevieve certainly hadn't, nearly losing her breakfast when she walked in on Ophelia finishing up the stitches—and Ophelia herself had waited until the last possible second to perform the necessary measures on their mother's corpse before the coroner arrived to collect the body.

"Never mind," Genevieve finished with a mutter. She reached into the folds of her dress and procured the paperwork she had worked on all morning. "Here's her birth certificate and the obituary we wrote."

The man scratched at his thick white mustache, eyes flicking between them as if he was wondering what to make of their strange manners. "I'll have a copy of the death certificate sent to Grimm Manor as soon as possible," he finally said, taking the papers from Genevieve's hand. "Take a moment to say your farewells. I'll be waiting just outside the door to lock up after you both."

The girls nodded in dismissal and turned back to their mother as he slipped out of the room.

"She isn't coming back, is she?" Genevieve murmured.

Ophelia took a deep breath. "Doesn't look like it."

"We'll be okay," Genevieve said, more to herself than to Ophelia. "If it was a problem with her heart, it was probably just a fluke. I'm sure she hasn't passed anything on to to us. After all, Grandmother was as healthy as a horse her entire life, and she probably would have stayed with us much longer if not for the accident. Mother wouldn't want us to worry."

"No, she'd want us to *move on*. It's just like her to leave me here, alone, to carry on our family legacy." The sound that came out of Ophelia's throat was something between a laugh and a sob. "I don't know how she expects me to do this without her. I will never be as good as her. I've only gotten half the training she did when her own mother died."

"No one can expect you to be perfect, Ophie," Genevieve reasoned.

"*She* did," Ophelia countered, memories of their mother's deep disappointed sighs every time she messed up reciting a spell or didn't think on her feet quickly enough. "She may have never pressured *you* to be perfect, but I was always held to a different standard. And even if Mother hadn't always expected greatness of me, I can't help expecting it of myself."

"Ophelia," Genevieve scolded. "That's hardly a fair thing to ask of yourself."

Ophelia wrinkled her nose but didn't comment further. Genevieve didn't understand. How could she? Genevieve had been allowed to roam free their entire childhoods while Ophelia had been cooped up inside Grimm Manor learning the family business. The Shadow Voice taunting her every time she made a mistake.

If Grandmother had been responsible for bringing the Necromancy industry to New Orleans, Tessie Grimm had been responsible for making it an attraction to both tourists and locals alike. Grimm Manor had a steady flow of foot traffic between the hours of dawn and dusk, Monday through Saturday, as the people of New Orleans ran to Tessie Grimm for just about every haunting request one could imagine.

Can you contact my brother on the Other Side so I can tell him I'm sorry?

Can you resurrect my girlfriend so she can tell the police I didn't do it?

Can you convince a Poltergeist to possess my husband and make him more tolerable?

All of which was now on Ophelia's shoulders alone.

"We have to move forward," Genevieve continued, interrupting her thoughts. "Find our closure so we can carry on her legacy."

"You mean so *I* can carry on her legacy," Ophelia corrected. "*You're* not tied to Grimm Manor. It is not your burden, nor would I ever wish it on you."

Ophelia bit her bottom lip and closed her eyes for a moment, taking a deep breath before her grief and anxiety boiled over. She'd much rather focus on her rage. Rage that her mother had left her here to take over the family magic, and Grimm Manor, long before she was ready. She knew it was probably in poor taste to be so angry with the dead, but her anger was easier to stomach than the grief that hid beneath her skin. Fury and spite could fuel her, propel her forward, but if she let her grief take over, she wasn't so sure she'd be able to dig herself out of that pit.

Genevieve gave her sister an indignant look. "For fuck's sake, I'm not going to up and leave you forever, Ophie. Besides, we don't have to make any decisions on Grimm Manor right away, okay? You don't need to take up Mother's mantle of helping every Tom, Dick, and Harry in New Orleans just because she and Grandma did. I know it seems overwhelming right now, but just because we inherit Grimm Manor doesn't mean we must—"

"*Stop*," Ophelia demanded as she looked back down into the casket.

Genevieve pressed her lips together. Ophelia didn't know how to tell her sister yet—Genevieve was still so full of dreams that the two of them would go off and travel the world together like they promised each other as children—but now that their mother was gone, the fate of Grimm Manor was pretty much made up in Ophelia's mind.

Ophelia reached over and brushed her fingertips against their mother's hollow cheek. Once she left this room, she would only be able to see Tessie Grimm in her memories. Memories of the eccentric woman drinking seven cups of tea a day until she smelled of vanilla and chai mixed with the scent of spell salts and magic. Of her soothing voice reading books aloud in the manor's library before lunch, and the metallic clanging of swords during fencing lessons in the evening. Of her teaching Ophelia all the rules of magic and dealing with the dead while Genevieve took her piano lessons in the parlor. Of the smell of gumbo and honeyed cornbread every Sunday in the winter.

"We'll meet again, some day," Ophelia vowed now.

If you don't knock on that door three times in the next five seconds, the insidious Shadow Voice in her head whispered, *you'll die too.*

Ophelia sucked in a breath as flashes of her own untimely death flicked through her mind. A shadowy figure standing in front of her, ripping into her soft flesh with claws as long as her fingers.

Tick, tock.

Her muscles seized as fear rushed through her, and her movements became frantic as she turned for the door.

"Ophelia? Shit. Is it the voice again?" Genevieve asked, dashing forward in her pink taffeta skirts, a hand reaching out with concern.

Tick, tock. Tick, tock. Tick, tock.

Ophelia tripped over her own hem as she lunged for the exit, rapping her knuckles against the solid door three times before the Shadow Voice counted off the last second. Then, silence. The voice was gone again, evaporating from her mind like mist.

"Dears?" the coroner spoke from the other side of the door. "Did you knock? The door isn't locked, you know."

Neither girl bothered to explain as Genevieve moved to wrench open the door. The man gave them a look of pity as they stepped out before locking up and leading the two of them to the exit. Genevieve shot a small glare at him. Genevieve hated pity.

"Good luck." The coroner bowed his head to them as they stepped into the late afternoon sun. Ophelia dipped her chin in thanks as she followed Genevieve, her younger sister not bothering with any niceties as they stalked away.

3

RUMORS

The air in New Orleans was still abuzz with the strange tension Ophelia had noticed on their journey to the morgue, but as they made their way home, it felt slightly different. The idea of saying goodbye to their mother had surrounded her with a fog of feelings so thick she had only been thinking of grief before. Now, however, she saw that New Orleans was in rare form tonight.

The streets of the Garden District were darker than usual, despite the lingering rays of the evening sun. The heels of Ophelia's boots clicked on the cobblestones of the sidewalk as she and Genevieve meandered down the road. Usually, the streets would still be packed with carriages and tourists heading to and from the Quarter, jazz music humming somewhere in the distance. Instead, the street that stretched before them was still, drenched in shadows and a quiet that was loud and clear to Ophelia: something insidious was in the air.

"We need to get home," Ophelia urged to Genevieve as her gaze darted around them. "This is not right."

"What are you talking about?" Genevieve asked with a raised brow. "Nothing seems wrong to me. No one's even out tonight."

"Exactly," Ophelia muttered. "It's tourist season—why is it so quiet?"

"It was quiet earlier, too," Genevieve pointed out. "Maybe everyone decided not to risk being caught out in the rain. Those clouds are getting awfully close."

Ophelia tilted her head back to peer up at the billowing, gray clouds in the distance. Maybe Genevieve was right, maybe no one wanted to risk the rain. But that still didn't explain the pit in her stomach. Or why the branches of the live oaks lining the street seemed more twisted than usual, the moisture in the air more suffocating.

Ophelia's pulse picked up its pace as something skittered deep in the shadows beyond the intricate wrought-iron fencing of the houses to their right. Ophelia huddled closer to her sister as they slowed to a stop next to a café at an intersection, a breeze fluttering through her thick, gray skirts, the familiar smell of fried pastries and powdered sugar hitting her nose a moment later.

"Oh!" Genevieve grasped onto Ophelia's forearm, tugging her toward the café. "Give me a moment, Ophie, I see a friend."

Before Ophelia could protest, Genevieve was entering the café, squealing a greeting to a girl Ophelia had never seen before. Ophelia pressed closer to peer through the door's glass panel as it swung shut. She watched as her effervescent younger sister threw both arms around the stranger with a familiarity that caused a lump in her throat. There wasn't a single person in the world, other than Genevieve, that Ophelia knew well enough to offer such a greeting.

But here was Genevieve, talking animatedly to this girl with flaxen hair, a sparkle in her vibrant cerulean eyes that had been long absent in Ophelia's presence.

While you were stuck inside, assisting your mother with calling upon the dead, your sister was making friends, the Shadow Voice told her. *Don't you hate her for it? Don't you wish you could make her hurt? Make her bleed? They think she's perfect, and funny, and pretty, and you're—*

"Stop," she whispered aloud, reaching out to tap her knuckle against the glass.

One, two, three.

The voice evaporated.

"...you hear? Farrow Henry claims he's entering. He's not going to make it two whole nights in that place if the rumors are true," a deep voice said from behind her.

Ophelia twisted around to see two men, about her age, heading toward her from across the intersection.

"Richard Henry's nephew?" The other laughed. "He was born with a silver spoon in his mouth. I bet twenty silver pieces he leaves the first night because his room isn't luxurious enough."

"He'll be lucky if he doesn't die from a heart attack in the first two *hours*," the first man agreed.

The first man, the taller one, barely spared Ophelia a glance when they made it across the street and shouldered past her into the café. The other took one look at her haunting eyes and flinched. They ambled right up to Genevieve, and she swallowed as her sister tilted her head back with a laugh, grasping onto the taller one with affection at whatever he had said. Despite the convincing show her sister was putting on that everything was just fine, Ophelia knew Genevieve well enough to see there was a mask to hide the pain. The news had not likely caught fire in New Orleans's social circles quite yet, and Genevieve was certainly not one to sour a good time with such a somber revelation.

Ophelia had to look away from the scene. Genevieve had an entire life outside of Grimm Manor. People she had made connections with, memories with, that Ophelia didn't even know the names of.

Before she could spiral too deep into that train of thought, a flash of light reflected in the glass from behind her. She stumbled back from the door and spun around, nearly choking at what she found.

There, a few feet away, was an Apparition. Its form was haloed in the same icy blue haze as the others she'd seen. Grimm Blue. Of course.

The Apparition tilted their head at her.

Ophelia swallowed. "I'm not her."

The Apparition hovered closer.

"Go away." Ophelia shooed the Apparition with a wave of her hand. "I'm not *her*, she's gone. I'll never be her. Leave me alone."

Because in New Orleans everyone knew the prolific Necromancer Tessie Grimm. Even the dead. Especially the dead.

The Apparition opened their mouth as if to argue with Ophelia's claim, but before they could utter a word, someone walked right through their transparent body. They blew away like smoke on the wind.

"It's come here, I swear," the man who had just unknowingly walked through the Apparition insisted to his partner as they strode by, heads bent together. "Out past the old cathedral, where the cemetery used to be. Emma said she saw it there yesterday."

Ophelia's senses stirred at the man's words. She had been right. The fact that the only thing in this strange quiet was hushed rumors surely meant something wicked was in the air.

Ophelia turned back to the café and pulled open the door. As she approached, Genevieve and her friends didn't even glance up from their conversation. A very hushed conversation.

Ophelia cleared her throat. "Genevieve?"

Genevieve stopped her whispering as her gaze shifted to Ophelia, a glint of surprise in her eyes. Like she had forgotten Ophelia was there at all. "Oh. Ophie."

"It's almost dark," Ophelia said. There was no need for any other explanation. Genevieve was well aware why that simple statement incited urgency.

Turning back to her friends, Genevieve sighed. "I'm sorry, I have to go. But I will absolutely let you know when I'm feeling up for dinner. We'll have a lot to talk about."

The others nodded in agreement, eyes flickering over Ophelia in curiosity, but none of them bothered to greet her or introduce themselves. Which was just as well—Ophelia wasn't in the mood to socialize anyway.

When they had stepped back outside, door firmly shut behind them, Ophelia asked, "Who were they?"

"Just some acquaintances," Genevieve answered with a flippant wave of her hand.

"Where did you meet them?" Ophelia pressed.

Genevieve's eyes slid to her sister with mirth. "Nowhere insidious, if that's what you're wondering."

"Of course not." Ophelia shook her head, hooking her arm through Genevieve's to pull them faster down the street as another flash of glowing blue appeared over her shoulder. "You just never mentioned them before."

"Are you alright?" Genevieve asked.

Another flash of blue to their right. Ophelia froze as her gaze clashed with the new Apparition's.

"Ophie? You look like you've seen a...*oh*." Genevieve's eyes widened. "That's it, isn't it? You're seeing them now."

"Distract me," Ophelia urged. "What were y'all talking about back there?"

They skipped over a hole in the pavement as they pressed on, away from the Garden District.

"Oh, um..." Genevieve hesitated. "Farrow Henry! Yes. That's right. Just petty gossip about New Orleans's most infamous bachelor."

"Do you know him?" Ophelia wondered. "Those other guys were talking about him when they walked in."

"No. Yes. No." Genevieve shook her head in frustration. "He asked me to one of last year's balls. His father is the head of one of the Mardi Gras Krewes. Mystick."

"I didn't think you ended up going to any of the balls," Ophelia commented.

Genevieve huffed. "I didn't. I had planned to, made my dress and everything, but then that asshole stood me up and took someone else. I still made sure to show up to Mystick's parade, though. Couldn't resist the opportunity to make him squirm."

Ophelia raised her brows at her sister's boldness, a laugh bubbling up in her throat. Genevieve had a mouth worse than a sailor at times. Though, the thought of anyone hurting Genevieve's feelings made her blood boil—not to mention it was laughable that anyone would find someone better than her sister. Genevieve would say Ophelia was biased, but the fact that there were multiple suitors sending love letters to the manor every month said otherwise.

"Well, he clearly doesn't have a brain if he threw away his opportunity with you," Ophelia commented.

Genevieve snorted. "That's alright. I fucked his best friend on the back of the float as revenge."

The sun dropped below the horizon now, and both of them instinctually picked up their pace as they passed the colorful rows of houses in the inner city. There were two golden rules their mother had taught them about roaming New Orleans after dark: the first was that if the dark looks at you, you *never* look back. That was a surefire way to be caught by a Devil.

Devils had roamed New Orleans as long as Witches and Vampires—longer even. Ophelia had never met one herself, and even with everything she'd learned from her mother about the insidious beings, she wasn't prepared for an actual encounter with one. Not yet.

The second rule was that if you *did* break the first, never *ever* make any deals with a Devil. Not unless you wanted to lose your soul. A concept many overly curious tourists never seemed to learn, flocking to places like New Orleans—places rooted in magic—in search of things they knew nothing about.

Those desperately fascinated with the types of beings who lurked in the dark hardly ever enjoyed the outcome of actually finding them.

Ophelia glanced around to see there were very few other stragglers roaming the streets with them. A couple shopkeepers getting off work, and brave street entertainers just beginning their days, which didn't help Ophelia's nerves. But at least they weren't completely alone.

To punctuate that sentiment, a carriage zoomed past, the clip-clop of the horse's hooves on the pavement melting into the sultry notes of jazz music that were climbing to a crescendo in the distance. A couple meandering toward them shook their heads at the sight of the sisters strolling arm in arm, and Ophelia wasn't sure if they disapproved of the two of them somehow, or if the gossip about their mother was already widespread enough for random locals to begin handing out their condolences. Regardless, the bone-chilling glare Ophelia shot in their direction was enough to make them flinch and hurry away.

"Looks like Mom's gift of unsettling the city folk has been passed to you." Genevieve wrinkled her nose a little. "I won't lie, Ophie—it is a bit harder to look at you now."

It was not shocking that Genevieve found the new color of Ophelia's eyes disturbing. Her younger sister had always had an issue making direct eye contact with their mother and had made it abundantly clear all their lives that should Ophelia tragically pass on without any heirs of her own, Genevieve would not be carrying on the family legacy.

The way people were easily vexed by their strange little family had always rubbed Genevieve the wrong way, and when Genevieve had reached a certain age, she even began to refuse to accompany their mother anywhere in town lest they run into any of her socialite friends. None of that had ever bothered Ophelia.

Maybe because Ophelia knew this would be her fate one day. Or maybe Genevieve was just embarrassed because her friends had told her to be, and Ophelia had never really had any friends of her own for such peer pressure to occur. The few times Ophelia had pursued suitors, they had ended with quick, passionate affairs that fizzled out as fast as they began. Not a single one ever made it to the stage where she might introduce them to her family.

Ophelia couldn't help but wonder if she was wildly unprepared to assimilate into normal society without their mother as her guide. Death she was familiar with. Living would be the real challenge.

Next to her, Genevieve suddenly shivered, turning to glance over her shoulder with a strange look in her eyes.

"What is it?" Ophelia pressed.

Genevieve hesitated. "Something one of my friends said earlier...about..." She shook her head. "Never mind. Let's just get home. I'm cold."

"Let's catch a carriage," Ophelia insisted as the night closed in. "I know we shouldn't waste the money, but I don't want to be out here a second longer than we have to."

One Night Until Phantasma

4

NECROMANCY BUSINESS

There was an incessant pounding on the front door.

Ophelia pried her eyes open at the noise. She reluctantly peeled herself out of her bed, fumbling around her room to pull on something decent before heading downstairs to see what all the racket was about.

Genevieve was poking her own head out of her doorway, eyes filled with rage at the untimely disturbance. By the puffiness beneath her sister's eyes, Ophelia concluded that neither of them had gotten much sleep the night before. Ophelia had lain awake well into the witching hours—the time between midnight and four in the morning when the veil between the mortal world and the Other Side was the thinnest—after returning from their hasty carriage ride, unable to stop thinking about her future, her magic, the strangeness of her locket pulsing around her throat...

Now, Ophelia rubbed at her eyes as she yanked open the front door, blinking rapidly against the morning sunlight that flooded through the entryway. When the spots finally cleared from her vision, she found two men standing on the manor's front porch, neither of whom she recognized, looking as if they'd rather be anywhere besides Grimm Manor at this early hour. Incidentally, she also wished they were anywhere besides her front porch.

"Ophelia Grimm?" the first man questioned.

He was an older, stocky gentleman with a thick, salt-and-pepper mustache that was ever so slightly crooked. His colleague was quite a bit younger, and leaner, his hair and beard a bright red color that contrasted greatly with his dull, gray, three-piece suit. Both of them were eyeing the unruly red roses that drooped from the porch beams as if they were knives and not flowers. Ophelia assumed it was odd for them to see roses growing in such a manner and place, but the roses were her mother's favorite way of keeping unwanted Apparitions out of the house and summoned Apparitions *within*. They had bushes and bushes of them bordering Grimm Manor's exterior, crawling up the latticework on the house's façade, as well as lining the front fence and gates.

Souls that are dead cannot cross roses of red, her mother had always chanted.

"Can I help you?" Ophelia asked, not unkindly, but in a way that indicated this wasn't necessarily a convenient time. Genevieve came to stand behind her, glaring at the men over Ophelia's shoulder.

"Who in the unholy fuck is knocking on peoples' doors this early in the morning? Our mother is no longer here to take appointments. If you have a dead relative, you're just going to have to suffer like the rest of us!" Genevieve huffed, and Ophelia had to press her lips together to keep from laughing. The men weren't as amused.

"Excuse the unscheduled house call. My name is Mr. Mouton, and this is Mr. Lafitte," the mustached man said. "We're from New Orleans City Bank. May we come in?"

"What for?" Genevieve snapped.

"There is some business with your, ah, mother. We were notified she recently . . . passed. Our condolences."

Genevieve narrowed her eyes. "Business?"

"Necromancy business, you mean?" Ophelia clarified.

"No." Mr. Mouton shook his head. "It's about the financial state of Grimm Manor."

"What are you talking about? The manor has been in our family for almost a century."

"Unfortunately, your mother seems to have taken out some loans and—"

"If you want to go back to sleep, Ophie, I can deal with this," Genevieve offered as she shouldered her way in front of her sister. "No need for both of us to have a migraine this morning."

Genevieve's words were nonchalant enough, but something about the tension in her sister's shoulders made Ophelia narrow her eyes.

Before she could decline Genevieve's offer, however, the red-haired man blurted, "This place isn't haunted, is it?"

"Oh, for heaven's sake, Mr. Lafitte," Mr. Mouton admonished before turning back to the girls. "I apologize, he isn't from here. He's unaware of the certain kinds of . . . beings . . . we have here in our little community."

"I thought you were joking about the Necromancy thing," Mr. Lafitte retorted, appalled.

"As I was saying," Mr. Mouton went on. "Your mother's debts. There are a few documents we need you to come in and sign and a few other things we should discuss. Would you be willing to come into town with us?"

"I'll go," Genevieve offered once again.

"Do you have any identification, Mr. Mouton?" Ophelia chimed before Genevieve could take a step over the threshold. "How should we know you aren't trying to kidnap us?"

The man scoffed at that as he shoved a hand into his coat pocket and pulled out a card. It had the official seal of New Orleans City Bank embossed in the linen paper, his name written below.

"See, Ophie? It's fine," Genevieve pointed out. "Go back to bed. I'll—"

"Unfortunately," Mr. Mouton interrupted, "since you both are equal shareholders in this estate, I'll need you both to come down with me."

Genevieve's jaw clenched a bit, but she nodded. "Give us a minute to lock up, then."

"As if anyone would break in here," Mr. Lafitte muttered at the same time that Mr. Mouton stated, "There's a car out front of the gates. We'll wait."

Ophelia retreated back inside to grab the key off the entryway table. A sinking feeling roiled in her stomach over what the man had said and Genevieve's odd behavior. There shouldn't have been anything wrong with Grimm Manor's finances. Their inheritance should have been enough to buy three estates if they wanted.

Ophelia took a deep breath and tapped the key in her hand three times before sliding it into the pocket of her black pinstriped skirts. She picked up the black velvet ribbon that she had left on the entryway table as well, slipping it into her soft curls and tying a bow at the top of her head, before scooping a few of the coins that had been sitting beside it into another pocket—just in case.

Once the house was locked up, the two of them started up the long driveway, toward the motorcar stalled past the gates. The noisy automobile was emitting a foul odor of smoke, and Ophelia made a face as she pulled her gloves from her pocket and slipped them over her hands. Mr. Lafitte stepped out of the passenger side, watching them approach with a skeptical expression as he pulled a metal lever behind the seat and folded it forward, gesturing for the two girls to climb into the back. Before they could squeeze themselves in, however, the rolling clacks of a horse and carriage sounded in the distance, making all of them turn as the vehicle approached.

"What now?" Ophelia muttered.

A woman, middle-aged, with dull brown hair, leaned out the carriage window. "Hello...I have an appointment. At eight o'clock—with Tessie Grimm. This is her residence, correct?"

Genevieve looked the woman square in the eye. "She's dead."

Ophelia made a disapproving noise as her sister turned back to the hand Mr. Lafitte was reluctantly offering and climbed into the motorcar.

Ophelia turned back to the woman. "I apologize, but all appointments are canceled. We just haven't gotten around to calling everyone yet."

The woman was gaping in shock, a hand fluttering to her chest with pity. "I'm so sorry to hear that, I had just spoken to her the other day—"

"So did we," Genevieve shouted from the car.

"You'll have to excuse my sister." Ophelia pinched her nose before waving the woman off and turning to stuff herself in the back seat next to Genevieve. When they were both fully situated, Mr. Lafitte lifted his seat back up and ducked inside, slamming the door shut.

"Must you be so brazen with people?" Ophelia whispered.

Genevieve rolled her eyes and sank back into the cushioned seat.

"The seats are comfortable, aren't they?" Mr. Mouton asked rhetorically as he shifted the stick between him and Mr. Lafitte forward. "It's the latest model."

Neither girl bothered with an answer as they neatly folded their hands in their laps and looked out their respective windows, watching as Grimm Manor faded from view behind them. The men carried on a conversation about cars for the next ten minutes, possibly the dullest conversation Ophelia had ever heard in her life, before they both became suddenly quiet.

"It's true, then." Mr. Mouton's voice was low as the two men gaped out the driver's side window.

Mr. Lafitte shuddered. "I *told* you. I heard it just...appeared."

Ophelia slid across the back seat of the car, pressing herself against Genevieve's warm side so she could peer outside. The locket around her throat immediately began to pulse, but all she could see out of the small window was a crowd of people. Genevieve looked back at her and shrugged.

"I always thought people were mad to believe those rumors," Mr. Mouton said. "The fools who enter those gates deserve everything they get."

Ophelia rested her head against the window, the glass sticky from the morning humidity, and tuned out their voices. She was so tired. And, worse, she was worried. She couldn't imagine what might be so wrong with her mother's finances that the bank would send someone to their house. Her mother had always implied their estate had long been paid off, their only expenses upkeep on the grounds and what it cost for them to live day to day. That didn't mean money hadn't been tight at times, of course. They still relied heavily on their mother's business and the regular income the people of New Orleans brought to their front door.

For a moment, she wondered if there was some sort of inheritance tax they needed to pay. If they'd have to begin hocking their valuables in order to transfer the estate into their names. Aside from a few pieces of jewelry and some of the antiques her mother collected, Ophelia couldn't think of anything inside Grimm Manor worth selling. The most valuable thing she owned was hanging around her neck.

As if it knew where her thoughts had turned, the locket began to pulse again. The golden bauble had been in her family for generations, enchanted with a powerful magic that bound it to its wearer. Her mother had always claimed it guided her through her toughest times and that one day it would guide Ophelia.

Ophelia looked down at the necklace, rubbing her thumb over the embossed, damask pattern of its outer shell, the crimson jewel nestled into the center on the front. She flipped it over and read the familiar words etched into the back: *Follow your heart.*

She almost snorted. A clichéd sentiment that was much easier said than done. Sliding a fingernail into the locket's clasp, she tried to pop it open. It wouldn't budge. Her mother hadn't been lying all those times Ophelia had asked to see what was inside.

"You're fidgeting," Genevieve murmured next to her, picking absentmindedly at her perfectly manicured nails.

Ophelia glanced at her sister. "I'm nervous. Aren't you?"

Genevieve dropped her hands back in her lap and turned to look out her window, hiding her expression from Ophelia. "Everything will be fine."

Ophelia narrowed her eyes. "Is there something you know?"

Before Genevieve could answer, the car lurched to the right, sending Ophelia sliding into Genevieve's side.

"Here we are," Mr. Mouton announced. "New Orleans City Bank."

5

THE SITUATION

"I...don't understand."

Mr. Mouton sighed again, either in frustration from having to explain the situation to Ophelia for a third time, or because he was starting to believe she didn't have the wits to grasp what was happening.

He fidgeted with his cravat as he leaned forward to point at the thickly inked words of the documents in front of her with his free hand. "Your mother stopped making payments on the manor earlier this year. She was a large part of our community, and we recognize how much she did for the grieving families of New Orleans. We tried to prolong this unpleasant part for as long as possible, but the bank started the foreclosure process two months ago. Today marks the countdown to the last thirty days until it becomes our property. We need you both to sign this document stating that you have been informed of the situation."

"But why did she take out a loan in the first place? Grimm Manor has been in our family for generations. My sister and I have lived there our whole lives, and not once have I ever seen a collection letter or—"

He cut her off, double-tapping a line in the document resting on the desk. "It says right here that she took out a cash loan against the manor's equity for personal use. Nearly thirty-five thousand dollars—with interest. She's only paid five thousand back. See? These are the carbon copies of the checks."

Ophelia reached out, almost subconsciously, and tapped her finger once over the line he had just been pointing at before dropping her hands back into her lap as she continued to study the slips of paper between them. He gave her a strange look, but she ignored him as her mind raced to process this new information.

Three of the one-thousand-dollar checks were made out in her mother's pristine handwriting. The other two, however... Ophelia narrowed her eyes. The slight shakiness of the connecting "S"s on Tessie Grimm's signature was the only giveaway that someone had forged them. She flicked a glance over at Genevieve, who was being oddly quiet in the face of this news, but her sister wouldn't look back at her.

"What can we do to stop this?" Ophelia demanded. "If it's foreclosed on, couldn't we buy it back from the bank?"

Mr. Mouton pulled out a pocket watch as he answered. "Unless either of you are going to come up with that money in the next month, I don't think there's anything you *can* do. The demolition date has already been set. The city has had its sights set on that land—as well as your neighbors' land—for some time. They want to install more modern housing, maybe even a hotel or two for tourists. My advice would be to sign over the rights now and give yourself a head start to begin considering other places to live."

"Well, then we don't need your advice," Ophelia told him before standing up and scraping her chair back. He winced at the sound. "We won't be signing anything. We're not going to hand over our home to you."

He shook his head in pity. "The house is getting torn down whether you like it or not, Miss Grimm. Signing the papers is merely a legal formality."

At that, Ophelia swiped the papers off his desk and stalked

out of the building, Genevieve silently following on her heels. Mr. Lafitte, who had been unable to join their meeting due to an irate client demanding his attention, gave them a smug look as they passed his desk. It took everything in Ophelia not to give him a crude gesture. Genevieve, however, didn't resist.

Ophelia pushed her way outside and rushed down the street, wanting to put as much distance between herself, those men, and the bank as possible.

"*Ophie*," Genevieve called after her. "Slow down!"

Ophelia turned into an alley, ducked behind a large stack of wooden crates, and leaned back against the dirty brick wall as she slid to the ground. Touching her forehead to her knees, she focused on steadying her breathing, clutching the crumpled papers for dear life.

You're failing your family's legacy already, and you haven't even begun, the Shadow Voice told her. **Knock on the wall three times and everything will be okay.**

She obeyed. *One, two, three.*

"Ophie," Genevieve said breathlessly as she finally caught up, wrinkling her nose at the grimy alley she now found herself in. "Ophelia, let's discuss this. We need to be realistic with ourselves about the situation."

"There's nothing to discuss." Ophelia's tone was drenched with bitterness. "We are not signing over our home to those scam artists. Didn't you see those checks? The signatures were forged on two of them, so who knows what else they could be lying about. I can't let this happen."

Genevieve bit her lip at the mention of the forged checks. "But if we're in debt...wouldn't it be better to take their deal and just be rid of it? This could finally be our excuse to leave— to *travel!* I know you feel like you have to stay here and take care of Grimm Manor forever but...maybe this is a sign."

Deep down, Ophelia knew that Genevieve was probably right. A normal person would be celebrating Grimm Manor's demolition. A part of her agreed that maybe this *was* finally the opportunity to be *free*. After all, this wasn't *her* doing. So, she couldn't really be blamed for the downfall of their family's legacy. But another part of her knew that if she didn't fight to keep it, she was making a clear choice.

Ophelia shook her head and whispered, "I can't be a failure. I won't."

Grimm Manor was their *home* and, dreams aside, Ophelia couldn't imagine leaving the place that raised her. The last place that she could feel her mother and her grandmother. The only place that *knew* her. Body and soul. Skin and bones. The manor's dust currently clung to the skirts of her dress, its dirt beneath her fingernails, the scent of wild roses woven in her hair. She had spent all twenty-three years of her life running around the creaking floorboards, playing hide-and-seek within its walls, falling asleep in the parlor after stealing sips of absinthe from its cupboards.

"I'm not giving up that easily, Genevieve," she said, louder now, pushing herself up from the ground.

"Why do you think that would be *giving up?*" Genevieve demanded. "Why can't you see that you're holding yourself back trying to fit into a mold Mother made for you? I know you, Ophie. You want to do bigger things than stay in Grimm Manor for the rest of your—"

"It doesn't matter what I *want*." Ophelia shook her head.

"But Ophie—"

"For fuck's sake, Genevieve, *stop*," Ophelia snapped, surprising even herself at the venom in her tone. Unlike her sister, Ophelia didn't use expletives very often. But Genevieve's optimism was wearing on her nerves. "I'm barely keeping it together, and you going on and on with this nonsense about leaving and traveling is not helping. We're not children anymore—Mother is no longer going to be there to coddle you whenever you make a mistake because you were too impulsive or didn't think your decisions all the way through. It's going to be *me* cleaning up your messes now."

"I've never asked for you to clean up my messes. I can take care of myself. I can help you take care of this, too. Why won't you just let me *help?*" Genevieve implored.

"Help how?" Ophelia challenged. "By forging checks?"

Genevieve winced. "I..."

"I knew it. I know Mother's handwriting better than anyone, Vivi," Ophelia said. "I've been reading her notes and spell books all my life while you've been out galivanting with your friends. Did you think I wouldn't notice such a detail?"

"I did what I thought was right at the time," Genevieve said, tilting her chin up in defiance.

"Why didn't you come to me?" Ophelia implored. "Why didn't you ask for help? And where did you even get the money from to write those checks?"

Genevieve looked away now. "It doesn't matter where I got the money. All that matters is I took care of things, alright? I bought us the time we needed then, but we have an opportunity to start fresh *now.* To stop trying to outrun a problem that will always be ten steps ahead of us."

"Where did you get the money?" Ophelia pressed.

Genevieve's fists balled at her side. "Why can't you just leave it alone?"

Ophelia shook her head. "That tells me all I need to know. Which is exactly my point—your good intentions won't matter if you stumble into a mess way over your head. And then it will be my job to fix it. Just like the mess we're in right now."

Genevieve's face drooped with hurt at Ophelia's words. In a blink, she spun on her heels and ran out of the alley.

"*Hell*. Genevieve, wait!" Ophelia called after her.

Genevieve rounded the corner and disappeared. Ophelia picked up her skirts as she chased after her sister, but by the time she made it out of the dank corridor, Genevieve was nowhere in sight.

TRESPASSING

Hours later, Ophelia found the day had come and gone as she'd meandered through the city streets. She'd decided Genevieve must have found a carriage home shortly after their fight, and thought it'd be good to give the two of them a little space before she followed. Unfortunately, she had not anticipated losing herself so completely in her thoughts, and it was now a much later hour than she'd like to have to walk all the way home. But they were in no position for her to spend any excess on a second carriage.

"They're opening the gates tomorrow night," a voice suddenly spoke from her right. "I heard the last competition had the most casualties in the last two decades. Twenty-seven reported deaths. It's a bad omen."

Ophelia turned to find that two young men had stopped only a few feet away, lingering before a newspaper stand at the entrance of a barbershop, their heads together over the gazette.

"Only twenty-seven? I thought there were almost a hundred who entered?" one of them said.

The other man shrugged. "Most contestants tap out before they die. The smart ones do anyway."

His companion scoffed. "The smart ones don't enter in the first place."

The first man nodded in agreement as he dropped a cigarette to the ground and smashed it with his boot, leaving a small smudge on the brick beneath. They closed the paper and threw it back atop the stack before hurrying up the street.

Ophelia strode over to the stand of newspapers, unfolding the top one and rifling through the pages until she found the article of interest.

October 23: Phantasma, the Devil's Manor, Arrives in New Orleans

She scanned the thick black print of the paragraphs beneath.

The competition's insidious reputation continues to terrorize the continent, leaving a trail of blood in its wake. A place where nightmares roam free, but the dream of winning a magical prize keeps participants rolling in.

Ophelia tucked the paper beneath her arm and took off for home. It couldn't be true. The Devil's Manor was just a rumor, a source of entertainment to fuel a media frenzy and sell more papers. But the conversation between Mr. Mouton and Mr. Lafitte in the car suddenly made sense. And it would serve Ophelia right for how she'd treated Genevieve to have to walk home in the dark, alone, well into the hour that Devils came out to play. Just as an insidious, Devil-riddled attraction came to town.

She picked up her pace as she headed home. The streets were lined with houses painted in hues of white and pink and green, each at least two stories high with bay windows and wraparound porches that featured brightly colored doors. She always knew she would stay in Grimm Manor, but sometimes she imagined herself in a pastel green house in the city, close enough to the French Quarter that she could walk to the cafés every morning and the bookstore every afternoon. But her mother was gone, and that dream was now buried six feet under as well.

Why can't you see that you're holding yourself back trying to fit into a mold Mother made for you?

She shook Genevieve's words from her mind.

Everything is going to be okay, she told herself.

Keeping her focus on steadying her breathing as she headed down the main road out of the inner city, she knew she couldn't let her fixations overrun her mind out here, alone in the dark. She counted out the minutes in her head, knowing there should only be about thirty-six more until she made it back to Grimm Manor's front gate. Before she made it even five more minutes down the road, however, she caught a ghostly blue flash out the corner of her eye.

Ophelia stopped in her tracks. This was about where the old cathedral should be, but she couldn't make out its shape through the sudden fog. Her heart thundered in her chest as she broke her mother's first rule—she squinted into the dark. She couldn't see the Apparition, but she knew it was there from the light vibration in the air that made the flesh on her arms pebble ever so slightly.

She approached the gates, searching for the telltale flash of blue, her heeled boots crunching on the oak leaves and acorns littering the ground. She leaned her hands against the bars of the gates and found herself pitching forward when they split open with a rusty creak. She righted herself quickly, brushing her hands off on her skirt as she slipped through the crack she'd opened between the parting iron.

"Hello?" Ophelia whispered. She practically heard her mother's scolding voice in the back of her mind. If she wasn't supposed to look at the dark, she certainly wasn't supposed to talk to it either.

But there was no Apparition in sight. She turned to leave. Odd. She had sworn there'd been a—

"Can you see me?" a small, squeaky voice asked.

Ophelia glanced around in the direction of the voice, but nothing was there. Her mother classified Ghosts on the Other Side into four categories: Ghouls, Apparitions, Poltergeists, and Phantoms. As the list went on, the abilities of the beings became stronger and more unpredictable. Ophelia knew that any being who was slightly transparent was just an ordinary Apparition— a deceased soul that had yet to cross over. All the other beings were more solid, possessing the ability to change their appearances in various ways, unlike regular Apparitions—who could only appear as they did when they were laid to rest. Still, all should be *visible*. To her at least.

"I can't see you, but I can hear you," Ophelia answered back, tone cautious.

"Are you here to entertain me?"

"No," Ophelia answered, breath hitching on the word as the energy in the air shifted. Where previously she had sensed it as a light vibration, the energy now settled over her skin as a warm, heavy static.

Is this some sort of trap?

Ophelia stumbled back toward the gates.

"Why not?" the voice pouted. "I'm bored. We can play games."

Ophelia opened her mouth to decline again when the locket around her throat suddenly began its unusual pulses. The sound of footsteps approached from somewhere in the distance.

"You shouldn't be here," a new, much deeper voice drawled out from the fog now.

"Uh-oh," the first Apparition whispered before their energy disappeared an instant later.

Ophelia swallowed. Like the other Apparition, she couldn't

see this new stranger, but she could *feel* them. And they felt much different.

The closer they got, the further the static spread across her skin, caressing every bare inch, making goosebumps perk up on her forearms and legs. And when...other things...began to perk up from the unnerving warmth as well, she blushed furiously and rushed to wrap her arms over her chest.

"Have you gotten lost?" the second stranger asked, a touch of humor in their tone.

If the dark looks at you, don't look back. But she couldn't help herself. Something was compelling her to stay in place.

"No?" she whispered.

"You sound very sure about that," the stranger quipped as they came even closer.

She squinted into the dark once more, trying to take another step forward, but it was as if there was an invisible wall in front of her, pushing her back.

"What the Hell...?" she wondered aloud.

"There are wards on these grounds," the deep voice explained. "Your trespassing seems to have awoken them. You cannot enter further unless you are granted permission."

"Like a Vampire?" she joked, though there was an edge of seriousness to her words.

She swore she could hear the smile in the stranger's voice as they questioned, "Who were you speaking to before?"

"I thought I had seen a Ghost..."

There was a whisper of breath suddenly next to her right ear. "*Boo.*"

Ophelia jumped as she felt the stranger's energy now pressing along the front of her body, making her flush even deeper.

Glaring at the empty space before her, she muttered, "Ghosts are such a nuisance."

"Who are you?" they asked as if she hadn't spoken, tone more serious than before. "You look so familiar..."

Ophelia sighed. She supposed she ought to start getting used to the Ghosts of New Orleans saying that to her now that her eyes nearly made her Tessie Grimm's doppelganger.

"Well, I can't see you," she told them. "So I'm unable to help with any insight on the familiarity front."

"Too bad," they said. "You're really missing out on my extraordinarily handsome face."

She resisted the urge to laugh. "I'll have to take your word for it."

Something brushed gently across her cheek then. "Angel..."

Her brow furrowed. "Oh, no, I'm not a—"

"What's your name?" they interrupted, demanded, with a new desperation.

Ophelia didn't know why, but she wanted to answer them, to tell her name to someone—or maybe some*thing*—new. Someone paying attention to her, making her heart race just as she liked to fantasize about. But she didn't dare answer. This wasn't a fantasy. No, this was very real. And she knew in certain places, to certain kinds of beings, names held too much power to freely give them away.

"What's *your* name?" she countered.

"Ah, good girl." Something in their tone seemed disappointed despite the praise. "You seem far cleverer than the tourists who've tried to sneak in here. Yet you're out in the dark, all alone. Don't you know what happens in the dark?"

"The dark is for people who are too cowardly to face their actions in the light," she automatically responded. It had been something her mother often said.

For a long moment, the stranger was silent, chirping crickets the only sound in the night. Ophelia might have started to wonder whether they had left, if not for the unmistakable warmth still engulfing her. And she knew she must be losing her mind for thinking that warmth felt...nice. For wanting to linger there just a little longer, to not be utterly, hopelessly, alone.

"You should hurry and find wherever you belong," they finally said, a hint of warning in their tone. "This isn't a place you want to be."

"Then why are *you* here?" she asked. "And who are you? Why can't I see you?"

"None of those are the right questions."

She narrowed her eyes at the empty space in front of her. "What is?"

The stranger's breath was next to her ear as they whispered, "How does one escape from here?"

She swore her heart was going to burst from her chest at those words, but she still didn't heed the warning bells in her mind, feet staying firmly in place. She was too intrigued. The touch she'd felt on her chin a moment ago now trailed along her jawline and down the side of her neck, to the crook of her shoulder, and she shivered.

"What do you mean, *escape*?" she rasped.

"I thought you knew where you were?" the voice questioned.

"Isn't this the old cathedral—" she began, but before she could finish her sentence, the realization hit her. There was a quiet laugh from the stranger as she finally peeled herself away and scrambled to wedge herself back out of the gates.

The wards. The missing church. The crowd they'd passed earlier in the motorcar. The whispered rumors. The news article.

She stepped backward until her eyes could finally make out the image through the fog as if her realization had pulled back a veil covering her eyes.

A calamitous, Gothic estate.

The wrought-iron gates that stood at the start of the driveway were at least twenty feet tall. The bars were woven with metal vines spiked with thorns and embellished with onyx roses. Above the left gate, the letters "PHAN" were written in metal, a "T" sat in the middle where the two doors parted, and "ASMA" was written out above the right gate.

Phantasma.

The Devil's Manor. A place often spoken about in whispered rumors and haunting cautionary tales in the dark.

Beyond the gates, which had been too crowded by nosy tourists before, sat the most expansive mansion Ophelia had ever seen. It was something out of the Gothic fantasy novels she'd read by candlelight in Grimm Manor's library, with menacing black spires that pierced the sky like needles, and east and west wings so long she didn't see how someone could live there without getting lost. The entire exterior was obsidian, so dark that even the live oaks that lined the grounds out front seemed to be leeched of color.

"Go home," the stranger advised. "A house of Devils is no place for an angel like you."

The way they continued to call her *angel* made her think they were teasing her.

And maybe she should have just heeded their warning and walked away. Maybe she should have been a lot more terrified than she was. But all she could think about was that, for now, she wasn't alone, and she wanted to linger in that feeling for as long as she could.

"Are you stuck here?" she asked.

No answer. She'd take that as a yes.

"Is there some way I can help you?" She swore the heat emitting from the stranger turned up tenfold.

Their next words were slow, deliberate. "Do you really care to know?"

"I did ask," she stated. "It's my job. To help Apparitions, I mean."

"And what if helping me would cause you harm?" the stranger posed. "Would you still be willing to assist me then?"

She stood there for another moment, debating, before her feet made the decision for her. Teasing or not, the stranger had been right—she needed to go. To put as much distance between herself and this place as she possibly could.

As she trailed away, she heard one last sultry whisper.

"A heart and a key would set me free," it said. "But you should hope we do not meet again, angel."

7

ALONE

About twenty minutes later, Ophelia was still trying to shake off the stranger's last words.

But you should hope we do not meet again, angel.

The two-mile walk from the cathedral—or rather, from Phantasma—to Grimm Manor was usually scenic. The road that led out of the inner city was lined with live oak and pecan trees, enormous homes sitting beyond them, away from the noise of the road. Marsh grass sprouted up anywhere untreaded on, and she could have sworn the air still carried the memory of magnolias from the spring. Tonight, however, the shadows and paranoia were drowning out anything Ophelia might have found pleasant. She'd stayed out much too late, and it was taking an alarming amount of time for the static sensation of the stranger's presence to dissipate.

If you don't get home in five minutes, Grimm Manor will crumble to the ground, the Shadow Voice whispered in her head.

Her shoulders tensed at the challenge. Five minutes wasn't enough time. And it didn't matter that she knew, logically, it was not possible for her to cause such a travesty with only her thoughts, yet she picked up speed.

Nothing is going to happen if I don't make it back within five minutes, she chastised herself. *The Shadow Voice isn't real.*

But it didn't matter how many times she told herself that. The intrusive thoughts always managed to make a traitor of her own mind.

Her heart begun to thunder louder than her footsteps on the ground. Her fists tightened at her sides as she passed the rose bushes that indicated the gates of Grimm Manor would not be too much further ahead.

Tick, tock. Tick, tock. Tick, tock, the Shadow Voice urged.

As the final two minutes counted down, she swallowed thickly, a pressure building right between her eyes as she pushed herself into a run. She was only a short sprint from the gates when she tripped over a fallen branch in the road. A burst of blue sparks, expelled from her palms as she shoved her hands out in front of her to catch herself. But she didn't have any time to be surprised at the first glimpse of her pent-up magic.

Tick, tock. Tick, tock. Tick, tock. Tick, tock. Tick, tock. Tick, tock.

Her legs were tangled in her skirts, panic seizing her as she thrashed on the ground. She twisted, rolling over onto her back—but her time was almost up. The crickets stopped their chirping as her body seized with fear at missing her self-imposed window of time. Grabbing up her skirts, she lurched to her feet.

Run.

Her hands balled at her sides. No. She was going to resist it this time. She took a single shaky step, then another. She was close, so close.

Snap.

She froze. Slowly twisting her head, she glanced behind her, scanning the dark for the source of the unnerving sound.

Nothing was there.

She took another step forward.

Crunch. A branch broke beneath her heel.

That was all it took for her to break into a full-blown sprint, shadows scattering out of her way as she pounded down the last stretch of road. She must have looked silly, running from nothing, but as she neared Grimm Manor's gates, the tightening in her chest began to loosen.

Thirty more seconds, the Shadow Voice warned.

She cursed and swerved to the right, cutting across the damp grass, her boots squishing through the mud as she ran. She hit the wrought-iron gate that opened to the manor's driveway with open palms, a metallic clang ringing out as one of them swung wide open. Thorns from the rose vines wrapped around the gateposts cut into her palms and blood began to swell from the shallow wounds. She didn't have time to think about the pain as she propelled herself further down the driveway and onto the front porch, patting the front pocket of her dress for her key.

Ten, nine, eight...

Another round of adrenaline flooded through her veins as she fumbled for the key, her blood-slick hand a hindrance. When she finally dug the key out of her pocket, her hands shook as she jammed it into the lock and pushed the door open. She stumbled into the house and slammed the door shut. Blood smeared on the locks as she turned them, but once the door was securely fastened, she leaned back against the frame, swallowing large gulps of air to steady her heart rate.

That was a close one.

She squeezed her eyes shut at the voice. It had only been in her mind. It was always only in her mind. She looked down at her hands, at the crimson coating her palms. The sight induced a visceral reaction in her core. Images of her mother's lifeless body in their living room flickered through her mind. Pictures of Genevieve's face after she had yelled at her sister so callously in the alley.

The blood needed to be washed away. She couldn't stand it on her hands.

She tripped over herself as she dashed to the kitchen, turning on the faucet to fill the sink. She began scrubbing at the blood on her palms, ignoring the stings from the thorns as the porcelain turned pink with her effort.

"I need it to come off," she sobbed. "I need it off."

Never feel bad for bleeding, Ophelia. Her mother's voice came back to her now. *Bleeding means you're alive.*

A sob caught in her throat, but she swallowed it. When her skin was as red and angry as the washed-away blood, she wiped her hands over the skirts of her dress to dry them.

"Genevieve?" she called out, voice shaky with desperation. "Genevieve? Where are you? I need to talk to you. Please."

The only answer was the echo of her own voice carrying through the dark. She made a beeline back toward the stairs, taking them two at a time, her breath shallow when she finally reached Genevieve's door. She knocked.

"Vivi, *please.* I'm sorry. Please, don't leave me alone."

No answer.

Tears stung at the corners of her eyes as she sank to the ground outside of her sister's door, pulling her knees into her chest.

"Please," she whispered one last time. "I'm so alone."

Eventually, she stood and made her way to her own room, taking time to bathe and wash away the rest of her sorrow before tucking herself into bed. She didn't fall asleep until well after midnight, and when she woke to the bell tolls that announced dawn, she knew something was very wrong.

The first place Ophelia checked was Genevieve's room. Nothing seemed off, but then again it was quite hard to tell when her sister's décor theme was *clutter.*

Thinking Genevieve might be in the library, Ophelia got

dressed for the day and made her way downstairs. Something small and pink caught her eye on the entryway table—an envelope. She must have missed it on her rush into the house. Her name written on the front in Genevieve's elegant penmanship. She dashed for the letter and tore it open, the foreboding that had been prickling through her body since she woke reaching a crescendo.

Dearest sister,

I hadn't meant for my departure to be in such haste, but after our conversation yesterday I see now that this is the way things must be done. What you said…I knew that if I told you my plans beforehand, you would try to stop me. So, I will be gone by the time you find this letter. Seeing Mother in that coffin was almost too much for me to bear, but seeing you with no hope for your future is something I cannot live with. If all goes as planned, I will return in no more than two weeks' time.

Let me be the one to bear the burden for once.

With all my heart,
Genevieve

"What have I done?" Ophelia whispered into the dark.

Ophelia stuffed the letter in her front pocket and hauled herself up the stairs. She pushed her way inside Genevieve's room, this time noticing things she hadn't before. It wasn't the clothes strewn all over the bed and sticking out of the dresser, or the bits and bobs scattered across the vanity—that was all normal. It was the absence of Genevieve's suitcases, the missing jewelry pieces she knew her sister never left the house without, and the stationery littering the desk.

Genevieve was really gone.

Ophelia began to rifle through the vanity and desk, looking for any hints or clues. She yanked open drawers, sifting through the baubles that rolled around inside. She tore the room apart all the way down to the floorboards. When she found the diary, shoved beneath a plank in the back of the closet—along with a brooch Ophelia had never seen before, and a wad of cash—she felt a heaviness settle over her shoulders.

Scooping the leather-bound journal out of its hiding space, Ophelia sat back and flipped it open to one of the middle entries.

April 30

I found another letter. I still haven't confronted Mother about the last one, and I don't want to tell Ophelia until I've spoken to her. I feel like Mother already puts too much pressure on Ophie and I worry what this might do to her. I also worry what this would do to my relationship with Ophie if she ever found out I hid this from her, but hopefully, I will be able to find out more from Mother when she's back from her trip this weekend. And hopefully, Ophie will never need to know.

X,

Genevieve

Ophelia squeezed her eyes shut. This was a violation, she knew that. Yet she didn't know where else to even start. Her mother was gone, Genevieve was missing—and keeping secrets—and the darkness in Ophelia's mind was beginning to wake up again.

No, she snapped at the Shadow Voice in her head. *I don't have time for distractions right now.*

Ophelia threw the diary into the wall with some strength,

and something fluttered out from between the pages. She scrambled forward on her hands and knees to catch the piece of paper floating down through the air, turning it over in her hands. A newspaper clipping.

Phantasma: Coming this Fall

"No," she whispered. She scooped the diary back up and opened it once more, shuffling through the pages for any other signs that Genevieve may have been collecting information about the Devil's Manor.

She turned numb as she uncovered more clippings shoved between the yellowed pages. She spread them all out in front of her and quickly realized that the articles spanned the last several years.

Ophelia's breath caught.

No. It couldn't be.

She hastily read each of the articles, once, twice, memorizing as much information as she could. Some were about the people who had died inside the macabre competition; others speculated about the Devil that ran it—rumored to be the most heartless and insidious of them all. One of the clippings was an interview from a past contestant detailing the horrors inside the haunted estate. She squinted down at the corner of that particular piece, noticing two words scribbled in the margin.

Find Gabriel

Ophelia flipped back through the journal looking for any signs of the name Gabriel, noting that some of the pages had been torn out. She finally paused on an entry from July.

July 23

I'm getting closer to finding Gabriel, I know it. I suspect Mother is becoming suspicious of my questions lately, so I have to pull back. But if my findings are correct, I know where he will be next.

X,
Genevieve

Ophelia gathered herself together, stuffing the clippings back into the journal and taking it with her as she stalked back to her room. She needed to pack.

Night One of
Phantasma

THE PRICE

When Ophelia stepped out of the carriage her locket's heartbeat kicked into overdrive. The driver gave her a dubious look as he took in the circus standing outside the gates. She handed him a bit of the cash she had pilfered from the wad in Genevieve's closet.

She'd pay her sister back by not strangling her whenever they were reunited.

"Thanks," the driver muttered, legs bouncing nervously as Ophelia gathered her things from the back seat.

As the carriage ambled away, Ophelia pushed herself through the throngs of captivated locals and tourists crowded in front of Phantasma's enormous gates. A few shocked looks were thrown in her direction as she made her way to the front, but she ignored them. There was only one person she cared to think about right now, but as she scanned the crowd, disappointment sank in her stomach like a stone.

Maybe she was wrong, and Genevieve hadn't come here. Maybe all the clippings had just been a morbid fascination. But her gut told her that wasn't the case. *Genevieve* and *morbid* had never belonged in the same sentence. And most damning of all was the locket around Ophelia's throat.

Follow your heart.

She took a deep breath.

At the helm of the mass of people was a well-dressed man in a black silk vest, with matching gloves and a top hat, just beyond the closed gates. His skin was a deep, warm brown; his eyes were rimmed with black liner and there was glitter smudged across his lids.

The stranger from last night? she wondered. The moment the man spoke, however, she knew it wasn't.

"Welcome to Phantasma," he told her as she stepped up to him. "Are you here to enter? Final call will close in fifteen minutes."

"I'm looking for someone," Ophelia explained. "A girl, twenty-one years old, with golden-brown hair and cerulean eyes. Much curvier than me. Probably wearing something pink."

He shook his head. "I cannot tell you who has entered already."

"Please—it's my little sister. I have no desire to enter if she's not here."

He raised a brow, unmoved. "Do I need to repeat myself?"

"What about someone named Gabriel?" she blurted out. "Is that someone who works here? Is it *you?*"

The man looked at her then, *really* looked at her, and an unnerving shiver ran down her spine.

"No," he eventually responded. "Now, either enter, or stop wasting my time."

What choice do I have?

She took a deep breath. "Fine. How do I enter?"

"First, entering Phantasma is not free," he said, his voice slipping into a tone that sounded rehearsed. "The price is your greatest fear."

She let out a relieved breath. Her greatest fears had already come true. She didn't imagine anything she revealed now would top the past week.

"Second," the man continued. "By entering, you are agreeing that neither Phantasma nor any of its staff can be held accountable for anything that happens within its grounds, as well as committing to fulfilling any bargains you make, down to every the last detail. This includes, but is not limited to, any physical or mental damage you may sustain once on the premises. You're also agreeing that you understand you're allowed forfeit during Phantasma at any time, for any reason, *except* within the actual trials themselves. Outside of the trials all you must do is state 'I, your full name, surrender to Phantasma' and you will be expelled from the game. Once you've begun one of the nine levels, your only saving grace will be the Devils who graciously answer your cries for help."

Ophelia noticed now that the crowd had hushed behind her. They were watching her. Carefully.

"In order to win Phantasma you must be the last person to leave, alive, after completing all nine levels—one level for each night, beginning tomorrow. The trials begin promptly at sunset, and if you are late, you are disqualified."

"What do the levels entail?"

"You'll have to see for yourself." He grinned with malice. "Lastly, and perhaps most important of all—fall in love within Phantasma at your own risk."

She almost snorted.

"Are you sure you still want to enter?" he prompted.

Her stomach clenched with uncertainty. This was her last opportunity to change her mind, but the weight of Genevieve's farewell note in her pocket made her lift her chin and answer, "Yes."

"State your full name," the man instructed, a curious glint in his depthless, obsidian eyes.

She paused for a second, thinking of how the stranger had asked for her name the night before. This time she answered. "Ophelia Marie Grimm."

She swore the whites of his eyes turned pitch-black for a moment after she spoke her name, and she felt an electric current zap through the air. Magic.

"This will be uncomfortable," he warned.

Ophelia squeezed her eyes shut. She focused on breathing in and out of her nose as she felt something dark creeping at the edges of her mind. Clawed hands made of smoke were prodding through her head, flicking through her memories and deepest secrets as if they were folders in a filing cabinet. He shuffled past memories of Ophelia and her mother reading together by a winter fire. The first time she snuck too much absinthe and threw up the putrid liquid all over the den's plush, sapphire rug. Scenes of her climbing into the branches of the enormous live oak trees and falling asleep atop pillows of spongy, gray moss until her mother called her inside for dinner.

Below the layers of those childhood visions were her greatest desires and then, deeper still, her fears. The foraging claws grazed over a few of her most prominent terrors—being buried alive, losing Genevieve, dying alone—and she shuddered.

The man lifted a brow. "I've never seen anyone with such a number of possible fears. It's a wonder you're able to sleep, with such darkness crawling in the shadows of your mind."

She gritted her teeth. She hated the idea of someone else being able to see the darkest parts of her subconscious. When the smoke abruptly plunged down into the depths of her mind and dragged out the one fear she thought had been buried forever, she had to choke down a scream.

Her breath was ragged when she blinked her eyes open again.

The man's eyes were sparkling with glee. "This will make the competition particularly hellish for you." A vicious grin. "And all the more entertaining for the rest of us."

Terror

I f Ophelia thought the outside of the Phantasma estate was something to behold, the inside was utterly magnificent. It had taken her almost ten minutes to walk up the long driveway that led to the front doors, and her arms now felt like gelatin from carrying the heavy suitcases, but when she stepped through the enormous, stained-glass entrance, she nearly dropped the trunks where she stood.

The windows stretched floor to ceiling and were draped with heavy black velvet curtains that matched the black and white marbled floors perfectly. The walls were dressed in ornate scarlet wallpaper, the color of new blood, and a grand chandelier made of iron spikes hung high above her like a medieval morning star. Before her was a set of onyx staircases that curved down in a crescent-moon shape on either side of the foyer.

She moved toward one of the curved staircases, still gaping in awe, when someone stepped into her path. Someone drenched in a blue glow.

"What is your name, lovely girl?" the Apparition asked, their mouth horrifically slashed at each corner in an eternal grin.

Blood bloomed down the front of the Apparition's shredded white shirt as their entrails fell out of their abdomen and pooled onto the ground. Ophelia felt bile rise in her throat, but she bit down on her tongue, hard.

How are you going to stay long enough to find Genevieve if you can't handle something as tame as this? Tighten up.

She tapped her fingers against her suitcase—*one, two, three*—forcing herself to look the Apparition right in the eye and answer their question. "I'm Ophelia Grimm. I was told to meet my group inside."

"Hmm. You're only the fifth contestant who hasn't lost their dinner or fainted."

"Someone fainted?" Ophelia didn't bother telling them just how close she had been to the former herself.

"Multiple people fainted," they corrected with a sinister laugh. "Several soiled themselves. One left Phantasma altogether. There's always at least one on the first night."

"Were any of them a girl about three years younger than me? Golden-brown hair—"

The Apparition shook their head. "I cannot disclose the names of any contestants outside of your group. Now, come."

Ophelia sighed in annoyance but still followed them down the center hallway, beneath the arch of the staircases, and through a large set of doors into a formal den where twenty or so other people were waiting. None of them Genevieve.

They turned toward her in sync, some sizing her up with curiosity, others sizing her up with something more insidious in their gazes.

"You are the final group," the Apparition beside her announced. "You are assigned your very own corridor of rooms. Dinner will be served an hour before dusk every night—and the first level will begin tomorrow at sunset *sharp*. If you exit your group's wing of the manor any time before you complete the seventh level, you will be disqualified from the competition. Good luck."

"Thanks," Ophelia muttered.

The first Apparition blinked out of sight without another

word, and another quickly appeared in their place. This one had a gash in their neck so deep, their head was barely attached.

"Your wing will be on the fourth floor," the new Apparition declared. "Follow me."

Ophelia walked with the crowd of strangers as they were led back to the foyer and up the right-hand staircase. Then up another flight. And another. By the time they got to the fourth floor, most of them were exhausted.

"Well, what do we have here?" a man asked as he dropped back from the rest of the group to linger beside Ophelia, matching her stride for stride. He was tall and lanky, his alabaster complexion managing to be fairer than her own, his dull brown hair slicked back from his face. "Aren't you a peculiar little mouse."

Ophelia wrinkled her nose but said nothing, hoping he might leave her alone if she ignored him. It didn't work.

"Who do you think you are, entering something like this?" the man prodded. "You must think you're special..."

"Couldn't I ask you the same thing?" she snapped.

"I bet you're—" he began, but someone cut him off.

"Go be an ass somewhere else, Cade," a soft voice admonished.

Cade's lips peeled back from his teeth in a look of utter contempt, but at least he obeyed, stalking away to catch up with another man walking ahead. Ophelia turned to her savior. It was a shorter girl, her flaxen hair plaited back neatly, her dress a bit worse for wear. Something about her looked familiar, but Ophelia couldn't quite put her finger on why.

"He's the worst," the girl offered. "Don't let him get to you. I'm Lucinda. But everyone calls me Luci."

"You know each other?" Ophelia asked, trying to sound vaguely interested, though she didn't really care.

"Cousins," Luci said, her tone almost mournful. "We're both here because our family has gotten into a bit of a financial, er, *situation*."

"I don't need to know the details," Ophelia said. "Thanks for saving me the trouble of punching him in the face, though."

Luci bit her lip. "You're Ophelia Grimm, aren't you?"

Ophelia heaved a sigh. "Yes, that's right. Now, if you'll excuse me..."

Ophelia picked up her pace, a slightly shocked look flitting across Luci's expression at her abruptness. She didn't bother to look apologetic as she pushed forward to reach the rest of the group, which had stopped in front of a set of large wooden doors. She wasn't here to make friends. She was here to find her sister and get the Hell out.

"Once you enter these doors, you cannot leave them until you complete the seventh level of Phantasma unless you choose to forfeit the game," the Apparition announced. "In which case, you will be immediately removed from the manor. Your rooms are divvied up between the four hallways at the back. The dining area is just inside to your left. Listen carefully for your room numbers."

The Ghost began calling out names and numbers in rapid succession. She memorized a few before they all began to blur together. *Luci, room 401. Cade, room 402. Beau, room 403. James, room 404. Eric, room 407. Charlotte, room 412.*

As each contestant heard their name, they left through the double doors to find their rooms while the others gossiped amongst themselves on why each person was here. Luci and Cade's family was bankrupt, as was Eric's. Beau's father was recently jailed after a sex scandal. James's wife died in childbirth. Charlotte was a total mystery, but someone floated the idea of murder being involved. Soon, the group dwindled down until only Ophelia remained, and she was grateful she wouldn't have to listen to anyone theorize about her participation.

"Ophelia," the Apparition finally addressed. "Room 426."

Ophelia didn't budge from where she stood. "How many groups are there in this competition?"

The Ghost tilted their head at her. "Including yours, there are nine total."

"Does each one have the same number of contestants?"

The guide shook their head as they said, "No. Some have more, some have less. This group already had two people tap out in the waiting room before you arrived. Now, are you entering or not? I can't leave until the last member goes through."

With that, Ophelia braced herself and pushed through the doors. As she stepped inside the corridor, she felt the Shadow Voice unfurl itself in the back of her mind, the weight of it seeming heavier somehow, making her temples throb. There were no signs in the wide hallway telling her where to go, she simply walked all the way to the back where it split into four further corridors and picked one. When she came to the first room with the number 420 decorating the wooden plaque on the wall to its right, she gave a small smile.

Lucky guess, the Shadow Voice whispered in her mind. ***Don't use up all your luck too soon...***

When Ophelia found her door further down the hall, she carefully poked her head inside, preparing for the worst. A stone cell, a cot on the floor, rats...but the room was completely normal, even charming. She set her trunks atop the large bed and sighed in relief as she shook out her aching arms from carrying their weight up four flights of stairs.

The patterned comforter and antique furniture made the small space feel homey. There was an old oil lamp glowing on one of the two bedside tables, and a hideous pink wing-backed chair in the far corner of the room that matched the jacquard design on the rug that blanketed the floor. She walked over to the bookshelf that sat next to the chair and peered at the odd titles and knickknacks decorating the shelves. When she reached out to pull one of the books from its place, a clicking sound rang out and the entire shelf shifted forward.

"The first thing I touch, and it's some sort of trick . . . just my luck . . ." she muttered aloud as she wondered if all the rooms had such a mechanism.

She couldn't help but think how much fun she could have exploring a place like this if she wasn't sure its entire design was meant to terrify or maim her. Or if it wasn't for the fact that her sister was lost somewhere inside.

A slow, eerie creak sounded from the bedroom door behind her, and Ophelia spun to see who was there. When no one appeared after a few minutes, she let her shoulders relax, turning back to the bookshelf—and then something blinked into view on her bed. She sucked in a breath, bracing herself, until she realized what it was.

"Oh." Ophelia narrowed her eyes at the fluffy white creature now sitting on her bed. "You're a Ghost *cat*."

The feline leisurely scratched an ear with its hind leg.

"Go on, shoo," she said, gesturing to it.

There was something in the cat's ghostly blue eyes that was wrong—something human-like that left an uneasy feeling in her stomach.

"*Shoo*," she said, a bit more aggressively now.

The creature gave a slow, unbothered blink before leaping from the bed and dashing through the hole she had opened in the wall.

"No way. I'm not walking through a random secret passage."

The cat meowed from somewhere beyond the dark as if it were telling her to hurry up. And damn her if she weren't curious. She took a hesitant step forward to peek into the inky abyss, knowing she should find a way to push the bookcase closed and not even think about where the passage led. But the locket around her neck had another idea.

She didn't know why, all she knew was that she had started, unwittingly, following the locket's lead—much as she suspected her mother used to do. She remembered times her mother would meet with clients, hand wrapped around the locket the entire time, as if assessing whether the necklace approved of their company or not.

Ophelia glanced around the room, spotting an ornate brass candelabra with three half-melted taper candles sitting on the dresser, and snatching it up. She concentrated her magic on the wicks until all three flames burst to life, and then stepped out into the secret passage. If it could be called that. It was alarmingly narrow, her shoulders brushing either side.

The cat was nowhere to be seen as she ambled down the dark space, the only light besides the candles coming from the glow of the lamp shining from the bedroom. She lifted the candelabra to the wall and scanned for any seams that might indicate there were more hidden doorways, but the alabaster paint was unblemished.

It's going to get you.

Ophelia flinched at the intruding voice that slammed into her mind. It was the Shadow Voice, but...different. Louder. Worse, was the disturbing dragging noise of the bookcase sliding closed behind her.

"Fuck," she said, tone shaky. Of course this was a trap. Why the Hell would she think it was a good idea to trust a cat and a necklace to lead her anywhere good?

You'd better start running, the Shadow Voice cackled in her head, its tone carrying an edge of maliciousness she had never noticed before.

She froze.

"Kitty?" she whispered into the dark, but the cat had completely disappeared.

And so had the locket's heartbeat. *Fuck.* A low, eerie echo emanated from the opposite end of the corridor, followed by a heavy thud. Ophelia squinted into the nothingness, every muscle in her body tensed.

Here it comes.

Just as the Shadow Voice spoke the words in her mind, something flashed red, several yards away. A pair of bloodshot eyes and a smile full of razor-sharp teeth.

"*Shit,*" she hissed, dropping the candelabra with a metallic clatter, and plunging herself into total darkness.

A high-pitched keening began as footsteps pounded toward her. Lifting her skirts, she turned and *ran.*

Getting closer.

She yelped as she tripped, managing to right herself at the last second, the raspy laugh that rang out at her misstep too close for comfort. As she rushed down the hall, unable to see even two feet in front of her, her locket grew warmer and warmer, its heartbeat rapid as it started back up and synched with her own.

Ten more seconds and you're dead.

Ophelia pushed herself harder, her calves screaming in pain.

Tick, tock. Tick, tock. Tick, tock.

With barely any seconds to spare, she reached the end of the hall, smacking into it so hard her entire body vibrated, teeth clattering together painfully. Her nose was crushed, blood gushing down her face, over her chin and onto the bib of her dress.

Tick, tock. Tick, tock. Tick, tock.

She let out a wild giggle as she roamed her hands over the wall in front of her, frantically searching for a doorknob.

"*Please, please, please,*" she whimpered, the iron taste of her blood on her tongue.

The footsteps were no more than a couple yards behind her now, a low growl roaring out of whoever— or whatever—was chasing her. She continued feeling for a way out and finally, *finally*, she found a handle.

Tick, tock. Tick, tock. Tick, tock.

She yanked furiously on the lever, pushing the door open a crack and lurching forward, shoulder first, to painfully squeeze herself through—

—just as a clawed hand latched on to her.

She yelped in pain as sharp, onyx nails ripped into her forearm. The hands that were trying to drag her back were gray and mottled, but she couldn't see anything else in the dark aside from the whites of wild, bloodshot eyes.

She let out a screech that was half frustration and half terror as she shook the creature off, squeezing her eyes shut and expelling out as much of the untouched magic in her core as she could. Blue sparks began rolling off her skin with small static pops, zapping whatever was holding her and making it let go with a hiss of pain. She snatched her arm through the opening and cradled it against her chest before slamming herself against the door, shutting it soundly.

She began fastening the various brass locks, hoping they were enough to hold the monster back. The creature pounded on the other side several times, shaking the entire wall with the force, but she kept her shoulder wedged against the door, waiting until the monster gave up its fight. She took several deep gulps of air. Looking down at the jagged wounds on her arm, her stomach dropped at the sight of crimson dripping to the floor.

Had that creature been her mind's doing? Or was it part of Phantasma?

Maybe it's both, the Shadow Voice suggested. **You let them dig around in your head after all. That means you'll have to be careful what you think in here, pretty little Necromancer.**

No. No. No. This wasn't supposed to happen. The things in her mind were never supposed to be *real*. The voice in her head had conjured so many deceitful, horrifying scenarios over the years, but she had always known, on some level, that's where they would stay. But here...An overwhelming sense of terror washed over her. She needed to find Genevieve and get them both out as soon as possible.

Pushing away from the door with determination, she scanned the space around her, looking for another exit. Her gaze snagged on the cat, its head tilted curiously at her, sitting on the corner of a table as if it had no cares in the world. The feline mewled, and she gave it a withering glare.

The ghostly creature leaped down from the table, entirely apathetic toward her scathing look as it pranced right over to a door on the far wall that she hadn't noticed. She cautiously made her way over, prying it open only a crack to assess exactly where it led. If it was another dark corridor, she would be staying in this small room forever. Thankfully, she found that it exited back into one of the main hallways leading to the contestants' rooms.

"That was quite enough excitement for tonight," she whispered, slamming the door closed behind her. She looked down at the feline, seething. "Thanks for leading me into a death trap, by the way."

The cat mewled at her, and Ophelia swore the sound was meant to be one of judgment. As if it thought she was absolutely mad for expecting help from a cat in the first place. She gave a discontented grunt as she hooked a right down the hallway—

—before snapping back against the doorframe.

Her skirt was caught. She pushed the door back open to dislodge the hem and stopped cold when she saw what was now beyond it. Gone was the small room she had just exited, replaced by a tiny, dank broom closet. She stood there for a long moment before hurriedly yanking it shut once again.

"No wonder this place drives people out of their sanity," she griped.

At that moment, something began stretching over the wall at the opposite end of the hall. A crackling sensation charged the air around her as she gaped in awe at the magnificent doorway forming in thin air. The cat trotted toward the surprising new addition to the corridor, head inclined in curiosity as two red mosaic panels and a gilded handle took shape as they watched.

Stranger still, a dark, weighted presence settled over her shoulders, and the palpable, inexplicable feeling of being watched sent a shiver down her spine. But when she looked around, she could see no one. It was only her and the cat.

Her locket began to heat as she stood there staring at the doorway. She had half a mind to ignore it after everything that had just happened—her face and arm were both still dripping with blood after all—but a part of her was inclined to give the necklace one more chance. If there was a reason that her locket was reacting to the doorway's appearance, she wanted to find out.

She reached up to tap the necklace.

One, two, three.

"Where are you leading me?" she wondered aloud, and headed for the door.

10

THE STRANGER

Ophelia yanked and prodded at the magic gateway for nearly ten minutes before she decided to give up. She had no doubt that her right shoulder would be purple by sunrise, having jammed it against the solid wood to make it budge—to no avail.

"You are the worst tour guide *ever*, you know," she admonished the cat, which was currently bathing itself at her feet.

"Well, he is a cat," a deep, vaguely familiar voice commented from behind her. "Do you need assistance with that?"

Ophelia startled, and the feline let out its own chirp of surprise. She spun to snap at whoever had snuck up on her, but as soon as she spotted them, no words came out.

The man, who looked to be in his mid-twenties, only a few years older than her, tilted his head in amusement as he opened his arms to allow the feline to leap up into them. For a moment, she wondered if he had been the one she had felt watching her, but his gaze didn't elicit the same uneasiness.

"You're..." she began, a bit breathlessly. "Um..."

The man smirked as he gave the cat's white fur a long stroke. The ghostly creature purred loudly as it rubbed its head underneath his chin with familiar affection. "I'm what? Very handsome? The most striking person you've ever seen?"

Ophelia began to nod, before realizing that perhaps that was a very embarrassing thing to do. She felt her cheeks flush as he laughed and let the cat drop back to the floor.

Others would probably describe him as being *very tall*, but at five feet and eleven inches herself, he only had about three and a half inches on her. He had shocking white hair and bright jewel-green eyes. The rest of his facial features were almost as sharp and delicate as her own—except *he* managed to look less gaunt than she did.

Another detail that spiked a small bit of jealousy in her stomach was how impeccably dressed he was. His waistcoat was made of deep viridian velvet that matched his eyes almost exactly, but his collared shirt and cravat were a rich onyx, the embroidered details of both pieces executed in a monochromatic silk thread. His pants were the same material as his shirt and tailored to perfection. If it wasn't for the disheveled state of his hair and the way he had his sleeves carelessly rolled up around his— surprisingly muscular—biceps, she would have thought he was some sort of aristocrat.

But what she really noticed most of all was that he was a Ghost, though not like any she'd encountered so far. The edges of his silhouette didn't have the same haloed blue glow that the other Apparitions had; rather, there was a faint white illumination about him instead. And there was very little transparency to his form unless she was staring very hard at him. Which she wasn't. At all.

Yes, he looked just as corporeal as she did, except she could *feel* that something was different. There was an intensely warm static buzzing over her skin just like...

The stranger.

"*You*," she said, a hint of accusation in her tone.

But there was no recognition in his emerald gaze. Only the briefest flash of confusion.

"Last night," she continued, "we...you were..."

"Here, as always."

"Yes, but—"

He gave her a pointed look as he lowered his voice and implored, "Be careful what you reveal out in the open. Even the walls have ears here, angel."

She scowled in confusion. She didn't understand what that meant. But all she said was "Stop calling me that."

His eyes turned sharp. "Are you implying I've called you that before?"

She thought of the night before. The feeling of his warmth making her want to linger in the dark despite knowing better. The way she had been desperate for him to know her name. The feeling of his invisible touch on her face...

"Are you going to act as if you don't remember me?" she demanded, kicking herself for holding on to the details of a moment that was clearly very forgettable for him.

"Unfortunately, many mortals come through here." He tilted his head, flicking his eyes up and down her figure. "Though, none have been as much a vision in red as you are."

She looked down at herself then, remembering how ghastly she must look. The blood that had been gushing from her nose had finally dried up, leaving only a dull throbbing and the gro-tesque scarlet stain behind.

"That looks like a nasty wound," he noted with a glance at her forearm.

She shrugged. The newly flowing magic in her veins had heal-ing properties. Her arm was already beginning to scab. From what her mother had taught her, it would take her a quarter of the time to heal than normal mortals, and she didn't need to worry about infections anymore either. Besides, she liked the sharpness of the pain. It reminded her that she needed to stay alert.

"If you don't remember me, why are you bothering me?" she pressed.

"Call it curiosity. Or boredom. Whichever you prefer, it's hard to ignore a contestant drenched in blood summoning a gateway in the middle of the manor." He snorted. "But why don't you jog my memory of our supposed meeting?"

"We met last night," she told him, trying to shove away the embarrassment she felt for remembering the interaction so viscerally. "By the front gates. But I couldn't see you, I could only hear you."

"Then how do you know it was me?" He lifted a brow.

"All Ghosts have their own energy—like a fingerprint—and yours is even more distinct than most. I've never come across anything like it before."

He smirked, and her defenses raised.

"I'm not crazy. I know it was you," she snapped. "Whether you want to admit it to me or not."

"You're not crazy," he agreed, gaze softening. "This is clearly your first time meeting a Phantom."

Phantom. That was it. They were the most powerful of Ghost. No wonder he was so . . . solid.

Apparitions were regular mortal souls that had died but not passed over to the Other Side. Completely non-corporeal and intangible by anything except each other and, of course, Necromancers. The worst type of Ghost, according to her mother, were the Ghouls. Apparitions that had stayed too long without crossing over, becoming zombie-like creatures as their ghostly energies began to fuse with that of this corporeal plane, making them strong enough to be semi-solid but also becoming mindless in the process. A horrible combination, to have power and no sense of morality. And she was beginning to wonder if that was exactly the sort of creature she had encountered in the secret corridor.

Poltergeists and Phantoms, however, were the rarest of the ghostly paranormal beings. The most powerful.

"When we met last night, what did we talk about?" he asked, interrupting her thoughts.

She gave him an exasperated look. "Are you teasing me? Do you really not remember?"

"My memories are . . . complicated."

"I asked if you were stuck here, if you needed help," she said. "You told me to go home. That a house of Devils was no place for me."

"I see you didn't heed my advice. Pity," he murmured. "It was an agreeable encounter, then?"

"Agreeable?" She snorted. "That wouldn't have been my first choice of words. Vexing, perhaps. As is our current conversation. But nothing unpleasant or insidious happened, if that's what you mean."

He nodded absentmindedly for a moment before flicking his eyes behind her. "How did you do this?"

"How did I do *what*?"

"How did you summon this door?" The undercurrent of his tone turned a little too serious for it to be a casual question.

"I didn't *summon* it. It just appeared," she explained.

"Hmm" was all he said.

"Do you work here?" she interrogated. "Are you part of Phantasma's staff?"

He slid his piercing eyes back to her. "Staff? No, not exactly."

"Well, is that *your* cat?"

"Poe belongs to me as much as he belongs to anyone else, I imagine."

She pinched the bridge of her nose and changed the subject back to the locked door. "Do you know how to unlock this?"

"Yes."

Ophelia waited for him to step forward and help, but when he didn't move, she tapped her foot impatiently. *One, two, three.*

·When he still didn't say anything, she finally implored, "*Would* you unlock this?"

"No." He smirked.

"Then why did you offer to help before?" she demanded, propping one of her hands on her hip. The one still smeared with blood.

His eyes immediately snagged on the crimson lines that stained her skin, but he only said, "I didn't, actually. I simply asked *if* you needed help."

"That's quite misleading."

"Sorry, angel, but I can't help any contestants during Phantasma."

She frowned.

"At least, not for free."

Before she could form a response, a piercing shriek rang out through the hall.

"*Genevieve?*" she called, pushing past the stranger, heart pounding at the sound of her sister's voice.

When she turned back to ask if the scream had been real, she found that the stranger, and the cat, had disappeared.

11

WHISPERS

As Ophelia made her way back to her room, she kept wondering if the scream she'd heard had really been Genevieve or if it was just another trick the house was playing on her. It occurred to her, of course, that her own mind might have been the one playing the trick.

The real trials haven't even started yet, she chided herself. *Don't psyche yourself out of the game before the competition gets a chance to.*

A few wrong turns and retraced steps later, she found room 426 exactly as she left it. Though, she regarded the bookshelf with a bit more suspicion now that she knew what was likely still lurking behind it. After a brief debate, she decided sliding the hideous wing-backed chair in front of the shelf was her best chance of getting a decent night's sleep.

Once that was settled, she opened her trunks and sifted through the contents to find a particular wine-colored dress she had packed. It was made of a lightweight chiffon, with a high collar and billowing sleeves that cuffed around her wrists. The skirt fell in tiers to her ankles, and that made it much easier to walk in than the heavy corseted ensemble she currently wore. In other words, it would be much easier to run away in, not to mention it was closer to the color of blood.

She stepped into the attached bathroom to wash off the remnants of crimson on her rapidly healing arm. Waving a hand through the air before her, she directed her magic toward the sconces on either side of the vanity's mirror. The flames flicked to life, licking up from the ivory candles and illuminating the reflection of her ghastly appearance.

She peeled off the ruined gown and filled the bathtub with water, as scalding hot as she could get it. Grabbing a washcloth and bar of soap off the vanity, she climbed into the water. Lowering herself until her shoulders were submerged, she relished the steam clouding the air around her. She needed this. A moment to breathe. To think.

She couldn't leave this wing of the house until level seven. Which meant she was stuck playing this game for at least the next week. It was important for her to maintain her sanity.

She leaned her head back against the edge of the tub and let her eyes fall shut as she worked on lathering the soap into the washcloth.

There would be no more exploring trap corridors or leaving her room unless absolutely necessary. She would go to the dining hall to eat, show up for the levels as directed, and that was it. Minimize the risks she took to avoid any more unwanted excitement.

She ran the washcloth over her flushed skin, gentle circles across her shoulders and décolletage.

Minimizing risks also meant no more encounters with certain green-eyed phantoms...Something about him disarmed her in a way that was concerning, and she didn't need such a distraction. Even if he was intriguing. And handsome. And exactly the type of being she had been trained to assist. Not that he seemed to need her assistance. Even if he did, he spoke in too many circles and she couldn't figure him out. His mouth much too smart.

Oh, his mouth.

She wondered what it would be like to have that mouth on her skin. Running along her clavicle, over her chest, down her stomach, to her...

Water sloshed out of the tub and onto the floor as she sat up, ramrod straight. The washcloth in her hand had been trailing down the planes of her stomach before she realized what she was doing, what she was thinking about. She hurried to finish bathing and drained the tub. Drying off and getting dressed for bed with lightning speed, she tucked herself beneath the covers and ordered herself to get some sleep.

This place was definitely going to drive her mad.

Ophelia awoke the next morning at a quarter past eight. Sitting up, she stretched out her limbs before climbing out of bed and headed to the bathroom. As she made her way through her morning routine, she refused to light the sconces, her eyes still too tired for the brightness.

Which meant it took her nearly ten minutes to see the fresh streaks of blood smeared across the wall next to the mirror. A shriek crawled up her throat as she realized that not only were the walls covered in gore, but blood was dripping from the faucet on the tub.

Drip. Drip. Drip.

One, two, three.

Another screech caught in her throat as something began to emerge from the pool of crimson as if it had been waiting for her to notice it. Something human-shaped with long, stringy hair covering its face. This time she knew, without a doubt, what the hellish creature was. A Ghoul. Mindless, deteriorating, with a hunger for mortal flesh.

She stumbled back and spun for the exit to her room. She twisted the knob with all her might, but it wouldn't turn. She pulled and pulled, her heartbeat erratic as she looked over her shoulder to see the Ghoul slowly dragging itself out of the bathroom.

"*What's with the damn doors in this place,*" she cried. "*Let me out!*"

Click.

She sobbed in relief as the knob finally turned and the door flung open, but it was not a hallway on the other side. Instead, the door had opened to a void of pitch-black nothingness. She halted on the very edge, almost tumbling over. As she checked back over her shoulder, she recoiled at the grotesque smile spreading across the Ghoul's face beneath their hair. Not waiting for another close call, she turned back to the inky oblivion, and braced herself.

She stepped into the darkness.

Ophelia couldn't tell if she had been falling for minutes or hours. There was not a single point of light around her. Only whispers.

As she fell, she passed through wisps of words. Shameful secrets and confessions of love. Snippets of conversations and hushed arguments. And one voice that seemed louder than the rest. A voice that felt hauntingly familiar. She strained to hear more from that voice, but she was falling too fast, and their words drifted away. She tried to call out, to scream for help, but no words would come out of her mouth. When she wondered if she would be adrift forevermore, she crashed through the floor.

"Quite an entrance."

Debris rained down atop her and the firm, cushioned surface she'd landed on. Sitting up slowly, she was too stunned to even grunt with pain. When her gaze locked with a pair of deep viridian eyes, she sucked in a sharp breath of disbelief.

"Missed my presence already?" the stranger drawled.

She dusted herself off with shaky hands, giving him as much of an indignant look as she could manage through the shock. "Ah, so *that's* the true distinction of a Phantom—an ego."

"That, and what I'm able to do with my hands," he taunted, lips curling up at the corners. "Shouldn't you be settling in before breakfast? Or was there something wrong with your room?" He lifted a crystal goblet of amber liquid to his mouth.

Her forehead wrinkled at the sight. "Are you *drinking?*"

"Would you like some? It looks like you might need it."

"No," she deadpanned, though the idea of having another conversation with him that went round and round in circles made her think perhaps a drunken stupor would be preferable.

"Here." He snapped his fingers, and she was instantly clean of the dust and chunks of ceiling clinging to her dress. He set his glass down on the table he was leaning against and moved to crouch before her. "How did you find your way to this room?"

It took everything in her not to flush at his proximity, which piqued her a bit.

"Ghosts can't eat or drink," she noted, ignoring his question.

"I'm special," he retorted. "Now, *focus*. How did you get here?"

"I'm not sure where *here* even is," she answered, waving him back so she could stand from the chaise she had fallen into.

He obliged, rising and stepping away. He was looking at her as if she were a puzzle and he was deciding whether to bother solving it.

She sighed, then explained. "I went to wash up in my bathroom and there was blood all over the mirror and in the tub—"

"Yes, I'm familiar with the scene," he told her. "The Ghouls and Apparitions haven't gotten very creative over the years."

"You mean they use the same tricks every time?"

"Yes. Ghouls don't have the capacity to be retrained once they've been stuck doing something for so long. Even the Devils use the same nine levels of terror for every competition—and yet there's still an incredibly low success rate." He shrugged. "Why fix what isn't broken is sort of the philosophy around here."

"Devils," she whispered, mostly to herself. She hadn't had time to add them to her list of worries yet. But it was only a matter of time before she came across one. It was called the Devil's Manor after all. They were the only beings with magic powerful enough to operate a place like this.

A slow grin spread over the stranger's face. "Don't tell me you've never seen a Devil before?"

"I don't make it a habit to seek out trouble."

He raised a single, silvery brow. "Don't you, though? You claim I took the time to warn you away and yet here you are."

She opened her mouth to retort until she realized he was right. To him, it probably did seem like she was a glutton for punishment.

"Well, I didn't use to," she muttered as she looked away from him and finally took in the room around them.

There was an enormous table dressed with intricate black and gold centerpieces in the center of the room, at least fifteen blood-red upholstered chairs lining each side. A large crystal chandelier hung from an ornate ceiling rose, sending scatters of rainbow light over the dark walls.

"Is this the dining hall?" she asked.

"Yes, and you shouldn't be in here while it's being prepped," he told her. "You shouldn't have been able to leave your room yet at all—you were supposed to be locked in."

"I *was*," she spat. "And then I finally got the door open, and the hallway was gone. There are too many magic doors in this place."

He opened his mouth to speak, but something stopped him. His eyes narrowed and began to dart around the room, and she was about to ask what was wrong when she felt it. That dark, invisible gaze.

Is something watching me? Or is it him *they're following?*

A beat later, a low sound of frustration came from his throat, and he moved into action. Guiding her around the chaise by her elbow, he gently steered her out of the room through its wide, arched entrance.

"Where are you taking me?" she demanded.

"Someplace we can have a conversation that won't get you into more trouble," he murmured. "Though, I'm starting to suspect that keeping you out of trouble wouldn't be an easy task."

She gave an indignant hum in protest, which he ignored. He led her down the main hall and into the first room they came to, which just so happened to be a broom closet, identical to the one in the other corridor that had magically appeared. He snapped his fingers as he kicked the door shut behind them, and a candle flared to life on one of the wooden shelves.

"Shouldn't you take me back to my room?" She lifted her brows as she soaked in the details of the dingy space, trying to put as much distance between herself and his towering figure as she could; the size of the room, however, made putting more than five inches between them rather difficult.

"Do you *want* to go back to your room and finish the haunt?" he asked, crossing his arms over his chest.

"Why do you care where I do or don't go?"

"I think you're grossly misusing the word *care*."

"What would you call it, then?" She shifted on her feet with impatience. "Concern?"

"More like self-preservation if we're going to continue running into each other," he corrected. "Now back to *my* question—tell me the rest of how you ended up falling through the dining room ceiling."

"But I don't *know* how I ended up there." She threw her hands up. "Like I said, I opened the door to my bedroom, and when I went through, I fell."

"Fell *where?*" he pressed.

"It was some sort of void. There wasn't anything around but pitch-black. Only...whispers."

He froze. "Whispers?"

"Yes." She felt her forehead wrinkle at his reaction. "A bunch of whispers of conversations and—"

"You found the Whispering Gate?" His eyes grew wide.

"What's the Whispering Gate?"

"A place that you should not be able to access. It's on the Other Side."

"The Other Side. You mean—"

"Only those who are non-corporeal, or Devils, should be able to access the Whispering Gate," he confirmed. "The fact that it showed up for you is...interesting, to say the least."

"I'm sure it was just Phantasma playing a trick on me," she reasoned.

"No, the Whispering Gate is *summoned*, and no normal mortal should be able to call it."

"Who said I was normal?" she challenged.

"Clearly, you aren't," he agreed with a slow flick of his gaze over her figure, not leering, but scrutinizing. "So, what sort of being are you, then?"

She lifted her chin. "I'm a Necromancer."

"Now that *is* something." His smile turned almost feline at her claim. "Which would maybe explain why we were able to meet yesterday."

"That reminds me...why do you think I wasn't able to see you then? And why did you bother to warn me away? Isn't everyone here supposed to want people to enter the competition?"

"There are wards around the perimeter of the estate to stop passing mortals from being able to interact with any beings beyond them unless they enter the competition. Your Necromancy abilities must have messed with their effectiveness. Stop thinking about any being in Phantasma as having good intentions or motives to help *you* and start asking yourself how their actions are really beneficial to *them*."

"I'm not sure I'm very fond of your riddles," she said.

The twinkle in his gaze turned sinful. "That's too bad. I find riddles and puzzles to be rather thrilling. Most mortals who enter this competition are usually fond of such things as well."

"I didn't enter because I wanted to. I'm here to find my sister." He didn't need to know all the murky details, like the fact that Ophelia was actually just making a very strong educated guess that this was where Genevieve had run off to. "I need to find her and convince her to come home before she can get herself killed."

"Don't you think if your sister came here, of her own volition, that she knows exactly what she signed up for?"

Ophelia shook her head. "Genevieve can be impulsive. I worry she didn't understand the full scope of what she was signing up for."

"If you're both already here, though, wouldn't you like to see if you could win?"

"I don't care about winning. I don't care about whatever prize this hellish place is promising. I just care about getting my sister home." She tore her eyes away from him when she felt tears prick at their corners. She would not show him any sign of vulnerability. "She didn't leave me much to go off of, and no one here will tell me if they've even seen her. Oh, and that she wrote in her diary that she's trying to find someone named Gabriel."

His eyes flashed when she spoke the name, and her guard immediately went up.

"Do *you* know a Gabriel?" she demanded.

His expression was carefully blank. "I know many people."

"That isn't a real answer," she chided. "And if you're not going to be helpful, then I would like it if you stopped holding me hostage in this broom closet."

"You shouldn't be exploring right now," he warned. "If the wrong person catches you outside of your room during a haunt, they'll know you're different. And who said I couldn't be helpful? What if I told you I could make sure you get to your sister?"

Now she was the one who crossed her arms. "And at what cost would you help me do that?"

"You're catching on," he murmured.

"I offered to help you yesterday, you know," she revealed. "And you pretty much told me that wouldn't be a good idea for my own health. Now, if you'll excuse me, I'd like to go, please."

Surprise shined in his eyes. "You offered to help me?"

"Yes. I'm a Necromancer. Helping wayward Ghosts is part of our job description."

His expression shifted to something like thoughtfulness. "What is your name?"

She stared at him for a long time, deciding if she should risk giving it over this time.

He gave a dramatic sigh. "If I give you my name first, would that help?"

"Possibly," she answered.

"You can call me Blackwell. It's nice to officially make your acquaintance...?"

A long pause. Then, "Ophelia Grimm."

"*Ophelia*," he repeated, tasting every syllable. Her name on his tongue sounded like a wicked prayer. "You are exactly the person I've been waiting for."

12

FAIR GAME

Ophelia looked at the stranger—*Blackwell*—as if he had just grown a second head. "What are you talking about?"

"I have a bargain for you," he told her.

"Sorry, but my offer to help you has expired. I'm not giving you anything, and I certainly am not going to trust someone who chooses to work for a place like this."

Ophelia made to step past him, but he shifted to block her path.

"Didn't I tell you that I'm not part of Phantasma's staff?"

"Not exactly," she echoed his words from earlier.

Wicked delight lit up his eyes as if he were a cat who'd found a mouse that might learn to equally enjoy the game.

"I'm not working against you like the others," he vowed. "In fact, I'll do the exact opposite—I'll help you win this competition."

Ophelia dropped her arms in shock. "How?"

"You cannot leave this wing to look for your sister until you manage to survive the first seven levels. From experience, at least half the contestants in this competition will die, or forfeit, by level five," he told her. "But I can make sure you survive long enough to reach the last two levels, and then you'll be able to learn your sister's fate. All I need from you is a blood bargain."

"A blood bargain?" A wild giggle escaped her throat at the ludicrous idea. Any being that possessed magic could offer a blood bargain to someone, an oath that was unbreakable until every term was fulfilled exactly. And the consequences of such contracts with more powerful beings, like Devils, were unavoidable even in death. "I don't make blood bargains with rogue Phantoms. Or anyone else, for that matter."

Even as she spoke the words, however, she had to admit he had intrigued her greatly. If he really could help her survive this Hell house and make sure she didn't have to deal with any more demonic surprises coming out of her bathtub, she could hardly put a price on the value of that. After all, her mother had always warned her not to make deals with Devils, but never told her anything about making them with Ghosts...

Blackwell leaned forward until their gazes were level with one another's, the tips of their noses nearly touching. "No one has ever turned me down before."

She felt her face twist into a mocking expression at his words, but her traitorous pulse was beating erratically at his further proximity. He smelled faintly of vanilla and tobacco, and it irked her greatly that she found it to be a delicious combination.

Clearing her throat, she retorted, "I'd say I find that fact surprising, except it is not the least bit shocking that any fool willing to enter this place would also be willing to enter such a foolish pact. Good day, Blackwell. And don't you dare follow me."

This time, she shouldered past him without hesitation and pushed her way out of the closet. As she strutted down the hall, something small blinked into view next to her, matching her pace.

"Hello, cat," she grumbled. "Did you come to plead his case? Or do you just get a kick out of watching me stumble around this wretched place?"

"The latter, definitely," Blackwell's voice rang out behind her.

Ophelia didn't bother looking back at the Phantom as she snapped, "I thought I told you not to follow me?"

"I apologize if I gave you the impression that I do what I'm told." His tone was anything but apologetic.

Now she did look back. "Do you truly not have anything better to do around here than stalk me?"

He was strolling leisurely behind her, hands shoved in his pockets. It was odd to see a Ghost walk so casually—usually they hovered. She was again struck with the desire to know more about him. Phantoms were rare, and her knowledge of their abilities was much shallower than that of other Ghosts. It took everything in her to shove her curiosity out of reach.

"I was trying to be helpful," he insisted.

"You were *not*," she scoffed as she hooked a sharp right down another hall. "A blood bargain is almost never beneficial for anyone but the one offering it."

Before she could take another step, he blinked directly into her pathway, causing her to pull up short before she smacked right into him.

"You're going the wrong way," he advised. "And you didn't give me a chance to tell you what the price of the bargain was."

Ophelia couldn't stop herself from saying, "*Fine*. If it's the only way to get you to go the Hell away, I'll bite. What is it that you're offering?"

"Don't forget, *you* keep finding *me*." He gave her a pointed look, and she was already regretting giving in to his antics.

"Yes, and I'm starting to wonder if it would have been less hassle to just get murdered by the Ghoul in my bathroom."

"They wouldn't have fatally harmed you on the very first day," he offered. "They like to play with their victims for a little while first."

"You have a response for everything, don't you?"

"Yes." He winked, and she hated herself for thinking that the gesture was attractive. She couldn't help it, though. *Everything* about him was frustratingly attractive. It was hard not to be keenly aware of that fact when he kept taking up all her space. Annoyingly, he seemed to be just as aware of his attractiveness, which was really starting to grate on her nerves. He was the sort of man that thought his face could get him anything he wanted, and she was determined not to prove him correct.

"Are you at least going to help me get back to my room first?" she quipped. "The cat was being more helpful, honestly."

"This way." He blinked out of sight and reappeared down the hall behind her, unperturbed by her obvious annoyance.

She sighed and pivoted, her gown swishing with the movement. Poe mewled as he winked out to reappear beside Blackwell, who scooped the creature up in stride. Ophelia tried to memorize the way back to her room as she followed, not wanting to have to rely on him again.

When they finally stopped in front of her door, she hesitated, worried about what she might find inside.

"Here's the first term of my offer," Blackwell said as he let Poe drop to the ground. "I will clean up any haunts that you may accidentally stumble upon outside of the nine levels. Within the levels, however, you will have to do the work yourself—but I can assist."

He opened her bedroom door and waved for her to step over the threshold before him. She hesitated, but he gave her an encouraging nod, and she lifted her chin and poked her head inside. There were bloody footprints all over the room. Long, jagged gouges ripped through the wallpaper as well as the doorframe. She shuffled forward and Blackwell began to close the door behind them, letting Poe slip through at the last second before pushing it all the way shut. The cat went straight for her bed, padding his white paws into the comforter before curling up on the corner.

Ophelia opened her mouth to comment on the state of the room, but shrieked instead. The bloody Ghoul was dragging itself into the bathroom. She stumbled back a step—right into Blackwell's surprisingly hard body. His muscles were even more toned than she had imagined they'd be.

She felt his chest vibrate with quiet laughter against her back as he leaned his mouth down to her ear and drawled, "Watch this."

Lifting a hand, he gave a sharp snap of his fingers and it all disappeared. The Ghoul, the blood, the scratches. Everything cleared in less than a second.

She swallowed. "Where did it go?"

"Somewhere on the Other Side. I can move things in and out of this corporeal plane."

She tilted her head. "Is that something all Phantoms can do? And if you intercept all of the haunts around me, is that considered cheating?"

"I don't know any other Phantoms," he admitted. "And if it's not against the rules you were given before you entered, it's fair game."

"Alright then, enough beating around the bush." She spun toward him. "You showed me what you're capable of, so what exactly do you want in return? That key, I assume?"

"Angel, you have not seen even a modicum of what I am capable of," he told her, his green eyes flickering down her figure with an emotion she couldn't quite catch before turning more serious. "And *what* key?"

"You know—the heart and the key thing." She waved an impatient hand in the air between them. "Before I left last night, you told me that's what would set you free—I'm assuming it's some sort of riddle, right?"

He froze.

She frowned. "What? What's wrong?"

"Tell me what I said *exactly*," he urged.

"Hell, you really do just walk around with holes in your memory, don't you?" she said, and she could have sworn her words made him flinch, but his ability to recover was impeccable.

"Something like that" was all he commented.

If she were a different kind of person, she might have pitied him. Instead, she simply explained, "I asked if you were stuck here and if there was a way I could help you, and you said..." She racked her brain for his precise words. "...*a heart and a key would set me free. But you should hope we do not meet again...*"

Angel.

She decided to take creative liberty and omit that last bit.

"Why didn't you mention that detail earlier?" he demanded, tone rather intense.

"How would I have known that I needed to?" she shot back. "What's the big deal?"

The glint in his eyes became slightly wild. "The big deal is that I have been trapped here for an amount of time I cannot even remember, because of the aforementioned holes in my memory. And I will continue to be stuck, eternally, unless I find whatever tether or anchor is keeping me bound to this place, and figure out how to free myself. And somehow you managed to catch me in a moment of clarity—a moment already erased from my mind—where I supposedly told you exactly what I needed to find in order to untether me. You have *no* idea how extraordinarily bizarre this is."

Her head was spinning as she tried to keep up with his words.

"You're trapped here *eternally?* You mean, you cannot choose to pass over like other Ghosts?"

"Correct." He shoved a hand through his hair in frustration. "Every time I get close to finding what is keeping me in this place—I lose it again. This is—*you* are—the first concrete confirmation I've had that there *is* something to find. That it is possible."

She propped a hand on her hip. "So, you were going to ask me to find something that you didn't even have any concept of?"

"Given your abilities to summon mysterious doors and magic parlors, I figured you'd still be the best hope I've had yet. And my gut was correct."

"But I haven't *meant* to do any of those things. It was purely coincidence that we met that first time. I wasn't even supposed to be out that night."

"Whether you meant to or not, you did them," he implored. "I don't believe in coincidences. You claim you weren't supposed to be out that night. But you were. And you found me. If you're truly a Necromancer, you will be able to see things others can't. Which means you can search this place like no one has been able to for me before."

"And if I don't find this key?" she asked. "What's the price of failing?"

"The blood bargain ensures I'll get payment if you fail your task," he told her. "If you succeed, you'll have nothing to worry about."

"That didn't answer my question," she pressed.

"If you fail"—one corner of his mouth lifted in a grim smile as he spoke—"one decade of your life span will be transferred to me."

Night Two of Phantasma

13

NERVES

"*Angel, you have not seen even a modicum of what I am capable of*," the handsome, green-eyed bastard whispered in her ear as he pinned her back against the wall with a hand at her waist. "*I could make you utter things you never thought you'd possess the will to say just to get a taste of what I have to offer...*"

His tongue flicked out to lick the pulse throbbing at the side of her throat to emphasize his point.

She hated the way her body arched into him, of its own volition, as it searched for the friction it craved. He kept his grip on her waist as he slid his other hand into her hair and angled her mouth up to his. She made a sound of breathy pleasure when he bit down on her bottom lip, hard. Her hips began to writhe forward, into the hardness she could feel growing at the front of his trousers, and his hand at her waist began to slide down, ripping away the skirts of her dress to—

A bell tolled.

Ophelia shot up in her bed, hair clinging to her forehead and temples with sweat. She glanced at the clock across the room and was unsurprised to find that she had dozed back off and slept through both breakfast and lunch. Her body and mind had been utterly exhausted from the past few days, not to mention her wounds, and sleep was when the magic in her veins took its time to heal her injuries.

Another toll.

She scrubbed a hand over her face before stretching out her limbs and assessing her clawed-up arm. The skin was as good as new. Her shoulders relaxed with relief. That was definitely one advantage to the family magic.

She pushed back the covers and stood to look around the room, confirming there were no grotesque Ghouls lying in wait for an ambush. The fatigue still clinging to her bones, mixed with the needling paranoia this place constantly bred in her mind, almost made her regret turning down Blackwell's bargain.

Almost.

She had sent him away after his ridiculous revelation, laughing at the notion of giving up a decade of her life when she could just find Genevieve all by herself. For one, who knew how many years she had left? Giving ten of them away would surely be a perilous decision. Besides, Blackwell hadn't put up a fight over her dismissal anyway. He had only nodded at her rejection and disappeared to wherever it was he went in the manor when he wasn't randomly showing up to vex her or intrude on her rest. As if her waking hours weren't filled with enough Ghosts, now she had a smug Phantom haunting her dreams.

As she started dressing for the day—or rather, night—she had a sinking worry that there might come a point when she'd pay an egregious amount to be able to sleep peacefully.

Shaking off that thought, she nimbly laced up the corset of her black velvet dress, pulling the strings as hard as she could until she was barely able to breathe. Something she would regret later when she'd have to wrestle with the stays to get them off. Sometimes, it took both her mother and Genevieve to undo her corsets with how tight she made them, but she didn't know what to expect out of Phantasma's trials, and the last thing she wanted was faulty knots being a hindrance.

Quickly tying a matching ribbon into her hair, she slipped out of her room, hoping it wouldn't take too much time to find her way back to the dining hall so she could squeeze in a meal before things began. She was already ravenous from skipping dinner the night before. Plus, she was hoping she might finally run into someone—fully corporeal—that she could ask about Genevieve.

It took a bit of trial and error as she retraced her steps, but eventually she found her destination. She walked through the familiar open archway and took in the extravagant display of food on the expansive dining table as her stomach growled. The architecture of the dining hall was more ornate than she remembered, but perhaps that was only because she had been too busy falling through the ceiling to notice. There was no sign of the ordeal now, the ceiling fully intact, the debris nowhere to be seen. There was a large black and gold rug that spanned the entirety of the floor, and the filigree wallpaper beneath the ornate picture-frame molding was the definition of opulence. As were the marble pedestals and statues that lined the walls on either side of the archway, identical chaises to the one she had crashed into sitting between each pair of stone columns.

When she had finished gaping at the elegant details, she was surprised to find she wasn't alone. The girl with the flaxen braids—Luci, she remembered—was hunched over a bowl of soup, looking alarmingly haggard. Large purplish bags now sat beneath Luci's hollowed eyes, her pale complexion almost gray, and it wasn't until Ophelia sat down at the table and began fixing a plate that her presence was noticed.

"Oh," Luci squeaked out in surprise.

"Long day?" Ophelia asked, tone neutral.

Luci nodded quietly and looked back down at her soup. Apparently, whatever had stolen her sleep had also stolen her friendliness—which was more than fine by Ophelia. The two of them ate in silence before a few other contestants in their group began to trickle in. One was a smarmy-looking man who had missed a button on his vest. A woman with wine-colored curls and an onyx hoop pierced through her septum filed in behind him. The woman looked content to keep to herself at the far end of the dining table, which officially made her Ophelia's favorite so far.

Especially when the man plopped himself in the chair to her left and caused the plates in front of them to clatter.

"Eric Greensborough," he greeted. "My father is Donald Greensborough, owner of the city's largest tobacco plant. You are?"

"Not interested in socializing," Ophelia answered. Her patience with the men in this place was wearing unbelievably thin.

Something tightened in Eric's eyes, but his smile didn't waver as he turned to Luci and tried, "You're Lucinda, right? Cade's cousin? Heard you barely survived last night."

Luci winced a bit but didn't respond, and Eric let out a deep sigh.

"I *would* get stuck with the most boring group in this place," he muttered, mostly to himself, before announcing a bit louder, "That's just fine. Makes it easier on me when you all inevitably drop out or get slaughtered. Don't expect any help."

"You can't even button your vest correctly," Ophelia pointed out. "I doubt you were going to be anyone's first choice for assistance anyway."

Luci's lips curled up in a small smile as she sipped another spoonful of her soup. Eric's mouth twisted at the insult, but he still looked down to check her claim, standing from the table to stalk away when he noted that she was, in fact, right about the buttons.

"He's insufferable," Luci muttered.

"That seems to be a running theme with every man here," Ophelia observed.

Luci gave a humorless laugh before leaning forward and whispering, "Rumor has it that his father's business is nearly bankrupt after a whole debacle with not paying their property taxes and that's why he's here. They used their estate as collateral. And I certainly have no room to judge..."

Ophelia nodded politely but didn't offer anything more, and they both settled into silence once again. She needed to get to level seven before she could look for Genevieve, and she suspected that blending into their group was a better strategy than sticking out too much, and she didn't want to risk making any attachments. She wasn't sure what game Phantasma was playing by forcing players into these groupings, but she was sure it wasn't in order to *help* them win—which meant trusting anyone here was not a strategic move.

By the time everyone in their group had finally appeared in the dining hall and she had finished eating, it was almost sunset. Their first trial was about to begin, and anxious conversations on what they might expect began to buzz through the room.

"The levels are based on the Nine Circles of Hell," said a middle-aged man named James with sandy hair and a thick beard. "I read an interview by a past contestant in the *New York Post* once. They described games of Deceit, Wrath, Greed, Limbo..."

"Are you saying they're going to transport us to Limbo?" Eric mocked, smoothing a hand down the front of his adjusted vest.

James huffed. "Not the *real* Limbo on the Other Side. At least, I don't think. It's more of an illusion from what I've heard. One that feels very real."

"We aren't going to have to work together, are we?" someone else asked.

"I sure hope not," Cade said from where he leaned against the back wall with a sneer.

"What? You're too good for help?" James countered.

Cade gave a quick, sharp laugh. "I have a bet running that you'll be the first one out, old man."

"When the Hell is this thing going to start so all of you can shut the fuck up?" the woman with the septum piercing muttered from her corner.

The second those words were out in the open, every light in the room snuffed out.

"Welcome to level one," a deep masculine voice boomed. Ophelia's eyes slowly adjusted to the dark as he continued, "I'm your host, Zel."

With that, a puff of smoke wafted up from the floor by the archway, and Ophelia's mouth went slack at the sight, her dinner forgotten. A Devil.

Gasps around the room resounded at the sight of the egregiously tall man dressed in an impeccably tailored crimson suit. The curved horns that adorned the crown of his head jutted out from bronze curls that complemented his dusky brown skin and amber eyes.

Horns. His Devil's Mark.

The grin on Zel's face stretched as he took in the terrified expressions around him as if this response was exactly what he was hoping for. Ophelia fought the urge to roll her eyes at the pure *drama*.

Zel's amber gaze flicked over to her for a brief moment then as if he could hear her thoughts. She froze.

Each Devil possessed a range of different abilities, which made it hard to anticipate exactly what you were dealing with if you ever met one. And Ophelia knew from her mother's lessons that mind-reading was not off the table.

"I have the pleasure of explaining how the events of each level will transpire—do listen carefully, because I do not repeat myself," Zel warned, waving a hand at the wall to his left, where a doorway now appeared. "This is the portal that will take you into the first level. Each of your hosts will provide you with a clue about what to expect inside. That will be your last chance to forfeit. Once you step through, the level will begin, and your only ways out are winning, bargaining, or death."

The tension in the room grew thicker as people began to shift uncomfortably on their feet, glancing around as if they hoped the others' presence would be a reassuring sign that they couldn't possibly be mad for participating in such a risky game when everyone else here was doing the same.

"If you complete the trial successfully," Zel continued, "you will be brought back to Phantasma and receive your winner's mark. Are you ready for this level's clue?"

Before anyone could confirm they were ready, the older man, James, chimed, "Winner's mark? What does that entail? Will it be permanent? And what happens if you don't complete the trial—is there a mark for losing?"

Zel's smile was unforgiving. "I suppose you'll find out if you fail, won't you? Now, pay attention, here is your clue."

They all watched with rapt focus as the Devil flicked his hand toward the portal and words began to burn themselves into the door's surface with his magic.

IN DEEPENING LIGHT, WHERE SENSES FADE, A LABYRINTH
VAST, A DAUNTING MAZE.

NO SIGHT, NO SOUND, NO TOUCH TO GUIDE, NAVIGATE TRUE OR
BE CRUSHED INSIDE.

BEWARE THE BEAST, WITHIN THE HEART, AND FIND THE DOOR,
BACK TO START.

Ophelia tried to commit as much of the riddle to memory as she could, but the Devil wasted no time moving on.

"When I call your name step through," Zel directed. "Lucinda."

Everyone snapped their heads toward Luci, who was now a sickly shade of white. Cade snickered when she hesitated. Something about the sound must have bolstered her determination, though, because she tilted her chin up, rolled her shoulders back, and took a step toward the door. The entire group waited with bated breath as she swung the entrance open. Ophelia wasn't sure what she expected to see on the other side, but it certainly wasn't a plain white wall.

"Step through," Zel ordered. Luci took a deep breath and followed his directions.

The room tensed, waiting for a scream of agony or some other sign of distress, but none came, and an instant later, Luci completely disappeared from view. The Devil called the others' names in turn, and when he finally got to Ophelia, there were only a few contestants left waiting. She could still turn around and leave—with very few to witness her embarrassment—but she steeled her nerves. She could do this. She *would* do this. For Genevieve. For Grimm Manor. For her family's legacy.

She stepped through the portal and into the nothingness.

LEVEL
ONE

14

ℒIMBO

I t was unnervingly silent aside from the high-pitched ringing in her ears when she exited the portal. Her eyes burned as she looked around at the too-bright stone corridor. Not a single other soul was around.

She tried to take a step forward and stumbled. A disorienting sensation rolled through her body, and she barely caught her balance against the opposite wall before she face-planted into the smooth, cement ground. A silent gasp fell from her lips, and she snatched her hands away from the stone in front of her, curling them into her chest. She couldn't feel the wall. She couldn't feel *anything*. Not a single one of her senses was working except for her sight.

Racking her brain, she tried to remember what the clue had said.

...A daunting maze...No touch to guide...Beware the beast...

Ugh. There hadn't been enough time for her to remember every detail, but so far, the bit about having *no touch to guide* was certainly accurate. She wondered what Circle of Hell this was supposed to be emulating.

All her mother's lessons on the Nine Circles of Hell began flooding back to her. Ruled by the King of the Devils, Hell and its Circles existed on the Other Side as a kingdom for all the different types of immortal paranormal beings. The immortal classifications of paranormal beings were able to access the Nine Circles whenever they desired, sharing the territories with the souls of the dead. The best perk she got as one of the mortal classifications of paranormal being was a longer than average life span here on earth before she crossed over to the Other Side.

Ophelia might have preferred Hell at this point.

Despite what some mortals believed, Hell was not meant to be a punishment for humans who lived sinfully before they died. Human morality was much too diverse and fickle to base an entire afterlife on, after all. Rather, those who were punished in Hell were often punished for their crimes against humanity or the fabric of the universe. The second major Kingdom on the Other Side was Heaven—home to all the classifications of Ephemeral beings. And despite what human lore loved to suggest, the beings that belonged to Heaven were no more good or bad than the ones of Hell. It just so happened Hell had been bestowed the task of punishing malicious mortal souls and Heaven the task of rewarding the ones who died with exceptional valor.

Ephemeral beings and their powers, however, were a subject her mother had never really expanded on. Which was just as well considering Ophelia thought she might find beings such as Angels and Seraphim, and the territories they ruled, rather dull in comparison. But there was certainly nothing dull about tales of the Nine Circles.

Those punished in the Circle of Violence were ripped limb from limb at the start of each day only to find themselves mended by the next dawn for the torture to begin again. Those punished in the Circle of Greed had to watch everything, and everyone, they coveted melt in a pit of boiling lava. Those punished in the

Circle of Gluttony were forced to run without stopping—for eternity. Those punished in the Circle of Limbo...

That was it.

This was Phantasma's version of Limbo. Complete sensory deprivation.

She wondered which Circle her mother had chosen to reside in on the Other Side.

You're never going to make it out, the insidious voice in her head whispered. **You'll die if you don't find your way out of here in exactly five minutes.**

"*Stop*," she tried to shout at the voice, but there was no sound. She reached toward the wall again, to tap her finger against it and neutralize the intrusive countdown her mind was trying to impose on her. But the comforting compulsion that usually overrode the inane tasks the voice ordered her to do didn't have the same effect when she couldn't feel it.

She felt the panic begin to creep in.

You're fine. There is no time limit. You just have to breathe.

She cautiously started forward, her steps a little wobbly as she got used to the inability to feel. Making her way down the long, narrow corridor, she eventually found an opening in the stone. There was another long corridor on the other side of the opening, which forked into two. The maze had begun.

She chose left. Picking up her pace, she made a few more turns before she realized she had gone in a giant circle. She was entirely disoriented and wanted to curl up on the ground and sob.

This is maddening. This is Hell.

And then it got worse.

The light around her dimmed, and dread bloomed inside of her. They were going to slowly lose their only remaining sense.

She needed a plan.

I need a way to mark the paths I've already taken.

She looked down at her hands. Her magic had to be useful for something. Concentrating on the tips of her fingers, she waited for the telltale sparks of her magic to ignite. Small, fizzling flares of light began to expel sporadically in every direction, and a sense of relief shot through her. She reached out to the wall and used the sparks to scorch the word *start* into the stone. Then she began.

Every time there was a split in her path, she marked her first chosen direction with a charred "X" and in the time it took to get through almost eleven unique passages, the light had dimmed twice more.

I can make it through about five corridors per round of light, she noted. *At this rate there's probably about ten more degrees of dimming before I'll be walking in the dark...*

At the next opening, she saw one of her "X"s marked on the left. She pivoted to the right this time and—

—the wall at the end of the corridor was moving toward her. Another line from Zel's clue came back to her.

...NAVIGATE TRUE OR BE CRUSHED INSIDE...

Fuck.

She spurred herself into action. Slipping through the next break in the stone, a few yards before the moving wall could reach her, she hoped to be in the clear, but what she found in the new hallway made her breath hitch in her chest. The walls in this corridor were moving as well. Which meant that if she didn't make it to the opening before they closed it off, she would be trapped.

She yanked up her skirts and rushed down the corridor. By the time she was halfway to the next opening, the moving wall was within inches of the gap's threshold, and she knew she had to push herself harder if she was going to reach it in time. Her breathing became labored, despite the fact that she couldn't feel the burning she was sure should have been igniting in her lungs. By the time she made it to the exit, the shifting wall was already halfway across it, causing her to wedge herself through the tight space and shimmy herself out the other side.

She hunched forward, dropping her hands to her knees to catch her breath. She knew she must be sweating, but she couldn't feel it. All she could feel was the pressure in her chest as her body begged for more oxygen, and the heaviness in her legs and thighs. When she finally straightened herself up, she stepped forward—

—but something snapped her back against the wall. Her damned skirts were caught.

She tried to scream in frustration, but no sound came out. Pressure pricked at the corners of her eyes, but if tears were sliding down her cheeks, she couldn't tell. She grabbed a fistful of her skirts and tugged sharply, causing the material to rip away with a jagged edge. When she'd spend her afternoons in Grimm Manor daydreaming about the sort of danger that could make her heart race, it had definitely not been anything like this.

A quick glance around the new corridor determined nothing was moving. For now. She continued her exploration, delving deeper and deeper into the labyrinth, her only measure of time the dimming light. Every time she entered a new corridor, the length of her walk grew shorter and shorter—she was getting closer to the center.

The light dimmed just as she marked another wall and started to the left, but it was immediately clear that it was the wrong way. The far left wall began to slide forward, just as before, and she pivoted on her heels and sprinted in the opposite direction.

As if in reaction, she caught the wall beginning to slide toward her faster out of her peripherals. Chasing her.

Damn it.

There was another moving wall ahead, and this time the exit looked to be out of reach. She sprinted as fast as her feet would carry her, the wall behind her staying on her heels.

A shot of fear speared through her as she reached the mouth of the exit, the wall behind her only inches from pressing into her back. When the one in front of her began to close in as well, she twisted her body to shuffle herself sideways, through the tightening gap.

In her mind, the Shadow Voice laughed. The notion of that laugh nearly tripped her up as she squeezed herself the rest of the way out into the next corridor, just before the two walls slammed together.

The anxiousness beginning to bubble up in her stomach should've come from the fact that she had just very nearly been crushed like an insect. Instead, it was the idea that the voice in her head had just chuckled at the prospect of her demise making her buzz with fear.

The Shadow Voice had always spoken to her, of course, but never had it been...this. Never had it taunted her or actively wished for *her* to be in pain. It had always been rather matter-of-fact in giving her the daily asinine tasks she had always been compelled to obey. As if it really didn't have a choice but to make her rush home in the dark within an arbitrary time limit, or knock on her headboard exactly nine times before she went to sleep in order to keep her family safe. And now it was laughing at her.

What's wrong, little Necromancer? it purred. **Can't handle the real me?**

Ophelia clenched her fists at her sides and shoved the voice away. She looked around, assessing the newest corridor, and was shocked to find that it wasn't another empty passage at all. She had finally reached the center of the labyrinth.

Her victory, however, was short-lived. Because in the heart of the maze, slept an enormous beast.

A Hellhound.

She recognized the monstrous beast from one of her mother's books on the creatures of Hell in Grimm Manor's library. The hound's leathery skin was white as snow, its talons and teeth a shiny ebony. The beasts had been created to guard coveted artifacts by the King of the Devils himself. They were vicious, with venomous bites, but they remained asleep as long as the item they were guarding stayed untouched.

Ophelia crept around the Hellhound, giving it as wide a berth as she could, but as she was about to get a glimpse of whatever it was guarding, two other contestants came crashing into the maze's clearing: Luci's cousin, Cade, and someone whose name she thought was Buford. Or Beau. Or Bradley. Whatever his name was, he barely spared her a glance as they gaped at the demonic creature sprawled before them. Cade waved to his friend to follow after him and Ophelia nearly choked on her shock as they took off straight toward the beast.

"*Don't!*" she tried to shout, but of course they couldn't hear her. She had a feeling that even if they could, they wouldn't listen.

They made their way toward its flank, and she finally caught a glimpse of what the monster was guarding. A gilded trap door.

She froze.

It was the exit. That's what the hound was guarding. And whoever went through first would get out unscathed.

But the rest of them would have to deal with the woken beast.

She gaped in horror at the realization. Cade and his friend

were going to escape, leaving the rest of them to be devoured. She jolted into motion, but it was too late. Cade had already reached the door and unceremoniously yanked it open. The hound woke in an instant.

A bursting pain shot through Ophelia's ears as her senses came roaring back. Her knees buckled and she tumbled to the ground, hands clamped over her ears. A flash of light shot across her vision as the two men stepped through the door and shut it behind them.

With no other beings around, the beast locked its eyes onto her.

"Fuck," she whispered.

The Hellhound lunged.

Ophelia lurched to her feet and headed back for the twisted bowels of the labyrinth, the Hellhound pursuing. She didn't have time to mark her path this time, only running faster than she ever had in her life and hoping she didn't turn into any dead ends. She dashed through the white stone corridors, feeling the rancid, hot breath of the monstrous creature thicken the air as it gained on her. The pounding of its paws shook the floor beneath her feet.

She gritted her teeth. This was those bastards' fault. Not that their selfishness should have surprised her. Desperate times, desperate measures, sure, but she would have at least waited for everyone who'd shown up to reach the exit before she went through it and woke the beast. The minor interaction she'd had with Cade had already left a bitter taste in her mouth, and when she saw him again, she was going to chew him up and spit him out for this.

"Assholes," she hissed as she hooked a right and—

—crashed right into another body. Spots flashed across her vision at the impact.

She couldn't remember this contestant's name. He was about Genevieve's age, scrawny with light brown skin and hazel eyes. She pushed off of him and regained her balance, opening her mouth to tell him to run, but the Hellhound rounding the corner did that for her.

"Holy—" the boy's eyes widened, but she didn't bother to stay and hear the rest of his sentence. He scrambled after her, clamoring to stay on her heels.

"Do you remember which direction you came from?" she shouted, her words ragged with effort.

"Left! Up ahead!" he answered, his own voice labored. "But it's blocked now!"

She nodded and hooked a right when they approached the next opening, hoping it might loop back around to the large clearing where they'd be able to make a break for the exit without the hound guarding it. The beast was gaining traction, and her new companion was slowing down.

Ophelia glanced over her shoulder with gritted teeth. "Faster!" she ordered.

His face was a mask of pain as he tried to push himself on—at some point during the sprint he had pissed himself—and she saw the moment the exhaustion took over his limbs. The Hellhound was getting too close. There was no way he was going to make it. She thought for a moment that maybe she should keep running anyway, that if the hound was distracted, it would be easier for her to get away.

The locket at her throat warmed. As if it was admonishing her.

Damn it.

Ophelia skidded to a stop and spun. Summoning every ounce of magic she had stored in her core, she pulled and pulled until she felt its heat slither through her veins, her limbs, to her hands. Then she released it all in a flurry of blue sparks right at the Hellhound's face.

The action lacked finesse—and aim—but it worked well enough. The beast let out a pealing whine as her magic hit its eyes, and Ophelia grabbed the boy's shirt and dragged him after her. They twisted down the corridors, having to backtrack a few times, but it seemed she had bought them just enough time to make those few mistakes. Then finally, the clearing came into view.

"Thank the Angels." The boy began to weep as they broke into the center of the maze once again, the gilded door just a few more yards away.

Relief washed over Ophelia's body when they reached the golden exit. Twisting its knob, she heaved the door open, and the boy didn't hesitate to jump through. Behind her, in the maze, she heard a blood-curdling scream and the echoes of bones snapping like twigs. The hound must have already recovered from her magic. She swallowed thickly, a knot of regret twisting in her stomach, and leaped through the door, letting it slam shut behind her.

15

VERMIN

The portal brought them right back into the dining hall; they dropped onto the floor with heavy thuds. Ophelia groaned at the ache of the landing as she made her way to her feet. The boy, however, stayed on the ground, losing the contents of his stomach all over the carpet. She cringed, sidestepping out of the onslaught's path, and looked around to find Cade and his accomplice shoveling food in their mouths at the far end of the table.

"You almost got people *killed*," she said, seething, stalking toward them, "and you're sitting here stuffing your faces?"

"Not our problem," Cade said. "You were there before me and Beau. You should've taken the opportunity when you had it."

"There can only be one winner," Beau added. "It's every person for themselves."

Ophelia wrinkled her nose at them. They were heartless scoundrels. She had been much too focused on the insidious dangers Phantasma would throw at her, and foolishly overlooked the threat that her fellow contestants posed.

"You could have waited a bit longer to make sure as many of us could get through as possible before waking the hound! You're both selfish *pricks*."

Cade laughed as he set down the leg of roast chicken he had been ripping into as if what she just suggested was the most ludicrous thing he'd ever heard. "Don't be so naïve, little mouse."

"Of the two of us, I think it's you who is closer to vermin," she spat at him.

His expression quickly turned to a sneer. "If it's between everyone else and me, I'm choosing me. You think I *want* to be here? My family gave me the option of going back with the prize or not going back at all. I don't give a fuck about your sense of nobility."

"Besides, that Devil, Zel," Beau chimed in before the vein in Cade's forehead ruptured with anger, "he already ran off to offer a bargain to whoever needed one in there. That's how this place works. And if they're smart, they'll take it. Otherwise, it's their own fault that they die."

"A Devil's bargain is not a mercy," she reprimanded. "It's deplorable of them to prey on victims like this."

It was becoming apparent that these were not the Devils of her sinful daydreams. The ones that *could* take advantage of defenseless souls but chose not to . . . using their magic for their sensual desires instead of insidious games . . . But isn't that why she had always so closely adhered to her mother's rules?

This was a Devil's true nature. It made her sick to think she ever imagined getting whisked away by such darkly perverse beings.

Beau wiped the back of his hand across his freckled face, smearing the shiny grease from his meal off his lips before he spoke. "That Devil made it abundantly clear that anyone could have forfeited before they entered. Not really the Devil's fault for taking the offerings of such fools."

Cade laughed in agreement. "The desperate will consent to the most egregious prices after all. I'd bet a Devil's success rate here is ten times what it is with tourists in the French Quarter after dark. And if you ask me, I'd much rather Devils reap their deals here than be roaming *our* streets."

"You're disgusting," Ophelia told them, backing away a step. "And if someone had to make a deal with a Devil in that maze, it's because you assholes couldn't wait a few minutes longer." Cade snapped out his hand to grab her wrist and hold her in place. "I don't like being called names."

"*Let go*," she demanded, trying to tug herself away, but his grip only tightened.

"You can't really think you're going to win this competition if you can't handle these harsh truths, little mouse," Cade taunted.

"Stop calling me that." She glowered as she pulled again.

"Make me," he bit out.

The malice in his eyes made her blood run cold. She could count on one hand the number of times she'd been alone in the company of a man. And she certainly had never been around a man like *this*. One who looked at her like she was prey.

She braced herself and gave another hard yank. When he still wouldn't let go, something strange happened. Her wrist slipped right through his grasp. Not because his grip loosened, but because her entire arm turned *transparent*. Her mouth fell open as she watched her limb return to its solid state a second later.

"What the—?" Cade scrambled back from her. "You're— you're one of them. One of the manor's Demons. This is a trap!"

Beau clamored out of his chair. "How did you even touch her, then?"

"I don't know! She was solid at first!" Cade swore.

Ophelia couldn't help it, she giggled. Her mind was finally reaching its breaking point after the terrors of the first trial. Out of the corner of her eye, she noticed the young man she'd saved passed out in a pool of his own sick, and her laugh deepened.

"Let's get the Hell out of here," Beau insisted, panicked. He pushed his way past Cade, his food completely forgotten.

Cade narrowed his eyes as he made to follow his companion, but they didn't get very far before the entire room went pitch-black.

"What is she doing now?" Beau shouted. "I can't see anything!"

A few candles flared to life as soon as he said those words, and Ophelia's eyes widened as she took in the scene change. The food on the table was now crawling with spiders and other rancid creatures. Centipedes and maggots writhed over the now-bare carcass of the roasted chicken; goblets of blood replaced the wine.

Beau retched and lost his dinner all over the rug.

"Stop it," Cade growled at her, an ominous orange glow illuminating his face from the dancing firelight. "Go away, Demon bitch!"

Her giggling stopped. "I am *not* a Demon!"

"I don't believe you," Cade snarled as he stalked toward her. "Make it stop or—"

He paused when he noticed a metallic flash atop the table. A silver carving knife had appeared. The damn house was spurring him on.

They lunged simultaneously. She was only a second too slow, and he managed to slip the blade off the table, brandishing it between them.

Adrenaline speared through her. "I'm not working for Phantasma," she implored. "This isn't happening because of me!"

"I saw your arm disappear, you lying bitch." He stabbed the silver blade in her direction.

There were several paranormal beings that could be killed by silver. If a Poltergeist managed to possess a solid form on this linear plane, silver could sever them from their vessel and send them back to the Other Side. If you could manage to stab a

Wraith or Demon in the heart with it, it would banish them to Hell—permanently. Necromancers, however, had no such magical weakness to the metal.

She would just bleed out the old-fashioned way.

Cade dove forward, tackling her to the ground. She struggled against his weight, thrashing her hips and legs to buck him off of her, but with him straddling her waist, it was hard to gain leverage. When he brought the blade down toward her heart, she threw her hands out, trying to block his swing, but the action was unnecessary. The knife plunged into her chest, but there was no blood. No pain. From her neck down she had *disappeared*.

A strangled sound caught in her throat at the sight.

"Don't tell me you're not going to fight back, angel," a voice drawled somewhere above her. "Careful, or I'll have to start believing you save all your moxie just for me."

Ophelia bristled at Blackwell's taunting words, while Cade remained oblivious of the real threat standing right over his shoulder. But Blackwell was right.

Before Cade could bring the knife down again, she summoned the small amount of magic she had left after her confrontation with the Hellhound and sent all of it right into the bastard's abdomen. Icy blue sparks crackled through the room from her palms, and Cade flew off her, passing through Blackwell's transparent form, and landing on his back with a thud. She scrambled to her feet.

Cade didn't waste any time recovering, pushing up from the ground more pissed than before. Blackwell was grinning down at her like a fiend, and her breath hitched as she watched him shift from his non-corporeal form to something just solid enough to grab the neck of Cade's shirt and yank him back before he could advance on her once more.

Cade stumbled in confusion, his arms flailing in panic as he tried to twist around and see what had caught him. Blackwell's grip held firm.

Cade looked at her and demanded, "Let me go!"

"I'm not holding you," she told him, palms up to demonstrate her innocence.

"Stop lying to me, bitch—*ah!*"

Blackwell spun Cade around to face him now, Cade dropping the knife to the ground in shock.

Then Blackwell solidified himself completely. "Call her a name one more time," he threatened, his tone bored but his eyes alight with mischief. "I dare you."

Cade gawked at the sight of Blackwell's tall frame, but his expression quickly soured as he spat, "Incredible, even Demons have whores—"

Blackwell grabbed Cade's wrist and twisted his arm until he screeched in agony.

"Incredible," Blackwell echoed. "The audacity of men worth less than dirt."

A surprised laugh fell from Ophelia's mouth, and Blackwell turned his face just enough to wink at her. Her amusement was quickly cut off by the feeling of something crawling up her right arm, however. She looked down to find spiders the size of her hand skittering over her dress. "*Gross.*"

While she began brushing the pests off her, Blackwell sent Cade flying into the far wall before blinking out of sight to reappear by her side, transparent once more.

"It's time for you to get out of here," he urged as he flicked another of the arachnids off her shoulder. "It's about to get much worse than a few bugs."

"Worse than the Hellhound?"

She regretted the question the moment it slipped from her

mouth. Spiders bigger than her head were dropping from the ceiling of the dining hall, and she swore she saw something *slither* out of a dark corner.

Phantasma certainly knows how to throw a victory dinner.

"It's too dark for me to see anything," she complained, spinning around to grab one of the candles on the table, sending bugs scurrying in every direction.

When she held the flame up to illuminate the space in front of her, however, the wax melted all the way down to the quick. She hissed as the hot liquid dripped onto her.

"Out this way," Blackwell advised, guiding her by her elbow. "Watch your step."

That was easier said than done, but she didn't resist as he led her toward the exit, kicking away another snake as they went. After a few careful steps, Blackwell's hold on her elbow tightened and he halted them in place.

Then, his mouth was right next to her ear. "Don't. Move."

She began to ask why, but his hand clamped over her mouth to stop her from speaking. She scowled, having half a mind to bite him for such a rude gesture, but then she noticed it.

Describing the creature in front of her as nightmarish would be an understatement. It was another serpent, but this one would not be so easily kicked away. Its fangs were the length of her forearm. The reptile's shrewd yellow eyes unsettling as it poised itself to strike. When it opened its mouth—which was big enough to swallow her whole—she noticed it had not one, not two, but three rows of razor-sharp teeth behind those fangs.

Blackwell slowly dropped his hand from her face when he was sure she was too frozen in shock to make another sound. He moved behind her, pressing himself flush against her back, sliding his hands around her waist to hold her steady. By the way the serpent didn't track his movements, she knew he had gone back to being only solid enough for her to see and feel. She was too terrified to pretend she wasn't grateful for his presence in that moment. Even though the stillness of his chest against her was oddly unnerving. There was no rise and fall with his breath—no heartbeat.

Ophelia's heart, on the other hand, was about to burst.

"You're going to slowly back away," he instructed. "And when I say run, you *run*. Got it?"

"Couldn't you just make it go away?" she whispered back.

"Not without payment," he answered. "Unless you're changing your mind about my offer, I don't have enough power to get rid of the serpent or transport you somewhere with me."

She balled her hands into fists. "I will not make such a life-altering decision because I'm *cornered*. That's as bad as making a deal with a Devil."

She felt him shrug. "Then get ready to run. On my word."

She took a deep breath, and he gave her waist one last reassuring squeeze before blinking away somewhere too dark for her to see. Now it was just her and the beast.

There was a crash of glass somewhere in the back of the room, and the snake snapped its head away to investigate. She waited for Blackwell's signal.

One excruciating minute passed. Then another.

When it failed to come, she wondered if the blackguard had abandoned her. The serpent was already turning back her way, and she knew she had a decision to make. Trust the Phantom she'd only just met with her life—or make a run for it.

She was hoping her locket might guide her through the decision, but it remained cold as ice against her throat. She gave Blackwell one more minute. When he still did nothing, she took a deep breath and broke into a sprint before the serpent's full attention locked in on her again.

Wrong decision.

Her movement recaptured the serpent's interest, and the creature darted forward, striking out with its head. She didn't even have time to scream as she dodged to the side, crashing into the sharp edge of a marble pedestal, and sending the stone bust that adorned the top crashing to the ground. As she fell forward to her hands and knees, one of the shards from the statue sliced open her left palm.

"*Fuck.*" She cradled her palm to her chest and twisted around to see the snake poising itself right above her. When it lunged out this time, she wasn't fast enough.

As the creature's fangs pierced through the soft flesh of her shoulder, the room shattered with the sound of her shriek.

16

SUCH TROUBLE

Warm blood soaked through her chemise and spilled down the front of her ruined corset. The serpent unclenched its jaw from her shoulder and readied itself to strike again. She lifted up her uninjured arm, trying to conjure even the slightest bit of her magic as she held her palm out toward the beast. She knew the well of power inside of her was nearly depleted, and just a few small blue zaps managed to putter out, the sparks quickly snuffing away like the last embers in a fireplace.

Her magic wasn't like a Witch's or Demon's—it could not transform into ice or fire, or any other element. A Necromancer's magic came out as pure energy. So, while she could light a candle with her magic's friction, she wasn't able to actually wield the flames. Necromancers were meant to be a bridge between the corporeal plane and the Other Side, to bring life and energy to that which was dead or undead. Replenishing that sort of magic quickly required one of two things: the life force of another being, or rest. Neither of which was currently an option.

Her tiny sparks made the serpent pause for all of ten seconds, but it was just enough time for her to spot a long sword hanging on the wall above the pedestal she had knocked over. She gathered the rest of her strength and hauled herself from the ground, reaching up to tug the sword from its mount one-handed. Just as she spun around to point it at the beast, the creature regained its bearings. It unlocked its jaw to strike at her again, and she shoved the sword, and half her arm, into its gaping mouth.

Blood spurted everywhere. The hot, sticky liquid splattered across her face and flooded down her arm. She let go of the sword and snatched her arm back out of the snake's mouth as it began to twist and writhe, swinging its head through the air as its long body curled into itself. A moment later, the entire reptile dissolved into a cloud of smoke, the illusion Phantasma had conjured destroyed.

Ophelia stared at the now-empty spot in front of her, chest heaving as she tried to catch her breath. That had almost been harder than the actual trial.

"Ophie?" a familiar voice gasped behind her.

"Genevieve?" Ophelia spun around. There, in the archway, was her sister's silhouette.

Ophelia staggered a step forward. "Genevieve—"

"Ophie! Hurry!" Genevieve urged, her face drenched in shadows as she turned on her heel and ran from the room.

Ophelia didn't hesitate. She stumbled after her sister into the hallway.

"Faster," Genevieve implored from the end of the long corridor.

Ophelia didn't know how her sister moved that fast, or perhaps Ophelia was just moving very slowly, but she spurred her feet on, ignoring the rippling pain coursing through her body with every movement. Just before she could reach Genevieve, her sister jetted around the corner and out of sight.

"Genevieve, wait!" Ophelia cried. She tried to pick up her pace, but something was wrong. Her feet weren't moving as quickly as she wanted them to and her vision was becoming blurry, the throbbing wound in her shoulder burning hotter. Still, she pushed herself on, turning the corner and scanning for her sister in the dark.

"Over here, Ophie," Genevieve directed, but something in her tone was off now.

"Vivi, I don't feel well." Ophelia swallowed as she stumbled closer, the room around her beginning to sway, and Genevieve's silhouette growing distant. "Where have you been? I've been looking for you..."

"I've been looking for you, too," her sister crooned, a hint of something dangerous peeking through the words. "Why don't you come closer, and I'll show you how much I've missed you."

"My feet aren't working..." Ophelia said, her words slurred to her own ears. "I'm so...tired."

The room was tilting now, darkness closing in on the edges of her vision as she tried to trudge another step forward. Her body became too heavy to move, but all she could think about was how close she was to reaching her sister. *Only two more steps.*

Before she could take them, however, she heard something thud in front of her and then a pair of arms scooped her up off her feet and carried her through the shadows.

"You're going to be such trouble," a velvet voice whispered above her in the dark.

She hadn't realized her eyes had fully shut until she tried to pry them open to see who was speaking. But she couldn't. Her lids were too heavy.

She knew the voice didn't belong to Genevieve, but she still tried to whisper back, to ask if they could take her home.

There was no answer. For a long moment, she felt like she was floating in the air, untethered by gravity. Then she was sinking into something soft. She thought she heard something rip, followed by words she didn't understand, and a beat later something cool draped over her feverish forehead.

The velvet voice said something else, but she was already slipping away.

Night Three
of Phantasma

17

OATH

Ophelia woke the next day drenched in sweat. A damp cloth was covering her forehead and something warm was pressed against her hip. As she struggled to sit up, a mewl of protest rang out.

"Careful," a voice warned, just as a shooting pain went through her arm.

She blinked her eyes open to find Blackwell sitting in the armchair across from her bed, and Poe lying by her side. The cat glared at her for disturbing his slumber.

"What are you doing in my room?" she croaked to them both, reaching up to remove the cloth from her face. No, not a cloth, a ragged piece of a... shirt?

"You almost got eaten by a giant serpent, and *that's* the first question you have?" He raised his brows and leaned forward to prop his elbows on his knees. "Not, 'are any of my limbs missing?' They aren't, by the way."

She took him in for a long moment, noting that something was different—his outfit had changed. Instead of the black jacquard suit and shirt, he was now wearing a three-piece ensemble made entirely of viridian silk. His long coat had polished gold buttons and his cravat was ever so slightly askew where it was tucked into his vest.

"What happened?" she finally asked, her voice still thick.

"What happened is that you're incredibly impatient," he answered flatly.

She tried sitting up again, wincing when she put pressure on her right arm. He shot to his feet to assist.

"The snake..." she realized as he gently propped her back against the headboard. "I thought you had abandoned me—"

"I told you to wait for my signal." His tone was irritated.

"And I'm supposed to trust you?" She wrinkled her nose. "This entire place is designed to kill me. I barely made it out of that first level, and when I did, there were more monsters waiting. Excuse me for not just taking the word of a Ghost who keeps stalking me."

"*Stalking* is a bit dramatic," he drawled.

She only glared at him.

He let out a frustrated breath. "I could have not offered to help you at all—does that not warrant at least a sliver of confidence that I'm not trying to get you killed?" He lifted a brow, growing more indignant with each word. "I also could have left you to be possessed by that Poltergeist you decided to traipse after in the hallway. I'd ask if you had any wits left in your head at all, except I'm fairly certain the venom in your system was responsible for that unadvised foray."

"Poltergeist?" she questioned.

Poltergeists were the souls of deceased Demons that had managed to weasel their way here from the Other Side and had the same abilities as regular Apparitions with one major addition—they could possess you. And if they possessed you long enough, they could steal your soul and resurrect themselves back to their original demonic forms.

He narrowed his eyes. "Yes. Another few seconds alone, and it would have swindled you into a possession. Poltergeists will shapeshift into people you care about and lure you in, so you shouldn't trust anyone you think you might know here. If your sister is in Phantasma, she is not in your group or this wing.

Until you reach level seven, it's safe to say you should stop looking for her. I thought a Necromancer would know to be more careful about such a trick."

The last bit brought her blood to a full-on boil.

"*Excuse me* for not being in the best mindset after fighting off a giant serpent! I don't think making one mistake under the influence of venom is an accurate reflection of my skills as a Necromancer." She glowered at him. "I did just fine against the Hellhound and getting myself out of that maze by myself. If you think I'm so incapable, why are you pestering me to help you with your silly little scavenger hunt?"

Blackwell snorted. "I didn't say you were *incapable*. In fact, I was mildly impressed with how you managed to get out of level one. And most people drop within two seconds of being injected with so much venom—if they don't faint from seeing a beast like that in the first place—so I think you're rather a force to be reckoned with there, too."

She gaped at him. "You saw me in the maze? How?"

He shrugged. "The levels of Phantasma take place on a different linear plane than this one. Corporeal souls can only see what has been created by the Devil who runs each level. But those of us able to shift between planes can watch the events from the outside."

"So, this is all some sort of sick entertainment to the Apparitions here?"

He shook his head. "The Apparitions don't really invest themselves much with the happenings in Phantasma outside of their debts. The Devils on the other hand...they have a betting pool for each group. Don't worry, you're not in their loser brackets. Yet."

Her nose wrinkled. "That's sick."

He shrugged again. "A Devil is a Devil."

"And you?" she asked.

"What about me?" He lifted a brow.

"Do you usually watch mortals run around like ants, trying to escape their deaths? Is that entertaining to you?"

"No, I'm usually helping my chosen contestant survive," he told her. "Since you turned down my bargain, I didn't have much else to do. Besides, I find the interpersonal group politics much more entertaining to watch. Two of your group members have already begun quite the sordid affair."

She ignored that last part. "So, you watched to see if I'd fail without agreeing to your bargain?"

He huffed a laugh. "Partially. You did well, but I do think you underestimate how much harder the trials can get. That first one was easy compared to the others."

"That was supposed to be *easy?*"

He smirked. "You get the picture, then."

She moved to hug her arms around her torso in comfort and flinched when the action pulled on the wound at her shoulder. She pulled her sleeve down to see a long, jagged bite mark marring her skin. And something else. A small golden star-like marking she had never seen before. Her prize for completing the first trial, she realized. She wondered if the glittering tattoo would be permanent.

"Your arm is in pretty bad shape," Blackwell cautioned as she tried to move again. "And I can't help heal you until…"

"*That's* what this is all about," she accused, jabbing a finger in his direction and disturbing Poe's slumber enough this time that the cat finally winked out of the room. "Let me guess—you summoned that serpent yourself so you could pretend to save me from it and trick me into trusting you."

"I had nothing to do with the serpent," he retorted. "That was a manifestation of one of the other contestant's darkest fears—the one you saved from the Hellhound. It was the secret he paid to enter Phantasma. The manor chooses when to utilize those. And I'm not trying to *trick* you into trusting me, I'm trying to show you that we can help each other. If you'd listen to me, that is." He muttered the last bit.

She had the sudden urge to stick her tongue out at him, but she resisted, and the corners of his mouth slowly turned up as if he knew that was exactly what she wanted to do.

"I don't need your help," she maintained. "And I can heal my arm myself. I just have to get a good night's sleep."

He snorted. "Yeah, good luck with that here. But that reminds me—you're stretching your magic too thin, too quickly. You're going to burn yourself out. I, on the other hand, would be able to heal your shoulder completely with very little effort. Even better, the next time you found yourself in a ghastly predicament, I could simply transport you away and you wouldn't have to worry about using up your magic before the next level."

"And why is it you can't do any of that without a blood bargain? You helped me back to my room, didn't you?"

"And being corporeal long enough to carry you back here took a great deal of effort," he revealed. "The only way I can do such things consistently is if I have a connection to something living."

"The decade you're asking for," she said with realization. "That's how you've become a Phantom. That's how you sustain yourself to become more powerful than normal Ghosts. More solid."

"Yes," he confirmed, and she could swear she heard a smile in his voice as if what she had said was an innuendo of some kind. "My powers are stronger during a blood bargain. You'd be able to summon me at will."

She bit her lip. She had to admit his offer was sounding more enticing the longer she thought about it. And like he pointed out, it wasn't as if she would be able to look for Genevieve unless she made it past the next six levels anyway, so she would have plenty of spare time over the next few days to search for his key...

"And if you take a decade from me and that's all the time I have left, I would *die*?"

"You could've died ten times in this manor already," he told her. "But you're right—that is a possibility. Still, it seems less painful to me than, say, getting ripped to pieces by a Hellhound?"

"Aren't you afraid that even if I do find this key, you still might not be able to pass over fully? That you'll be able to leave Phantasma but not have any other place to go?"

"That's a risk I'm willing to take. Life happens. Even in death. No use worrying about things that haven't occurred yet."

She was silent for a long moment as she mulled over his words, but she knew in the back of her mind she had already made a decision. She could hear her mother's voice scolding her for what she was about to do, but she ignored it. Her mother wasn't here.

She shooed him away from the side of the bed so she could stand, her right arm hanging uselessly as she straightened herself up before him. "What are the terms, *exactly*?"

His green eyes blazed with excitement as he cleared his throat and declared, "If you agree to this blood bargain, I vow to use our connection only to answer your summons and to help you in any dire situations. In exchange, you have until you leave Phantasma's grounds to find my anchor. A heart and a key, according to you. Failure to find it will result in you transferring ten years of your life span directly to me through the blood bargain—not a second more or a second less."

"And if I *do* find this key?" She tilted her head. "I want payment for that."

Something sparked in his eyes at the request. "What would you like?"

She didn't hesitate. "My family has a debt against our home. I need money to pay it off."

"I'm a Ghost," he deadpanned. "I don't have access to mortal currencies."

"Well then, how about finding and keeping tabs on my sister? You should be able to see if she's in another group, right?"

"You don't get your prize until *after* you complete our bargain," he reminded her. "But if you win the competition, a gift from me seems moot anyway considering Phantasma's prize is better than anything I could offer."

"I don't care about winning," she told him.

"You should. The winner gets a Devil's Grant—one of the most coveted, omnipotent favors there are—and you could use it to settle your debt. Make it to level seven, find your sister and convince her to forfeit, then stay and let me help you win. Why go through seven levels of Hell to find her just to give up and go home when you've only got two levels left?"

She hated to admit that he had a point. As she searched his eyes for a sign of sincerity, he reached out and lifted her left hand, turning her palm face up. He traced one of the long lines in the center with his index finger, and she felt her locket warm against her skin.

"This is your lifeline," he told her, and she watched as her arm broke out in goosebumps. "I see a very long life here. But I don't think that's something you should bother worrying about anyway."

"And why not?" she breathed. The sensation of him touching her so delicately sent a whirlwind of butterflies through her stomach.

"Because I have a feeling you're not going to fail," he answered seriously, his gaze even more intense than before. "Not with your abilities. You're..."

He trailed off as if he were trying to decide if what he wanted to say was advantageous to his cause.

"I haven't been this hopeful in a very long time," he settled on.

"I think you're putting a lot of stock into abilities I can't even seem to control," she muttered. "When Cade tried to stab me, I *disappeared*. I've never done that before. My mother never mentioned that's something Necromancers were even capable of."

"Maybe that power is particular to your personal brand of magic," he suggested. "It's possible for the same types of beings to have unique abilities."

She sighed. "My mother is turning in her grave somewhere at me having this conversation with you. Though, I think she'd be more upset that I drove Genevieve away in the first place."

"Do we have a bargain or not?" he prompted.

"One last thing," she pressed. "The bit with the heart—I'm not capable of killing anyone. We'll have to find a way to get that piece of this puzzle ethically."

"You'd be surprised what you're capable of doing under the right circumstances," he said.

"Let me rephrase, I don't *want* to be capable of that." She looked down at her hands. "It's enough that so many people already think Necromancers are dark, even evil. I will not stain my hands with blood and prove them right."

He sighed. "Hearts are everywhere here. Let's focus on the key first and cross that bridge when we get there. Do we have a deal?"

She took a deep breath and finally nodded. "We have a deal. Make the bargain."

He disappeared abruptly and then reappeared a second later, now with an ornate onyx dagger in his hand. He held out his palm for hers, and she gave it to him, watching intently as he ran the steel blade across her delicate skin. She hissed at the pain while he lifted his own hand and made a similar cut before clasping their bleeding slashes together and closing his eyes. He said a few words in a language she recognized from all the times she eavesdropped on her mother's appointments, and sucked in a sharp breath when her entire body flushed with a pulsing heat. The sensation was the closest thing she could imagine a high would be, but it faded just as quickly as it had come on.

He dropped her hand gently. "Whenever you need to summon me, all you must do is recite my name three times. I'll come."

Three times, the Shadow Voice purred, satisfied.

"Whenever?" She lifted a brow. "So, if I want you at my beck and call every second of the day—?"

"Yes," he confirmed with amusement. "You can summon me any time you want. The morning. The afternoon. The middle of the night..."

She cleared her throat. Wherever his thoughts were trailing off, she did not need to follow. "I got it. What about my injuries?"

He placed a hand over her shoulder, causing her to grit her teeth, and after a few more words in that same language, all the pain melted away. She looked over to inspect his work, rolling her arm in its socket to make sure it was good as new. The only evidence left of the ordeal from the night before was the dried blood crusted on her skin and clothes.

"Thank you," she told him sincerely. "Now what?"

"Now, we begin."

18

Burning Question

By the time Ophelia changed out of her bloody ensemble and into something fresh, there were about two hours left before dinner was served and the next level began. While she stripped off her ruined garments in the bathroom, Blackwell had made her list out all the places she'd already been in the manor and she'd made the mistake of mentioning the terrifying passageway. Now, she was reluctantly watching him move the chair she had used to barricade the bookcase so they could access the secret door behind it.

"Are you going to need me to hold your hand while we walk through?" he taunted over his shoulder with a smirk.

"Oh, bite me," she deadpanned.

His smirk grew wider. "Is that an invitation?"

She ignored his teasing and asked, "Why don't you just do your little disappearing act and transport us where we need to go? Or do you only pop into places that you're uninvited?"

He gave her a pointed look now, a tad incensed. "I can only transport myself into places I've already physically been. Plus, traveling in and out of this corporeal plane is not as easy as I make it look. And it's certainly harder with a person in tow. I'm trying to conserve my energy for your next trial...unless you've decided you'd rather take a stab at it solo?"

She rolled her eyes to the ceiling. "I cannot believe I'm stuck here dealing with a sarcastic Ghost while my sister might be getting maimed."

"Is she that incapable of taking care of herself?"

"No," Ophelia admitted. "In a lot of ways Genevieve is much more capable than I am. I was alone with our mother a lot growing up while she was...out. But it seems like she became infatuated with this place for some reason, collecting newspaper clippings from all the cities the competition has traveled to over the last few years. I worry she was too enchanted with the prospect of the prize being able to fix all of our problems and didn't think through the consequences of coming here."

He tilted his head thoughtfully. "And it wouldn't? Fix all of your problems, I mean."

"Paying off the debt we have, sure. Fixing everything else in our lives...doubtful. It wouldn't make our mother's death any easier. Or fix our fighting." She knew she was probably oversharing, but aside from Genevieve she'd never had anyone to open up to. And though Blackwell wasn't exactly her first choice, he was her only option at the moment. Besides, she was going to milk this blood bargain for all it was worth.

"When did your mother pass?"

She stared at him for a lingering moment, trying to gauge if his curiosity was genuine.

"About five days ago now," she shared.

He didn't pry any further, and a moment later, he'd opened the secret passageway. "So, the disappearing room was through here?"

"Yes." She swallowed as she peered into the darkness, half expecting the demonic creature from before to come flying out. "It should still be there, right?"

Blackwell shrugged. "The manor moves its rooms around for its haunts and traps all the time. If you found it and nothing happened to you inside, it was definitely by accident."

"So, explain the haunt system." She crossed her arms. "Is

there a custom plan for each contestant? Do you have a Ghost secretary in the back keeping track of the schedule?"

"No secretary," he told her as Poe suddenly reappeared, rubbing his furry head against Blackwell's leg. "Just Devils, Ghosts, and Phantasma itself. The manor has a mind of its own, if you haven't noticed. It chooses when to manifest its guests' greatest fears, and enlists the Apparitions and Ghouls for help, but the Devils coordinate other haunts as they get bored. And if none of that drives people out—the levels and other contestants take care of the rest."

"Right," she muttered as Blackwell shooed the cat into the dark with his foot. "Who is in charge, then?"

"Only the Devils know—and they've been sworn to secrecy. The only other beings to meet the creator are the contestants who complete level eight and win the bid to enter level nine."

"What bid?" she asks.

"If there is more than one contestant that completes level eight and survives the night to get to level nine, they must either eliminate each other until only one person remains or offer the highest bid to enter the level."

She shuddered at the thought of the death matches that must ensue when too many people make it that far. She couldn't imagine killing someone else just to have a shot at meeting the monster who created this place.

Blackwell walked over to the wooden dresser in her room and grabbed two unlit candles from one of the drawers, snapping his fingers and igniting the wicks as he handed one to her. "Ready?"

She gave a tense nod, blood running cold as her body begged her not to go back through the demonic passage, but she refused to let that fear take over. She stepped through the doorway and raised her candle to the shadows, making extra sure the creature from the other night was nowhere to be seen. A shiver ran down her spine at the memory.

"Something wrong?" Blackwell asked, a glint of amusement in his green eyes as he watched her pause.

"No," she told him before he could tease her anymore. The look on his face said *doubtful*, but she ignored it, changing the subject. "If you are not one of the Ghosts who perform the haunts, how did you end up trapped here?"

"*That*," he said, "is the burning question, isn't it?"

Blackwell let her lead the way, staying close on her heels as they walked down the corridor, one of his hands lightly resting atop her shoulder to assure her of his presence. She must have been unconvincing in her nonchalance about re-entering the dark passage, and she found herself touched by the considerate gesture. As they moved, the flame of her candle danced higher, throwing her shadow onto the stone walls. His silhouette was notably missing.

"The only reality I can recall has been here, in Phantasma," he divulged, the words smooth and even as if he had recited this many times before. "I have no memories of how I got here or why I can do as I please but the other Ghosts can't. The only routine I know is making my bargain with contestants, watching them fail, then waiting for Phantasma to move to another city so I can find someone new when the next competition begins. Over and over. Other Ghosts are tied here because they died within these walls or made poor bargains with a Devil in their past lives and have to stay until their debts are fulfilled and they can pass on. Some aren't successful, and over time they've become the Ghouls Phantasma uses for haunts."

"What happened to all the other contestants who failed your bargain?" she whispered.

"Very few died, if that's what you're getting at," he assured. "A lot of them forfeited—but most of them have won Phantasma."

She looked over her shoulder at him. "They won their prize, but you won a decade of their life."

His green eyes met hers with no hint of remorse. "Exactly."

If they were smart, they would have just asked to dissolve their blood bargains, she thought. But now that such a prospect occurred to her, she wondered if that's what she'd waste her own Devil's Grant on if she won it. Ten years of her life back or anything she wanted in the world...

"Was it hard to watch the ones who died?" She paused her stride to face him, her head tilting with curiosity. "I don't think I could stomach such a thing over and over again."

"Being too compassionate in a place like this is a mistake," he warned. "Soft hearts don't survive here."

"What kinds of hearts do?"

He leaned down until their eyes were level. "Hearts with teeth." He reached out and gently gripped her chin in his hand, rubbing the pad of his thumb across her full bottom lip.

She was frozen in place.

"C'mon, angel, show me your teeth."

Her breath became shallow at his proximity, so close that she could see the firelight reflected in his emerald irises. Her eyes flicked down to his mouth, and like her brief lapse of control in the bathtub the night before, she wondered what it would be like to kiss him. Would he taste like the notes of vanilla and tobacco that lingered in the air around him? Would his ghostly nature make it feel cold?

Blackwell's lips began to curl up at the ends, and she realized she had been staring at him, silent, for just a little too long. He huffed a deep laugh and reached for something behind her, his lips dipping even closer to hers as he leaned over. She turned her head to the side and swallowed. When she glanced behind her, she saw that they had made it to the end of the corridor. He pushed on the door's lever and let it swing open.

"Look"—he waved a hand at what they'd found, a glint of satisfaction still shining in his eyes—"a regular broom closet."

Poe meowed at their feet and Ophelia jumped in surprise, having forgotten about the feline. When she spun around to investigate the open doorway, she saw that Blackwell was right— it was just a broom closet.

"Maybe I have to be the one who opens it?" she said, voice a little too thick, as she pulled the door shut again. She didn't wait more than a second before pushing it back open, and a noise of disappointment hummed in her throat when it still hadn't changed.

"Take your time," Blackwell asserted. "Imagine the place you want to go in your mind, first. Then open it."

She gave him a skeptical look but shut the door a second time and closed her eyes in concentration. This time she pictured the plain hidden room, the long tables that had sat in its center, and the bare shelves that had lined the walls. She recalled Poe hopping up onto one of those tables to bathe himself and silently judge her.

A creak echoed in front of her and then, "Ophelia."

She blinked her eyes open, and her jaw went slack as she took in the new room before them.

Blackwell gave her an appraising look. "Nice job, angel. Now let's see what else you can find."

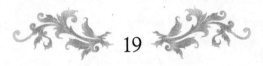

19

AMBIANCE

An hour and a half later, and they had already searched three different places top to bottom for any sort of key, or clues that might trigger Blackwell's memory as to its whereabouts. All to no avail. The plain room at the end of the secret corridor hadn't had much to look at, so it was easy to rule out. The next place Blackwell suggested had been a drinking parlor, complete with a stocked bar and a hair-raising chill.

"Did you only bring me here so you could get a drink?" she accused.

"Of course not," he had told her right before knocking back an entire glass of amber liquid in two gulps. "I brought you here for the romantic ambiance."

The room had been slathered in cobwebs and grime.

The final place Blackwell had suggested was the library. The massive room was covered wall to wall in dark oak bookcases that were stuffed with novels and journals. In the center of the back wall of shelves was an enormous brick fireplace, a gilded oculus mounted above its intricately carved mantel. It smelled like charred earth and old books and was much less drafty than the rest of the manor.

Blackwell was lying back over a chartreuse chaise in the sitting area before the burning hearth, and after digging through two of the bookshelves by herself, Ophelia was ready to throttle the Phantom. While he had his nose stuck in some old fairy tale, she was choking on dust, pulling out tome after tome and checking to see if any might be hiding hollowed out spaces for stowing objects such as keys.

"Does anything here feel familiar to you at all?" she threw at him after another coughing fit.

"Maybe," he said as he flicked his gaze leisurely over the book she currently held—a thick encyclopedia wrapped in distressed brown leather and embossed with gold foil. "Maybe not."

That was it. She chucked the tome at his head with all her might. He switched into his non-corporeal state a second before the projectile would have smashed into his face.

How unsatisfying.

When he solidified himself once more, there was a lazy smirk on his face. "If you want to play rough," he drawled, "I have better games we can play. Ones that involve less clothing—"

"Ugh," she groaned, fists balling at her sides. "No wonder no one has ever been able to find what you're looking for. You're *impossible* to work with."

"Have you ever thought that, just maybe, I've already looked through all of this before? I'd remember if anyone had ever found anything of interest in these books."

"Would you? Because you didn't even remember you met me and told me about it."

"That's because I met you before the competition. Which has never happened before."

"So, you can remember everything within the competition, but nothing that you do in between," she realized. The way he'd made sure to ask if their first encounter was *agreeable* suddenly made sense.

"Correct."

She threw her hands up. "Then *why* are we in here getting my dress covered in dust?"

He blinked out suddenly and reappeared right in front of her, making her startle.

"Boo." He grinned.

"Oh, I'm so glad to see that's a habit of yours," she said, tone dripping in sarcasm.

He gently pried the next book she'd been ready to launch at his head from her grip, discarding it to the floor as he explained, "I chose you because you have been able to see and find things none of the others could. But right now, you're still looking on the surface. I need you to dig deeper."

"Would it torture you to speak plainly for once?"

He reached out and placed a hand against the frame of the bookshelf at her back. "Something you need to understand if our partnership is going to work—we are on the same side. I want you to be successful more than you do, I *promise*. You found the Whispering Gate and you made that room in the secret passage appear just fine. That's what I mean when I say 'dig deeper.' Find things I haven't looked through a million times already. Look beyond the books, the obvious."

"Fine, I get it." She crossed her arms over her chest, trying to ignore the way every time he got this close to her, it sent her pulse into such a frenzy the only thing she could hear in her head was the roar of her own heartbeat. "In the meantime, it would be helpful if you made yourself useful in *some* way. Perhaps helping me get to know you? It seems when I find these places by accident, it's because something inside me needs to at that exact moment in time. I need to feel...connected to whatever it is I'm looking for."

Blackwell tilted his head. "Alright. What would you like to know?"

She looked him square in the eyes. "What's your earliest

memory of being here? Do you remember ever existing any-where else?"

He contemplated her question for a moment, tapping his fin-gers against the shelf above her head as he searched through his memory. *Once, twice.* She reached backward and tapped her fin-ger against the shelf to complete the trifecta he had started.

His green eyes tracked the gesture, but he didn't bother to comment on it; he only answered, "No. There is no *before* in my mind. I remember every contestant I've worked with, and every city we've traveled to, but nothing outside of Phantasma's competitions. A shame, too. I feel robbed of my first time laying eyes on you."

Heat bloomed on her cheeks as a ripple of butterflies went through her stomach. He was too charming for her own good.

"What if..." She cleared her throat. "What if you died in Phantasma?" she pressed on. "Maybe you were a contestant at one point and that's why you're tied here?"

"I've thought of that possibility." He nodded, his expression turning morose. "But a lot of Apparitions who are here were contestants who died in the competition. Yet I became a Phan-tom rather than a regular Apparition. Thankfully, the bargains I'm able to make ensure I don't become a Ghoul."

"Phantoms can be created in several different ways," she told him. "Most often they are created when an immortal dies and does not pass over—something about the power of an immor-tal's soul creates a stronger type of Ghost. But there are defi-nitely other ways, too."

Especially because immortals didn't die often, given the fact that they never aged and were semi-invincible. But still, it wasn't impossible, and she wondered if something of the sort was at play here. Unfortunately, Phantoms were elusive enough that her Necromancy studies hadn't taught her much more about the subject than that. She wasn't sure her mother had ever even met one.

"Hmm," he said thoughtfully. "Perhaps that is it. I was an immortal in my past life. A Vampire, maybe. I do like to bite." He clacked his teeth together in demonstration before giving her a wink.

She made a noise of surprise, her cheeks heating at the prospect of his teeth sinking into her skin...

He grinned at her involuntary blush with satisfaction.

She quickly changed the subject. "Maybe we should just start with the basics. What's your favorite color?"

He lifted a brow at the mundane question but reached out with the hand that wasn't propping him up and tugged at the tail of the velvet ribbon tied in her hair. "Red."

The ribbon perfectly matched the rest of her ensemble: a high-collared, scarlet chemise with long gossamer sleeves that puffed at her shoulders and tapered then flared at her wrists, beneath a black velvet corset.

"That's at least one thing we have in common," she noted. "Do you have a favorite book?"

"There's a book here about a doctor who uses a bunch of different dead bodies to create his very own monster. I enjoyed that one."

She straightened up with excitement. "I know that book—"

Before she could finish her thought, someone else blinked into the room, humming a tune reminiscent of the jazzy melodies one might hear in the French Quarter. It was the man who had let her into Phantasma, his top hat and black-lined eyes unmistakable. His song paused when he noticed the two of them.

"Blackwell." The man dipped his chin in greeting to the Phantom, but his shrewd eyes stayed on her.

Blackwell straightened himself away from her, crossing his arms over his chest as he gave the other man a measured look. "Good evening, Jasper."

Jasper removed his top hat and set it down on a table. Ophelia swallowed a gasp. The hat had been hiding a third eye embedded into his forehead. A Devil's Mark.

Jasper gave her a knowing grin. "I wouldn't have pegged you as Blackwell's first choice. What did you do to get his attention?" He flicked his gaze over to Blackwell now. "Or is this one of those rounds where you just picked the prettiest contestant in hopes that you'd get to ravage them in dark corners?"

"Jasper," Blackwell murmured, a hostile edge beneath his smooth tone. "Get lost."

"Sorry, handsome." Jasper shook his head. "No can do. Why don't the two of you rip each other's clothes off elsewhere?"

Ophelia's entire body flushed at the suggestion. "We aren't—that's not—"

"Don't tell me he hasn't even kissed you yet?" Jasper flicked his eyes between them. "Taking it slow this time, Blackwell?"

Blackwell didn't deign to answer, the look on his face somewhere between bored and irritated.

"There have been a few past contestants he made a deal with that damn near broke Phantasma's cardinal rule for our handsome friend here," Jasper continued. "Might want to mind your heart around him, or the trials won't be the worst that'll happen to you."

"Let's go," Blackwell told her, gesturing with his head for her to follow him out.

She eyed Jasper warily as she went, and the Devil's third eye winked open. The third eye wasn't the same warm brown color as his other two, but a bright gold—and the way it homed in on her face sent a shiver down her spine. She rushed out of the library and down the hall after Blackwell. Back in her bedroom, she could tell that Blackwell was tense, though he was trying to pretend otherwise.

After a few beats of silence, she finally said, "Is kissing usually part of your bargains? Am I just not your type?"

Blackwell froze for a moment. Then he tilted his head back and let out a deep laugh.

"I have no type," he told her with a pointed look, turning to face her fully. "Jasper was just keeping up his habit of being a pain in the ass. There's only *one* contestant I've kissed in recent memory, and that's because they were a dreadfully dull conversationalist and absolutely horrid at searching—there weren't a lot of options for me that round. I figured we might as well do something to pass the time."

"I suppose I should really start thinking of more interesting topics of conversation, then," she told him.

"Is the thought of kissing me that horrible?" he murmured.

No.

"Yes," she answered.

"Did you know that every time you lie, your left eye twitches a little?"

She crossed her arms. "It does *not*."

Blackwell opened his mouth to say something else, but the dinner bell tolled through the manor. A glint of something she couldn't name sparkled in his eyes.

"I suppose we'll have to table this argument for later," he said as he went over to open the door for her. "Better hurry so you can get something to eat before level two begins. Once you're in the trial, you need to make sure to summon me so I can guide you out of it."

As she shuffled past him in the doorway, she asked, "Do you know which Circle of Hell this one will be based on?"

Blackwell pulled the door shut behind them and then brought his mouth down to her ear to whisper a single, spine-tingling word.

"*Lust.*"

LEVEL TWO

20

LUST

Before the shiver finished running through Ophelia's body, Blackwell was gone. It wasn't until she stepped into the dining hall that she remembered the two mortal enemies she'd made less than twenty-four hours ago. The moment she passed through the archway, every single contestant snapped their head in her direction, and it all came roaring back to her. Blackwell and his blood bargain had distracted her from the memories of the nightmarish serpent, the spiders, the knife plunging into her transparent chest...

She wondered to what extent Cade had sensationalized his version of events.

"Here we go," someone in the back muttered. It was the older man—James.

"Do you think she's really a Demon?" a young woman with golden hair and severe eyebrows wondered aloud. "Didn't she complete the first level?"

"Look at her eyes. They're fucking creepy. I wouldn't be surprised at all if she's one of the hauntings," the towheaded man next to her commented. He was unusually tall, his hunched posture almost painful to look at. Ophelia wondered if he and the girl with the eyebrows were related, noting their resemblance and familiarity they seemed to have with one another.

"*Demon*," Cade spat, scraping his chair out from the table with an ear-splitting screech. The rest of the room fell silent as

Cade and Beau stood from their self-appointed spots at the head of the table and took a threatening step toward her.

Ophelia didn't cower. She didn't care what any of these people—people who would most likely be dead in just a few more days—thought about her. They could take their insults to their graves.

Instead, she fixed a sultry smile on her face. "I'm so glad to see you both made it through the night." Her eyes flicked over to Beau. "I was concerned you might have drowned in your own vomit."

Eric let out a low whistle in the back of the room. Cade and Beau charged at her.

She stood her ground as they came closer. "You both look as if you should be carrying torches and pitchforks. Honestly, if *I* rile you up this much, the Ghosts in this manor must be having an absolute *ball* haunting the two of you."

With lightning speed, Cade reached out and slapped her clean across the face. Her head snapped to the side, and she stumbled back in shock. A choked gasp came from someone to her right. Luci.

"*Cade!*" the girl exclaimed, expression aghast.

"Shut up, Lucinda," Cade growled.

Luci obeyed, her expression pained.

Ophelia's face was tingling from the assault, but a sharper stab of pain was pulsing from the corner of her bottom lip. She reached up and gently brushed the new split in her mouth, bright red blood coming away on her fingertips. A laugh bubbled up in her throat.

Beau sucked in a breath. "She's bleeding."

"Yes, she's bleeding." Charlotte pushed out of the crowd, a look of disgust on her face at the entire spectacle. "Which means she's not a fucking Demon or a Ghost."

"You don't understand—she *disappeared*," Cade insisted to the group.

"Her blood is red," James pointed out, tone firm. "She might not be entirely human, but she's a mortal, just as the rest of us are. Leave her alone."

Cade's jaw clenched at the admonishment. The grin slowly spreading over Ophelia's face must have been terrifying given the way Beau paled. He was definitely the sheep in this situation, Cade the wolf. Blood dribbled from the slice in her lip and down her chin as her smile tore the gash wider, but she didn't bother to wipe it away as she spoke.

"If either of you had a brain, you'd have realized that believing me when I said I wasn't a Demon would have been a lot less risky than making me an enemy."

She felt a sense of pride at the strength of her words. It might have been mostly bravado, but *they* didn't know that. Cade didn't bother with a retort as he gestured for Beau to follow him and return to their spot at the table, his eyes shining with a level of malice no other being had ever had for her before. The rest of dinner was awkward to say the least.

Ophelia didn't eat anything. She stood alone in the back of the room and counted those who were left, making a mental file of their names and features. Twenty contestants, including herself. That meant six people didn't make it past the first level. She wondered how many of those six had forfeited and how many had died in the labyrinth.

When the lights flickered out a few minutes later, there was almost a collective sigh of relief. Almost.

"Welcome to level two," a sultry voice announced as the Devil made her entrance. A curling cloud of red smoke caressed its way through the room, the powerful scent of Louisiana magnolias arriving with it. This Devil had bright scarlet hair and warm ivory skin. Her voluptuous body was draped in black silk that left little to the imagination, and Ophelia was pretty sure a few of the contestants had drool hanging from their mouths at the sight.

Ophelia subconsciously wiped the back of her hand over her own mouth to make sure she wasn't drooling as well.

"My name is Drima," the Devil declared. "My specialty is *lust*."

Someone coughed. Someone else made a lewd comment.

Drima whipped her head toward the source of the comment, and the rest of the room followed suit. The Devil stalked toward the contestant. It was the towheaded man. As Drima slinked up to him, Ophelia made out something twitching behind the Devil from beneath her silk dress. A tail.

"Quite a creative mouth you have," Drima purred to the man. "I think I'd find you more pleasing without it, though."

Everyone watched with bated breath as the Devil reached out and waved her perfectly manicured hand in front of the man's face. It took everyone a second, including him, to understand what she had done, but when the realization hit, the piercing scream of the girl next to him was so loud Ophelia swore one of the glasses on the table shattered.

His mouth had completely disappeared.

"*Mmm!*" he tried to scream, but it was a choked, muffled sound. His hands flew to his face, clawing at the grotesquely blank space where his lips once were.

Drima addressed the rest of the room with a sinister smile. "Let this be a lesson to not give in to your lusts so easily, or your ability to speak won't be the only thing you lose. Now, let's begin."

As Zel had demonstrated for their first trial, the Devil summoned a doorway to portal them into the level, and with a flick of her wrist, their clue began to etch itself into the door's surface same as before.

IN A REALM OF DESIRE, ILLUSIONS ENTHRALL,

CONTESTANTS BEWARE, LEST YOU SUCCUMB TO THEIR CALL.

AMONGST THE LUSTFUL VICES, YOU MUST PICK ONLY ONE,

WHEN THE FIRST BELL TOLLS THE TRIAL HAS BEGUN.

BEFORE THE FOURTH CHIME, THE TRUTH YOU MUST FIND,

AND THE KEY TO YOUR FREEDOM BENEATH A BED LIES.

Drima began calling out names while Ophelia recited the clues to herself over and over. Most of it meant nothing to her—yet—but one thing that stood out was the part about the tolling bell. She had a sinking feeling that this trial had a time limit.

As members of her group passed through the portal one by one, the man who disturbingly parted ways with his ability to speak was still writhing on the ground in tears, broken, smothered sobs nearly choking him. Ophelia had to admit she felt sorry for him, if only because she thought such a fate should have been Cade's instead. What a dream to never have to hear *that* man talk again.

"Edna," Drima called out.

The girl kneeling by the crying man's side looked up, gnawing on her lip, unsure.

"Now or never," Drima snapped.

Edna swallowed and stood, whispering, "You have to get up,

Mason. We have to win. Think about Michael." With that, Edna walked to the door and, with only a single glance back, stepped through.

The Devil called out a few more names and then finally, "Ophelia."

Ophelia was disappointed that she wouldn't get to see if Mason rallied the courage to get up or not, but she didn't waste any time stalking toward the door. She was ready to get this over with. Taking a deep breath, she stepped into the dark portal.

This time when Ophelia stepped out of the portal, she didn't find herself in a labyrinth of nothingness. No, this time it had transported her to the most opulent display of debauchery she had ever seen.

The walls were draped floor to ceiling in swaths of black silk, the plush carpet beneath her feet littered with what looked to be precious gemstones of all colors and shapes. Circular beds dressed in black satin sheets and scattered with more of the loose jewels took up most of the space throughout the enormous room. Couples and trios in ornate masks writhed atop them, the air flush with heat and sweat. The lighting was dim, the only illumination coming from piles of lit black candles surrounding the beds; for a moment Ophelia worried one of the lust-fueled partiers would knock them over and set the room ablaze.

The heady erotica on display around her was the most sensual thing she'd ever witnessed. When she tried to look away from it, glancing up, she saw that mirrors covered every inch of the ceiling above her, making it impossible to avoid the salacious acts around her. Men feasting between their partners' legs, making their backs arch with pleasure. Women hoisting themselves atop their lovers and riding them with abandon, rolling their hips while their partners spoke the filthiest words Ophelia had ever heard strung together.

A part of her was darkly fascinated. What would it be like to have someone so enraptured with you that they forgot everything else around them? Not to be embarrassed to speak every unfiltered thought with reckless abandon?

"Drink?" someone asked her.

She turned to see a waiter, face covered with a raven mask, holding a tray of oddly colored drinks, each bubbling enticingly. Red, green, blue, pink, or gold.

"Pick your poison," the waiter urged as a cacophony of moans vibrated through the room.

She hesitated. "What will it do?"

"Depends," they answered. "But you have about one more minute to choose before you're taken from this place."

"Taken? As in disqualified?"

They didn't bother with an answer, only shoved the tray of drinks closer to her face. She swallowed and chose the red one.

"That's my personal favorite." The waiter winked behind their mask. "Cheers!"

Ophelia peered down at the effervescent drink, as light and enticing as a glass of champagne. When she looked back at the room, she saw a fleet of waiters flooding through a door at the back, each holding a tray of the same red drink she had chosen, handing one to each masked partier. The attendees toasted each other, sending a melody of clinks throughout the room.

"Here goes nothing," she muttered to herself as she brought the glass to her lips and drained its contents. Every last drop.

Somewhere in the room, a bell chimed.

A bell...there's something I'm supposed to remember about a bell... she remembered faintly. But as quickly as the thought had entered her mind, it faded. Washed away by the heady feeling of ecstasy now swimming through her blood.

The feeling started at her crown. A warmth that dripped down over her face, her neck, her shoulders. Her head became light as her limbs grew heavy. The champagne flute rolled from her grasp and shattered on the floor, and she stared at the sparkling pieces of glass with a languid smile.

She felt *incredible. Indestructible. Free.*

The clothes draped over her skin felt softer than clouds, and she began to rub her hands over her arms and torso, soaking in the heavenly feeling of the fabric. Her hands moved up over her stomach, to her breasts, and she moaned as she felt them peak beneath her palms. She reached beneath the collar of her dress and began scraping her fingernails over her skin, leaving angry red lines. She didn't know why, but she needed to bleed. Needed to release the heat inside of her somehow.

"Come over here, lovely, come sit with us," a saccharine voice purred at her.

She twisted around to see a masked woman draped only in strings of sapphires and pearls, lounging back on one of the beds, someone massaging her shoulders from behind. The woman patted a spot next to her on the black satin sheets in invitation. Ophelia's feet began moving of their own accord, and when she reached the edge of the bed, the pair gave each other a conspiratorial look.

"Won't you play with us while we watch the show?" the woman grinned. "We could have a lot of fun together."

Ophelia's brow furrowed. "What show?"

A second bell chimed.

Silk sashes dropped down from between the mirrors on the ceiling, spaced evenly across the room. A flurry of people, dressed in the same red and gold outfits, each claimed one of the sashes and began twisting the silk around their bodies, climbing, twirling, and dancing in the air. Ophelia watched in awe at the gravity-defying stunts, the fluid way the performers were able to move above the crowd, and when they were done, she found herself clapping with the others.

"Come, lovely, sit down. This is the good part," the bejeweled woman coaxed.

Ophelia sat and the woman immediately positioned herself to kneel at Ophelia's back. Ophelia found herself sighing with pleasure as the woman gathered the heavy tendrils of her curls and moved them to gain access to her bare neck.

Ophelia didn't know what the woman's intentions were, and she didn't care. She was too enamored with the performers, now draped horizontally in the air, sashes wrapped around their middles to keep them suspended securely. A few of the party-goers began to approach the dancers, touching them in places that should have been too intimate for so many lingering eyes, but everyone here looked positively greedy for the displays of intimacy. And when the screaming began, Ophelia barely even noticed.

Someone was holding a knife over the performer closest to her, and before she could really register what was happening, they plunged the knife through the performer's throat. Blood spurted and poured out of the dancer as their limbs grew limp, the people around them crowded forward in a frenzy, lapping at the blood like...Vampires.

What did those drinks have in them? They couldn't have transformed them all into Vampires...right?

"Hold still, this will only hurt for a second," the woman purred in her ear.

"Hmm?" Ophelia murmured, dazed. She tried to twist around to see what was happening, but her head wouldn't move.

"I said hold still," the woman growled now, hands tightening painfully on Ophelia's biceps.

"This one is mine," a deep voice cut in.

Ophelia's eyes snapped to the stranger towering in front of them as the woman hissed a curse in her ear. The stranger looked so incredibly familiar, but she couldn't put her finger on why...

"I got to her first," the woman growled, clinging to Ophelia possessively.

"That doesn't matter if she isn't willing," the stranger countered. Then, turning to Ophelia, he reached out a hand in offering. "Would you like to come with me instead?"

Yes. Very much.

"No!" the woman exclaimed. "You want to stay with me, don't you, lovely? We can have so much fun together if you'll just let me taste..."

The stranger's emerald gaze met hers. "It's your decision."

Ophelia reached out and grasped the stranger's hand without hesitation now. As soon as she had made her choice, he wasted no time pulling her up from the edge of the bed and whisking her away, leaving the woman howling curses at their backs. He moved them blithely across the room, slithering through the crowd of people drinking each other's blood. A couple in the center of the room was practically bathing in a pool of crimson, and it made Ophelia shudder.

The stranger brought her to an empty bed in a far, unwatched corner, sitting her down and warning her, "Don't move."

As she watched him disappear back into the crowd, she began to panic. She didn't want him to go, didn't want to be alone.

You're a foolish, foolish girl.

Her chest tightened at the raspy voice in her mind. She needed to get out of here. She needed—

"Hey," the stranger soothed, interrupting her thoughts. He crouched down before her, placing a steadying hand on her knee as he brought his eyes level with hers. "I'm right here. I had to go get you the antidote."

"Antidote?" she whispered.

He lifted the hand that wasn't touching her, a glass of pink liquid in it. "The drink they gave you at the start was a slow-acting poison. Each color would make you, and the rest of the room, experience one of five types of lust and it would slowly kill you unless you broke through its effects and realized you needed an antidote."

AMONGST THE LUSTFUL VICES, YOU MUST PICK ONLY ONE...
BEFORE THE FOURTH CHIME, THE TRUTH YOU MUST FIND...

Fear rippled through her. The bells had already chimed twice. "Which type of lust did I choose?"

He smirked. "Bloodlust."

The red bubbly. The blood drinking. Of course.

"Here," he urged, pressing the glass to her lips. "Drink."

She did. And just like the first concoction, this one spread through her in seconds. Her head went from fuzzy to clear, and the writhing room around her suddenly seemed less opulent and much, much colder.

She looked back at her savior and breathed, "Blackwell."

He grinned in satisfaction. "How do you feel?"

"Okay..." she trailed off, rubbing at her temples where a headache was beginning to form. "If you hadn't come to help—"

"But I did," he said. "Now, here's the catch of this trial—you can't get out of here until you perform a task themed after the type of lust you chose."

"What does *that* mean?"

"It means that because you selected Bloodlust as your vice," you have to drink someone's blood and let them drink yours," he deadpanned. "Now, if you want me to help you choose someone—"

"*No,*" she choked. "I am not drinking a stranger's blood!"

He gave her a devious grin. "You're in luck that I enjoy biting, then."

"This is a nightmare," she muttered.

"Then your nightmares must be absolutely riveting," he noted. "Do you want to drink first, or do you want me to?"

She swallowed thickly before she finally answered, "You first."

He pulled her to her feet, shifting to take her seat on the bed before pulling her to sit across his lap. He wrapped one of his arms around the back of her waist. She wiggled against him, making herself more comfortable, eliciting a groan from his throat.

"Unless you want this to go in a much different direction, I wouldn't do that again," he admonished.

She blushed.

"Tilt your head for me, sweetheart," he requested, voice still gruff.

She did as he asked, exposing her throat to him. When his cool lips grazed her pulse, something inside her became uneasy. Something about his touch felt...off. Cold. Maybe it was the remnants of the potion, or maybe she was paranoid, but—

—another chime of a bell made her jump, and she recalled that there was something she was supposed to remember.

BEFORE THE FOURTH CHIME, THE TRUTH YOU MUST FIND,

AND THE KEY TO YOUR FREEDOM BENEATH A BED LIES.

The truth you must find.

"Blackwell? How did you know to come help me?" she wondered, almost absentmindedly. "You said I'd need to summon you so you could help guide me out...but I never said your name."

"I decided to check in just in case you had forgotten. I was worried it would take you too long to figure the illusion out. Good thing."

She let him trail his lips over her skin as he reached up with his free hand to angle her chin down, until their lips were nearly touching. Her breath caught. She desperately wanted to kiss him. She wanted to experience the sort of passion the room around her was feeling. It was almost painful how attracted to him she was.

"Can I..." he trailed off, letting the unspoken question hang between them.

She nodded and that's all it took for his lips to crash onto hers. His lips were cold, hard, not at all like she thought they might feel. And the adrenaline that went through her as he began to deepen the kiss was not from passion.

She pulled back. "I..."

"What's wrong, sweetheart?" he asked, impatience bleeding into his tone.

Sweetheart. Blackwell had never once called her that. She narrowed her eyes now and looked at him. *Really* looked at him. And the first thing she noticed was that the spark in his eyes wasn't the glint of humor she was used to...but rather something harder. Darker. The second was that the locket around her neck was utterly lifeless.

The truth you must find.

"You're not Blackwell," she whispered, the oxygen rushing from her lungs as a spike of fear speared through her.

The imposter's mask immediately began to slip. Beady black irises overtaking the green, a too-wide smile stretching over Blackwell's stolen face. He moved like lightning, grabbing her by the arms and moving her back into the wall next to the bed.

She began shoving at the imposter's chest, clawing at any bit of skin she could get her hands on. "*Get away from me!*"

An insidious laugh came out of his mouth as their grip on the back of her neck turned painful. "What gave it away? Was it the voice? The way I kiss? I could try it again, I could reach into your mind and get every little detail right to make your deepest, wildest fantasies come true. All you have to do is grant me access..."

"*No,*" she screeched and shoved the heel of her hand into his nose, making the bone *crunch* and *pop*, though there was no blood. "*Leave me alone, asshole.*"

The imposter dissolved into black smoke, and she crashed to the ground with a surprised yelp. She scrambled back to her feet as the smoke enveloped her vision and made it impossible to see the room beyond it. Squinting into the darkness before her, a tall silhouette began to take shape, the wisps of obsidian slowly dissipating. She braced herself.

"It's about damn time—" the silhouette began.

She lunged. Tackling him to ground, she wrapped her hands around his throat, determined to cause as much harm as she could while he was still solid.

"I don't care if you're already dead," she hissed. "I'm going to kill you again."

"Is this your attempt at flirting, angel?" he choked out despite the pressure she was putting on his neck.

Her lip curled up in disgust. "Both of my hands are wrapped around your throat!"

"That doesn't make it any clearer," he responded, blinking out from beneath her and letting her fall forward on her hands.

A second later, he was standing above her, arms crossed over his chest.

She hauled herself up to rush at him again, but before she could strike, he caught her wrist, his grip firm but gentle. She was about to hurl out another insult when the locket around her throat began to awaken, and a warm, familiar static sensation emanated from where his skin was touching hers.

Is this your attempt at flirting, angel?

Angel. That ridiculous fucking nickname, the locket's steady heartbeat, the strange power that pulsed in the air around him...

All her energy deflated as she realized. "Blackwell?"

One of his brows shot up. "Obviously. You summoned me."

She shifted on her feet. "I didn't do it intentionally. I forgot, actually."

He tilted his head. "You didn't say my name three times?"

She squeezed her eyes shut in embarrassment. "I did."

"Why were you saying my name if not to..."

When his words trailed off, she let her eyes flutter back open, and the moment they refocused on his face, she regretted it. His grin could have blinded the stars.

"Do you want to know what the goal of this trial is?"

"Considering the ridiculous smile on your face, I have a feeling that I absolutely do *not*," she grumbled.

"The trial presents you with a choice to pick a type of lust. From all the blood on the floor, I'm going to assume you chose bloodlust," he commented as he looked around at the undisturbed bloody orgy still happening around them. Not a soul seemed to have noticed her confrontation with the imposter or Blackwell.

"Unknowingly," she reasoned.

"The trial then presents you with an illusion of the person

you lust after most," his expression turned taunting, "in order to entice you to lose in one of two ways: giving in to the theme of lust you chose, or keeping you here until the bell chimes a fourth time by distracting you with said illusion. You didn't drink any blood, did you?"

She shook her head. "And what of the antidote? Will I be okay now?"

"Antidote?"

"Yes, you—er, the illusion—gave me this antidote. It cleared the haziness from the first drink. You know, the one that made me think everyone stabbing each other to supply the party with refreshments didn't seem so bad."

Blackwell shrugged. "If they gave you something to clear your head, it was purely strategic. I've never had a contestant they *didn't* try to drown in a lust-filled daze, truth be told."

"It was to lure me into trusting them," she realized. Then muttered, "To think I thought this trial would lead to something a lot sexier than fighting an imposter version of you and drinking blood."

"Don't tell me you're *disappointed* you didn't get to live out a wild illusion of another nature?" He started to scoff, before pausing thoughtfully and saying, "Actually, *do* tell. I'm desperate to know what sort of wicked fantasies live in your head."

Her face flushed at the way his voice deepened with those last words, a sensuality bleeding into them that she had never experienced before. The only person who ever shared her bed had been neither sensual nor passionate. Elliott Trahan, the nephew of the older couple who owned the estate across from Grimm Manor, had been visiting New Orleans for the summer while his parents were overseas. Ophelia was pretty sure he had been hoping to find Genevieve the day he knocked on her door three

Julys ago. Instead, he found Ophelia—bored, frustrated, and home alone.

Their brief affair ended with little ceremony the day he'd left New Orleans in late August. It had felt more transactional than anything; two twenty-year-olds ready to see what all the fuss was about and finding that it was far more lackluster than the novels made it seem. Now, she was getting the distinct feeling it might have been the person and not the act or lack of experience.

Blackwell huffed a laugh. "What's wrong, angel? Too many salacious scenarios to choose from? Or are they too scandalous for you to say aloud?"

She swallowed. "No, they just don't concern *you*."

"Maybe I'd believe that if I wasn't pretty sure you almost just let someone with my face—"

"Do not finish whatever it is you're about to say," she inserted, jabbing a finger at his chest. "Just do your job and help me get out of here. The Devil's clue said the key to freedom lies beneath one of the beds, right?"

His lips curled up in amusement as he nodded. "There's a trap door hidden beneath one of the beds. It's a random one each time."

They began with the bed closest to them, working together to shove the heavy mattress aside. Nothing. They moved to another, Blackwell unceremoniously kicking off a couple in the middle of their passion, the woman straddling the man in a reverse position, moaning as he cupped her breasts from behind. Ophelia pried her eyes away and got back to her task. She toed the mattress to the side with some effort. Nothing.

They checked two more beds to no avail.

On the next mattress was a lone man, his black eyes piercing into her from behind his mask.

"Aren't you stunning?" he leered at her, sitting up from where he was lounging to wrap an unwanted arm around her waist and drag her toward him. "Let me have a taste, won't you, sweetheart?"

She shoved at his chest with both hands, trying to wiggle out of his hold.

Smash his face in. Gouge his eyes out. Break his nose. Tear out his hair.

She froze at the sudden appearance of the Shadow Voice, and the man wasted no time reeling her back in. Then he began to change, his face slowly morphing into one with a familiar, square jaw. The eyes behind his mask turning from black to green as his hair became the color of fresh snow.

"Let me kiss you," the man pleaded in Blackwell's voice, with Blackwell's mouth. "I can make you feel ecstasy like you've never felt before."

Her mouth parted in awe as he tilted his face closer to hers. She knew it wasn't real, that it was an illusion, but she couldn't control her reaction to the words *let me kiss you* coming from Blackwell's lips. Even if it was an imposter.

"I sure as Hell hope I've never sounded so ridiculous," the real Blackwell said behind her, snapping her out of her momentary lapse in judgment.

She cleared her throat as she answered, "Oh, you absolutely have."

Then she brought her knee up between the imposter's legs, as hard as she could, making him release her as he howled in pain. She shifted her eyes to the real Blackwell, and he gave her a small smile.

"Nicely done," he praised. "Though, for the record, I'd like it to be known that *I* am personally rather fond of choking as the method of attack if you're ever compelled to brawl with me again."

Her look of exasperation was completely ignored as he moved to kick the bed aside. The imposter Blackwell still moaning in pain atop it. And beneath the mattress—there it was.

Blackwell pulled the trap door open. He offered a hand to her and said, "I'll jump with you."

She grimaced down into the dark abyss beyond the trap door, remembering the unpleasant collision with the dining hall's floor from the first level.

"I've got you," he reassured her.

Her locket warmed against her neck as she nodded and grasped his still outstretched hand. She let him wrap a secure arm around her waist to tuck her in close.

"Ready?" he prompted.

"Okay," she said.

They jumped. And as they fell through the portal, the final bell chimed above.

21

You Called

When they landed back in the dining hall, there was no aching crash like before, Blackwell keeping them both on their feet. He wasted no time guiding her back to her room.

"Well, I suppose the debate on whether or not you think it'd be terrible to kiss me has been settled," he declared as he kicked the door shut behind them.

She jabbed a finger into his chest. "Do not tease me right now. That was *horrible*."

"Of course it was," he agreed. "No illusion could possibly replace my—"

"That is *not* what I meant," she gritted out. "Imagine you believe, with every fiber of your being, that something is real, and suddenly you get an inkling that it is *not*. I have to live that nightmare every single day in my own mind! Do you have any idea how terrifying it is to have your reality so distorted that you can't trust your own thoughts, your own *sight*?"

"No," he answered, sincere. "But it's over. You figured it out before it was too late. You finished the level."

"But how do I know that!" she exclaimed, fear creeping into her voice. "How do I know *this* is real and I'm not being tricked by another illusion into a false sense of security?"

He watched as she began to pace back and forth, the amusement in his eyes slowly dissipating the more anxious she became.

"It was too easy to get out of there." She shook her head.

"I can't trust my own judgment, clearly. I have to get out, I have to—"

"Ophelia." Blackwell sidestepped into her path, making her stop short. "That's the point of this place. It's desperate to make you question your sanity. That trial is set up the way it is to make you paranoid the remainder of the time you're here. It's a mind game."

"How can I trust you?" she sniffed, refusing to make eye contact. "You were there too. You were there and you were pretending to be protective of me, you *kissed* me, but it *wasn't* you—"

"Look at me," he demanded, reaching out to lightly pinch her chin and tilt her face up to his.

She swallowed as she allowed her gaze to slide back to his.

"This is real," he promised. "I'm real. I'm sorry the illusion used my likeness to trick you. I need you to know if you were to ever let me touch you, in any way, the moment you wanted to stop—I would. No hesitation."

He spoke with such vehement intensity that she didn't have a single doubt in her mind they were true.

She swallowed. "Okay."

His shoulders relaxed a little and the corners of his mouth tilted up again. "I'll try not to be insulted that you believed whatever stale pleasure that imposter was giving you could have come from me. I think in the future it would be objectively beneficial to let me prove to you exactly what it feels like to be kissed by me, just in case such a thing were to ever happen again."

"Alright, maybe I am inclined to believe this is real." She rolled her eyes as she grumbled, "Your face might be able to be replicated, but your ego can't. What if I had said it was the greatest pleasure I've ever known?"

The mischievous glint in his eyes was back in full force as

he leaned down. "If you thought that was your threshold of pleasure—imagine being worshipped by the real thing."

Her breath caught in her throat and any ability she had to form a coherent retort was lost then and there. A response wasn't needed anyway as his focus shifted to her mouth. He reached out and rubbed his thumb over her split lip, eliciting a quick, sharp pain. He brought his thumb to his mouth, now painted with a smear of her blood, and licked it clean. She had to swallow the whimper crawling up her throat at the sight. Something about him consuming any part of her made her belly warm.

Get it together, she admonished herself internally.

"It looks like you gave that imposter a Hell of a fight at least. Good girl." His fingertips warmed as he reached out to brush them over the wound once more, and she relished the relief of his magic as it healed her. "There."

"The illusion wasn't the one who did that," she corrected, lightly brushing her own fingertips over where the split had been moments before. "Actually, I had completely forgotten about that."

He stiffened as he asked, "Who was responsible, then?"

She shrugged. "One of the other contestants."

He narrowed his eyes. "Which one?"

"Who cares? I'm fine. You healed me. We need to get back to our quest."

"I care. We have a bargain. I'm supposed to protect you from harm while you're here," he told her, his tone a little too casual. "So again. Who did that to you?"

"The one named Cade," she admitted. "Happy?"

Without another word, Blackwell disappeared.

Phantasma's library was back to its original, orderly state. After Blackwell's abrupt departure, Ophelia had spent an hour pacing her room, too much anxious energy pent up inside of her to be still. And the moment the Shadow Voice had begun its whispering, she knew she needed to occupy herself with something other than worrying about Genevieve and reliving her kiss with the fake Blackwell over and over and over. Especially because the latter led directly to her thinking about kissing the real Blackwell— and that was officially forbidden territory in her mind.

"He's done nothing *that* special," she muttered to herself as she strutted through the library. "And he's got me on a wild goose chase. There is no reason to let him linger on my mind like this."

Someone cleared their throat.

"Oh." Ophelia came to a halt when she spotted Luci, huddled near the fireplace with a book. "I didn't see you there."

Bash her face in, break her nose. She didn't help you, she was a coward, the Shadow Voice hissed in her mind at the sight of the girl. *It would be so easy to make her hurt, make her bleed*—

Shut. Up. Ophelia ordered the intrusive presence, giving her head a vigorous shake as if it would make the voice leave her alone. Luci gave her a strange look.

"Are you alright?" Luci asked.

"Yes," Ophelia answered, the response automatic, practiced. "What are you reading?"

Luci shrugged and stood. "Some romance about Angels and Demons. It was the first one I picked."

Ophelia nodded like she was listening, but her feet were already itching to turn around and leave. Luci noticed.

"Wait," the girl pleaded. "I wanted to tell you I was sorry. About what Cade did."

"It isn't for you to apologize for," Ophelia told her.

Luci bit her lip. "I know, but we all just stood there and let it happen. He had us convinced that…"

"I know." Ophelia waved off the words she knew were coming next. "It doesn't matter. No one owes anyone anything here, right? We are all going to do what it takes to survive. When you see Cade again, you can remind the bastard of that for me."

Luci's eyes widened a bit at the darkness that had bled into Ophelia's tone. The Shadow Voice's influence, she supposed. But for this, she didn't mind. She hoped Luci took her words seriously and delivered the message.

"It's just...I of all people should have known better about you. But Leon said you did something in the first level," Luci disclosed, "to make the Hellhound—"

"For fuck's sake." Ophelia pinched the bridge of her nose. "The way people will find a way to gossip throughout even the direst of circumstances. I'm assuming Leon is the scrawny kid I had to haul out of there? Maybe he should be talking less about me and work on his stamina. He could barely keep up—and I was wearing a corset."

"He's not scrawny," Luci defended, blushing. "He's just lean—"

"Oh no..." Ophelia cut her off. "You *like* him? If I could give you some advice? This place seems to like to twist good, sweet things until they break. Don't let it."

Soft hearts don't survive here.

The girl became visibly flustered at Ophelia's words, but Ophelia couldn't have cared less. She was right. Blackwell was right. She didn't know what stakes in Luci's life led her to this place, but anyone could see the girl's soft heart from a hundred miles away.

"It's lonely in here," Luci confided. "And the haunts...I've never had nightmares like this before. We made a pact to take turns sleeping and watching each other's backs. It's nothing more."

Before Ophelia could say *yeah right*, someone else entered the room.

"Speak of a Devil..." Ophelia murmured.

But it was no Devil; it was Leon. His gaze darted between the girls as he approached. There were beads of sweat on his temples and his breathing was a bit ragged, and Ophelia wondered if he had just been running.

"There was a haunt in the dining room," he panted. "Spiders and snakes and—"

"I know the scene," Ophelia interrupted before he conjured up the grotesque vision in her head. "Anyone dead?"

His eyes widened a bit at the directness of the question, but he answered, "Not that I know of. But Mason forfeited. His sister's room is right next to mine, when she made it out of level two, she found him gone. I've never heard crying like that before."

"I'd leave if I got my mouth magically sealed, too," Luci said with sympathy. "I just feel bad for Edna."

Leon nodded in agreement. "It's on her shoulders to bring back their brother now."

Ophelia lifted a brow and Luci explained. "They lost their younger brother a couple months ago in an airboat accident. Their family runs swamp tours for tourists out on the Atchafalaya Basin. It was a nasty ordeal."

Ophelia made a face. "Does everyone here know each other?"

Luci and Leon shared a look, then Luci said, "Many of us have met previously, yes. We run in the same social circles— or our parents do. I have a few friends who entered in earlier groups."

"So do I," Leon inserted.

"And you...you're Genevieve Grimm's sister," Luci finished.

Ophelia rocked back a step. "You know Genevieve?"

"It's why I wanted to introduce myself," Luci revealed. "It's why I shouldn't have let Cade influence anyone into thinking you could possibly be anything insidious. I met Genevieve last year at a gathering on the riverfront in the French Quarter. She was being courted by a good friend of mine at the time. I just thought she was so lovely, if a bit rambunctious, and we became quick friends. We always told her to invite you along when we made plans, but she said you weren't one for leaving the house. I was surprised to see you here that first night."

Ophelia stared at Luci in shock, and, as if the girl's words had made something click in her mind, a memory suddenly came rushing back. Of her and Genevieve leaving the coroner's office and Genevieve going inside the café to greet a friend...

"Did you know she was going to come here?" Ophelia demanded, ignoring the jealousy suddenly burning in her belly at the recollection of the way Genevieve had run up to Luci and hugged her. "Did she ever talk about this place?"

Luci gaped. "No, she never—you mean, she's here too?"

"She never once said anything about Phantasma?" Ophelia pressed on.

"I swear." Luci shook her head. "Phantasma wasn't on anyone's mind until recently, but even so, Genevieve never talked much about her home life. She seemed to be very private in that area and we never pushed."

"Who is *we*?" Ophelia narrowed her eyes.

"There were five of us. Myself, Genevieve, Iris Saloom, Farrow Henry, and Basile Landry."

Farrow Henry. Genevieve said he'd stood her up for the ball. The name was unmistakable. Ophelia wondered how much Luci knew of that situation, but even more she wondered why this was the first time she was hearing that Genevieve had a close group of friends. Did her sister not trust her enough to tell her about those sorts of things? Or had she just been too wrapped up in herself to notice Genevieve had an entire social life outside of Grimm Manor she knew nothing about?

She hates you, the Shadow Voice laughed. *She hates you and she will always hate you and she will probably die in here and—*

Ophelia reached out to one of the oak shelves and knocked on it. *One, two, three.*

The Shadow Voice vanished.

Leon scratched the back of his neck. "Um, I should go back to my room and get some rest. It's been quite a day. I'll leave you two to finish your conversation…"

"No," Ophelia retorted. "Our conversation is done. I don't know how close you and Genevieve were, but that does not make the two of us allies. If you were smart, you wouldn't be making allies at all. It will only lead to heartbreak."

Luci didn't look Ophelia in the eye as she shoved the book she'd been reading back into the stacks on the shelf and hurried after Leon without another word. Leon placed his hand on the small of Luci's back in comfort as he guided her out, throwing a loaded glance back at Ophelia before they disappeared.

Fools.

Alone at last, she began to dig through the shelves again, but this time she took Blackwell's advice and went deeper. Using the rolling ladder abandoned on the west side of the room, she climbed up to begin clearing the very top shelves first. Thick novels rained to the ground with heavy *thumps* and clouds of dust, and while treating books so callously was, without a doubt, a form of sacrilege, she didn't exactly have the time to gently place each one in a tidy stack below.

As soon as the shelves were emptied, she began running her hands over the wood panels inside, feeling for anything out of the ordinary: switches, uneven planks, buttons, hinges. Grimm Manor's library had quite a few hidden compartments of its own, and she and Genevieve had always made a game of seeing how many they could find. She was sure there were many they had yet to discover.

Almost an hour later, she finally felt it. Two cases to the left of the fireplace, third shelf from the top. A slightly indented square, about an inch wide, with something springy beneath. A button. Before she could shift her weight forward enough on the ladder to press it all the way down, however, the temperature of the room dropped five degrees.

"Well, well," a deep voice rumbled behind her. "Look at what I've found."

Ophelia held herself as still as possible as Jasper faded into view below. His unsettling third eye was, thankfully, shut, but his too-observant gaze was hardly any better as it assessed her current predicament.

"Doing some redecorating?" He grinned. "Would you like some help?"

She snatched her outstretched hand back from the hidden mechanism she had found and glared down at him. "Leave me alone."

"Or what?" he taunted. "You'll call Blackwell? Please do. I could use the entertainment of pissing him off."

Ophelia swallowed. "Are the two of you friends?"

"Devils don't have friends, darling. Not in the same sense that mortals do."

"You seem to know each other well, though," she reasoned.

He crossed his arms. "When you share a space with the same beings for as long as we have, you tend to find those who annoy you less than others."

"The other Ghosts here must be *very* annoying, then," she murmured, mostly to herself.

Jasper laughed. "You've got a silver tongue. I see why he likes you."

"He doesn't *like* me," she snorted. "He's using me. As I'm using him."

A strange glint of something she couldn't read entered the Devil's eyes, but all he said was "Have you ever thought about... other arrangements?"

She didn't like where this conversation was heading. "No."

I should never have thought about the first one.

"How many years did you promise him?"

"None of your business," she bit out.

"A decade is a long time," he stated. "What if I told you I could get you out of your bargain and make you an offer for a whole lot less?"

She glowered. "I'd tell you to go back to Hell. I don't make deals with Devils."

He opened his mouth to spear her with a retort, but before he got the chance, something suddenly appeared out of thin air and crashed into the chaise in the center of the room. No, not something. Two *someones.*

She recognized the Devils from the first two levels—Drima and Zel—within seconds, even with both of them trying to eat each other's faces off. She was officially alone with three Devils, and two of them didn't have a single stitch of clothing on.

She flushed and averted her eyes from the spectacle. Jasper only laughed.

"If you change your mind, the offer stands. Enjoy the show." With a teasing wink up at her, he disappeared.

Moans began to echo through the room, and for a moment, Ophelia was frozen in utter shock. The way the two Devils were moving together made her skin break out in a feverish sweat.

Their performance was somehow more salacious than the pairings in the second trial had been. She knew she ought to look away, scandalized, but a part of her was...curious. The same part of her that had been so easily fascinated in the second trial.

Until the claws came out.

Drima yanked Zel's head to the side by his hair, exposing his neck so she could rip her sharp fingernails through his skin.

It's time to go, Ophelia told herself as she began to plan her escape route.

Press the button before you leave, the Shadow Voice demanded. **Press it, press it, press it.**

Ophelia twisted back toward the shelf. She had spent all this time searching and finally she'd found something...she might as well see what it did, right? Besides, it's not like it would hurt anything, considering the Devils probably wouldn't notice if the room around them burst into flames.

She hauled herself forward as much as she could on the ladder, gripping a rung for balance with one hand as she reached out to slam the button down with her other. There was a sharp click followed by a metallic groan, and a moment later, the ground below began to move. Ophelia cursed as one of her feet slipped from the ladder and she lurched forward to cling on for dear life as the entire shelf began to *turn*. Before she could blink twice, the shelf had done a complete one-eighty. She was now on the inside of Phantasma's guts, and it was so dark that she could barely see her own hands in front of her—which made for a clumsy climb down. When her feet reached the ground, the planks beneath them groaned.

She shuffled forward a bit, hands outstretched to feel her way around. It took nearly fifteen steps before she reached what felt like a stone wall, but as she ran her palms over the cold bricks, she couldn't locate so much as a sconce or torch. Anxiety sank in her stomach like a stone. The last time she'd been in a dark, secret corridor alone...

The Shadow Voice's crackling laugh resounded in her head. *You'd better get ready to run.*

"No," she breathed, core tightening with fear.

It's going to get you, it's going to—

"Blackwell, Blackwell, *Blackwell*," she recited in a rush.

The Shadow Voiced hissed. *If you don't find a source of light in the next ten seconds, it's going to devour you.*

Her chest heaved as she tried to shake the words from her mind. She needed to stay alert and find her way back to the ladder. Hopefully, pushing the button would return the shelf to its original position in the library without any fuss. Turning and counting her steps back in the direction she had come, she only reached number seven when she felt the telltale static raise the hairs on the back of her neck.

"Where the Hell are we?" Blackwell's voice rang out from her right, clear and strong. Any hint of the Shadow Voice lingering in her mind evaporated like smoke.

The faint white haze that always clung around Blackwell's form illuminated the space and filled her with such a strong sense of relief that before she realized what she was doing, she was launching herself in his direction. He caught her against his chest easily, and she wrapped her arms so tightly around his neck that it was a good thing he didn't need to breathe.

She buried her face into the crook of his throat. "You came."

"You called," he answered.

After a long moment, she took a deep breath and unwound her arms from his neck.

He narrowed his eyes. "What happened?" he asked. "Don't tell me absence really does make the heart grow fonder?"

"Nothing in particular," she admitted. "Between Devils

going at each other like rabbits in the library and accidentally getting myself stuck in here, I may have panicked a little."

"Sounds like quite the ordeal indeed." His eyes sparked with amusement. Whether at the mention of the Devils and their sexual escapades or getting herself stuck, she didn't know. "And where is *here*, exactly?"

"I found a mechanism in that library shelf"—she pointed to the bookcase in the center of the wall—"and it flipped around into whatever this place is. A secret tunnel that runs through the bowels of the manor, I presume."

"Clever little Necromancer." He grinned.

He snapped his fingers and two brass candelabras appeared in his hands. Shifting one into her waiting grasp, he snapped a second time to light all ten tapered candles, illuminating a good amount of space around them. Enough to see that his outfit was splattered with crimson. The reason for his earlier disappearance came rushing back.

"Is that Cade's *blood?*" She gaped. She knew he was more than capable of changing his clothes, which meant he'd left these in their current state intentionally. "What did you *do?*"

"Nothing permanent." He shrugged. "Not physically at least."

"Well, it isn't like he didn't deserve it," she muttered.

"We're on the same page, then," he agreed before waving at her to follow after him.

22

PLEASURE

It turned out that the corridor wasn't very large. Just a hollow, stone room.

"There has to be something more," Ophelia muttered from one end while Blackwell examined the other. "Why would there be a secret passage to nothing?"

"Here," he called.

She rushed over to see what he had found, and he tilted the candles toward the wall to reveal three tally marks carved into one of the stones.

"Hmm." She squinted as she ran her fingertips over each of the grooves. Once. Twice. Three times. Blackwell didn't rush her, quietly waiting for her assessment. "I wonder if..."

She pressed on the rectangular brick and the rock scraped back noisily. Her breath hitched with anticipation, but when they looked around, nothing else happened. A moment later, the stone shifted back into place like it had never been touched.

"Three lines," she realized once the brick was fully reset. The locket around her throat began to hum to life as excitement pulsed through her veins. She turned to Blackwell and instructed, "Start searching for others with the same sort of markings on them!"

They got to work on opposite ends, scanning the stones in the dim light of their candles. Ophelia was grateful for her above-average height during this task, able to stretch her arm high enough to see the stones that lined the ceiling. It didn't take long for Blackwell to find another marked stone and seconds later she found a third.

"Five lines," he declared.

"Two," she returned. "Which means we're missing numbers one and four at least."

A beat later, he said, "Four."

They checked every single brick several times over, but all they came up with were stones numbered two through five. Ophelia was growing more exhausted by the minute and was just about to suggest they give up for the night when she stepped on something in the center of the room and felt it move. She looked down, swishing her skirts out of the way to see the floor beneath. She sighed at the mark in the center of the tile beneath her feet.

"Now we press the rest in order," she instructed when Blackwell crouched beside her to inspect the shifting plate on the floor.

"Does it feel like it can go down further?" he asked.

She lifted herself up onto the balls of her feet to bounce her full weight down a few times and, sure enough, the button was able to go down further. Blackwell stood and pressed himself closer, until the front of his body was completely flush with her back, to use their combined force on the tile. She wobbled a bit as it sank into the ground, lowering nearly half a foot, and Blackwell placed a steadying hand at her waist before she tipped to the side.

"Quick!" she implored as they stepped out of the shallow hole and made their way over to the next numbers. She retraced her steps to relocate stone number two and shoved it inward. "Two is done!"

"Three... four..." he counted aloud as he pressed each one.

She met him at the final brick, and he waved for her to do the honors. Smiling, she proclaimed, "Five."

The room began to shake. Ophelia rocked back into Blackwell, and he wrapped an arm around her waist as their gazes darted around. Rocky debris rained down from the ceiling and clacked to the ground. They looked up to find the roof was now pocked with small holes.

Odd.

"Is that it?" she whispered, glancing over her shoulder to gauge Blackwell's reaction.

He lifted his chin to point at something a few feet ahead. "Look."

She traced his gaze until her eyes landed on an opening at the bottom of the wall. It was about five feet wide, but only three or four feet tall. Still, plenty of space for them to crawl through, though she really wasn't looking forward to doing such a thing. They ambled over and lowered themselves to the floor to peer inside. She couldn't make out any distinguishable details. Only a deep, dark abyss.

Darting her eyes over to Blackwell, she quipped, "Rock, paper, scissors on who goes first?"

He snorted and began to unbutton his ruined overcoat. Discarding the heavy article of clothing, he started on the cuffs of his shirt next, loosening them until he could roll the expensive material up to his elbows on each arm. She watched with what was surely too-rapt attention, but he only lifted a brow at her in amusement as he finished by removing the cravat from around his neck.

"Much better," he murmured. "Now I'll be able to—"

Something dripped down from the ceiling and splattered on the now-exposed skin of Blackwell's forearm, interrupting his thought. His skin turned an angry, blotchy red in an instant. Blisters bubbled beneath the mysterious substance, and though Blackwell didn't indicate that he was in any pain, just looking at the way his flesh boiled churned her stomach. An instant later and the wound melted away, his fair skin unblemished once more.

"Ophelia," he said as his form flickered from its corporeal state to its transparent one. "Move. *Now*."

The gravity of his tone felt wrong to her ears. And when every hint of amusement slid from his face, her chest began to tighten. She tilted her head back to peer up at the ceiling.

That's when the onslaught began.

Blackwell turned solid just long enough to shove her toward the tunnel. She scrambled forward on her hands and knees, barely ducking her head and shoulders out of the room in time before the acid began to pelt down. The burning liquid singed holes through her bodice and skirts, but fortunately the layers helped keep it away from her skin. Blackwell cursed as he transported himself into the tunnel just ahead of her and grasped onto each of her biceps in order to drag her headfirst through the crawl space with him.

Blackwell let her go just long enough to kick in the small wooden door at the end of the passageway before hauling them both into another pitch-black space.

"Hold on, angel," he reassured.

She worked to gulp in breaths of air, trying to push away the panic settling into her bones at their near escape. Blackwell snapped his fingers and two brass candelabras appeared in his hands. He hastily set them both down so he could see what he was doing.

"We have to get that dress off of you before the acid touches your skin," he told her.

Not even a second after the words were out of his mouth, something began to burn at the small of her back. She hissed and he moved into action.

Kneeling behind her, Blackwell expertly unlaced her corset, pulling the ribbons free and loosening the boned contraption enough to tug it over her head and throw it off to the side. Next, he tore at the linen buttons down the back of her chemise, sending the small pieces clattering over the floor. The dress was discarded with the corset, as well as the remaining threat of her flesh melting off her bones. Cool air hit her exposed skin, and she sighed in relief. A glint of gold flashed in her peripheral vision, and she noticed the first level's star tattoo had been joined by another for the second level.

"Thank you," she said as she twisted around to face Blackwell, watching the candlelight dance over his grim expression as he hovered above her. "What's wrong?"

"I should have been able to transport you away. But I wasted too much energy on revenge," he admitted.

"On Cade, you mean?"

He shifted his eyes away from hers as he nodded. "I won't make such a mistake again, don't worry."

She tilted her head. "You got me out of there. It could have been worse."

"You don't get it," he said, gaze locking back on hers. "Every time I allow you to get hurt, the bond unravels a little. Eventually, it will make it harder to hear when you summon me. That could have been catastrophic."

"Oh," she breathed. "Why didn't you tell me that little detail before?"

"I should have," he admitted. "Especially considering your ability to find trouble."

She once again fought the urge to stick out her tongue at him. "No more mistakes, then."

"No," he agreed, firm. "Which means I should take you back to your room before we trigger any more fatal traps—"

"What? No," she argued. "I did not risk getting rained on by *acid* to quit now! We have to see where this leads us."

Blackwell lifted his eyes to the ceiling with exasperation but didn't bother to refute her request as he leaned over to snatch up one of the candelabras to illuminate more of the room. The space was half the size of where they had come from, and unlike the room before, the ceiling and walls were paneled with planks of dark, knotted oak. On the far side of the room was a single bookshelf.

"I'd venture a guess that leads us back to the library," he remarked.

"*Damn it*," she fumed. "All of that for nothing? Just one big path to nowhere? I fucking *hate* this place!"

A small smile found its way back onto his lips. "Welcome to the club."

She waved her hands with conviction as she spoke. "All of that pain and effort and it's just an ugly, bare room? *No.* I am going to rip every single one of these boards up if I have to."

"Angel?" Blackwell murmured.

"I swear I will burn this forsaken place to the ground," she went on as if he hadn't spoken.

"Ophelia."

"*What?*"

A familiar wicked gleam lit up his emerald irises as he mused, "As much as I'm enjoying this rant, perhaps it would come off more threatening if you weren't practically nude."

The realization that she was sitting there in only her under-garments hit her like a freight train. A squeal choked out of her mouth as she hurried to fold her arms over her torso.

"Turn around!" she ordered.

He lifted a brow. "I think it's a bit too late for modesty, don't you?"

"Says the one who isn't almost naked!" she threw back.

His smile turned into a full-on grin now. "I could change that if you'd like."

"You are such a thorn in my side." She glowered. "Honestly, I'm surprised you got my corset off so easily in the first place."

He leaned in close enough that the tips of their noses nearly touched as he spoke. "There's no article of clothing I don't know how to take off efficiently."

A shiver ran down her spine at the sensuality laced into his words, and her eyes flicked down involuntarily to his infuriating mouth.

"You know, I'm still waiting to know exactly what happened with that imposter during the trial earlier, angel," he drawled. "I've been wrought with curiosity to know exactly what experiences I need to replace in your mind."

She flushed but tilted her nose up at him, refusing to give him the satisfaction of a response.

"If you don't want to tell me, I'll just imagine my own version of events. I'm sure it would be more creative anyway."

She narrowed her eyes and said, "Okay. Go ahead."

A spark of shock flitted over his expression, chased by wicked determination.

"Well?" she prompted. "Let's hear it. How would things have gone if it had really been you and not an illusion?"

"Are you sure you want me to *tell* you?" He shifted until their lips were practically touching. "Or would you like me to show you instead?"

Ophelia wasn't sure what was coming over her. His intoxicating proximity, the last three days of near-death experiences, or maybe it was the fact that witnessing so much lust tonight made her realize she'd never once come close to feeling that way about anyone. She desperately wanted to feel *passion*, even if it was only for a moment. And the way Blackwell set her nerves on fire made her certain he'd be the perfect one for the task.

"Show me," she implored.

If he was shocked by the conviction in her voice, there was no indication. And as soon as the permission fell from her mouth, he was moving. Capturing her lips with his own, no hesitation, no timidness. As if this had been inevitable to him all along.

She let her eyes flutter closed and sank into the feeling of his mouth against hers.

Electrifying.

His lips *were* warm, unlike the illusion's had been, and her toes curled as the static she had grown to associate with him zapped through her entire body, searing her from the inside out. When he pressed closer to deepen the kiss further, her hands came up of their own accord to plunge into the soft tresses of his moonlit hair.

The kiss, the utter earnestness of it, knocked all the air from her lungs. She didn't know if his ardor was real or if he was just an incredible actor, but she didn't care. Never had she felt something so raw before. It was as if he had suddenly woken her and made her realize just how untouched she'd been all this time and now she would starve without his hands and mouth running over every inch of her skin. Hunger burned in her core as his tongue expertly tangled with hers, and she had to pull back for a moment, gasping for air. Blackwell changed courses seamlessly, letting her catch her breath while he dipped his head to press a line of scorching kisses into her collarbone. She felt one of his hands slowly slide down to the back of her thigh, the other drifting up to gently cup the back of her head.

In one fluid motion, he shifted forward and pressed her back against the ground so he was hovering above her. He lifted up her leg and hooked it around his waist, while using the hand behind her head as a buffer against the hard stone floor.

"At any point, if you want to stop," he said, his voice thick with his arousal, "we stop. Understand?"

"Yes," she confirmed, tugging gently on his hair to bring his mouth back down to hers.

Their lips slammed together once again, and their moans were swallowed with equal fervor. For once her head felt crystal clear. No intrusive voices or thoughts of danger and violence. There was only Blackwell and the sensation of his weight pressing into her, his hands tracing their way down her sides as his mouth learned the shape of her kisses.

A deep, primal sound came out of his throat when she gently nipped his bottom lip, something between a moan and a growl, and it ignited a need deep in her core. She could feel the slickness between her thighs grow as she arched her chest up into him, desperate for friction. He responded by dragging a hand between their bodies, rubbing his thumb over one of the tight buds poking from beneath the sheer lace camisole she still wore. It was her turn to moan.

She felt him hum in satisfaction at the breathy sounds coming from her throat and gently rolled her nipple between his fingers, making her entire body writhe beneath him with pleasure. Her hands began ripping at his shirt as she broke their kiss, panting. She wanted it *off*. She wanted to know what his bare skin felt like when they moved together like this.

He huffed a laugh at her eagerness and snapped his fingers. The shirt was gone before she could blink.

"That is incredibly convenient," she noted.

He smiled down at her with an alarming amount of mischief. "As is this."

He snapped again and her camisole disappeared, letting the cool air hit her chest and send a ripple of goosebumps across her skin. Then she watched as he slipped out of his corporeal form and felt her own body become lighter than air. Before she understood what was happening, she found herself straddling his lap, his back propped against the wall for support.

"What—?" She blinked, placing her palms flat against his pectorals to hold herself upright.

"Transporting can be disorienting," he told her as he angled her body back against his raised knees so he could have better access to her bare chest. "Give your head a moment to clear."

"You're really making that an easy task right now," she retorted as he leaned in to press a kiss on the underside of her jaw.

She felt his smile against her skin, but he didn't stop his ministrations. His mouth just continued lower and lower and lower until she felt his breath against her nipple. When he didn't immediately press his lips there, a sound of annoyance hummed in the back of her throat.

"Exquisite," he remarked as his eyes roamed over her bare body.

She followed his gaze to glance down at herself. The dusty pink of her nipples was stark against her ivory skin, even though she was flushed with arousal. She had always wondered what it would be like to have the voluptuous curves she thought were so lovely on her sister, but the way Blackwell was looking at her right now eradicated any thought of self-consciousness from her mind. She let herself unabashedly take in every inch of his body as well, the way his muscles were so well defined, the chiseled planes of his abdomen.

The self-satisfaction on Blackwell's face at her gawking made her want to stick her tongue out at him. She had never been so

affected by someone's attractiveness as she was his, and it drove
her wild that he seemed to know it. She was surprised to find
herself bolder, more confident than she imagined she might be
in this moment. But something about the frenzy she currently
felt overrode any modesty she might have had before. Not to
mention the fact that she'd never see Blackwell again after this
week anyway.

A pang of something she couldn't quite name shot through
her at that last thought, but it was gone a second later when
Blackwell's tongue flicked against one of her nipples.

Holy shit.

He gently grazed his teeth over the rosy bud of her breast,
sucking it into his mouth and wringing a blissful gasp from her
lips. She wriggled in his lap, looking for pressure where she
needed it most, and immediately felt the length of him strain-
ing against his trousers. He worked his way over to her other
breast and repeated the spine-tingling swirl of his tongue until
her skin became so heated with pleasure, she worried she might
combust.

When he brought his mouth back to hers, he threaded his
hands into the long tendrils of her hair, tugging on it affectionately as she continued to writhe against him. He lifted his hips
ever so slightly to grind the hardness in his trousers against her
own movements and before long both of them were becoming
more and more unwound. Her underwear was utterly soaked
between them.

His hands never stopped moving. Brushing over her pulse
points, tugging at her hair, rubbing circles into places on her
body she didn't realize could bring her such delicious sensations. She whimpered as she pressed herself into his length even
harder, and he met her with a thrust of equal fervor.

"Good girl," he murmured as he licked and nipped at the

sensitive skin behind her right ear. She preened at the praise. "Let go."

The words snapped something loose inside of her. It was all too much. Too intense, too hot, too *good*. And soon there was a sharp, carnal sensation tightening deep inside her core, climbing, and twisting until it reached a crescendo and she came crashing down in a wave of pleasure.

Her chest heaved as she blinked open her eyes to find his smug face peering back at her.

"I imagine that's right about where you would have lost the trial if it had really been me," he told her. "And that was barely a taste."

"I think I might hate you," she said, but it didn't come out with nearly as much heat as she wanted it to. "That was...Does it always feel like that?"

His brows shot up. "Have you never—"

"I've had a lover," she interrupted before he could jump to any conclusions. "But he never made me do *that*."

"Then he was useless and a waste of your time," Blackwell told her as he tightened his arms around her waist and lifted them both from the ground. He slowly lowered her to her feet—as if he had pleasured her so intensely, he was worried she wouldn't be able to stand on her own now. She huffed and stepped away.

Then she did hesitate. "Wait, did *you*—?"

"No. That wasn't for me," he told her as he picked up his shirt and tossed it over to her. "Here. Let's get you back to your room. I'm sure you need to rest." He winked as she slid her arms into the button-down, and she shot him a disparaging look.

"There will be no living with you after this," she muttered. "That...That can't happen again."

He lifted a brow. "Are you trying to convince me or yourself of that, angel?"

Myself, she thought, but aloud she insisted, "I'm serious. Our relationship is complicated enough what with the blood bargain and all."

He tilted her chin up with a single finger until she was looking directly into his eyes. "Whatever you say, but don't be surprised when you find yourself having to resist begging me for more."

She glared at him.

"I will never beg you for anything," she said.

He grinned. "Famous last words."

She ignored him as she gathered up her discarded clothes, very careful not to touch the side that had been ruined with the acid. When she backed up a step to make sure she had grabbed everything, she accidentally knocked over one of the candelabras. Rushing to pick it up before she actually made good on her promise to burn this place to the ground, she noticed something strange where it had landed. Etched into the oak flooring were several words. The first was unreadable, having been scratched out so many times there was a deep gouge in the floor, but the ones beneath were crystal clear.

And Gabriel Forever.

NIGHT FOUR OF PHANTASMA

23

ODDLY COMFORTING

Blackwell was leaning against the dresser watching as Ophelia paced back and forth through her room. She had already explained the entire ordeal of her sister's diaries in excruciating detail—more detail than he probably wanted, but he was patient enough not to complain—and now she was trying to connect those pieces with what they had just found.

"Gabriel is a common name," Blackwell reasoned.

"My sister was secretly harboring an obsession with Phantasma for *years* and wrote that she needed to find someone named Gabriel, and then we find the name Gabriel carved into a floorboard within Phantasma, and you think I should write it off as *a common name?*" she said in disbelief.

"Point taken," he allowed. "But there's nothing more you can figure out tonight. Why don't you get some rest and I'll see if I can track down one of the Devils and find out where the contestant logs are kept?"

She perked up. "Contestant logs?"

Blackwell nodded. "Yes. The Devils are vigilant about keeping track of every soul that comes through here, but they don't share that sort of information with just anyone. I'll have to see what I can do. If anything."

"Please," she whispered. "Please try."

He pushed away from the dresser to place his hands on her shoulders, turning her around and ushering her to the bed. "I will. Now, get some sleep. You're going to need it for the next level."

She pulled back her comforter and tucked herself beneath, still wearing his shirt from earlier. The material was luxurious and soft against her skin, and best of all, it smelled like him. Vanilla and tobacco. It was becoming oddly comforting.

He stretched the blankets up around her shoulders and made to turn away, but she reached out and snagged his hand. "Are you leaving? What if there's a haunt in the middle of the night?"

"I can stay until you fall asleep," he told her, gently tugging his hand out of hers to take up residence in the armchair a few feet away.

Closing her eyes, she tried to force herself to go to sleep. But it was no use. Her mind was racing. Thinking about Genevieve and the mysterious Gabriel and what it could all possibly mean. Thinking about Blackwell's lips on hers. Which turned to thinking about what led them to that moment in the first place. Acid burning through her clothing, the next trial of torture she would soon have to endure. It was all enough to keep her awake for the rest of her life.

And then, right on schedule, the Shadow Voice made its nightly appearance.

You need to knock on the headboard, it told her. *Three sets of threes. Then name the people you want to keep safe through the night. Or they'll all die. Every last one.*

As discreetly as she could, she reached over her head to tap her knuckles against the headboard. *One, two, three. One, two, three. One, two, three.*

"Genevieve," she whispered to herself.

"What are you doing?" Blackwell wondered softly.

Damn it. Not subtle enough.

Her mother and Genevieve were the only two people who

had ever known about the extensive list that was the Shadow Voice's nighttime ritual. And not because she had told them— more that they had spent every single night witnessing it for themselves. Something about it had always deeply embarrassed her. To be at the mercy of knocking on her headboard or wall or doing whatever other ridiculous tasks the voice demanded of her just so it would shut up and she could sleep without the ominous blanket of existential dread.

"I was pleasing my inner demons," she finally said, only half joking.

"Anything I can do to vanquish them, so you can go to sleep?" he offered.

The genuineness in his tone made her chest tighten with an emotion she had never felt before and couldn't quite name.

"If only," she whispered. "Besides, if all of my inner demons were destroyed, there wouldn't be much left of me."

He was silent for a long moment. Then, "Nothing is going to hurt you while I'm here, Ophelia. Rest."

She took a deep breath and sank further into the mattress, counting the heartbeats pulsing from her locket—which had not let up since their kiss. Soon enough the necklace and the steady buzz of Blackwell's energy lulled her deeper and deeper into subconsciousness, and she finally let go.

The next morning, Blackwell was nowhere to be found, but Poe was curled up beside her, purring in contentment. Ophelia patted the cat's ghostly head before stretching out her limbs and getting ready for the day. She decided on a simple white chiffon gown and strapless front-lacing corset. Both relatively easy to move in.

The clock on the wall told her there were still hours before dinner, and that meant she had plenty of time to sneak back to the secret room before she and Blackwell crossed paths again.

She wanted to go inspect it by herself and take a moment to grieve the fallacy she had been living: her belief that she knew Genevieve better than anyone in the world. Genevieve certainly knew her better than anyone else. At least, before Phantasma. Now, Ophelia felt they were strangers to one another. Maybe that was a bit dramatic, but the hurt that had been hiding beneath the adrenaline of the past few days was finally working its way to the surface, and it heightened every hue of betrayal in her mind.

Ophelia was running around making blood bargains with Ghosts, getting bitten by venomous serpents, and risking her life every night, and it probably never even crossed Genevieve's mind that Ophelia would dare come after her.

Which perhaps wasn't giving Genevieve enough credit, but at this point Ophelia had no idea what her sister could be thinking. The worst part was that right now, Ophelia wanted nothing more than to just speak to Vivi. Despite the secrets, their fight, or the ire Ophelia had for Genevieve's impulsive nature, she desperately wanted to know that her sister was safe. And to tell her *everything*. What she had been through inside Phantasma, how strange her new magic felt, the weird pulsing of the locket, and—most of all—Blackwell.

She wanted to tell Vivi about their ill-advised bargain and how infuriating she thought the Phantom was. She wanted to tell her about the annoying way he gave her half-answers to every single question and made her want to stab him, just for him to turn around and save her life or make her laugh. And she absolutely, desperately, wanted to tell her sister about the mind-blowing way he touched her, how intoxicating his kisses were and how one erotic encounter with the Ghost made her realize that maybe she wasn't broken after all. The complete opposite of how Elliott had made her feel during their brief affair.

Part of her was devastated she couldn't experience Blackwell that way ever again. Not unless she wanted to be a hypocrite.

What makes you think he'd ever want to experience you that way again? the Shadow Voice hissed. **You're pathetic, undesirable. You're creepy. He probably thought the way you acted last night was embarrassing.**

Embarrassing. *Embarrassing.* *Embarrassing.*
Embarrassing. *Embarrassing.* *Embarrassing.*
Embarrassing. *Embarrassing.* *Embarrassing.*
Embarrassing. *Embarrassing.* *Embarrassing.*
Embarrassing. *Embarrassing.* *Embarrassing.*
Embarrassing. *Embarrassing.* *Embarrassing.*
Embarrassing. *Embarrassing.* *Embarrassing.*
Embarrassing. *Embarrassing.* *Embarrassing.*
Embarrassing. *Embarrassing.* *Embarrassing.*
Embarrassing.

"*Stop!*" she cried aloud, slamming her hands against her forehead as if she could physically dislodge the voice from her mind. But it wouldn't stop. The word looped on repeat until Ophelia was practically ripping the hair from her scalp.

Embarrassing. Embarrassing. Embarrassing. Embarrassing.
Embarrassing. Embarrassing. Embarrassing. Embarrassing.
Embarrassing. Embarrassing. Embarrassing. Embarrassing.
Embarrassing. Embarrassing. Embarrassing. Embarrassing.
Embarrassing. Embarrassing. Embarrassing. Embarrassing.
Embarrassing. Embarrassing. Embarrass—

"Ophelia," a deep voice said.

The Shadow Voice slinked off into the depths of her mind and finally it was quiet.

Blackwell was suddenly there, gently prying her hands from her hair. "What's going on?"

"It wouldn't stop," she groaned.

"What wouldn't stop?" he pressed.

"The Shadow Voice," she gritted out, squeezing her hands into fists to resist the urge to plunge them back into her disheveled tresses. "It kept telling me I was embarrassing last night—when we, you know—and it wouldn't stop. Over and over and over and over and over—"

"Hey. Look at me."

She hadn't even realized her eyes were closed.

"Take a deep breath," he instructed when she finally opened her eyes. "In. Out."

She did as he said.

"Again."

In. Out.

"One more time."

In. Out.

"You have nothing to be embarrassed about," he vowed. "Next time your mind tries to convince you otherwise, remember this: there is nothing about you that I find undesirable. Okay?"

She looked away. She never wanted to believe something more.

You can't, though, can you? The Shadow Voice laughed. ***They are just pretty words from a pretty face. You can believe me, though, little Necromancer.***

"Ophelia," Blackwell called her back. "Every time your eyes glaze over like that... where do you go?"

"Nowhere," she lied.

His eyes narrowed. "Who is the Shadow Voice?"

Her blood froze at the sound of someone else naming the insidious entity in her head. She couldn't speak. She didn't know what to say, and even if she did, she didn't want to explain something so intimate to him, afraid it would make her break down. The panic in her eyes must have been blatant because he decided to let it go, changing the subject.

"I made a deal with Jasper," he informed her. "We'll be able to see the contestant logs soon."

She sucked in a surprised breath. "That easy?"

He grimaced. "I wouldn't say *easy*. But it's done."

"What did you promise him?"

He shook his head. "Nothing savory. Don't worry about it."

She heaved a sigh. "Well, when can we see them?"

"In about an hour, so we have some time to kill."

She couldn't mention that she had intended to sneak off to the secret corridor without him. She would just have to table that idea for another time.

She grabbed her brush and began smoothing out her tangled curls. "What would you suggest we do to bide our time?"

A wicked smirk. "Nothing that involves keeping our clothes on."

"Please don't make this hard."

The smirk grew into a full-blown grin. "Well, technically you're the one—"

"If you are about to make some ridiculous innuendo involving the word *hard*"—she pointed at him with the hairbrush—"swallow your tongue."

He made a show of sighing heavily as if not getting to finish his joke was deeply inconvenient for him. "Fine. How about we use this time for something I've been wanting to address—your magic."

She inclined her head. "What about my magic?"

"You need to learn how to wield it better, control it. It's driving me mad watching you waste so much of it. Plus, I want you to learn how to control your little disappearing act before the next few levels."

"I think I'll pass. I'm not sure I could tolerate you as a teacher. And what exactly does the next level entail?"

"A lot of death if you don't utilize every advantage," he said.

"Helpful as ever," she quipped.

"Well, I'm trying to be helpful, and you're being difficult," he countered. "The first two trials were child's play compared to what's coming next. I can only help so much within some of these levels. The rest will be on you. I want that to be a hopeful prospect—not a risky one."

"Aw." She pressed a mocking hand to her chest. "Are you saying you'd be sad if I were to get maimed or die?"

He gave her an odd, inscrutable look. "Tell me, angel, do you believe me to be heartless?"

The gravity of his tone made her squirm a bit, but she only pointed out, "Technically, you *are* heartless."

"Until you successfully complete our bargain, of course," he said. A clever joke considering the items they were searching for. "Right?"

She wasn't sure where he was going with this. "Yes..."

"Then let me train you so you don't end up perishing tragically," he pressed.

"Fine. I suppose your tutoring cannot possibly be worse than whatever creative death the next level has planned."

Blackwell laughed. "That's the spirit."

24

LESSONS

To Blackwell's credit, he was a decent instructor. Though she could do without the smug grins whenever she tried something contrary to his suggestions and it backfired.

Though their magic wasn't the same, he was able to break down the mechanics in his lessons well enough to give her an idea of what to look for within herself. How to feel out the different sensations in her body in order to concentrate her power in a way that gave her more control. Though, that effort became muddied up by the butterflies in her stomach every time he got a little too close to demonstrate something.

He was a bit firmer in his instruction than her mother had been—probably because her mother hadn't been able to do anything but describe magic to her, and now Ophelia was actually able to feel it firsthand. But all of Blackwell's critiques were constructive in a way that encouraged her to elevate herself to his level, rather than break her down.

"You're losing concentration right before you expel," he told her. "You can't let go of your focus just because you feel your magic ready to fire. Make sure to follow all the way through. Go again."

They had been at this for a little over an hour in the cobweb-filled drawing room, facing each other a few feet apart so she had something to aim at. She'd summon her magic, point, and expel, then Blackwell would turn transparent just in time for the blue sparks of her power to pass through him and scorch the wall. The summoning part had become easier the more she flexed that muscle in her core. It was the aiming part she was having difficulty with. No matter how much she tried, the zaps of power always came out scattered instead of streamlined, and though Blackwell never seemed to run out of patience with her, she was running out of patience with herself.

"I'm tired," she told him. "And I don't have a lot left in my reservoir."

Plus, the room had begun to smell strongly of petrichor and salt, a side effect of all the magic that was beginning to make her lightheaded.

He nodded. "Alright. Why don't we shift our focus to the disappearing?"

"I told you," she said, sighing. "That was an *accident*. I wouldn't know where to begin."

"What triggered it before?" he prompted.

She crossed her arms over her chest. "Cade attacking me with a knife—"

Before she could finish the rest of her sentence, Blackwell snapped his fingers and a knife suddenly appeared in his hand. There was not even a second of hesitation as he launched the blade right at her.

She choked on a squeal as she tried to dive out of the way, but she didn't move fast enough and the knife—

—went right through her now-invisible chest. She gawked at Blackwell, half in disbelief, half in rage. He met her gaze evenly, quite satisfied with himself.

"It's definitely a self-defense mechanism," he confirmed with a wink.

"You're a *menace*!" she barked at him. "What if that hadn't worked?"

"It did work, so there's no point in being upset about it," he countered as he procured another knife, tossing it into the air and catching it by its hilt.

"I swear if you throw that at me—"

He whipped the blade in her direction. This time, she managed to dive out of the way, but he already had another knife on deck. She didn't even bother to protest as he aimed the next one, instead focusing on the way her skin pricked as she traced the knife's trajectory through the air. When it came closer, a shot of terror went through her veins and an odd sensation—that she could only describe as what she'd imagine evaporating would feel like—rippled through her. The knife passed clean through her chest.

"I got it," she realized.

This time when he threw the blade, she planted her feet shoulder-width apart and braced herself.

With a sharp nod, she instructed, "Aim for a different spot this time."

He whipped it toward her left shoulder. Now that she knew what feeling to anticipate, she homed in on that warm tingle, and before the knife was even within arm's reach, she made her entire left arm disappear.

"Hell," she gasped as she lifted her invisible limb. Instead of it immediately returning to its solid state, as it had when this happened involuntarily, she found that she had to will it to reappear. It took a bit longer than she expected, but eventually it came back, fully intact.

She looked back over to Blackwell and found a knowing glint in his eyes, as well as another emotion she couldn't quite place. "Did you see that?"

"Yes," he crossed his arms over his chest. "Now, you just need to keep up the practice until you can fade in and out in a split second."

"Have you ever heard of a Necromancer who could do such a thing?" she wondered, looking down at her hands in awe.

"No," he told her. "I think maybe—"

"Blackwell," a voice suddenly boomed through the room.

Ophelia spun around to find the owner of the voice was Jasper. In the Devil's hands was a leather-bound book so thick, she wondered how the spine was able to hold all of the pages without coming unglued. The contestant logs.

"You've got twenty-four hours," Jasper warned as Blackwell transported himself over to take the book out of the Devil's hands. "If anything happens to it—*she's* the one who will deal with the consequences. Understood?"

Blackwell dipped his chin in a single, sharp nod and then both men flicked their eyes over to her, waiting for confirmation that she understood the stakes. She nodded profusely and Jasper disappeared. Running over to Blackwell, she greedily took in every detail of the book as he flipped the cover open. A language she couldn't read was written in thick, black letters on the title page. A few more pages in and the list began. Names in tongues from every corner of the world, including those that had been forgotten, were listed one by one. Most were crossed out in red ink, though some were struck through in black, and every hundred or so, one was circled. She didn't need an answer key to put the pieces together. Killed, forfeited, won.

"This competition must be centuries old," she whispered.

"Yes," Blackwell murmured back.

"But if Genevieve knows this Gabriel person, then he cannot be *that* old," she reasoned. "Which means we can flip to the end, right?" She flipped a large chunk of the book to the left as she spoke. "And Gabriel had to have been a contestant. Genevieve would never be in contact with someone who worked here—someone of the paranormal variety. She disliked our mother's practice greatly. As soon as she was old enough to go into town alone, she'd take every opportunity to get out of Grimm Manor."

And make a bunch of friends I didn't know about.

Blackwell nodded, the movement oddly tense. "If you're sure, we'll start at the end."

As soon as the words were out of his mouth, a bell tolled through the room. It was time for dinner—and level three.

Blackwell sighed and slammed the book shut, tucking it beneath his arm. "We'll get back to this after the trial. Listen—from here on out, the second you step through the portals you need to summon me, alright?"

"Got it." She waved at him and made to move for the door, but he sidestepped in front of her.

"I'm serious, Ophelia." The earnest way he spoke her name gave her slight pause. "If you don't summon me quickly enough and get distracted, you could easily get killed."

She held his gaze as she promised, "I understand."

With that, they went their separate ways—her toward the dining hall, and him out of sight to hide the book for safekeeping. As she walked down the corridors, she dragged a finger along the intricate damask wallpaper, watching as she left a trail in the dust as she passed. The open hallways here always carried a draft, but the air was surprisingly not stale. The rich scent of something warm and musky, notes of magnolia lying beneath it, actually reminded her of her mother's favorite perfume. She wondered if it was one of Phantasma's tricks.

She couldn't help but think that with a little soap and water, and fewer Devils, this place had the potential to be truly magnificent. For a moment, she let herself imagine that Phantasma was not a horrific competition, but an opulent estate hosting an annual Mardi Gras ball. A place she could don an ornate mask and an egregiously lavish gown and dance and drink until she passed out.

A vision flashed into her mind of her being twirled around a ballroom by a handsome suitor.

The full skirts of her vermilion gown swished effortlessly with each spin and were layered like delicate rose petals. The top of the dress was a structured drop-waist corset made of rich silk, which pointed down in a "V" just below her bellybutton before the skirts began. Matching silk opera gloves stretched all the way to her elbows, and her neck glistened with a choker of glittering rubies. As the dance wound to an end, her suitor led her from the dance floor and pulled her, giggling, into a dark guest room down the hall. He slowly rolled her gloves down her arms and tossed them aside. Next, he discarded the dress, and her lacy undergarments, until all that was left was the ruby necklace . . .

As he dipped her down, arms wrapped around her waist, lips pressed against the pulse at her neck, Blackwell whispered, "You look ravishing tonight."

Ophelia snapped back to the present. Just in time to run smack into someone's back.

No, not just someone. Cade.

He looked at her like a hunter staring down a fox. Ophelia worried that whatever Blackwell had done had reinforced Cade's desire to eradicate her more than it had inspired the man to stay away.

"You can sic your Demon friends on me all you want, you bitch," he snarled at her. "But I promise, one of these nights I'll be getting the final laugh."

She glowered. "I'm getting really tired of being called a bitch. I didn't intentionally sic anyone on you, but I can if you'd like."

He sneered at her threat, but didn't linger, turning on his

heels and stalking into the dining hall. She kept her distance as she followed, silently wishing that Blackwell had drawn more blood. Cade was definitely going to become a problem if his hatred for her influenced the other contestants and they had the chance to band together against her in one of the trials.

In the dining hall, however, the other contestants—aside from Beau and Eric—looked equally as wary of Cade's presence as they did hers. She wondered what Cade held over the two men for them to be so loyal to him. Or maybe it was just that insipid sense of comradery assholes always seemed to have with other assholes that made them stick together. Regardless, she liked that they took the guesswork out of who she needed to avoid.

The only person who bothered greeting her was Luci, lifting her hand in a small wave as Ophelia went over to the dinner table to grab some fruit. Leon was uncomfortably stiff by Luci's side, and Ophelia wondered if Luci had told him about the rest of their conversation in the library.

The silence as everyone ate was thick, and the appetites around the room had gotten noticeably smaller. Most people had a few grapes or a slice of buttered French bread on their plates. Leaving the richer dishes—crawfish étouffée, red beans and rice with honeyed cornbread, fried boudin, and praline bread pudding—completely untouched. Any other circumstances and Ophelia's mouth would have been watering, but the image of the dining table crawling with maggots and spiders was still too fresh to make even her absolute favorite of their local cuisine tempting.

"I think the cruelest torture this place enacts is feeding us right before each trial," James muttered as he dusted crumbs from his single slice of bread out of his mustache.

A few grunts and mutters of agreement resounded before the

tense blanket of quiet fell over the room once again. Ophelia stared at the clock on the far wall, willing the time to tick by faster as she picked grapes from their stems and absentmindedly arranged them by size on the plate in front of her. She began to pop them into her mouth, smallest to largest, one by one, letting the sweet juice run down the back of her throat as her knee bounced beneath the table.

Tick, tock. Tick, tock. Tick, tock.

She was anxious for the trial to begin, and she wasn't sure why. Maybe it was the warning Blackwell had given her. Or maybe it was the anticipation of seeing him again as soon as she stepped through that portal...

He's been gone for less than an hour, get a hold of yourself.

Kissing him had been an astronomical mistake.

Go back to finding him annoying, she told herself. But the problem wasn't that she had stopped finding him annoying—the problem was that she had started finding him enticing.

A flash went through the room, and Ophelia swallowed the last of her fruit, twisting around to get a good look at their newest host. The Devil was wearing little more than a bolt of gold fabric strategically tied around their body and their platinum hair was so long it pooled on the ground at their bare feet. With so little on, their Devil's Mark was easily distinguishable—a series of bone-colored spikes lining their forearms. A vicious smile.

"My name is Devon. Welcome to level three," they said as they summoned the portal and revealed this level's clue. The routine was becoming familiar to the point that people were nudging each other for a spot at the front so they could get the best look at the incendiary script.

ABOVE A FIERY ABYSS, YOUR GILDED CAGE MUST RISE,
BUT WHEN IT DOES, OTHERS WILL DIVE.

GOLDEN WEIGHTS AROUND YOUR CHAINS,
GREED'S ALLURING SONG, A DANGEROUS GAME.

A SEA OF TEMPTATION, A CHOICE TO UNFOLD,
DECIDE IF YOUR LIFE IS WORTH ITS WEIGHT IN GOLD.

Ophelia watched as one of the other contestants procured a pen and paper in order to scribble the clues down. Smart. At least, it would have been, if the words didn't fade away as soon as they were jotted down. Ophelia watched with rapt curiosity over the contestant's shoulder as they tried over and over to make the ink stay on the page—to no avail. Phantasma would not let the clues be written.

Devon began calling names, and Ophelia took the opportunity to update the roster of the group in her head as she braced herself to enter herself. A fiery abyss being mentioned in the very first line of their clue did not bode well. Neither did the realization that there were only seventeen of them left and they had only completed two levels.

Summon Blackwell immediately, she reminded herself as she took her turn stepping through, letting the portal's magic envelop her.

The moment she stepped out, however, everything except the crisp feeling of fear flew from her mind. She was trapped in an enormous, gilded cage hanging in the air. And a thousand feet below was an ocean of boiling lava. A fiery abyss.

LEVEL
THREE

25

GREED

The only thing more eye-watering than the charred smell of lava was the scent of burning hair and flesh. Both of which permeated the foggy air around the cliffside.

Her golden cage was floating just in arm's reach of a rocky mountainside above the great sea of fire. As she squinted through the rolling steam to her left, she could make out the glistening of another cage about a hundred feet away and could only assume it contained another contestant. Before she could summon Blackwell, her cage shook violently. She stumbled forward and gripped the bars for balance.

**Above a fiery abyss, your gilded cage must rise,
but when it does, others will dive.**

For a second, a part of her was impressed at her increasing ability to remember the wordy clues under such pressure. The other part of her was acutely aware that she was slowly being lowered toward the sea of lava.

Scanning the golden vessel for anything that might make it stop moving, it became clear that there was nothing special inside the cage—no levers or cranks to lift it back up. Behind her there was a thick chain that descended all the way down into the fire, but when she reached out to tug on it, the metal scorched her skin, and a scream of agony ripped from her throat.

"*Hell*," she hissed between her clenched teeth when she finally managed to catch her breath from the blistering pain. A nasty burn was bubbling up on her palm, the charred skin turning a grotesque mottled brown, and she worried for a moment that the heat had melted her skin down to her bone. Tears slid down her cheeks, and she swatted them away with her good hand.

I never let pain get the better of me, Genevieve's voice pierced through her panic. *I'd much rather let it bring me clarity.*

Her cage dropped again, and this time it knocked her to her knees.

She took a deep breath and pushed the throbbing fire in her hand to the back of her mind. She wondered if everyone else's cages were moving as well, and when a few shouts of panic echoed somewhere out in the thick mist a moment later, she got her answer. Enough of this.

"*Blackwell,*" she summoned, repeating his name twice more while the cage bounced down another foot.

Her stomach was beginning to roll from the suffocating heat of the atmosphere, her hair sticking to the back of her neck with sweat.

"I'll have to strip down to nothing just to avoid a heat stroke," she gasped to herself, wiping the back of her good hand across her forehead.

"As much as it pains me to say this," Blackwell's voice rang out, "keep your clothes on, angel."

She spun to face the direction of his voice, but he was nowhere to be seen. A wave of paranoia washed over her. "Blackwell?"

"Yes, I'm here," he assured her. "The magic of the cages balances each contestant's exact mass. And even in my most ghostly form, energy carries weight. Which means I can only project my voice in here."

"And how do I know it's really you?" She narrowed her eyes at the empty space before her.

"How shall I prove it? List out every biting remark you've given me over the last few days?" She could hear the amusement in his tone. "Or maybe I can go into detail about the expressions you make when I bring you to the edge of pleasure—"

"Okay, enough." The burn on her hand was beginning to ache with an unbearable pain and her patience was wearing thin. "I believe—"

The cage dropped again, two feet this time, cutting off the rest of her sentence as her teeth clanged together from the abrupt halt.

"The wall in front of you," Blackwell directed with haste. "You'll have to reach between the spaces of the bars and climb your way up to find circular weights embedded in the rock. You'll clamp those weights around the chain behind you—carefully—and the enchanted pulley system will lift your cage. Each time you make it up a yard, however, the magic will counter the movement by lowering the other contestants. And considering the rate this contraption is falling, I'd bet several others have already begun to figure out their task."

Her breath hitched. "You mean... surviving might mean killing someone?"

"If the others aren't fast enough to recover. But that's not your concern," he told her. "Remember what I told you about having a soft heart. Now isn't the time or place."

"My hand," she blurted, sticking it out toward his detached voice to show him the angry, blistering welt. "I touched the—"

"*That's* why your summons felt so faint," he murmured. "What did I tell you about getting injured? And summoning me immediately?"

"I don't know what to tell you if you don't think being distracted by a giant abyss of lava is a reasonable excuse to make a couple of mistakes," she retorted.

He was quiet for a moment, and she could just picture the look of exasperation on his face. Then, "I can't heal you."

She swallowed. "But...I have to use my hand to climb."

"I know." A loaded pause. "I can only heal you in my fully corporeal state, and that amount of weight would trigger the cage to drop too far down."

His voice sounded strained now, his words taut with something she couldn't quite place, and she wondered if it was anger or frustration at her foolishness for touching the hot chain, or if it was...something else. Something considered dangerous here.

She shook her head. There were too many other things to focus on right now than whatever was going on between the two of them. Taking a deep breath and rolling her shoulders back, she braced herself.

She put her hands through the bars of the cage, grabbed a rock protruding from the cliff, and pulled down as hard as she could. The motion propelled the cage upward on its pulley. The pain that clawed through her wounded hand from the rough rock and the effort of hauling herself and the cage upward was almost enough to make her pass out. Even the skin of her uninjured hand was becoming chafed with the grueling effort, and just when she wondered if she was capable of doing this trial, she saw something shining within the rock above.

Gritting through the agony, she hauled herself up another foot, toward the golden weight peeking out of the cliffside, and began digging to unearth it. Bits and pieces of the mountainside crumbled to her feet and wedged itself beneath her fingernails. The heavy ring-shaped piece was thick, almost bigger than her head. And when the weight finally came free, her pride spiked with the accomplishment.

She felt the cage shake and bounce down a few feet as she walked across it with the new added mass. The weight had hinges that allowed her to pry it open before clamping it shut around the scalding chain on the outside of her cage. When she let it drop down the chain, like an enormous charm around a necklace, several clangs vibrated up the metal links, until the distinct sound of a hiss reverberated from below as the gilded hoop plunged into the sea of lava.

The cage shot up several feet.

"You're doing excellent," Blackwell praised. "Keep going."

His encouragement made her push herself harder. As much as she hated to admit it, she craved confirmation when she did something well. Something her mother hadn't often bothered with.

She managed to haul herself up the rocky surface a few more feet before her injured hand began bleeding profusely, sending lightning pain shooting up her arm. But she ignored it.

"That's it, angel," Blackwell continued. "The next one is just a little further."

She didn't bother to wipe away the tears that streamed down her cheeks, any qualms about being vulnerable in front of Blackwell replaced by the pride his words were igniting in her belly.

A few excruciating minutes later and she found another weight. This time, when she sent it into the fiery sea below, however, the splash it made was accompanied by a string of agonizing screams. Worse was the whiff of charred hair and flesh that permeated through the bars of the cage a moment later.

No.

Ophelia leaned through the bars and heaved up the contents of her stomach.

No.

She could feel the Shadow Voice begin to unfurl in the back of her mind, eager to feed into whatever spiral was about to take over her senses. If the contestants' screams didn't haunt her for the rest of her life, the Shadow Voice would be sure to.

You killed someone, little monster. What a terrible sin to have forever marring your soul. But if you knock on the rock three times, you can absolve yourself of murder, the Shadow Voice tempted.

And damn herself to Hell if she didn't rush back over to pound her knuckles into the mountainside.

One, two, three.

Again, it laughed.

One, two, three.

Again.

One, two, three.

"Ophelia."

At the sound of *his* voice, the Shadow Voice shriveled up and disappeared. A sob caught in Ophelia's throat as she spotted the blood now coating her knuckles.

"The Shadow Voice..." she whispered. "It won't stop unless I do what it says."

"Tell me who the Shadow Voice is," Blackwell pressed gently.

She squeezed her eyes shut and shook her head.

"Angel?"

"I don't know," she finally answered, sniffing. "Sometimes, I think it's *me*. All the bad parts of me. But the things it tells me to do...I know I would never want those things. I *hate* it."

"Hey," he murmured, and she suddenly felt a warm static sensation envelop her, like he was wrapping his arms around her even though he wasn't physically there. "Listen to me. It's just the two of us here right now, alright? Take a deep breath."

She did.

"Two more," he directed, knowing.

She took two more gulps of air as instructed, something inside her swelling with a foreign emotion that he had so shrewdly observed such a specific detail. Always in threes. Her locket began to warm.

"Now, we will get to the bottom of this Shadow Voice later, but right now I want you to listen to *my* voice and my voice only," he directed. "You only need about five more weights. We're going to take this one at a time."

She let his voice steady her nerves, clung to the reassurance lacing his tone. If he thought she'd be fine, she'd be fine. He wouldn't lie to her. He *needed* her to get through this competition unscathed. To succeed. With him was the safest place she could be.

"Okay," she whispered.

"Ready?" he prompted. "Start climbing."

She did. As Ophelia pulled herself up one foot at a time, her biceps were screaming at her to stop, and she was chiding herself for having such a lack of upper-body strength. She was going to start lifting books in the library after this.

A few minutes later, she found another weight. Then another. When she came across a third, her bones felt like gelatin from the strain, but Blackwell's encouragement and confidence never wavered.

"Two more," he promised.

When she pulled herself up another couple of feet, searching for the next piece of gold, she reached a thick patch of fog. Coughing, she hauled herself out of the damp, white mist and into the clear air above. She gasped when she saw at least six cages already sitting at the top of the cliff, empty.

"How did they get up that *fast*," she complained.

Then, immediately to her left she saw none other than Cade, clawing his way above the haze. She was actually quite shocked to see that he—being in such good shape—hadn't already completed the trial. Then she saw what was sitting at his feet. At least six of the gold weights.

"Why would he keep them—? Wait."

...DECIDE IF YOUR LIFE IS WORTH ITS WEIGHT IN GOLD, the clue had said. Apparently, Cade thought his was.

"Level three. *Greed*," Blackwell said. "The weights are pure gold. If you can manage to haul them up with you, you can keep them, but it's a risk. Those with the most weights fall the furthest when someone else moves up."

And as if Cade had heard Blackwell's words—which for all she knew, he *had*—his gaze cut to hers. Mouth twisting with determination, he began pulling himself up at twice the speed he had been moving before, the veins in his arms protruding so distinctly they looked as if they were in danger of bursting through his skin. Scrambling back into action, she began pawing her way up the side, her injured palm nearly useless at this point. Still, she kept going, slow and steady, and soon enough she found another weight. This one was so deeply embedded into the rock that she tore her fingernails apart trying to excavate it. Soon, enough of it was out, and though Cade had already added his weight and moved up a story above her, the moment she sent her own down, she watched him plummet with a scream back below the mist.

Blackwell laughed in delight as a small pang of guilt shot through her core. Only a small one, though.

"You're almost there," Blackwell announced as the cage rose. "One more."

She could see the glorious edge of the cliff so clearly now she almost wept. Well, she was already weeping, but this time it would be in joy.

When she found the final gilded weight, another two cages sprung up in the distance to her right, but she didn't allow her gaze to linger on them. Blackwell was right, she could not have a soft heart in this moment.

I can do this, she told herself as her jaw clenched with the strain of her movements. *I can redeem my soul later. Genevieve is waiting for me somewhere. I will make it back to her.*

Flesh shredded around the tendons in her hands, blood splattering the charcoal-colored earth before her. Her body ached like it never had before, her limbs and muscles growing tauter by the second, until she worried they'd seize up and stop working altogether. But she didn't stop digging. Blackwell's presence never wavering in the air around her.

With a guttural heave, she dragged the final weight from the cliffside and hauled it to the chain. Forcing open its hinge, she let it snap shut and fall into the chasm below, propelling her up to freedom. When the screams rang out beneath the mist, she didn't even flinch. Her focus was set only on the exit.

Crawling through the portal out of the level, Ophelia barely made it to the edge of the arched entryway of the dining hall before she fainted.

26

TASTE

"Come on," a deep voice murmured, cool hands running over her face, brushing back the hair on her forehead. "Wake up for me."

Ophelia didn't want whoever was touching her to ever stop.

"Mmm?" she muttered, trying to open her eyes, but they were much too heavy.

"I'm going to start healing you," the voice told her.

She hummed an incoherent response as they began running their fingertips over the damaged skin of her hands and arms. A staticky, vibrating sensation rippled through the places they touched, and she found herself giggling.

"That tickles," she gasped.

It didn't take long for the strength to return to her limbs, the pain fading so quickly she nearly forgot how it felt only seconds before, and when she finally opened her eyes, a beaming smile stretched across her face as she gazed up into Blackwell's emerald eyes.

"I think you must have been heaven-sent," she told him as her head finally cleared.

He lifted a brow in amusement. "That's a new sentiment for me. Here."

He offered his hand and pulled her to her feet. She stretched her arms out above her, inspecting the now-smooth skin of her palm where the wounds had been festering just a moment before. Brand-new. Meanwhile, Blackwell's hands were now covered in her blood.

"Sorry about that," she told him sheepishly.

He lifted a shoulder with a smirk. "It's only blood."

She reached out to give his hand a squeeze. "Thank you. You got me through that."

He took a step toward her, lifting her chin with his finger so he could look her square in the eyes. "You got yourself through that. I'm proud of you."

Her breath hitched. No one had ever said those words to her before. Not Genevieve. Not her mother. Her mother might have told her she'd done something well, but never that she was *proud*. Tessie Grimm had never been the kind for flowery sentiments.

As quickly as his words had warmed her, his next sentence made her blood run cold. "I want to talk about the Shadow Voice."

She ripped her chin from his grasp and shook her head. "No. In fact, why don't you just wipe everything that happened in that level from your memory forever?"

There was something about being in excruciating pain that had postponed her embarrassment. But now that her senses had returned, sharpened from the power of his magic, she couldn't help but be mortified by everything he just witnessed. She had *cried*.

Next time, just take the plummet into the ocean of lava, she chided herself.

His expression turned frustrated. "If this voice is making you hurt yourself—"

"I can fix myself without your help." She huffed. "I was just under a lot of stress. It gets louder when I'm stressed."

"Ophelia." His tone was firm now. "You don't need to *fix*

yourself. You're not broken. But it's okay to get outside help if it gets too loud."

"I can control it," she insisted. "Just drop it."

"It was making you beat your hand into a bloody pulp," he stated bluntly. "Excuse me for being concerned."

"You don't get it," she whispered. "No one gets it. They only judge. The girl who has to tap on walls before she leaves a room—or everyone she's ever talked to will die. The girl who can't run a simple errand because a dark thought popped into her head that something catastrophic would happen if she left the house that day. Meanwhile, I'm just trying to satisfy the voice long enough to get a break from having to listen to every single sin I've ever committed on repeat."

"Listen, if you need to punch a wall to relieve yourself from whatever insidious voice is in your head, I'm not going to *judge* you. That is one of the least strange things I've ever come across in Phantasma, I assure you." He narrowed his eyes. "But letting yourself believe you've done something so sinful that you deserve to be in pain is another sentiment altogether. And if you're upset about what may have happened to the others in that trial...taking care of yourself first is not a sin. You understand that, right?"

She looked down at her hands. "It's just...all my life people have had thoughts about what my mother was—what it is that *I* now am. Necromancer. Blasphemous. Demon. It's all the same to some people. Sometimes, it's easy to listen to the voice in my head when it tells me I don't deserve something. Who wants to be around someone tied so closely to death and darkness? It's morbid."

"Because I, of all people, wouldn't understand what it's like to be surrounded by death and morbidity?" he responded dryly.

Point taken.

"Can we please talk about something else?" she implored.

"After everything that just happened, Hell, I just want to feel *good* again."

The intensity in his eyes heated at her words. "And what would make you feel good right now, angel?"

She swallowed thickly. The answer was on the tip of her tongue, but she couldn't bring herself to say it. It was unequivocally a bad idea to even be *thinking* it. And he was taunting her, challenging her. She knew that. Yet, still—Hell if she didn't deserve a little fun after all the blood and sweat she had just shed, if all she was guaranteed in this place was pain, why not seek out pleasure when and where she could?

He took another step closer, and she backed up into the wall behind her. They were still in the corridor just outside of the dining hall.

He placed a hand above her head for balance as he leaned in and taunted, "C'mon, angel. Tell me what I can do to make you feel *good*. I'm at your service after all."

She tilted her head up, her lips brushing over his as light as a feather, but still she said nothing. A low, sensual sound hummed in the back of his throat, and he lifted his free hand to the front laces of her corset, skimming the backs of his fingers over the material across her stomach. He slowly tugged at the laces holding her corset closed, nimbly undoing them, one pull at a time, the blood still covering his hands smearing across the delicate white gossamer of the gown beneath.

"Tell me what you *want*," he murmured.

Her breath hitched as the corset finally fell away and he began flicking open the buttons running down the front of the dress beneath one by one. All the way to her navel. The cool air of the open hallway hit her feverish skin, and his fingers moved to lightly trail down between her breasts, leaving a faint crimson line in their wake.

"You first," she whispered. "What do you want?"

He moved in, turning his head so he could lightly touch his lips to the underside of her jaw. "I want you to let me see you." His mouth began tracing up her jawline, languidly, torturously. His words tickling her skin. "*All* of you. There is nothing I have seen yet that has made me look away. No atrocity you could commit to make me not want you like this. No matter how forbidden." He seared a kiss into the sensitive spot at the end of his trail. "I want to know everything. I want to see all the darkest corners of your mind." He tilted his face up to whisper his next words right into her ear. "I want to taste your sins."

The moment those words rolled off his tongue, something possessed her. She leaned back briefly, her hands finding their grip on the front of his shirt to steady herself before she rocked up on the balls of her feet and slammed her mouth into his. This kiss was not gentle or shy. It was all-consuming. Fire—the good kind—erupted in her core as he greedily gathered her body up into his, twisting one hand up into her hair as he wrapped his other arm around her waist like a vise. She moaned at the sensation of him deepening the kiss even further, plunging his tongue into her mouth and scraping his teeth against her bottom lip. When he pulled back to give her a chance to catch her breath, her mouth was swollen and throbbing.

He kissed his way down her throat, nipping at her pulse before lowering himself down to his knees before her. Her heart thundered in her chest, her locket nearly fusing with her skin it burned so hot, and she frantically looked around the corridor to make sure they didn't have any witnesses. He huffed a laugh at her nervousness as he gathered her skirts and pushed them up over her hips.

"I dare someone to bother us right now," he threatened.

Her voice was shaky as she asked, "What...what are you doing?"

He gave her a wickedly roguish look. "*Tasting.*"

She nearly choked on her shock, but there was no time to respond before he leaned in and began kissing the sensitive skin of her exposed inner thighs. A shiver ran down her spine the higher his mouth traveled, and her chest heaved with ragged breaths of anticipation. He slid a hand slowly up the side of her leg, toward the delicate material at her hip, and the next thing she knew, he was ripping through the lace of her panties and discarding them.

That's when she felt the dark gaze return. The same one she swore she had felt that time she first met Blackwell within Phantasma—and the other instance after she had crashed through the dining room ceiling. When Blackwell had become paranoid as to who might be listening and dragged her into a broom closet...

She went utterly still, scanning the hallway, but there was no one she could see.

Blackwell instantly froze his movements when her body language changed, looking up to assess what had made her tense.

"Is something wrong?" he asked. "Do you want me to stop?"

She took a deep breath and shook off the paranoia. There was no one there. She looked back down at Blackwell. "*No. Don't stop.*"

That was all the permission he needed. He placed kisses around her navel as his hand wandered closer to the spot that had been aching for him since their first kiss.

When she felt the pad of his thumb brush over her core, lighter than a feather, she made a sound that was somewhere between a moan and a purr as she leaned her shoulders back into the wall and arched herself closer to him, desperate for more pressure. The slickness between her legs grew as he drew lazy circles around the bundle of nerves at her center, his mouth moving in closer and closer and closer.

Dropping his hand, he flicked his tongue out, to taste her arousal, and they both groaned in unison. She began to pant, needing more, more, more. But he was taking his sweet time. Plunging his tongue in and out of her core, but never against *that* spot, and after a minute she'd had enough of his teasing.

"I can only imagine death is more kind than you." She peered down at his smug face as she practically writhed against the wall.

He laughed and continued his teasing until she was whimpering for relief.

"You taste like *heaven*," he murmured.

"Blackwell," she pleaded, tugging on his hair with her impatience. She needed relief. This teasing was too much.

Finally, he gave it to her. His tongue flicked over her clit, sending a piercing wave of pleasure through her body, making her toes curl, her stomach clench. She tightened her hold in his hair as if to keep him right there forever. He swirled his tongue in lazy circles and sucked gently until her legs almost gave out beneath her. Her body was building to that beautiful apex of bliss with each stroke, each hum of satisfaction from his throat in response to her sounds of ecstasy, but just before she reached the place she was climbing toward—he pulled away.

She was going to murder him.

27

NEW SUSTENANCE

Blackwell's shoulders shook with quiet laughter at her murderous expression as he pulled away, dropping her skirts and standing. He recaptured her mouth in a heated kiss before she could pelt him with the million curse words on the tip of her tongue. Winding his arms around her waist, he transported them away.

When they blinked into her bedroom, it took her a moment to shake off the disorienting feeling of being transported. But Blackwell didn't miss a beat. He stripped away his jacket and unbuttoned his shirt, and she was once again taken aback by his beauty.

"God," she whispered as she flattened her hands against the six distinct muscles of his abdomen, tracing a fingertip over the perfectly cut "V" of his hip bones. "You're so beautiful. It's quite irritating."

"I know," he said wryly.

She rolled her eyes, but before she could knock him back down a peg, he swiftly bent to lift her up by the backs of her thighs, hooking her legs tight around his waist. She greedily pressed her lips back to his and let him kiss her until her head was swimming from the lack of oxygen. He walked them over to the bed and gently laid her all the way back against the plush comforter. She unwrapped her legs from his waist, letting her knees fall open as he snapped to remove the dress from her body, leaving her utterly bare before him.

The expression on his face as he stood there, peering down at her, was one of sincere awe.

"You're..." He rubbed a hand over his mouth in wonder. "Stunning. Angelic."

She snorted but resisted the urge to cover her blushing face with her hands. She had only let her last lover see her briefly, between the sheets. With Blackwell, he'd made it clear there was nothing she felt like she needed to hide. He'd seen some of the worst parts of her already, and by the end of this, she was sure he'd see it all. The woman. The Necromancer. The monster.

"Come here," she whispered, reaching out for him.

He undid the belt of his pants with a single hand and tossed it aside before lifting a knee onto the bed, placing it between her legs. He planted a kiss on her belly, just above her navel, before licking and nipping his way up to her breasts. He gently clamped his lips down over one of her pert nipples and her back arched off the mattress as the fire inside of her reignited.

She tugged his head up by his hair and brought his lips back to hers. She gripped his sides and slowly rolled their bodies over until she was lying on top. Pushing herself up, palms flat against his chest, she maneuvered herself until she was straddling his upper thighs.

She smiled. "It's my turn to taste."

Scenes from the second trial flashing through her mind. Of lovers feasting on each other in ways she had never before imagined. And she wanted to try it for herself.

There was something deep inside of her that was still unsure how much further she was going to make it in this competition. Especially after that last level. There was another part of her that knew this would likely be the one and only time she could allow herself to be close to him like this. Which meant she was going to take the opportunity to do every single thing she wanted to do before it was gone forever.

Reaching between their bodies, she unbuttoned his pants before lifting herself up just enough for him to kick them off to the floor. She looked down.

Holy. Shit.

The impressive length was considerably more than she had realized the previous night when she had ground herself to a climax against him. Part of her worried that what she was about to try wouldn't work. She reached out, tentative, and wrapped her fist around his shaft—her hand too small to encircle it fully—then gave the hard length a single stroke.

His hips bucked.

"*Fuck*," he groaned. "I take back what I said about you being angelic."

She cleared her throat. "Is it okay if I—"

"You can do anything you want, angel," he inserted, voice gruff. "I'd let you drag me to the depths of Hell right now if that would please you."

"This is a version of you I can work with," she quipped as she gave him another stroke.

"Fuck," he hissed again.

She braced her unoccupied hand on his stomach to steady herself as she leaned down and gave the tip of his cock a tentative lick.

"*Ophelia.*"

She had always adored the way he spoke her name. Like a wicked prayer.

She gave another lick, and his hand flew to the back of her head, wrapping itself in the tendrils of her hair, almost involuntarily, as she slowly lowered her mouth down the first few inches of his shaft. It took a moment to get used to the feeling, but soon enough she found a rhythm between her mouth and hand, adjusting her speed and pressure to his responses. It wasn't long before she could feel the muscles in his stomach clenching tighter and tighter, and when she was sure she had brought him just as close to the edge as he had brought her in the hallway—she stopped.

A sensual curse fell from his lips.

She lifted her head, wiping her mouth with the back of her hand, and grinned down at him. "Payback."

"You're a fiend," he told her, voice thick with lust and affection.

In a blink, he transported them both into a new position, pressing her back into the pillows at the head of the bed, his body hovering over hers. He reached a hand between their bodies, moving it down to her core to rub circles against her clit with the pad of his thumb, kissing her until she could hardly remember her own name or the fact that she was required to breathe in order to live. He was her new sustenance.

There was nothing slow or lazy about his attentions now as he worked her back into a writhing, moaning mess. She could feel herself soaking the plush comforter beneath them, drenching his fingers with her wetness as he slid two of them inside her. He curled his fingers in a beckoning motion, hitting a spot that made her clamp her teeth into his bare shoulder to keep from screaming with pleasure. A guttural moan tore from his throat at her bite, and he used his free hand to tilt her face back to his, kissing her with the hunger of a man starving. He added a third finger inside of her, and she moaned as he pumped them in and out, so slow it was almost agonizing. And just as she wondered if he was going to wait for her to beg—determined to prove that what she'd said about never begging him for anything were, in fact, famous last words—he removed his fingers and placed the tip of his cock at her entrance.

He broke their kiss and pulled back just enough to read her face in the dark. "Tell me you want this."

"I want this," she swore, breathless. "Very much."

He sighed in relief and rocked his hips forward, sheathing himself inside of her, all the way to the hilt. The way he stretched her was sinful, euphoric. He was so deep she swore she could feel him in her *soul*. Her eyes rolled into the back of her head as he pulled out, slowly, before rocking forward in another languid movement. She twisted her fists into the comforter at her sides as she rode out each wave of pleasure.

She didn't know it could be like this—*Hell*, if only she had. She wouldn't have wasted time with anything less. And now she understood why some people sold their souls to experience even a fraction of this feeling.

The feeling that she'd never be able to get enough, that she needed more or she might explode, overwhelmed her. Every thrust of his hips and she saw the stars. So clear in her mind, she had forgotten how much she missed them these past few nights until now.

"Blackwell," she whimpered, her body beginning to tighten beneath his. "More. More. *More*."

"You can have everything, angel." He leaned his forehead down against hers as he pumped into her, harder, faster, driving them both wild with each stroke. She moaned as she lifted her hips off the bed and met his next thrust with her own. Sweat beaded at her temples as she finally unraveled. Completely undone.

When she began to float back down to earth, he flipped their position in one fluid motion, fixing her to straddle him once again. She leaned forward to balance her weight against his chest. His cock had slipped halfway out when they moved and yet she somehow felt it was even deeper than before. Biting her lip, she slowly slid herself all the way down onto his shaft, taking him completely despite the more intense angle, whimpering when their bodies became flush together.

Blackwell reached up to gather her hair out of her face, pushing her long curls over her shoulders so he could see her fully. She couldn't help blushing as she met his gaze and slowly rolled her hips forward before grinding them back down again. Over and over again she moved up and down his cock, his hands coming up to grip her waist and guide her into a smooth, steady rhythm. Teaching her how to ride him perfectly.

This time, when she began climbing back to that place of ecstasy, she could tell he was climbing with her. Rocking all the way forward, until only the tip of him remained inside her, she slammed herself back down a second later, eliciting a noise from him that wasn't entirely human.

"You're such a good fucking girl," he growled as she shifted forward again, moving one of his hands between their bodies to rub his thumb over her clit. "Come for me again, angel."

"Blackwell," she whimpered as his thumb rubbed faster and faster between her legs, sending every nerve in her body into a lust-filled frenzy.

"Fuck me," he told her. "Harder, angel."

She ground atop him even harder, until the sound of them joining together over and over thundered through the room.

And then an actual clap of thunder echoed around them.

Ophelia's movements slowed as the two of them gaped up at the ceiling and the curse that left Blackwell's mouth now was not said in euphoria. Because above them, crimson rainclouds began to manifest, a foreboding, swirling tempest. When the first drop of blood rained down, splattering onto Blackwell's chest, Ophelia smeared her finger through the bright red drop-let in disbelief.

"I forgot about this haunt," he said, seething, more blood pitter-pattering over their skin. "If you let me up, I can take care of it."

The rain turned into a drizzle, the warm splashes of scarlet dying his hair pink, sliding down the bridge of her nose, running over more sensitive areas...

Ophelia began moving against him again, and his brows shot up in utter shock.

He quickly recovered and a devious smile slowly curled up at the corners of his mouth at her boldness. "Are you sure?"

She shrugged and repeated his own words from earlier. "It's only blood."

He hummed in approval and twisted his hands into her damp hair, angling her face down just enough for him to meet her in a rapturous kiss. It didn't take long for them to return to their previous pace, their blood-slicked skin making their bodies slide together in a way that was utterly sinful. The storm came down stronger and stronger with each passing second, building to a crescendo at the same time that they were building to their own, and this time, when she reached the edge, he crashed over it with her. Not even the thunder overhead could drown out the sound of his name being wrought from her lips.

When they both finally came down, he gently separated their bodies and rolled her over to lie back against the pillows before standing from the bed. Her eyes widened as she took in the scene around the room without the sex-fueled haze in her mind. It looked as if a massacre had occurred.

"*God*," she exclaimed at the sight.

Blackwell smirked. "I could get used to that name, I suppose."

She rolled her eyes at him. "Please. Your ego is big enough."

He huffed a laugh as he turned to clear the carnage. By the time he was done, not a single splatter of red could be found in the room, or on her skin. When he began to dress, pulling his trousers on and fastening the button with a single hand, she pushed herself up onto her elbows to watch.

As evenly as she could, she asked, "You're leaving?"

He glanced at her as he bent to swipe his shirt from where it had been haphazardly discarded on the floor. "Do you want me to stay?"

A beat.

She felt strangely more vulnerable in this moment than she had during their throes of passion, but she swallowed and whispered, "Yes."

"Then, I'll stay," he avowed.

He left his shirt unbuttoned and returned to the bed by her side, tucking one of his arms back beneath his head and lifting the other so she could press herself into his side. As she laid her cheek against his chest, over the place where his heartbeat should've been, neither of them spoke another word.

Blackwell traced affectionate circles over her back and down her spine, and in no time, she drifted off to sleep. But not before something forbidden unwittingly began to take root inside of her. And soon enough she'd find that she wouldn't be able to stop it from growing.

Fall in love within Phantasma at your own risk.

28

DIVULGE

When Ophelia woke, deep into the witching hours, Blackwell was still beside her. Back in his ghostly form, he had moved to sit up against the headboard with the book of Phantasma's past contestants open before him. A wave of his hand in the air and the page he was reading turned in tandem.

"Clearly, I didn't wear you out enough if you're already awake," he drawled.

She flushed a bit at his words, so casually said for what they had experienced together. But she supposed that was a good thing.

It had only been sex, she reminded herself. *Plenty of people just have sex and nothing more.*

Genevieve had always been an advocate for women to indulge in intimacy just as casually as men did. A trait Ophelia had always admired, though now she thought it might be easier said than done for herself. It had probably been a mistake that she asked Blackwell to stay the night—especially because waking up to him was more comforting than she'd like to admit.

So, she forced herself to murder every butterfly fluttering in her stomach as she sat up and stretched, holding the covers he had tucked around her at some point tight against her bare chest. She was surprised to find the exhaustion that had lingered in her bones over the last week was gone. It seemed that for the first time since her mother died, she had slept well. Refusing to look too closely at why that may be, she distracted herself with the list of names Blackwell was scanning.

"How many pages have you gone through?" she wondered.

"About two hundred," he answered.

"I can take over for a while if you need a break," she offered. "I just need to get dressed—"

He snapped his fingers and suddenly she was fully clothed beneath the covers. The silk dress was a sensual burgundy color, like the ripe seeds of a pomegranate, and was definitely more luxurious than anything she had brought with her—or ever owned. The boned bodice was molded to her like a second skin and pushed her bosom up in such a flattering way that it managed to give her a semblance of cleavage. The sleeves were draped in a way that hung off her shoulders and the same meticulous draping detail was featured in the skirts, which had a slit on one side that reach all the way up to the middle of her thigh. She'd never worn anything so risqué. He'd even added a matching ribbon to her hair.

"This is gorgeous," she said as she gaped down at the elaborate garment, brushing her hands over the butter-soft fabric of the skirts. "Where is it from?"

"My fantasies." He winked.

She cleared her throat, "*Anyway*. Do you want me to help you search or not?"

"No need," he said. "I've already found a few handfuls of entries with the first name of Gabriel; I've bookmarked them all so you can look through and see if any seem familiar to you. You should get some more rest, though—it isn't even dawn. You need another few hours at least."

She sighed. "I won't be able to go back to sleep now, plus my entire sleep schedule has been ruined by this place anyway. Also a few *handfuls?* This is going to be a waste of time if there are already that many."

"I told you it was a common enough name. Not as bad as William or James, though. Humans have gotten increasingly less creative in the past few decades."

She snorted and reached out a beckoning hand. "Show me the pages you've marked."

He made to move the book closer to her when a rippling shriek rattled the hallway outside of her room. She raised her brows at the eerie sound.

"There's another scheduled haunt going on right now," he explained. "I took care of yours before you woke up."

She didn't bother to thank him. It was the least he was supposed to do as part of their bargain. Another thing she needed to constantly remind herself of. Hell only knew what sort of perverse violations they committed by having sex with each other with a blood oath in place. Her mother's grave was probably nearing seven feet deep with how many times she'd made the woman roll over in the past week.

She asked, "Is there somewhere quieter we can go? The screams are going to give me a migraine."

"Your wish is my command." He smirked as he took her hand and transported them away.

Blackwell ended up bringing them to the dining hall first, which had quickly become her least favorite room in the house. But he insisted on snagging her some food—careful that they were in and out without being caught by any roaming Devils or Apparitions—since she hadn't managed to digest the last meal she'd eaten. After making sure that was taken care of, he brought her to what she was starting to suspect was his favorite place in the manor—the dusty old drinking parlor.

While he toiled over which amber liquor to pour himself, she sifted through the pages he had dog-eared. Tracing her eyes over each letter of every entry of strangers named *Gabriel*, she waited for one of them to jump out at her, to feel familiar in some way. A part of her even hoped her locket might respond and give her an inkling on which lead to follow, but no such luck. Not a single one of the names inspired anything. She slammed the book shut in a defeated huff.

"I'll look through some more the next time you're resting," Blackwell told her as he took a sip from his glass, ice clinking with the movement.

"What's the use?" She shook her head. "We should be spending time looking for your key. And even if we did figure out who he was, what would I truly do with the information without Genevieve here? She's the missing piece to this puzzle now."

"Have the two of you always been so at odds?" he asked, genuine curiosity in his tone. "You don't make it seem like you're very alike."

"We aren't," Ophelia admitted. "But I never thought...I never thought we were *this* far apart. She's kept such intricate secrets from me. I knew she could be a bit impulsive at times, but this is all downright *foolish*."

"Perhaps it only seems foolish because you don't have all the pieces of the puzzle," he reasoned.

"And whose fault would *that* be?" She wrinkled her nose. "For the last twenty-one years Genevieve's made a point of avoiding all things even remotely *strange*—our mother's practice, visiting relatives at the cemetery, any mention of our family's magic—but *Phantasma* she jumps right into? And then I find out she has an entire social life I've known nothing about. From a contestant here, of all people!" Her voice grew thicker now. "Genevieve and I had an understanding. She got to be the one society considered *normal*. And I would never once complain about having to take over our family's legacy if she would just let me live that sort of life through her. I don't know when she stopped telling me everything. And it hurts to think that all this time I thought I knew exactly where we stood, and she was somewhere else completely."

He steadily sipped from his glass during her rant, not offering any reaction in his expression, but she could tell he was listening to every word intently. When she finally finished, he turned back to the crystal decanter on the bar and replenished his glass.

"Here." He held the bourbon out to her. "Drink."

She took the glass. "The only thing I've ever really drank was absinthe that my sister and I stole from our mother's liquor cabinet."

"This ought to be mild, comparatively," he told her. "Try it. I can only imagine your poor nerves are at their wits' end."

She took the glass with a begrudging mumble beneath her breath, and he watched in abject amusement as she lifted it to her mouth to take a tentative sip. She felt her expression sour as soon as the brown liquor hit her tongue, its deep vanilla undertones not enough to mask its burn. He tilted his head back and laughed.

Her lips curled, aghast. "How in the Hell can you drink this stuff?"

"You learn to tolerate it," he said.

"Sort of like your personality?" she quipped.

He smirked and crossed his arms over his chest. "Are you admitting I'm not so bad?"

"Never," she answered as she took another sip. The liquid burned all the way down her throat.

"For what it's worth," he started, "being normal is incredibly dull. Almost as dull as living vicariously through someone else. Why rely on your sister to divulge her adventures to you for the rest of your life when you can live your own?"

"And when can I do that?" Another sip. "When I'm finding a way to pay off my mother's debt—another thing Genevieve knew about that she didn't tell me—or when I'm taking calls for the citizens of New Orleans day in and out to resurrect their dead relatives? My mother spent her youth traveling and seeing the world before she tied herself down to the family business. I'll never get to do that."

"Then don't take up your family business." He shrugged. "Who's going to die if you decide not to keep it? No pun intended."

"Me," she whispered into her now-empty glass. "Twenty generations of Grimm women have taken on the responsibility of being Necromancers, and I will be damned if I let all of them down because I'm too selfish to carry on."

She hiccuped and held the glass out to him. She was beginning to feel all warm and fuzzy and she wanted more. He obliged. She tipped the glass back, draining it in three gulps this time.

"Well, that's one way to drink bourbon that's taken three decades to age," he noted.

She held out her glass again. "More."

About an hour and two more glasses later, Ophelia was feeling amazing. Blackwell, however, almost seemed stressed as he ushered her over to the jacquard silk couch in the center of the room, a hand at her waist as she wobbled a bit on her feet. She sank into the couch cushions, a giggle bubbling in her throat as she grinned up at him.

"I think maybe I'm drunk."

He crouched down in front of her, until they were eye level. "Yes, I think maybe you are. Do you feel any better at least?"

"About what?" she questioned, the only thing on her mind the warmth spreading through her blood and the vibrant emerald of his eyes.

"Perfect." He smiled, content.

She trailed her finger down his cheek. "You have pretty eyes."

He reached out and cupped her face, brushing his thumb across the apple of her own cheek. "So do you."

She shook her head. "Everyone thinks my eyes are creepy. They used to be different—before I got my magic, I mean. Like turquoise instead of ice."

"And what do *you* think?" he prompted.

"I think..." She stared into his eyes, so clear she could see her own reflection. "I think they look like my mother's." She leaned forward and placed her forehead against his, let her eyelids flutter closed. "Why do I feel like this?"

"That would be the four glasses of liquor you downed," he murmured as he leaned back so he could brush the hair from her face.

"That's not what I'm talking about," she whispered, then she blinked her eyes open and tilted her chin up until her lips brushed lightly against his. "You...and I..."

"Need to sober up before there's any more kissing," he said firmly, pulling away.

She tried to protest, but he ignored her, standing to scoop her up and lay her out horizontally on the couch. He blinked out for a moment and returned with a blanket. Once she was tucked in, he took up post on the ground against the armrest near her head, leaning his back against it and propping his elbows onto his bent knees. She squirmed into a position on her side to face him—or rather, the back of his head. In the silence she softly brushed her fingers through his hair, sifting through the strands at the nape of his neck to admire all the silver threaded throughout the white. She'd never known anyone with such striking features as his, and something inside her was saddened that soon enough she wouldn't know him any longer either. That one day she might forget how vibrant a green his eyes were. The way his smirk was slightly crooked on the left. The sound of her name on his lips. The way he called her angel. The way he kissed her and how she was positive no one else would ever be able to live up to that experience.

"Go back to sleep, angel," he murmured. "Right now, I'm here."

She hadn't realized her eyes were already shut, and for a second, she wondered if she had been talking aloud, but before she could ask, she was slipping under.

NIGHT FIVE OF PHANTASMA

29

Villainous Theatrics

By the time Ophelia woke again—sobered but with a pounding headache—Blackwell had gone through another hundred pages of the book. He'd fixed her a glass of ice-cold water while she gritted through the pulsing in her temples to sit up on the couch, and he took her barrage of insults for pouring her that third and fourth glass of bourbon without complaint.

"The water will help. Or so I've heard," he said.

"Have you never been hungover?" she asked.

"Not that I can remember," he answered with a smirk. "The dead don't get hangovers."

She gulped down half the glass. Then, "What's it like to have no recollection of anything beyond this place? I feel like that would drive me mad."

He shrugged, lifting her outstretched legs so he could sit on the cushion beside her before lowering them back over his lap. "I don't know any different, so it's hard to say."

"What's your earliest memory here?" she asked, scooting herself closer to him until her thighs were resting perpendicular atop his.

"I'm not sure," he murmured. "If I think about it hard enough, I can remember plenty of competitions and specific contestants—especially the most recent ones—but when I try to search too far back, it all just...fades. It's as if I'm being haunted by my own memories, but I don't know what's eating them away other than time."

A pang of sadness ached inside her at his words.

"What's it like being a Phantom?" she whispered. "Is it terribly lonely?"

He shifted his eyes to her, a loaded emotion in them. "Most of the time." He reached over to cup her cheek in his hand, brushing his thumb over her pouted lips. "But not always."

Her chest tightened. "Did the past contestants you made bargains with try and get to know you?"

"No."

She swallowed, trying to work up the nerve to ask her next question. "Not even the others that you kissed?"

"Not even them," he answered. "But there weren't many contestants that I kissed anyway. And there were none that I..."

The jealousy that had been swelling in her gut dissipated ever so slightly as she boldly suggested, "Fucked?"

He gave a single, surprised laugh, eyes lighting back up with his usual mischief now. "That isn't exactly what I was going to say."

She wanted to ask what he was going to say, but before she got the chance, something ghostly popped into view on the opposite end of the couch.

"Poe." She smiled. "I haven't seen you in a bit."

Poe meowed and trotted over to where they were draped over each other, padding his way onto her lap and rubbing his head beneath Blackwell's chin.

"Hello, you miscreant," Blackwell said with affection, scratching behind the cat's ears.

Ophelia sighed. She wished they could stay like this for the rest of the day, but with less than a week left of Phantasma, she knew they couldn't waste any more of their time. She said as much aloud.

"We should start another magic lesson if you're feeling up

for it," he agreed. "Our time is dwindling. I probably shouldn't have poured you that fourth drink. Or the second or third."

She shooed Poe off her lap so she could stand. "You know, my mother taught me the basics of her practice. How to call upon a soul, how to communicate with them on the Other Side, all the different types of Ghosts and other paranormal beings. But your lesson was a lot more tactile. I never realized I was capable of using my magic like that."

"Does this mean I have your permission to throw the knives this time?" he drawled.

She rolled her eyes. "Within *reason*."

The grin that began to stretch across Blackwell's face as he got to his own feet made her instantly regret her request.

Hours later and Ophelia was a sore, disheveled mess. Over and over, they had practiced summoning her raw energy and aiming it accurately at various objects around the room. A few broken glasses later and she found that she was getting pretty good at it. Her reflexes still weren't as quick as Blackwell was hoping for when it came to expelling her magic—taking a moment for it to warm up each time she used it, and the lower her reservoir got, the longer that delay grew—but he was patient, and every time she made a particularly good shot, he rewarded her with a dazzling smile.

Then the knives came into play. Whatever muscle she used to turn parts of her body invisible was growing stronger, and if it weren't for the fact that she thought Blackwell was having a little too much fun launching blades at her, she might have thanked him for discovering how to help her develop this new ability.

Just then, a particularly large cleaver passed through her sternum and embedded itself into the picture-frame molding of the wall behind her. Blackwell made a sound of satisfaction.

"I think you're ready for level four," he commended.

"What's the theme of level four?" she questioned.

"*Gluttony.*" He enunciated the word with flair. "There's this whole bit with collars and chains... you wouldn't happen to enjoy being choked, would you?"

She spluttered a bit. "I—"

"I'm kidding, angel," he snorted. "But if you ever get curious, I'm always game to try *anything.*"

Her cheeks heated profusely. He had a knack for making everything sound sensually appealing. It drove her mad with want. Something he must have sensed because a blink later and he was right in front of her, reaching around to pull the cleaver from where it was wedged into the molding and discarding it so he could press her against the wall.

"That's enough training for now," he murmured, tapping beneath her chin with his index finger until she tilted her mouth up toward his. "I think you deserve a reward for how well you did today."

She felt the corners of her lips curl up. "If I get to choose the reward, may I suggest you get on your knees again?"

"Hmm," he hummed as he slid his hands around to cup her ass. "First, I want to—"

The lights in the room suddenly flickered, cutting off the rest of Blackwell's words and making him freeze before her.

"Whatever you do," Blackwell told her beneath his breath, an eerie calmness to his voice, "do not show him an ounce of vulnerability."

Ophelia didn't bother to ask who he meant by *him*—she didn't need to when a second later a Devil appeared in the center of the room in a cloud of black smoke. The man was only an inch or two taller than Blackwell, with combed-back, raven hair and a porcelain complexion even more fair than her own.

Though most would probably describe him as dangerously handsome, his maroon eyes were unsettling, and as he began to prowl closer to them, she saw that his pupils were vertical slits—reminding her of a feline's. Something about the heaviness of his gaze felt eerily familiar.

"Well, what do we have here?" the Devil purred as his shrewd eyes shifted between Ophelia and Blackwell's compromising position. "A pretty little plaything you've chosen, Blackwell."

Blackwell dropped his hands from her body and fixed his expression into one of boredom. "Sinclair. We were just leaving."

Sinclair's eyes lit up with the sort of deviousness that promised pain. "It didn't look like you were just leaving. What's the matter, Blackwell? Don't like to share your toys?"

Ophelia remained utterly frozen, her eyes tracking every movement the Devil made. She wasn't particularly keen on being in the presence of any Devils, but there was something very different about *this* one. Something vengeful beneath the surface. A stark difference between the uncomfortable presence of Jasper and the palpable darkness Sinclair seemed to emanate.

As if he could hear her thoughts, Sinclair's eyes slid to her face, the slits of his pupils dilating as they took her in. She kept her face unmoving, Blackwell's warning not to show any hints of vulnerability on loop in the back of her mind.

Sinclair's scarlet eyes narrowed while his grin widened. "Have we met somewhere before?"

That seemed to push Blackwell over the edge. "We're leaving."

Blackwell wrapped his arm around her and gently, but firmly, began to usher her away. But it was the wrong move. Sinclair noted the familiarity between them in an instant, and Ophelia had a sinking feeling that something very bad was about to happen.

Sinclair gave a menacing laugh. "Tell me, Blackwell, is this one a good fuck?"

Ophelia hardly felt the insult, more focused on the barely contained rage rolling off of Blackwell.

"If she gave me a ride, do you think—"

Blackwell snapped. Tucking her behind his back, he lunged forward and slammed his fist into the Devil's face. Sinclair's head whipped to the side, but his feet stayed planted in place. The Devil was now grinning, his pupils expanding so wide they swallowed the vermilion of his irises whole.

"That was a mistake." Sinclair laughed.

In a split second, Blackwell disappeared from between them, the warm energy of his presence snuffed out completely. Then thick black smoke began to seep in across the floor, billowing in the air around her, until Sinclair was the only thing she could see clearly.

"Blackwell," she whispered beneath her breath as quietly as possible. "Blackwell—"

"Don't bother summoning him, girl," Sinclair threatened. "It will only cause him harm when he is unable to come to you."

To his point, there was a loud pounding on the door to the room. She could hear Blackwell shouting her name, but his voice was muffled, like he was yelling underwater.

"What the Hell do you want from me?" she spat, lifting her chin with bravado.

"It's not you I want something from," Sinclair avowed. "I apologize for my crudeness; I couldn't help getting a rise out of him. And unfortunately for you, you seem to be something he cares about. Which means you're the key to his undoing."

"*Undoing?*" She gave a mocking laugh. "Could you be any more cliché with the villainous theatrics?"

Sinclair slinked closer to her until she was cowed against the wall. He reached out to grip her face in one hand as he brushed the hair away from her face with the other. Her blood ran as cold as ice.

"I could," he assured. "Would you like a demonstration?"

Ophelia didn't say anything or dare to move—she hardly dared to breathe.

Sinclair grinned, satisfied. "I have a proposition for you."

"No—" she began, but her words were quickly choked off by a painful squeeze of the Devil's hand.

"Do not interrupt me," he snapped. "My proposition is simple. You forfeit this competition, and I will grant you a single favor."

She recoiled in disbelief.

"Rumor has it you're looking for your sister," Sinclair continued. "I'll tell you *exactly* where she is. Or maybe you'd prefer money? Fame? Name it and it's yours."

"Why do you want me to forfeit so badly?" she questioned, eyes narrowing. "We've never met before now. What concern is it to you if I stay in this competition?"

Sinclair's expression soured. "*Just take the deal.*"

Her lips curled in disdain as she ripped her chin from his hand. "*Fuck. Off.*"

"Do you really think if you win this competition there's a happy ending for the two of you?" he crooned, but his velvety smooth tone was laced with malice. "Blackwell cannot leave. Forfeit now, and I will not only grant you a favor—I'll also break your oath to him."

She swallowed, ignoring the way his words sliced through her heart. She and Blackwell were using each other as frivolous distractions. Nothing more. "Where is this coming from? Why are you suddenly in this equation?"

"Because there have been rumblings about the pretty little

Necromancer who's helping Blackwell and finding things in this manor she shouldn't be." He glowered at her. "It's only a matter of time before you uncover something you have no business poking around in. And I'm willing to do what the other Devils aren't."

A realization hit her. "You know where the key is...don't you? You know things about him, and why he's here, and you don't want me around long enough to figure them out."

"And they say mortals are fools," he mocked.

She gave him a taunting smirk. "I'm a threat to you. Is that why you've been watching me all this time? It has been you, hasn't it?"

The darkness in his eyes deepened and his expression turned hostile. "I am the last person you want to make an enemy of."

"Right, because a Devil threatened by the presence of a mortal is the epitome of terrifying," she retorted. "As I said before—*fuck off.*"

To that, he did something surprising. He took a step back and gave her a smile. "You think you know him so well? Page eight hundred and eighty-two. Ask him why he didn't show it to you."

Ophelia's stomach dropped, but she was careful not to show any reaction to his words. "Asking him a question would require you to let him back in here."

Sinclair leaned in. "We'll meet again soon."

With that lingering threat, he disappeared, along with the smoke, and there was barely time for her to take in a relieved breath before Blackwell blasted open the door to the room, sending shards of wood flying in every direction. In a blink he was back in front of her, concern visible as he frantically traced his eyes over every inch of her, his hands coming up to wipe the disheveled strands of her hair from her face.

"Are you alright?" he demanded. "Did he touch you?"

"I'm fine." She pulled away a bit, and there was a flicker of hurt in his eyes as he dropped his hands. "Show me page eight hundred and eighty-two."

He swallowed and looked away. "Ophelia."

She sucked in a surprised breath. It was true. There was something he was intentionally hiding from her.

"Show me," she ordered again. "*Now.*"

His jaw clenched before he blinked away for a moment, to grab the book from the floor beside the couch, and when he returned with it, he handed it over in silence.

She held her breath as she flipped through the pages until she landed on the one she was looking for. She scanned carefully over each name, and when she reached one of them, adrenaline sliced through her veins.

Gabriel White.

Her breath hitched as she continued through the rest of the list. And the name she spotted just a few lines below buckled her knees.

Tessie Grimm.

30

SECRETS

The problem with secrets was that they festered and tore open wounds that were starting to scab. Kneeling there, tears pricking at her eyes, Ophelia was beginning to question if anything she had ever known was true. Or if she had just been going through the motions of a distorted reality for her entire life.

Growing up, she hadn't questioned her mother often. After all, Tessie Grimm had experienced so much more life than her, had been kind even when she wasn't necessarily *warm*, and only harped on her strange rules out of protectiveness of her daughters.

Don't make deals with Devils. Don't stay out in New Orleans after dark. Don't sleep with an oculus in front of your bed. The voice in your head will ignore you if you ignore it. One day, you will be at the helm of this family, Ophelia, and I know you will carry on our legacy with grace.

Her mother's voice followed her everywhere she went, colored everything she did. And when she felt suffocated by the weight of what it meant to be the eldest Grimm heir, she reminded herself that her mother gave up a life of adventure when Grandmother died to be loyal to her birth-gifted destiny. How could Ophelia be so resentful of being the firstborn when magic was an *honor*? How could she be jealous of her own sister who was only ever bright-eyed and loving? But something about all these secrets made the already dulling, rose-colored lenses shatter entirely. The only reason she was in Phantasma was because her family didn't trust her with their secrets, and she *hated* it.

She hated that she had never known that her mother had been one of Phantasma's contestants, but Genevieve clearly had. Her sister had spent years obsessed with the Devil's Manor, and it seemed she was trying to contact another contestant that their mother presumably had known. And Ophelia suspected this was all much more intimate to her family than Gabriel White just being a random player. Something she couldn't look at too closely at the moment, or she worried she'd lose another meal all over the ground.

She hated that Genevieve had also known about their family's debt and had forged their mother's signature at the bank to keep Ophelia in the dark. Was forced to do Hell only knows what to get the money to help out. And Ophelia had to wonder whether her mother and sister did not believe she could handle such information. That her mind was already too fragile, had become too *crowded* by the Shadow Voice to take on anything else that might be considered stressful.

But what she hated most of all was that the only person she wanted to see right now, to talk to about all of this, was Genevieve. And Genevieve was missing. Because of Ophelia.

What a broken little family, the Shadow Voice whispered, awaking in her mind. **Broken. Broken.**

"*Ugh!*" Ophelia screamed. She pushed herself up from the ground and jabbed a finger into Blackwell's chest. "I was foolish for coming here, and I was even more foolish for ever trusting a single word you said."

He curled his hand gently around her wrist to keep her palm against his chest. "Angel, please listen—"

She ripped herself from his grip and stumbled back over the forgotten book on the floor.

Quickly righting herself, she said, "I am *not* your angel, but I will be your nightmare. If you sabotage my chance of getting my sister back, I will find a way to haunt *you* until every single one of your inner demons looks like me. You will never know a moment of peace again."

His jaw clenched, but he didn't offer up a retort. Just stood there and braced himself against the venom in her words.

"Did you not bother to show me my mother's name because you thought it would distract me from our bargain?"

"*No.* It isn't like that. I just needed more time to tell you."

"Tell me *what?*" she demanded.

Blackwell took a deep breath. "I knew something about you was special the very first time I saw you. Of course, I know I do not remember our true first meeting, but I suspect if I was somehow a different being then, one with all my memories, I was clearly still enamored with you enough to tell you about the key that would bring me my freedom. Something about you calls to me in a way I cannot explain, and your essence has always felt *familiar*, but I couldn't figure out why. You mentioned you were looking for someone named Gabriel"—he took another deep breath—"and things slowly began to click."

Her gaze was razor-sharp as she asked, "Who *is* Gabriel?"

He winced. "Gabriel White is your father."

Ophelia felt like the floor had dropped from beneath her feet and she was freefalling as the words echoed through her mind again and again and again. She squeezed her eyes shut.

Gabriel White is your father.

Find Gabriel.

When she opened her eyes again, she demanded, "Tell me everything."

Holding out a hand, he implored, "Can I take you back to your room first?"

She gave a single, sharp nod and grabbed onto his hand, hating the way her stomach fluttered whenever their skin touched. He transported them back to her room, and she pulled her hand from his the instant they arrived, taking a few steps back to put some distance between them as she crossed her arms over her chest.

"A few days before Phantasma came to New Orleans, Gabriel lost his second attempt at this competition." Blackwell shook a hand through his hair as he searched for his next words.

"I'm unsure of exactly what happened because halfway through the trials, he had stopped summoning me and I lost track of him entirely. What was abundantly clear by the end, however, was that he lost."

"Summoning you?" Ophelia gasped, hand flying to her mouth. "You mean—?"

"I offered him my bargain and he took it," he confirmed. "I knew I recognized something in your essence when we first met here. Half of your essence comes from him and the life force he owed me is what's currently sustaining me."

"Is that why you couldn't leave me alone?" she asked. "Something about my essence called to you because of him?"

He hesitated for a moment. Then said, "Perhaps."

"I can't do this," she whispered. "*You've* met my father and yet, before now, I hadn't even known his full name. My mother always refused to talk about him. I just don't understand."

"There's more," he told her. "Your disappearing act? You get that from him. It's how I knew the knives wouldn't hurt you."

"*What?*"

"Your father was a Specter," Blackwell explained. "It was the reason I chose him for my bargain. In hindsight, he was one of the worst contestants I've ever offered it to. Stubborn. Distracted. But he could shift himself in and out of visibility and pass through solid objects and walls if he chose. Specters are incredibly rare beings, and I suspect that if he met your mother during his first experience with Phantasma...well, it doesn't surprise me that two paranormal beings might find a connection with each other."

"I need to...process this," she told him. "You've been testing me this entire time? To prove your theory that he and I were connected. And didn't bother to tell me."

"I know. I didn't do things in the right order." He stepped closer. "I just need you to understand that Sinclair wants to create a divide between us to make it harder for you to succeed. And that must mean he believes you're truly capable of finding out how to release me."

"What is Sinclair's vendetta against you?"

"I'm not entirely sure," he admitted. "The holes in my memory won't allow me to go that far back. All I know is that any time I've gotten even remotely close to figuring things out here, he intercedes and makes sure I fail."

Ophelia was quiet for a long moment. Her mind didn't know what information to focus on first. Her father, her mother, or the Devil determined to make her a new enemy. Finally, she said, "I'm still not sure how I feel about the fact that you weren't going to tell me who my father was."

"I only had a strong suspicion at first, which is why I suggested checking the contestant logs in the first place. It was our lessons together that I finally felt very sure of what was going on. And then I found the page while you were sobering up in the drinking parlor to confirm my theory before I upset you for no reason. I made the mistake of mentioning my hunch to Jasper when I was convincing him to let me see the book. Sinclair must have caught wind of what I was looking for and waited for the prime opportunity to make you as paranoid as possible. He was watching us. The only reason I was going to wait until after the next level to tell you was so your head could be clear."

"I get it," she said.

He sighed in relief.

"I just have one more question. Why didn't you seek him out when he stopped summoning you? Why didn't you watch him in the trials on the Other Side as you've done for me?"

The light in his eyes dimmed a little bit as he answered, "I think I had begun to give up. That last round when it was clear that he wasn't trying...I didn't have it in me to try anymore either."

The sadness in his voice made her heart ache. So much that she had the urge to throw her arms around him in comfort. Instead, she said, "I need to be alone. I need to think."

He gave a single nod. "When level four begins, summon me."

"Okay," she said and then he was gone.

Finally alone, she threw herself onto her bed, face down, and let herself mourn the version of her life she once knew and would never have again. The idea of never knowing her father had never bothered her the way it seemed to have bothered Genevieve. Which made the fact that her sister had unraveled all of this the least shocking part of it. But the idea that her father had been here, of all places, had known Blackwell, of all people, made her participation in this game almost inevitable. Perhaps she would always be destined for darkness no matter what she did or where she went.

She sniffed and wiped at her face, trying to pull herself together, despite the evidence of her devastation soaking the blanket beneath her cheeks. The next trial was starting soon, the anticipation of a different sort of pain twisting her nerves into knots. She knew she needed to keep her morale strong until she got through this competition and she had more space to mourn. But she couldn't help but feel the walls were going to close in on her long before she got the chance to escape.

LEVEL
FOUR

31

GLUTTONY

By the time the dinner bell tolled, Ophelia had been to Hell and back in her mind. She knew she needed to get out of bed and make it to the dining room, but her appetite was completely gone and part of her thought that maybe if she just got herself disqualified, everything would be so much easier. The other part of her wanted to prove, *needed* to prove, she was capable of doing this.

She rolled out of bed. Scrubbing a hand over her face, she hoped her tears hadn't stained her cheeks as noticeably as they had stained the silk of her dress where they fell. There was no reason to bother changing, however, so she straightened her skirts and braced herself to face a crowd of people.

"I can do this," she told herself. "Just six more days."

Dinner was more than halfway over by the time she finally made it to the dining hall. Luci spotted her and came rushing over.

"I was worried you weren't going to make it," Luci whispered, eyeing the extravagant gown Ophelia still wore. The dress looked sorely out of place amongst the casual attire of the other contestants but blended in with the dark opulence of Phantasma's décor perfectly.

"You shouldn't be worrying about me," Ophelia said flatly.

Luci flinched a bit, hurt shining in her eyes, but Ophelia didn't apologize. How many times would she have to warn the girl of getting attached? They weren't friends.

As Luci trailed back to her spot next to Leon, Ophelia took up post against the wall, observing each contestant as they ate. She noted three people were missing after the last trial, leaving only thirteen members of their group left—including herself, Luci, Leon, Cade, Beau, Eric, Edna, James, and Charlotte. The remaining four contestants, whose names she didn't know, hadn't really stood out before, when there were more people to get lost in, but now she committed their features to memory. She wondered how many contestants were left in Phantasma overall. If any of the other groups had completely dissolved already.

The Devil finally arrived. Ophelia was not expecting it to be Jasper. He came in whistling, that same jazzy tune he always seemed to have on the tip of his tongue, and when his eyes landed on her, he gave her a wink. Out of the corner of her eye she saw Cade, Beau, and Eric stiffen at the interaction. Her face remained carefully blank.

Jasper clapped his hands together. "Alright, you miserable souls, it's time for *my* game. If you thought that last level was hard, well"—he tipped his head back and laughed—"you might want to tap out of this one now."

Everyone glanced around at each other, wondering if this would be level someone finally forfeited before they entered. But they all seemed equally as determined to dig in their heels. After all, they did not go through that last grueling level for nothing.

Jasper waved a hand next to him and summoned the door to this level, revealing their next clue and causing a few murmurs amongst the different alliances that had formed over the course of the last few days. Ophelia was the only one standing alone.

A DEADLY GAME UNFURLS, UPON A TWISTED BOARD,
WATCH EVERY STEP YOU TAKE, OR YOUR FATE WILL BE UNTOWARD.

> To gain the upper hand, levers are in play,
> but be careful which you choose, the pendulum
> swings both ways.
>
> Temptations in numbers, don't overcount,
> forward or backward, a single key to get out.

"My name is Jasper," he introduced himself as he twisted the door's knob and swung the portal open. "I have a feeling some of us are about to get very well acquainted. Hope you all know how to negotiate under pressure." The Devil's eyes found hers again, a smirk curling up on his lips. "Ophelia, you're first."

She tilted her chin up as she walked to the door, ignoring the pointed looks that speared through her at the way the Devil said her name. Too familiar.

When she stepped up to the portal, Jasper whispered, "Good luck."

At first, there was nothing around her but gray. It wasn't long before the details of the room came into view, however. It was made completely of dull stone bricks and was a similar size to the opulent party room from the second trial. A large grid was etched into the floor. Like a chess board.

The only other notable details were the thirteen pairs of levers on the far wall. Each set of levers had a single golden plaque beneath them bearing the name of one of the contestants. All the levers on the left were marked with check marks, the ones on the right with crosses.

Ophelia tried to take a step forward but found that her feet were frozen in place. Other contestants began to appear, one by one, and immediately her defenses went up. This was the first time they had begun a level in which they could all see each other from the start. When the last of their group of thirteen stepped through the portal, Ophelia noticed that they had been arranged in a single line across the middle of the room facing the wall of levers. Each one of them stood in the exact center of one of the squares on the grid, with five empty squares between each person so that they were evenly spaced apart. As everyone else looked around nervously, Ophelia suddenly remembered something that Blackwell had said.

There's this whole bit with collars and chains . . . you wouldn't happen to enjoy being choked, would you?

As soon as the thought entered her mind, the iron collar appeared around her throat. Sounds of alarm echoed through the room, and she heard a hastily whispered prayer on her left. She glanced sideways to see that it was James, sweating profusely, tugging at the metal collar. He caught her stare, and before she could look away, she saw the absolute terror in his eyes.

If you knock on the ground three times you'll survive, the Shadow Voice whispered to her.

Despite knowing such a thing would not have any effect on her chances whatsoever, she still lowered herself to the ground to knock on the stone. While she was crouched, two chains dropped down from the collar, one at the front of her throat and one at the back. The heavy metal links clattered to the ground and snaked their way to opposite sides of the room. The chain in front of her pierced through the wall beneath the levers, and when she twisted to look behind her, she saw the second half of the chain had fastened itself on the other side. The boundary was clear: they would only be able to move on their designated paths.

In front of them, hovering in the air, three solid bars of gold appeared.

"I don't get it," a deep voice on her right said. Eric. "What are we supposed to do?"

Surprising no one, Cade was the first to move. The chained collar only allowed him to step forward, of course, and the moment he shifted out of their orderly line and stepped onto the square before him, the square sank down nearly three feet. One of the gold bars disappeared from before them and reappeared in Cade's hands. There was a pregnant pause as the rest of them glanced at each other. Then three people moved at once: James, Eric, and the contestant named Becca. James's and Eric's tiles sank down first, and each of them received their own gold bar just as Cade had. Something strange happened with Becca, however. Her tile didn't move, and there was no more gold left to claim.

The girl rubbed at their throat where the iron collar was digging into her neck, confused. "What do I—"

That's when the jagged circular blade, swinging like a pendulum, dropped from the ceiling. The contestants who were still standing on their sunken tiles were able to easily hunch down out of the saw's path, but Becca barely avoided getting cleaved in two. She flattened herself against the ground just before the pendulum swung through her torso. Her scream filled the tense silence in the room as everyone gaped at the spectacle in horror.

"Becca!" one of the other contestants screamed. Ophelia wasn't able to see who it was.

Becca sobbed as she tried to drag herself toward the next tile on the row in front of her and out of the pendulum's path. But when she moved onto the square, her weight triggered another pendulum to drop down. This pendulum swung perpendicularly to the other, creating a cross-shaped path of death. They all watched, horrified, as she crawled forward again, and another saw dropped, swinging parallel to the first.

Then it only got worse. The saws were dropping lower with each swing, only about an inch each pass, but soon Becca wouldn't be able to avoid their blades, and neither would the others. And if she continued to move to the other squares, the room would quickly become a grid of saws and death.

"Help!" she cried. "*Help!*"

"Call for the Devil before you summon any more and get us all killed!" someone yelled. Beau.

Becca took a ragged breath as she looked up at the pendulum, face blotchy and red with her tears. "What was his name—*Jasper*. Jasper! Help! Please!"

Not even an instant later Jasper was there, scooping the girl up and over his shoulder like a sack of potatoes and disappearing. To everyone else's dismay, the two extra saws Becca triggered did not disappear with them, though the first one did.

Before any of them had a chance to grasp what had just happened, another group of gold bars appeared. This time, there were four to claim. Six people scrambled forward, including, to Ophelia's shock, Luci. Fortunately for Luci, she was one of the four who made it to the bars quickly enough. Cade and James were the ones too slow this time—having to climb their way out of the hole they'd been sunken into first—and just as before, two pendulum saws dropped from the ceiling as soon as they moved too late. The men hit the ground, James immediately beginning to panic, but Cade looked fiercely determined. Cade began to crawl forward, the gold bar he'd won from the first group wedged in the crook of his elbow, triggering pendulum after pendulum, and soon Ophelia could hardly see anything but lines and lines of swinging blades. Back and forth. Back and forth. Back and forth.

Each pendulum swung at different times, creating a chessboard of death, all because of their collective gluttony. Which was, of course, the point of this level. The rest of them considered their next moves. As things became increasingly dangerous and another pile of gold appeared to entice everyone, Cade had slithered along the ground all the way to the wall of levers. And that's when Ophelia realized the space around the grid was free of saws—the entire perimeter a clear zone. Cade had once again managed to get to safety while leaving the rest of them in the worst situation possible.

Cade immediately pulled one of his levers and then twisted around to search for someone. Ophelia. His grin was sinister as he held her gaze, reaching for the lever to the right above her name, the one with the "X", and slamming it down. Then they all watched as his collar and chains disappeared.

The room descended into a rage of chaos. Ophelia didn't waste another second as she began chanting Blackwell's name. The metallic, slicing clang of blades cut through the room and the screaming began seconds later. There was so much mayhem around her, it was hard to tell where she could safely move. Then she remembered the grid on the floor. Scanning the ground beneath her feet, she quickly put together that the lines were the paths of the blades. As long as she stayed in the middle of the empty squares, she would be safe.

When Blackwell appeared, he was in his non-corporeal state. He raked his eyes over her, head to toe, and though she knew he was only assessing her for injuries, her stomach still flipped. She needed to find a way to make that stop.

She cleared her throat. "What's the best course of action?"

"You have two options," Blackwell told her as he assessed the situation around him. "On the wall behind you is the key you need to release you from your collar and open the door to exit this level."

Ophelia waved her hand impatiently. "And the second option?"

"You go for the levers in front of you," he continued. "Every contestant has two levers; pull the one with the checkmark and it will give that contestant an advantage in a future level. Pull the one with the cross and it will give them a disadvantage. If both levers are pulled, it will neutralize the outcome."

"Cade just pulled two levers."

Blackwell nodded as if this wasn't shocking news. "It's time to move, then."

"First things first," she said, looking down at the collar.

She focused on her body from her neck down, invoking the prickling sensation she needed to turn herself invisible. Slowly, inch by inch, she began to disappear, and the collar clattered to the ground. She sighed in relief as she rubbed at the sensitive skin of her neck.

"As it turns out, I don't like being choked," she muttered.

Blackwell shrugged. "Not by metal collars at least."

She shot him a hard *look* and stepped past him toward the path of the swinging pendulum in front of her. She counted the seconds between each swing, and Blackwell was blessedly quiet while she concentrated. Gathering up her skirts, she waited for the saw to pass in front of her three times before making the leap.

One.

Two.

Three.

Jump.

She landed easily in the next empty square, Blackwell on

her heels. The only problem was that her movement triggered another pendulum to drop down to her right.

"Forward one, then left two," Blackwell directed.

She dashed across the grid with his help. Forward...Left... Waiting for the next pendulum to reach the top point of its trajectory, she jumped over its path and then pivoted to look behind her from where she'd just come—

"*Ophelia*," Blackwell yelled.

She lurched another square forward, her right arm disappearing in the nick of time before it was severed from her shoulder by one of the dropping blades. She paused, chest heaving as she began to panic.

Blackwell popped into view right in front of her. "Hey. You're fine. You used your abilities perfectly."

A howl of agony sounded from a few feet over, and she whipped her head to see James hit the floor, clutching at his right shoulder as it gushed blood onto the ground. She sucked in a breath at the poor man's pain. He began calling Jasper's name without hesitation.

"I have to help him," she said, shuffling a step forward, but it was too late.

Jasper appeared in front of James and tutted. "That's going to bleed out."

James was paler than a Ghost as he looked up at the Devil, his eyes pleading for mercy. "I want to leave. Take me out of here."

Jasper smiled and reached out his hand in offering.

James gulped, his wound spewing more and more blood. Then with great effort, he clasped the Devil's hand.

And then there were eleven.

"You have to move," Blackwell told her. "Other contestants are halfway through already."

Ophelia took a shaky breath and turned back to the grid.

"Forward two, right two," Blackwell assessed for her. "Ready?"

She nodded and took off. Her dress was not the easiest thing to move in, and after she cleared the next few squares, Blackwell crouched to grab her hem. He ripped the fabric until it was just above her knees, tossing it away. She felt practically naked, but it made it so much easier to move she didn't even care.

"Thanks—" she began, but her words were cut off by the jet of water that gushed from the ceiling.

"From the levers Cade pulled," Blackwell told her. "Each one triggers more obstacles. This trial is all about not giving in to gluttony. Excess that you don't *need*. And it punishes everyone collectively every time you do."

She sobered and sprang back into action, nearly slipping on the damp stone beneath her feet, but Blackwell was there to steady her, a firm hand on her waist, a constant presence by her side. Hopefully, the other contestants were too distracted to see him in the brief seconds he was solid.

"Right next," he said as she jumped across the next blade's pathway. "Two forward."

She prepared to follow his directions, but as she counted the swings of the next jump, someone suddenly rammed into her from behind. She hit the ground and Blackwell cursed, not having noticed Eric sneaking up on them.

Ophelia scrambled back to her feet, narrowly clearing the pathway before the saw severed her in half. She spun to see Eric glowering at her on the other side of the pendulum's trajectory.

"What the fuck is wrong with you?" she hissed, shoving her soaked hair out of her eyes. The water coming from above hadn't let up for a second.

"I saw what you just did. Cade was right, you turned *invisible*,"

Eric accused, raising his voice over the noise of the rain. "And you've been talking to someone. Someone none of us can see—except I just saw them. They're helping you. You're a Demon and you've got friends here."

"I thought we already established this. My blood is *red*," she retorted.

"Then it's a trick," Eric said. "Either way, I'm going to see to it that your blood spills all over this floor, just to be extra sure. And if I'm wrong, that's just one less person in this competition, right?"

"Angel, you have to run," Blackwell told her. "Disposing of him myself will drain too much of my magic at once."

"Men are always *useless*," she growled to them both, half-exasperated, before pivoting and dashing for the next square.

Eric followed her, the chains of his collar clinking as he moved. At least she had that advantage. She moved to the left, and he tried to follow, but his chains pulled taut. Her relief didn't last long, however, when another one of the pendulums forced her right, back directly in Eric's reach. She could see the wall of levers just ahead now, the space in front of them clear. She braced herself to jump, but it was too late.

Eric slammed into her again, and she struggled against him for a minute, but he was too strong. Ophelia kept thrashing out with her arms and legs as Eric tried to push her to the ground.

"Forget what I said, I'm going to fucking kill him," Blackwell snarled as he began to shift into his corporeal state.

But before Blackwell got the chance to lay a hand on Eric, Ophelia managed to twist in Eric's grip just enough to slam her knee up between his legs; he howled and released her as he hunched forward. She stood and regained her bearings.

There was a saw mid-swing behind her.

She turned to face Eric fully as he regained his composure

and straightened himself up. She backed up a step, directly into the path of the pendulum's downswing. Eric braced himself to lunge.

When he leaped forward, too distracted by his rage to realize the trap she had set, Ophelia let him seize her. And when the blade swung back down, he never saw it coming.

32

DISTRACTION

Blood splattered across Ophelia's face and the front of her dress as she stumbled back and returned herself to her solid state. Eric's mutilated corpse dropped to the floor with a sickening thud. As his blood pooled beneath her feet, the guilt hit her full force.

"Well, that saves me the trouble," Blackwell muttered.

"What did I just do?" she whispered.

"What you had to," he stated. "You can't stop now. One more path to clear and you're there."

She nodded numbly, turning away from the corpse. The rain above turned to hail, indicating another lever had been pulled, but she barely felt the ice pelting her skin.

What did I do?

"*Ophelia*," Blackwell implored. "You have to move, angel."

She swallowed thickly and took a single step forward. Her hands were shaking at her sides, and she couldn't tell if it was from the sudden drop in temperature as ice was thrown around the room, or if it was from the horror of what had just happened. Another step.

She waited for the saw to swing down and finally jumped to the strip of clear space before the wall. She looked around, but no one else was there.

"Where are the others?" she asked. "Have they cleared the field?"

"They're still at the mercy of their collars or gambling for gold," Blackwell answered. "It looks like you're only the fourth to make it here."

She observed the levers before her with a healthy dose of skepticism, knowing what she was about to do would add another deadly obstacle to the room.

Aside from hers and Cade's, two other levers had been pulled so far—Edna's and Charlotte's. Both checks.

She spotted her own lever all the way to the left and scurried forward to pull the checked one down and neutralize whatever Cade had done. The punishment for touching it descended on the room in an instant. A ball and chain appeared around each of her ankles. Someone screamed. Another cursed. But Ophelia was out of the chains in seconds.

"Let's go," Blackwell urged. "You have to get all the way back across for the key..."

Ophelia went over to Cade's lever and slammed down the one with the cross.

Every pendulum in the room began to speed up, and Blackwell looked at her in shock for a moment before a proud grin spread over his face. "Look who's finding her teeth."

She didn't respond as she turned back to the chess board of death and braced herself against the gore she found there. She didn't linger. She simply took off through the clearing, racing around the safe perimeter of the room until she made it to the opposite wall.

"The tool to unlock the door," Blackwell reminded her, pointing toward a spot on the wall where a small, odd-shaped tool hung from a hook.

The moment she snatched it down, another appeared to replace it for the next contestant and a door popped up before her. She slid the small metal piece into a similar-shaped hole in the center of the door and watched as it shimmered open. She exited back into Phantasma's dining hall. Blackwell was nowhere to be seen, but she found she wasn't alone. The last person she had expected, however, was Luci.

In fact, now that she thought about it, aside from the purplish bags beneath Luci's eyes that suggested a serious lack of sleep, Luci had seemed to float through the competition so far. Running around with Leon, taking time to read books in the library.

Unless the girl had her own ghostly guide, Ophelia couldn't help but wonder how Luci, with her sweet demeanor and timid nature, was taking this competition in such strides. It was almost as if...

Ophelia's eyes narrowed in on a gash at the top of Luci's right shoulder. It looked fresh, the skin around it slick and shining with something, opalescent? Yet the cut had already begun to scab. Meanwhile, Luci was gaping openly at Ophelia's appearance.

"There's so much blood," Luci whispered. "Is it—"

"It's Eric's," Ophelia interrupted. "Not mine."

A hand flew to Luci's mouth in surprise. "Is he...?"

Ophelia nodded. Then she did something shocking. She laughed. "I killed him." Another giggle, this one coming out a bit breathless. "He tried to kill me first, of course. But I...I killed him."

Luci stood wide-eyed as Ophelia began to break down in a fit of laughter. "He tried to kill you?"

Ophelia swiped tears from her face as she sobered. "Yes. They're still convinced I'm some sort of Demon. I suppose I didn't help my case."

Luci was quiet for a long moment. Then, "I'm glad you didn't let him get away with that."

Ophelia lifted her brows, shocked at the girl's support. Luci seemed so quiet, so reserved, not an ounce of menace in her demeanor. But maybe Ophelia had the girl pegged all wrong. Maybe because it was hard for her to imagine Genevieve being friends with anyone so blasé about a death. Genevieve hated the dark and macabre.

Luci, however, didn't even flinch at the idea of Ophelia having committed murder. Which only deepened Ophelia's suspicion that the other girl was not all she seemed on the surface.

Ophelia cleared her throat. "Are you waiting in here for a reason?"

Luci bit her lip and flicked her eyes away. "Leon still hasn't come out yet."

Ophelia's chest tightened, but she didn't offer any critique. It would be hypocritical considering what she was about to do herself.

Before she left the girl to worry alone, however, she couldn't resist saying, "That looks like it was a nasty wound."

Was, being the operative word.

Luci bit her lip and shifted her eyes away from Ophelia.

"Did one of the pendulums do that?" Ophelia asked though the both of them knew it was rhetorical. Luci hadn't had the injury before the trial.

A tense beat of silence passed between them.

Finally, Luci whispered, "Please, don't tell anyone."

"What would there be to tell?" Ophelia wondered, real curiosity this time.

Luci shook her head as she reached up to comb her long hair over her shoulder, to hide the cut. Ophelia noticed the girl's hands were smeared with the same odd opalescent substance as her clavicle and chemise.

"I hope Leon makes it out safe" was all Ophelia offered as she strode out of the dining hall.

When Ophelia got back to her room, all she wanted was a distraction. Something that would get the image of Eric's massacred corpse out of her mind.

She stripped away her ruined dress before padding to the bathroom to draw a bath. Slipping into the tub, she scrubbed away every drop of blood on her skin until it was raw. Until she felt clean of her sins. When she was finished, she pulled the drain and made her way back to her room, leaving a trail of water in her wake.

Standing in the middle of her room, without a stitch of clothing, she chanted Blackwell's name.

It took almost an entire minute for him to arrive. "I'm sorry, I was returning—"

He stopped short when he spotted her. His gaze instantly heated, but he remained planted in place.

Each word he said next was slow and deliberate. "What are you doing, angel?"

"Distract me," she told him.

He brushed a hand over his mouth in contemplation. "I... don't think this is a good idea."

She stepped closer, and his expression became pained. "I need a distraction."

I need that trial wiped from my memory forever.

"The last real conversation we had, you were very upset with me," he reasoned. "You're only doing this because of what happened in that trial. You only ever want me after near-death experiences."

"So?"

He leaned down until their eyes were level. "So, maybe I don't want to just be a distraction to you."

She balled her fists at her sides. "Fine. Then go away. I'll take care of my own distraction."

He crossed his arms over his chest, amused. "Alright, then. Go ahead."

She wavered a bit. "I will as soon as you leave."

"And miss the show?" He smirked. "I think I'll stay."

She narrowed her eyes. "You don't think I'll pleasure myself with you here?"

"No, I don't," he taunted.

Something inside her had come further undone tonight, and he had no idea how bold she was feeling. He thought he was calling her bluff, but little did he know she was about to play all her cards. She gave him a mocking smile as she made a show of crawling onto the bed and settling back against the pillows. Her skin was still glistening with droplets of water, and she could see the hunger in his eyes as he watched every movement she made, enraptured.

She bit her lip as she gently cupped her breasts, rolling her taut, pink nipples between her thumbs and forefingers until they perked up. She gave a breathy moan as she continued to pinch them, pleasure shooting through her belly right to the apex of her core. She could feel herself getting wet. Blackwell watched her intently, and she held his gaze, making it clear she wasn't about to stop.

She trailed her fingers over the skin of her stomach and thighs, circling her navel, before inching her way down, down, down. When she touched that sensitive spot between her legs, she threw her head back and squeezed her eyes shut, moaning with sweet relief. She made slow, languid circles over her clit, her fingers becoming slick with her wetness as her body melted with pleasure. For a moment, she forgot that she had an audience or where she was—there was only the ecstasy building in her core and the sound of her moans.

As she moved closer and closer to the edge, she slipped two fingers inside of herself and pumped them in and out.

"*Fuck.*" Blackwell's voice had turned husky, and she opened her eyes just enough to see him approaching the foot of the bed. "Why are you torturing me?"

She only pumped faster in response.

"Fuck, that's it," he grunted.

The next thing she knew he was hovering over her, kneeling between her legs. He grasped onto her wrist and pulled her hand away from herself. She made a noise of protest, but a shot of excitement ran through her as she waited for his next move. He brought her fingers, slick with her arousal, to his mouth and gently sucked them clean. Something primal erupted inside her at the sight.

"*Delicious,*" he said.

"Touch me," she breathed. "Please."

He lifted a brow. "I thought you said you'd never beg me for anything?"

She pressed her lips together as she glared at him, indignant. He laughed.

"Hmm," he hummed as he leaned in to run his lips along the underside of her jaw, grinding the hardness in his pants between her legs until she was whimpering with need. "I think I *should* make you beg. As punishment for teasing me."

"I hate you," she said, but it came out too breathless to be convincing.

"Good," he murmured. "Try and hold on to that while I do this. I adore a challenge."

One thing about having a Ghost as a lover: changing positions was always smooth. She was on her back one second and the next he had flipped their positions.

"Reach up and grab the headboard," he demanded.

She didn't argue. Stretching herself up, she grasped onto the top of the scrolling baroque frame, her knees straddling his sides. He reached around to grip the back of her thighs, using them as leverage to slide himself further down the bed until his mouth had perfect access to the apex between her legs. When his tongue flicked against her clit, her legs nearly gave out, and his arms had to support her weight for her to remain upright. He didn't seem to mind.

He gave another lick, this time lapping at the slit of her entrance, and she could feel herself growing wetter and wetter with each stroke of his tongue. Until the heat pooling between her legs was dripping down her thighs. Her chest heaved with the effort of stamping down the moans and whimpers clamoring up her throat, and Blackwell made a noise of discontent.

"Stop holding back," he commanded beneath her, moving one of his hands between her legs to slip a single finger inside her. "I want to hear you."

When he added a second finger and curled it inside her, hitting that sensitive spot deep within, she let go. A moan slipped from her lips as she threw her head back in ecstasy, using her purchase on the headboard to lift herself up and down on his fingers, desperately needing more friction.

"Blackwell," she whimpered as she slammed down on his hand harder and harder.

"Good girl, use me to fuck yourself," he praised, his voice deepening with lust. "Faster."

As she sped up her movements, he added a third finger. As she rode his hand, he brought his mouth back to her clit and sucked until she thought she was going to combust with desire.

"Yes," she urged him on. "Please . . . please don't stop."

His tongue made lazy circles around the sensitive bundle of nerves, and it didn't take long for her to reach her climax. The muscles in her core clamped around his fingers, and while she slowly came down from her high, he disappeared from beneath her. A moment later, she felt his bare chest against her back, his arms wrapping to the front of her body to cup her breasts as his lips left searing kisses against her right shoulder.

"Please," she whispered as he pinched her nipples not caring about the desperation in her voice.

"Please what?" he murmured as he moved one hand up to gather her hair and toss it over her left shoulder, giving his mouth access to the side of her throat. He nipped and licked his way over her feverish skin, and she shivered. She could feel the head of his cock pressing against her entrance and it was driving her wild.

"I need you," she gasped, "inside of me."

"You need me. As a distraction." Something in his tone making it sound like a test.

"I need a distraction, yes," she admitted. And then, "But more than that—I *want* you. Even though I shouldn't. You make me feel . . ."

She could feel the planes of his body tense behind her as he cautiously prompted, "I make you feel . . ."

"Good. Safe." Her locket warmed, its pulse becoming more erratic with every word she confessed. "Not so alone. I want you."

"Then you'll have me," he told her, and without preamble, he sheathed himself inside of her, all the way to the hilt.

"*Blackwell*," she cried.

One of his hands splayed across her stomach while the other rested on her hip, helping keep her steady as he pulled all the way back out to the tip and then slammed forward once more. Soon he was pumping into her with a steady rhythm and her head lolled back against his shoulder as she enjoyed the sensation of him filling her so completely.

"Ophelia," he grunted. "Fuck, angel, I never want to be anywhere else but right here. Inside you."

She whimpered with pleasure as she glanced down at herself, to where his hands were splayed over the planes of her stomach, and she could see the swell of his length moving inside her beneath them.

"I think you might be the closest to heaven I'll ever get," he whispered.

She turned her face toward his just enough for his mouth to capture hers in a sloppy kiss. He licked and nipped until her lips were swollen, and as their tongues lathed at each other, his hips pumped faster, deeper. The hand he had splayed on her stomach came up to massage her breast, rolling her nipple between his thumb and forefinger just hard enough that pleasure mixed with pain, and she let out a cry against his lips. The sounds coming from her spurred him on faster and soon a thin sheen of sweat covered their skin, but Blackwell's pace didn't let up. Driving them both to the edge at the same time.

"Come for me," he implored as the hand on her breast made its way down to her clit, flicking the swollen bundle with his index finger and making her buck at the overwhelming stimulation.

"I'm close," she told him.

"Good girl," he encouraged. "Go all the way for me."

"Blackwell?"

"Yes, angel?" he asked, nearly breathless.

"I think, I think maybe I..." she trailed off as his fingers pinched her clit and her entire body lit up with unprecedented pleasure. A surge of sparks erupted from her hands at the sensation, their union creating literal magic.

She had been on the verge of unraveling for a while, but now she was crashing headfirst and she was determined to bring him there with her. She slammed herself all the way down against his length, grinding hard against him and making him hiss out a string of expletives. She felt the muscles in his arms tighten, and she knew he was about to tumble over the edge as well—so she let herself go for the second time, right beside him.

Every bone in her body felt like gelatin as he slowly pulled out of her and disentangled himself. Her chest heaved as she tried to catch her breath, and he gently pulled them both down onto the mattress, pillowing her head against his chest as the final waves of pleasure dissipated. They stayed like that for a long time, basking in the silence of the afterglow.

Blackwell was the one to speak first. "I feel less alone with you, too."

Her chest swelled with a dangerous emotion and tears pricked at the corners of her eyes. What she had been about to admit to him...

I think maybe I'm falling for you.

A deep sense of dread began to sink into her gut that being within Phantasma wasn't going to be the thing that broke her.

She pushed herself up from Blackwell's chest and climbed out of the bed. Going over to dig around in her suitcase, she pulled her crimson nightgown from the trunk and hastily threw it on. Blackwell watched her with a blank expression.

"Going somewhere?" he questioned.

"I can't waste time lying around when I should get back to searching for your key," she answered. "We've been too distracted lately."

He stood, snapping his fingers to redress himself. As always, he had impeccable taste. High-waisted black satin trousers with a monochromatic brocade embroidered over them. His shirt was a clean-cut, cream button-down, tucking neatly into his pants and just ever so slightly oversized on his lean, muscular frame. There were expensive-looking onyx cufflinks at each of his wrists and a matching necklace beneath the open collar of his shirt.

He looked so devilishly handsome that she had half a mind to damn it all to Hell and drag him back into bed, and that was exactly the problem.

"Something's wrong," he stated as she busied herself with fixing her sex-disheveled hair. "What did I do?"

"You didn't do anything," she said back easily. "Nothing is wrong. Like I said, I just can't waste time lying around."

He sighed. "Alright, then. Where are we going to start looking tonight?"

"There is no *we* tonight," she told him, adamant. "I want to explore alone."

"There's no *we*?" He raised his brows. "You were just begging me to fuck—"

"I did not beg." She wrinkled her nose, cutting him off before he could finish that thought. "But . . . we aren't being careful. Everything that just happened . . . what was said . . . consider it the last time. We cannot become attached to each other. I cannot want you like this. You leave for an hour, and I'm craving your company. That's not just foolish, it's *dangerous*. And I cannot rely on you to save me from everything when in less than six days I will never see you again."

The emerald of his eyes deepened with anger. "Then what do you propose we do? Not speak for the rest of the competition?"

"As if you could go two seconds without popping in to

bother me," she muttered. "I'm not saying we can't *speak*. I'm saying no more kissing, touching, or sleeping in the same bed. We need space."

He gave a single, sharp nod. "Understood."

Then he disappeared.

NIGHT SIX OF
PHANTASMA

33

FRIVOLOUS FANTASY

This time when Ophelia went back to the secret room to revisit the carving of her father's name, she made it a point not to get burned by acid. Crawling through the tight tunnel, she could hear the pitter-patter of the burning rain behind her, but she reached the small, paneled room without incident. She tried not to picture the last time she and Blackwell were in here together, scrubbing the intimate scene from her mind before she spiraled any further tonight.

Finally alone, the Shadow Voice hissed in her mind, startling her. She hadn't realized it, but the voice had been bothering her less and less with every passing day she spent in Phantasma. A shocking pro amongst a massive list of cons.

She shoved the Shadow Voice from her mind and set down the lit chamberstick she'd brought with her. The soft, dancing firelight illuminated the planks of wood before her, revealing the carved words she'd come in search of.

She traced her fingers over the letters of *Gabriel Forever*, one by one, wishing she felt some sort of magical connection in them, but she didn't. Her locket didn't react either, just stayed silent and cold against her throat. Turning her attention to the scratched-out words at the top, she leaned in, trying to decipher what letters might have been there before they were gouged beyond recognition. If she didn't know better, she would have sworn the first letter was a "T".

A sob racked through her chest.

"Momma," she whispered as her tears hit the ground. "Why were you ever here?"

She curled up beside the words and let herself cry. Shedding tears for her mother's untimely death. Too sudden, too soon. Tears for the relationship with her sister she wondered if she'd ever get the chance to mend. Tears for the father she never got to know.

But most of all she shed tears for herself. And the soft heart she would never have again.

Ophelia woke to the gray light of a nearly extinguished candle. The wax of the tapered column had melted down to the quick, and she wondered how many hours she had been asleep. Stretching out her limbs, she pushed herself up from the ground, chamberstick in her left hand, and padded toward the bookcase on the far wall of the room.

She set the brass candleholder down on one of the empty shelves and ran her fingers over the panels of each shelf's alcove, looking for a button to trigger the turning mechanism like the one that had led her here. At first, she didn't find anything, and she made a noise of annoyance low in her throat that she'd once again have to summon Blackwell to help her out of a sticky situation. Upon a second inspection, however, she found a small indention on the shelf just above her eye level. She rolled to the balls of her feet, hopping a bit to push it down.

The shelf began to turn, spinning a hundred and eighty degrees until she was returned to the library. No one seemed to be around, and she sighed in relief. But she didn't make it two steps toward the exit before smoke began to crawl across the floor from beneath the shelves, billowing through the room like rolling storm clouds. She felt Sinclair's presence before she saw him.

"Hello, Necromancer," the Devil greeted her as all the light in the room snuffed out.

" 'Fuck off' doesn't seem to have the same potency here as it does in the French Quarter," she muttered as she crossed her arms over her chest.

"I come in peace," he said as he began to circle her. "I've decided I didn't make the best impression before."

"What do you mean?" she said, tone dripping in sarcasm. "You were downright *charming.*"

He tipped his head back and laughed. "You have a decent sense of humor for a mortal."

She didn't respond. She had no desire to keep this conversation going. He cleared his throat at her silence, a phony gesture meant to feign an aura of humanity he did not possess. Devils loved to play at being human to lower mortals' defenses.

"I thought perhaps I'd show you that I'm not so terrible as you might think," he offered. "Give you a small reprieve from the sadness plaguing you here and offer you some fun."

Ophelia's walls immediately came up at the mention of *fun.* She was certain their definitions of that word varied drastically. "I'm not interested in fun. Now, if you don't mind—or even if you do—I'd like to go back to my room."

"Aren't you a tad bit curious about what I have in mind?" he teased. "I swear it won't cause you any physical harm and I won't even ask for anything in return. I just want to show you what someone like me can give you. Have you ever truly seen what a Devil can do? A *powerful* one, I mean?"

She hesitated. She hadn't had a single experience with a Devil before Phantasma because of her mother's strict rules and even stricter curfew. She had only ever heard of their abilities secondhand—ranging from parlor tricks to omnipotence. It wouldn't hurt to at least ask what he had in mind, right? To sate her curiosity?

Do it, the Shadow Voice urged. ***This ought to be good.***

"What is it, exactly, that you want to show me?" she appealed.

Sinclair's answering grin was dazzling. "Tell me your most frivolous fantasy."

It took her a moment to think about that request. Truthfully, for most of her life her favorite daydream involved exploring the French or Italian countryside with Genevieve, somewhere completely uncharted to them both. The new scene forming in her mind, however, was much more alarming. It was of her and Blackwell, sitting in the drawing room of Grimm Manor. Him sitting upright with a book in his hand, her lying on her side with her head pillowed in his lap as she read her own novel.

Her breath hitched in surprise, and she shook away the image as quickly as she could.

"A ball," she blurted out, picking the next random, frivolous thought that popped into her head. "I've never been to one. Which is practically blasphemous as a New Orleanian. I want to wear a ridiculously lavish gown and dance with handsome suitors."

Sinclair stepped closer. "Close your eyes."

She hesitated.

Do it, the Shadow Voice commanded now. ***Do it!***

Her eyes fluttered closed. A cold gust went through the room, making her skin pebble as she shivered. Then a bright light flashed behind her lids and the silky sound of violins began to play somewhere in the distance, the romantic notes caressing her mind.

"Open your eyes," Sinclair murmured.

Ophelia nearly fainted with shock at the room before her.

Gone was the library, replaced with a dazzling, gilded

baroque ballroom. A phantasmagoria of splendor and grandiosity. The checkered floor was made of gold and cream marble and the scrolling filigree molding that climbed up the walls and over the fifty-foot ceiling was brushed with gold foil. Between the molding were various painted scenes of Angels and Demons in pastel oranges and pinks amongst clouds of swirling blue. In the center of the room hung a massive chandelier made of what had to be at least a thousand individual hanging teardrop crystals. The entire back wall was made of glass, the band set up before it to the left, and Ophelia sucked in a breath when she saw the twinkling stars.

If she didn't know better, she'd have sworn they were real. She said as much aloud.

"They're as real as you believe they are," Sinclair responded. "Now, would you like to dance?"

He held out a hand, and she narrowed her eyes as she took it. He immediately swung her into his arms, the movement smooth, flowing, and soon they were engaged in an easy waltz across the dance floor. The music began to play louder, and soon other dancers emerged from the shadows beyond the pillars that lined the side of the ballroom. As other couples swirled and danced around them, Sinclair spun her out by one hand before expertly reeling her back in, and as she turned and turned, she felt the fabric of her nightgown grow heavier until it transformed completely into a dress even her wildest fantasies could not have come up with.

The dress was made of ruby silk and shimmering gold embroidery. The bodice looked as if it had been painted onto her skin. The sweetheart neckline of the red corset plunged scandalously low, and gold brocade appliqué was layered atop in an intricate, swirling pattern, accentuating her bosom. The appliqué climbed all the way up the straps and draped over her shoulders, sweeping down her back in a deep "U" shape. The gown's full skirt was made of the same scarlet silk as the bodice, pleated in a most flattering way, lending hourglass curves to her usually shapeless figure. Golden opera gloves stretched from her fingertips to her elbows and a ruby pendant the size of a quarter hung around her throat just below her beloved locket.

"It's quite something, isn't it?" Sinclair jutted his chin at the dress. "You look positively *exquisite*."

"Yes," she breathed as he spun her again and she watched her skirt twirl as if it were lighter than air.

"All of this took less than an ounce of my energy," he revealed. "Imagine the things I could give you if I really took my time."

"I'm not making any deals with you," she informed him once again, her tone absolute. "I don't care how many pretty dresses you give me."

"But you made a deal with *him*?" he implored, the slits of his pupils tightening ever so slightly with frustration. "Why? What was his secret to convincing you to agree?"

"For starters, he isn't a Devil."

"Ah." Sinclair rolled his eyes. "It's Devils you hate. Original."

"Self-preservation," she countered. "No deal with you would lead to anything good. But Blackwell is helping me just as much as I am him—more, actually."

"Until he steals away a decade of your life," Sinclair reminded her. "Is that truly something you're prepared to lose?"

She swallowed. No, it wasn't. But she would never admit that to him of all people.

"I'm not going to lose," she stated.

Sinclair laughed now, his maroon eyes lighting up with amusement. "Oh, sweetheart, but you will. You have no idea what you're up against."

"Then tell me," she pressed. "What am I up against? And

why do you hate Blackwell so much? What could he have possibly done to you?"

The hand on her waist tightened as his face soured with her last question. "He had my freedom stolen. I am tied to this fucking Hellhole for the next few *centuries* because of that bastard."

"What do you mean? I thought the Devils that ran this place were here of their own volition?"

"The rest are. It is only me and Phantasma's creator—Salemaestrus—who are not here by choice," Sinclair told her.

Salemaestrus. She filed that name away for later.

"The manor's creator is forced to be here, too?" she questioned.

Sinclair sighed deeply and pulled them from the dance floor, pushing past the faceless crowd of dancers toward one of the massive pillars on the edge of the room. He leaned back against the marble column, crossing his arms over his broad chest as he began his story.

"No one in Phantasma can speak of the creator to anyone." He gave her a loaded look. "Except for me."

She propped a hand on her hip and tapped her foot impatiently. "Why?"

"It's part of their contract. I, however, am not bound by the same sort of contract—I am indebted, not employed. And the boundaries of my debt do not include any sort of clause that keeps me from speaking about Salemaestrus himself," he explained. "Only certain details of his situation."

"How did you become indebted?" she wondered.

"I was foolish enough to once consider Salemaestrus a friend." He seethed at the memory, shaking his head as he spoke the word *friend*. "When his father chained him to this place as punishment for treason, I was given a sentence for conspiring with him."

"His father?"

Sinclair's smile was all teeth, a fiendish sight. "The King of the Devils."

She gaped in horror, rocking back a step. "*What?* Phantasma is run by—"

"The Prince of the Devils himself," Sinclair finished, nodding in confirmation. "Salemaestrus fell irrevocably in love—and chose his lover over his father. As punishment, his father had his lover killed, and Salemaestrus is now forced to run the Devil's Manor for eternity as a lesson. Or until his father gets bored and ends his sentence early. Whichever comes first."

"And how do *you* fit into that?"

His upper lip curled. "I tried to help him hide his lover."

She frowned. She hadn't expected anything so noble from a Devil.

"And Blackwell?" she questioned. "Where does he fit into the story?"

Sinclair straightened up, fury flitting across his expression at the mention of Blackwell's named. "That Phantom bastard has *sabotaged* me time and time again."

She almost laughed. "How?"

"The details don't matter. What does is that I had an opportunity to get the fuck out of here, and that damned Ghost ruined it. I'm going to make sure he never sees the light at the end of the tunnel as long as I'm stuck here."

"That's why you want me to forfeit," she realized, the puzzle pieces falling into place. "You don't want him to be released—as revenge."

Sinclair's smile turned tight. "It's nothing personal, sweetheart."

"See, I was about to say the same thing to you." She made to turn away from him. "Sorry about your vendetta, but I've got

one of my own and I don't plan to fail. I will be finding Blackwell's key whether you like it or not."

His laugh made her pause. She twisted back just in time to
see him begin to fade away.

"We'll see," he whispered.

Uneasiness sank in her stomach as she spun around, searching for him. The Devil was nowhere in sight, but the ballroom
was still perfectly intact. Another song began to play, another
round of dancing rippled through the crowd. She turned toward
the shadows just past the columns and tried to step into them,
but an invisible force slammed her back. That asshole had
trapped her here.

She gathered her skirt up in her hands and ran. Slicing
through the dance floor, shoving bodies out of her way, she tried
every corner of the room for another exit, but her search was
fruitless.

"*Damn it,*" she seethed before chanting Blackwell's name. She
loathed that she needed him to get her out of here. Except that
he didn't come.

She tried summoning him again.

No response.

Again.

No response.

No, this can't be happening. Why isn't he coming? Where is he?

The Shadow Voice cackled. **This is what you deserve, foolish girl. Why don't you try smashing the windows? Jump to your
doom.**

She twisted to face the glass wall. The night sky beyond it
was still so clear. The stars smiled at her, twinkling in greeting
as she padded closer, her silk skirt skimming the ground. Oh,
how she had missed the stars. When she reached the glass, she

placed a palm flat against its cool surface. *Would* breaking the glass shatter the illusion?

Here goes nothing, she thought as she wound her fist back, bracing herself for the pain that was about to come.

A split second before she could throw her punch, however, someone tapped her on the shoulder. She whipped around to find the most handsome man she had ever seen. With eyes of crystal blue and dark hair that curled onto his forehead.

He reached out a hand in offering. "Would you care to dance?"

She stared at his hand for a long moment. For some reason, she did want to dance. Even though she was pretty sure she shouldn't.

"I promise I don't bite." The man smiled kindly, the corners of his eyes crinkling adorably.

She slowly lifted her hand and placed it in his. "Sure..."

He swept her into his arms and turned her around the dance floor. Song after song she waltzed, passing from partner to partner. Soon she felt herself grow tired, exhaustion settling deeper into her bones with each spin, each beat of the music. The faces of every suitor began to blend together, and there was an ache of emptiness deep in her core.

How long had she been dancing? Her feet were so sore...

Another spin, another—

Suddenly, she was being ripped out of her dance partner's arms and into someone else's embrace. She stumbled, eyes widening as she looked up and found a very pissed-off Blackwell.

"Are you out of your damned mind?" he reprimanded. "What the Hell are you *doing?*"

"I..." she started, but her mind was still fuzzy and she didn't know how to explain. Then a name came jolting back to her. "Sinclair."

Blackwell let out a string of curses that would have made the King of the Devils himself blush. Then, "What is it that you're seeing right now?"

"What do you mean?"

"Around you, what exactly are you seeing?"

She glanced around them. "A ballroom. There's a band, and dancers, and—"

"Fucking Hell," he interrupted. "Alright, prepare yourself. This next bit isn't going to be fun for you."

Before she could ask him what the Hell he meant, he bent down and lifted her up, throwing her over his right shoulder like a sack of flour. He walked toward the opposite end of the ballroom, and the closer they got to the wall, the more she thrashed in his arms to let her go. His grip never wavered.

"You don't understand!" she screamed at him as she beat her fists against his back. "There's no way out. There's a forcefield—"

Blackwell reached the wall and stepped through it, cutting off her words as the illusion around her shattered and a piercing pain exploded through her body.

LEVEL FIVE

34

WRATH

The scream that left her mouth as the ballroom dissolved around her could've turned a lesser place into rubble. She only quieted because her voice became too hoarse, and every inch of her skin felt as if it had been sliced by a thousand cuts. Not to mention the shooting migraine that had her rolling to her side and heaving up bile. Blackwell cursed from somewhere above.

He crouched down next to her, reaching out to run a soothing hand over her back. "Breaking that sort of magic wreaks havoc on your senses. You're going to feel like shit for a little longer—but you have to get up."

"No," she moaned, pressing her forehead to the cool ground. "Leave me alone."

"Ophelia," he said, voice turning firm. "You have to get up. Level five is beginning."

That jolted her from her pain-induced haze. "What? It should be hours from now!"

"Sinclair's illusion really made you lose track of time," he said. "Dinner has already finished. I have to transport you to the dining room now, before you're disqualified."

She grunted in discomfort as she heaved herself up from the ground, wincing at the pounding in her temples. "Okay, okay. Take me there."

He pulled her into him by her waist and blinked them out of the corridor in front of the library. When they appeared at the archway to the dining room seconds later, there were no other contestants in sight. Just the door that would port her into level five, and a smug-looking Devil leaning on the wall next to it. The woman was nearly Blackwell's height, with straight black hair and blunt bangs, and a face people would start wars over.

"Without a second to spare," the Devil commented as Ophelia rushed toward the portal. "Need to keep your little mortal on a tighter leash, don't you think, Blackwell?"

"Fuck you, Rayea," Blackwell told the Devil, but the words didn't have as much bite as Ophelia would have liked.

"Are you offering? Because my answer would be yes," Rayea purred, making Ophelia pause, hand on the doorknob. "It's been a while after all."

A ripple of jealousy burned through Ophelia's veins at the sultry way the Devil was watching Blackwell, at the implication of those last words. Ophelia glanced at Blackwell, but his expression was carefully blank.

Rayea flicked her eyes to Ophelia. "You'd better get going, girl," she spat. "Or you'll find yourself outside Phantasma's gates."

"What about the clue?" Ophelia gritted out.

Rayea shrugged. "Should've been here on time if you needed the assistance. Now, if you'd like to give Blackwell and I some privacy." The Devil made a shooing motion with her hand.

Ophelia scowled as she threw open the door and stepped through, shaking off the envy she had no right feeling as she prepared herself to face whatever was about to come. Exiting the portal, she found herself in a tight room, no larger than five square feet. The room had no door or window. It was simply a hollow box, and Ophelia's breathing quickened at the absence of any obvious exit. She really was beginning to hate such enclosed spaces.

As she inspected the small room, scrutinizing the smooth alabaster walls for any sort of indication that there might be a way out, her mind wandered to the way Rayea had been looking at Blackwell. She hadn't liked the way the Devil had said his name. Like it was a name she had once screamed in the throes of an orgasm.

And did you see her body? the Shadow Voice laughed. *As if you could compete.*

Ophelia gritted her teeth. No. She would not let herself be distracted by what may or may not be going on with Blackwell and his sex life. This was precisely why she wanted space. Getting distracted in the middle of a life-or-death trial was not how she was going to leave this place.

She focused her attention back to the walls around her, resisting the urge to summon Blackwell for help. One, because there wasn't enough room here for two people, even if one of them was a Ghost. And two, because she needed to start figuring things out for herself. After a minute of being stumped as to what move to make—and realizing that she probably had a limited supply of air—the scraping of rock against rock rumbled through the small space, and she spun to find a small square panel in the wall lifting up to reveal a hidden alcove. The indented space contained two chains with metal handles dangling from them. Below the one on the left was the word *forfeit*, and below the right—*wrath*.

She sighed. "Well, here goes nothing."

She pulled the handle on the right.

A panel of buttons flipped up beneath the handles. Each button had a contestant's name etched beneath it. Ophelia gulped.

She didn't have any clues to go off of. She could only assume after having picked wrath that she was now supposed to pick who to enact that wrath against . . .

Her fingers hovered over the button that was marked with Cade's name.

Two breaths later and the walls around her began to shake and crack apart. One by one, each fell to the ground, revealing a larger room behind them—and all seven of the other contestants standing in the rubble of their stone chambers. As she took in their faces, she was able to determine the five people that either died or took a Devil's bargain in level four. James, Eric, Becca, and two of the other contestants she'd never bothered to remember were officially gone. The last people standing in her group were herself, Cade, Beau, Luci, Leon, Edna, Charlotte, and a quiet man with an unfortunate cowlick in his mousy brown hair. Maybe she'd actually learn this one's name before he left.

"Everyone picked wrath," Luci observed, voice barely above a whisper.

Cade sneered at her. "No shit, cousin."

Leon visibly tensed at Cade's tone. "Don't talk to her like that."

"We're family, I can talk to her however I please," Cade spat at the boy.

"Would you all shut the fuck up?" Charlotte demanded. "God, the most torturous part of this fucking place has been being stuck listening to your insipid conversations."

"Who the fuck made you the boss?" Cade snarled.

"Better than you, asshole," Edna quipped, crossing her arms over her chest as she glared at Cade. Something about her was different, and it took Ophelia a moment to piece it together; she had chopped off all of her long, blond hair. Now it didn't even brush the tops of her shoulders, swishing with every little movement she made.

"Careful, bitch, or you'll lose your ability to speak, just like your brother," Cade threw back.

Edna hissed at the mention of her brother's unfortunate maiming, lurching across the circle at Cade.

Beau, ever the good henchman, stepped between them, pointing at something beyond the group. "*Look.*"

They all turned in sync. Seven stone pedestals had risen from the ground. There was a beat of intense silence, all of them glancing around at each other as they did the math in their heads.

"That means everyone picked the same person," Leon said.

"What were the clues?" Ophelia asked, the question directed mostly at Luci.

"It was something about a unanimous decision," Luci told her. "If six of the seven of us chose the same person, only one of us wouldn't be able to make it to the next level. If the decisions had been split any other way, there was something about extra choice to be made."

"Cade was the obvious choice," Charlotte spoke up then. "Even his friends knew that, apparently, so I think it's clear he's the one who doesn't get a pedestal."

Cade's lips curled as he spat, "Over my dead fucking body."

And then the rush came.

Cade pulled no punches shoving people out of his way with brutal force as he lunged toward the pedestals. Edna took off after him, making a point to slam her palms into his back when she caught up, sending them both tumbling to the ground in a mess of thrashing limbs. Beau descended on Edna, snatching her back by her hair and pulling her off Cade. Cade slammed his fist into Edna's stomach, making her grunt in pain, and as he wound his hand back to do it again, the mousy-haired man yanked Cade back by his shirt.

"Stop it," the man ordered, voice level but firm. "What is wrong with you?"

Cade whipped around. He was about a foot taller than the other man, an advantage he made sure to take as he loomed down over him menacingly.

"Only seven of us can get out of here. Which means one of us isn't making it. And I don't give a fuck if you all voted it should be me—that was when all you had to do was push a button. Now is the real test. Try and take me out. I dare you," Cade snarled.

"You're not seriously going to murder someone, Cade," Luci said, aghast. "What is the matter with you? I know things have been hard back home. I know your father gave you an ultimatum, but this is more than fighting to win. This is *evil*. How could you have expected all of us to unanimously agree on anyone *but* you at this rate?"

"Evil?" He gave a single hard laugh. "All the things you've seen in this place, cousin, and you think I am the evil thing here? Because I'm not a coward? Because I'm willing to do what the rest of you won't?" Cade twisted around to look at everyone in the room with disdain. "You should all thank me!"

And when he spotted Ophelia, as if just remembering she was there, he paused. Ophelia didn't break his steely gaze even to blink.

"Beau," Cade called out to his friend, who was still holding on to Edna. "Drop that one. I have a better target in mind."

Ophelia's fists balled by her side as she lifted her chin in challenge. "I'd like to see you try."

"You got Eric killed, you Demon *bitch*," Cade accused, stepping toward her. "Beau saw you."

"Then he also saw that your friend was a fucking fool," she snorted. "He got what was coming to him for *attacking* me. As will you if you get any closer."

Cade made to charge at her, but Leon jumped between them before Cade could reach her.

"*Stop*," Leon insisted. "We aren't going to jump to murder, Cade."

"Look around and tell me what other options we have," Beau inserted.

"Someone could just call a Devil and make a bargain," Luci stated, voice soft. "Wouldn't that be better than murder or death?"

"Oh." Beau blinked. As if that thought would have never even occurred to him. It probably wouldn't have.

"Where's the fun in that?" Cade sneered. "After all, we all picked *wrath*, didn't we?"

"I say this sincerely," Ophelia spoke, curling a lip in disgust at Cade. "You need an exorcism."

"Don't act like anyone here is going to willingly forfeit after coming this far," Cade shot back. "I sure as Hell am not."

Ophelia made a show of pressing a hand to her heart in mock surprise, staggering back a step as she exclaimed, "Truly shocking!"

"Let's see *you* forfeit, then," Cade taunted.

Leon gave a frustrated sigh as he addressed the entire group this time. "Raise your hand if you're inclined to forfeit."

They all glanced around at each other. Not a single hand went up.

"It seems we're at an impasse, then," Charlotte stated.

"Not as long as I'm around." Cade grinned.

And before anyone could stop him, he wrapped an arm around Edna's neck in a chokehold. The girl's entire face turned red in an instant as she slammed her fist against Cade's bicep, clawing at his skin with her nails, but Cade only squeezed harder. All of them were frozen, watching the grotesque scene in front of them in horror, none of them moving until Edna was almost purple from the lack of oxygen.

Cade looked around at each of them in turn, eyes wild. "If you all watch her die, you're just as responsible for her fate as I am. Someone forfeit—or we will all have blood on our hands."

Ophelia swallowed. He was, for once, right. But she still didn't move. Not even when Edna grew limp in Cade's arms. Not even when she could see the light begin to drain out of the girl's eyes.

And maybe it was because her hands had already been stained with blood after what she let happen to Eric. Or maybe she just decided getting to Genevieve was worth a few strangers.

Or maybe you're just as much of a monster as me, the Shadow Voice whispered.

Or that.

Let her die, the Shadow Voice insisted. *Let him drain all the life from her. It's what they deserve.*

"No," Ophelia whispered.

Everyone shifted their uncomfortable gazes to her.

"What was that, Ghost whore?" Cade questioned. "You give in?"

"*No,*" Ophelia growled, loud enough to boom through the room this time. "Let her go. Now."

"Or what?" Cade retorted.

Ophelia smiled slowly, making sure to show him all of her teeth. "Or I'll give you a demonstration of exactly what I'm capable of."

Cade narrowed his eyes now. "I don't believe you."

No! Let her die! the Shadow Voice screamed. *You're a monster!*

Maybe I am a monster, she thought back. *But not the same sort as you. Never that.*

Edna's eyes were beginning to flutter closed for good. That's when Ophelia went completely invisible. A few choked gasps rang out as they stared at the spot she had been standing moments before. Cade visibly paled.

"Where is she?" he demanded, a tinge of panic in his tone. "Where the fuck is she? I told you all she was a Demon!"

His hold on Edna had slackened, and Ophelia positioned herself behind him, unsure how long she could hold herself in this state, and gave a hard kick to the back of his knees. He yelped in surprise, going down like a sack of potatoes, Edna's limp body hitting the ground with a heavy thud moments before he followed.

"She needs air!" Ophelia yelled at them. "Someone check her pulse!"

Everyone sprang into action at once, Luci, Leon, and Charlotte going for Edna, beginning the motions to resuscitate the poor girl. Meanwhile, the mousy-haired man and Beau were watching intently for Cade's next move.

Cade spun around in her direction, grasping at the air to find where she was. She easily dodged his arms before pulling her fist back and jamming it so hard into his face that she felt the skin of her knuckles split open. He grunted in pain as his nose began to gush blood, but when he sprang himself forward, she dodged him again. She got in one more good hit, to his jaw, before she couldn't hold her invisibility anymore, and she found herself flickering back into her solid state. Now that Cade could see her, his rage increased tenfold, reflecting the theme of this level perfectly.

"Hey! She's breathing!" someone exclaimed. Leon.

Ophelia heard Edna choke on a ragged breath, sputtering as a hoarse sob heaved from her chest while trying to suck in as much oxygen as she could. But Ophelia didn't take her eyes off Cade for a moment. Disappointingly for Cade, he didn't get a chance to launch another attack.

"I give up!" Edna cried. "Please! I'm done! I'll make a deal! Any deal! Just let me *leave*. I'm so sorry, Michael. Please forgive me. I'm sorry. I'm sorry. Rayea! *Get me out of here!*"

The moment the last words were out the girl's mouth, Rayea appeared. Not bothering with a greeting or any sort of ceremony, the Devil clasped onto Edna's arm and transported the girl from the room.

35

MORTAL FOLLY

The rest of the level was uneventful, a somber silence settling over the room from everyone except Cade—whose rage was still rolling through the air around him. Each of them climbed onto one of the stone pedestals, and when they were all in place, a single door appeared before them.

No one hesitated to exit, and they were promptly deposited back into the dining room where they had begun, albeit with even more paranoia than they had started with. Everyone watched each other with apprehension, but they especially kept an eye on Cade. His true colors were out for everyone to see. Blessedly, Cade didn't bother to stick around for long, Beau hot on his heels.

"That guy is a bastard," Charlotte commented, then looked at Luci. "Did he call you his cousin?"

"Our mothers are sisters," Luci confirmed reluctantly. "We were never close, though. I'm sure you can guess why."

Ophelia snorted.

"I just feel horrible about Edna." Luci bit her lip. "Her little brother Michael...this was her only chance to bring him back."

I'm so sorry, Michael, the girl had sobbed. Ophelia's chest tightened with empathy. She knew all too well the feeling of being helpless at the death of a family member. She hoped the girl found peace.

Luci turned to Ophelia now. "You...turned invisible."

"Yeah, I suppose that cat's out of the bag," Ophelia muttered.

"I knew your family were Necromancers, but I didn't realize you could do something like *that*," Luci said. "Genevieve never liked when we asked questions about magic and such."

"Sounds like Genevieve. But in fairness *I* didn't even know I was capable of such an ability until a couple of days ago," Ophelia admitted.

"Well, you did a good thing, you know," Luci said. "When none of the rest of us did."

Ophelia shrugged. "The idea of Cade getting something he wanted didn't sit well with me. And no one deserves to die like *that*."

Luci nodded and then without another word, they all trickled out of the room. Ophelia lingered. Partially because she was absolutely ravenous since she missed dinner, and partly because she felt a familiar gaze settle over her and did not have any intention of luring the owner of that gaze back to her room to be cornered in the one place she felt semi-comfortable in this manor.

She plucked a bunch of grapes up from the table, popping one of the sweet green spheres into her mouth as she said, "Hello, Sinclair."

Sinclair faded into view on the opposite end of the dining table, leaning forward, hands gripped atop one of the chair backs as he watched her eat. "Please, darling, call me Sin."

She glared at him.

He flicked his eyes over her lazily. "I see you made it out."

"Of the level? Or your tricks?" She tilted her head, popping another grape between her lips.

"Both," he allowed. "Can't blame me for trying, though, can you?"

"Keep that sentiment in mind for the day I try to banish you to the pits of Hell," she quipped back. "Although, I truly hope you're tied here for the rest of your miserable eternity."

His answering grin was vicious. "As long as Blackwell is tied here with me."

"What do you want?" she demanded.

"Just thought it'd be fun to be the one to inform you that if you're looking for our aforementioned Phantom friend, he ran off with Rayea shortly after you went through the portal. Did he ever tell you they were lovers, for quite some time?"

The jealousy was back in full force. She set down her grapes, appetite gone.

"Ah, I see he didn't." Sinclair laughed. "Rayea always claimed he was one of her favorites, in fact. Something about the way he eats her—"

"*Stop*," she snarled. "I don't want to hear this. Leave me alone."

Sinclair shrugged. "Just thought you should know who you've been sharing your bed with and who he's been sharing his bed with. You *have* been sharing your bed with him, haven't you? I saw the two of you in the hallway that night."

She blushed furiously but didn't dignify any of that with a response.

"You may think the two of you are close," Sinclair warned. "But nothing in Phantasma is ever as it truly seems—I'm pretty sure I taught you that lesson well enough already."

"Oh, I don't know," she quipped. "You seem like an utter bastard and that's holding up so far."

He glowered, opening his mouth to return her biting remark, she was sure, but a telltale whistle began to carry down the hall just outside the room and the Devil disappeared. As predicted, Jasper passed by the entryway moments later, only halting when he spotted her standing there, alone.

"Hello, sweetheart." Jasper roved his eyes over her, head to toe, as he leaned a shoulder against the doorframe. "I heard you nearly missed that last trial after an unfortunate scene in the library."

"And who did you hear that from?" she asked. "Is there some sort of Devil gossip mill here?"

"Us Devils enjoy following petty mortal folly just as much as your kind does." He smirked. "But this I heard from the horse's mouth himself."

"Blackwell?"

Jasper shook his head. "Sinclair. Blackwell's . . . occupied."

She froze. "Occupied?"

The Devil's three eyes assessed her closely, scrutinizing her for something she hoped he didn't find. "Yes."

He was going to make her ask.

She made her tone as nonchalant as possible. "Occupied with what?"

"It's not really my business to tell," Jasper answered. "Which is my favorite kind to tell. He's with Rayea, I believe. Not unusual."

Her stomach churned. The jealousy was writhing beneath every inch of her skin now, and she didn't know what to do about it. This was bad. So, so bad.

Blackwell possibly fucking a Devil somewhere should not elicit this sort of response in her. In fact, it should be a *relief*. The more time he spent pleasuring someone else, the less time he spent distracting her. Unfortunately, the ache in her chest was not soothed by that logic.

"I have to go," she muttered.

Stalking back to her room, she wanted nothing more than to climb into a scalding hot bath and scrub away the feeling of betrayal she had no right to claim.

⚜

The water in the bathtub was not nearly as hot as she wanted it to be, but it would have to do. She sank into the porcelain tub, submerging herself up to her chin, letting her dark tresses float out around her. For a sweet, blissful moment, her mind was quiet. The only sound was the calming lap of water against her skin.

But the Shadow Voice never missed an opportunity to disrupt her peace.

He's probably fucking that Devil against a wall somewhere in the manor, the insidious voice cackled. *If you knock on the side of the tub three times, maybe you can stop it from happening.*

Her fists clenched by her sides. She refused to give in to such a ridiculous compulsion. If Blackwell *was* fucking someone against a wall right now, why should she stop him? He didn't belong to her and never would.

Did you see how pretty she was? the Shadow Voice continued. *Ebony hair, violet eyes, sinful smile. What do you think* her *name sounds like on his tongue?*

Shut. Up. Go away.

Knock three times and I will, it demanded.

Her hand twitched and she gnashed her teeth together. No. She would not give in.

Knock, it continued to growl. *Knock. Knock. Knock. Knock. Knock. Knock.*

She gave in.

Three quick taps of her knuckles against the porcelain and the voice dissipated like smoke, making her rage. She *hated* that giving in to it made it quiet. Worried that one day she'd slip and accidentally give in to something unforgivable it asked of her. She hated that she wasn't strong enough to shut it out completely. And that she thought a little bit less of herself each time she didn't.

Now, she submerged herself fully beneath the water, letting her eyes stay open to watch the bubbles drift to the surface above. She stayed like that, hair floating all around her, tickling her skin, until her lungs burned and screamed for oxygen. Just before she pulled herself up, a face appeared above the tub. One with piercing green eyes.

Pulling herself to the surface, she gasped for air, droplets rolling down over her skin and falling from her thick lashes, her hair pasted down her back, heavy from the water. Blackwell was standing beside the tub, arms crossed, shielded expression on his face as he roamed his gaze over her naked form.

"Glad to see you made it out of another trial," he commented. "Were you planning on letting me know?"

She raised her brows at his audacity. "Letting you know? I didn't realize that was an obligation of our bargain."

He didn't react to the bite in her words. If anything, he looked bored. "The last time I went looking for you somewhere, I found you ensnared in Sinclair's illusion, dancing around the library, alone, in a complete trance. I don't think it's unjustified that I might like you to check in and let me know that you're still alive after completing a level you didn't summon me to help with."

She sighed heavily and gestured down at herself. "You can see I'm alive, can't you? As for not summoning you—I didn't need your help. So, I didn't summon you. See how that works?"

Her tone was dripping in sarcasm, and a flicker of something she couldn't quite pinpoint went through his gaze. "Are you going to refuse to talk about what happened with Sinclair?"

"I don't see why that matters," she said.

"You don't see why it matters?" he scoffed. "You were lured into one of his tricks because you needed *space*, and damned near got disqualified because of it."

"But I *didn't*," she pointed out, shifting forward in the tub to sit up on her knees and sloshing water out over the sides as she moved. "And if you really cared about me getting stuck in Sinclair's trick, you would have come one of the three times I tried to summon you!"

Her voice cracked at that last bit, and his expression finally broke, morphing from apathetic to pained.

"Where were you?" she demanded. "*Where were you?*"

"I couldn't hear your summons through Sinclair's magic," he told her, head shaking with regret. "He's...he's much more powerful than I am."

"We're supposed to have a bond," she swallowed. "That's the deal. I call, you come."

He kneeled down before her and grabbed her face in his hands, eyes piercing into hers with sincerity. "I need you to know if I had heard you, there would have been *nothing* that could've stopped me from getting to you. Hell, nothing did stop me from getting to you. I went looking for you because I got the strangest feeling that something was wrong. I had every intention of respecting your request for space until then."

"I was scared," she whispered. "When I realized he trapped me. I called and called for you, and you didn't show up and..."

He leaned his forehead against hers. "I'm sorry, angel."

The truth of his words was palpable in the air around them.

She swallowed. "Where did you come from? Just now, I mean."

She knew she shouldn't have asked, but here she was—naked, vulnerable, and on the verge of asking him to hold her closer—unable to get one little thing off her mind.

He pulled back, searching her face for the underlying motive behind the question. "Why?"

She sat back once again, bringing her knees up to her chest and wrapping her arms around them to hide herself—a move that definitely did not escape his notice. "Sin said you were with the Devil from level five. I forgot her name," she lied.

"*Sin?*" he practically snarled. "Have we not learned our lesson about listening to *Sin* yet?"

"Jasper confirmed it as well."

Blackwell rolled his eyes to the ceiling, muttering something that sounded like *nosy bastard* under his breath, before fixing her with a pointed look. "Rayea only said those things in front of you because she knew she could get a rise out of you. Teasing mortals delights her—don't give her the satisfaction."

"So you *were* with her."

When the slow smirk began to curl up at the corners of his mouth, she knew she'd made a mistake. "Jealousy is a sexy color on you. Almost as sexy as blood."

I'm not jealous, she wanted to scream, but it was too late. She had already given herself away. Instead, she said, "Please go away. I need to finish bathing."

"With what soap?" He glanced around. "And what washcloth?"

Her face heated with frustration. Of course he couldn't just spare her some dignity.

"Don't worry, I got it." He winked as he snapped his fingers and a small glass vial of liquid soap appeared in his hand, along with a washcloth. He kneeled forward on the ground and reached over the lip of the tub to dampen the cloth before pouring some of the soap into the middle of it and lathering it up. "Give me your back."

For a moment she didn't move, wanting to protest that she did not need to be bathed as if she were a child. But when he waved an impatient hand at her to turn, she sighed and caved in. She curled her torso forward and rested her chin atop her knees while he gathered her hair and twisted it out of his way over her left shoulder. He began rubbing the washcloth over her bare shoulders and down her spine, sending a shiver through her at the intimacy of the moment. The sweet floral smell of magnolias hit her, and she recalled the walks into town with her mother, the scent of the trees drifting alongside them. As he continued his ministrations, her body relaxed, the emotional exhaustion of the day finally sinking into her bones.

"Rayea owed me a favor, and I called it in to pay Jasper back for lending us the contestant logs," he began.

She began to pick at her nails as she said, "I don't want to talk about her."

"Rayea and I haven't had an intimate relationship in a very long time," he pressed on as if she hadn't spoken. "And even when we did, it was purely physical."

She twisted around to give him a hard look. "This is *exactly* what I didn't want to talk about. I don't need the details of your past debaucheries, thanks."

He shrugged. "There aren't many details for me to give anyway. It was all very forgettable; I can hardly remember anything other than being distracted from the consuming loneliness of living eternally without a single person who knows me. Because of my limited recollection, I barely know myself."

The sadness in his tone made her heart bleed. She faced him fully now, and he brought the washcloth to the side of her neck, running it down to her shoulder, across her clavicle, then lower, between her breasts.

"But you..." he told her as he brushed the rag beneath the swells of her chest and over her smooth stomach. "You are apparently anything but forgettable."

"You forgot the first time we met," she reminded him.

"Did I?" he murmur. "Because I felt you the *moment* you stepped into Phantasma. It was an undeniable, magnetic pull that led me to finding you that first day. Yanking on that door, making conversation with a cat, dressed in blood." A soft smile began to curl at the corners of his lips at the memory. "I wanted to offer you my bargain then and there, but I knew I had to be patient. So, I made myself leave you, determined to give you space for the rest of the night—and then you found me. Because it seems that's what we do. We find each other."

The corners of her eyes began to prick at his sweet words. "You only felt my presence that first day because you recognized the essence of my father. Not me."

"No, that's just what I let you believe," he told her, determined. "I didn't want to scare you further with the intensity of it all in such a vulnerable moment. The familiarity of your bloodline helped with the part of connecting you to your father, yes. But it's *you* I am drawn to, Ophelia. You claim that I told you to stay away from here the very first time we met. Then you were erased from my memories and yet..." he shook his head with slight disbelief, "...yet we still found our way back to each other. Because even with my memory gone, you marked me somehow."

"You don't have to sugarcoat anything," she whispered. "I know whatever it is we're doing has an expiration date."

His hand stilled for a beat, his jaw clenching at her words.

"I saw you save that girl," he told her, meeting her eyes. "When you didn't summon me, I became worried and went to the Other Side to watch the trial play out. You saved that girl when not a single other soul would. You joined this competition knowing it would cause you harm not because you want money or fame or a stupid fucking prize, but for your sister. There are times that you're afraid of yourself, but you'll look a Devil right in the eye and insult them. You have learned so much about your magic in just a few days than people do in months, even years. You...you figured out that imposter in level two wasn't me and you had barely known me for three days. I can't think of any other person who knows a single thing about me. I am honored that I have gotten to spend this time with you. I only wish we had more."

A tear rolled down her cheek. "I killed someone."

"I know," he told her as his eyes tracked the tear over her skin and into the tub.

"The voice in my head has told me to do worse," she confided. "It's always telling me to harm someone no matter how much I beg it to stop."

He tilted his head. "And do you?"

"No," she whispered. "But it makes it easy to think anything good about myself is simply neutralizing all the darkness in my head. I've done nothing extraordinary—all of my energy goes toward trying to atone for the negative energy I put into the world every time the voice awakens."

He huffed a laugh. "That's not how things work, angel. Life is not measured in good or bad *thoughts*—it's how you treat the world around you despite them. All the people who only do good deeds because of what that might gain them in the afterlife are no better than those who indulge in a little sin every once in a while."

"Eric *died* because of me," she reminded him.

"He was trying to kill you," he deadpanned. "*That* is what I call neutralizing."

He continued lathering every inch of her skin until it was covered in suds. Cupping his hand into the water, he scooped it over her pebbled flesh to rinse away the soap.

"Blackwell?"

"Yes?" he murmured.

"Part of me wants to ask you more about my father. But

another part of me doesn't want to know what it's missing if I never get to meet him. I've never really thought about him this much before. My mother and sister were always enough," she told him.

Something in his eyes dulled a bit at her words. "Not asking is probably for the best, then."

She nodded. Then, "I'm sorry that I fell for Sinclair's tricks so easily. And for...getting jealous. I know I don't have a right to be, especially after I said we needed space. I don't own you."

His expression heated, and he stood, offering a hand to her to help her out of the tub. She took it.

"Is space still what you want?" he asked, roving his eyes from her crown to her toes as she dripped water onto the floor before him.

A shaky breath. "I shouldn't have a choice at this point."

"But since you do?" he implored.

"No. I don't want space," she breathed. "I want anything but space."

Their collision was earth-shattering.

36

CURSED

The entire front of Blackwell's ensemble became soaked with the bathwater that lingered on her skin as he gathered her body into his to deepen their kiss. This kiss was a little wilder, a little more desperate than any of the others had been. Without breaking it, he hauled her up into his arms, and she wound her legs around his hips like a vise. The tip of his tongue massaged hers with long languid strokes as he turned toward the vanity and placed her on the edge of the counter. Her hands twisted into his hair as his reached around to unhook her and push her knees apart. When he finally pulled away, she made a sound of disappointment, and he smiled.

Kissing the underside of her jaw, he assured, "I promise you'll prefer where my mouth is going next."

She whimpered with anticipation as he stepped back and undid the belt of his trousers with one hand, flicking open the button with his other. His eyes didn't leave her face as he liberated his cock from beneath its fabric cage and gave it a single pump with his fist. Her blood boiled with her need as he lowered himself to his knees in front of her, the counter she was sitting on the perfect height for his mouth to access the apex of her arousal.

Spreading her thighs wider with one hand while he continued to pump the other over his thick shaft, he leaned forward to taste her arousal, and she swore her moan of pleasure could probably be heard across the entire manor. He gave a pleased grunt as he lashed his tongue over her swollen clit and pumped his hardness to the same rhythm of his licks across her sex. It didn't take long for him to send her over the edge, and as the orgasm washed over her, she called out his name.

He stood and she grasped his shirt, pulling his mouth back to hers, loving the taste of herself on his tongue. He aligned the tip of his length with her entrance and wasted no time sheathing himself inside, swallowing her moans as he deepened their kiss once more. His thrusts were slow, deliberate. His hands were roaming over her body like he was trying to memorize the shape of her.

She broke their kiss, eyes half-lidded, mouth swollen, as she said, "Let me down."

He didn't hesitate, pulling out of her in an instant and stepping back to help her to the ground. Confusion flitted across his face at what her next move would be, but when she lowered herself to her knees, his expression turned positively feral with lust.

"Don't hold back," she told him before slowly licking her own arousal from his shaft, running her mouth from base to tip.

"If I don't hold back, I'm not going to fucking last," he groaned, a hand flying out to sink into her hair at the nape of her neck.

She had never taken the full length of him all the way down her throat, but now she was determined to try. Wrapping one of her hands at his base, she sucked the tip of him into her mouth, making his hips buck forward with a curse and sliding a few more inches between her lips. He used the hand in her hair to gently guide himself even deeper, and she took it greedily. She brought her unoccupied hand up to rest on his thigh for balance as she took him further and further, one inch at a time, until he hit the back of her throat.

"*Fuck*, angel," he panted. "Your mouth feels like fucking heaven."

She adored the way he always praised her when she did something he liked, the raspy little breaths that came out of his throat as he pumped into her mouth letting her know he was enjoying himself as much as she was. He made her feel safe to explore him without worry of judgment or fear.

As she sucked harder, keeping up with the steady rhythm he had set, his hand began to tighten in her hair, and she knew he was getting close.

"You're doing such a good job," he encouraged. "Eyes up for me, angel."

She flicked her gaze up to his face, holding his lust-filled stare as she moved her hands to the back of his thighs to take him as deep as possible for the last few strokes. He practically growled in satisfaction as he came harder than he ever had before with her.

She wiped the back of her hand across her mouth as he helped her rise, circling one arm around her waist while he reached around with the other to massage the back of her head where he had been tugging on her hair. She hummed in contentment as he pressed hot kisses over the base of her throat and behind her ear.

"If there were ever a divine entity I'd worship," he murmured, "it'd be you."

"My body, your altar," she offered.

He whispered her name—no, he didn't whisper it, he *invoked* it.

The bathroom disappeared as he transported them to the bedroom. He pinned her beneath him as he snapped away his clothes, and with a single thrust, he buried himself back inside of her. Their kisses turned sweet now, lingering, the connection between them strengthening with each thrust of his hips, each ragged breath. It was something that transcended the boundaries of the living and the dead. He wasn't a Phantom in this moment, nor she a mortal. And this was not a melding of their bodies, but their souls.

"Ophelia, I—"

He didn't get a chance to finish. Someone popped into the room, at the foot of the bed.

"I love a good show after dinner." Jasper laughed at the compromising sight of them, Poe lounging in his arms.

Ophelia was sure the cat threw her and Blackwell a look of judgment as she squeaked a sound of surprise and scrambled to cover herself. Her entire body flushed pink at being caught in such an intimate moment.

Blackwell used his magic to clothe them both before hopping off the bed to confront Jasper. "You're early."

"Am I?" Jasper asked ruefully, his tone suggesting that he knew precisely what he was doing.

"Early for what?" she asked, climbing off the bed to smooth out the delicate black gown Blackwell had dressed her in. It had ribbons and bows and little red roses embroidered around the hems.

"Lover Ghost, here, asked me to track down what happened to your parents," Jasper told her. "Made me an offer I couldn't refuse. I'm pleased to inform you both I got the intel you're looking for."

Ophelia gaped at Jasper in shock before swinging her gaze to Blackwell. "What did you offer for this?"

"Nothing important." He shook his head. "Don't worry about it."

"He's being modest." Jasper smiled, though it was not necessarily kind. "He gave up three years of his memories for this information. When you get back into bed, you should thank him nice and hard—"

"Shut it, Jasper." Blackwell glowered at the Devil before looking back to her. "You don't have to hear anything he found if you don't want to. Don't worry about what I paid for it—it's your choice."

They watched her as she cycled through an array of emotions. On the one hand, if her mother had wanted her to know her business, wouldn't she have told her herself? On the other...

"Is it bad?" she asked Jasper.

"Depends on your definition of *bad*," he said. "Must I keep reminding you that I'm a Devil, sweetheart? I doubt we have the same system of measurement for good and bad."

She took a deep breath. "Okay, what did you find?"

"Why don't we go somewhere else for this conversation? Somewhere that doesn't reek of flowers and sex," he suggested. Turning to Blackwell, he said, "The drinking parlor?"

Blackwell nodded, and Jasper disappeared, along with Poe. Blackwell turned to her, gently pinching her chin in his hand to angle her eyes up to meet his.

"Are you sure you want to know whatever he's found? You can still change your mind."

"I'm sure," she said.

He nodded in acceptance, kissing the bridge of her nose with affection before pulling her to him so he could transport them after Jasper.

"I hope you know we'll be finishing what that bastard interrupted, later," he promised.

"I'll hold you to that," she answered just before they blinked away.

⚜

Jasper hummed as he fixed himself and Blackwell a drink, Ophelia making herself comfortable on the couch next to Poe. Jasper held out a glass of the brown liquor to her in offering, and Blackwell's smirk was knowing as she made a face and politely refused.

"Alright, where do I start?" Jasper said as he stirred his glass.

"How about the beginning?" she suggested.

"That's no fun." Jasper shook his head. "How about, do you want the good news first or the bad news first?"

"Bad," she said without hesitation.

"Your parents fell in love during Phantasma," he said cheerily.

She made a face. "Then what the Hell is the good?"

"You were conceived here during that time." He raised his glass to her. "Isn't that neat? A first, I do believe."

"We absolutely do not have the same definitions of good and bad," she told him, aghast. "Explain to me the whole ordeal with people falling in love here. I don't get it."

Blackwell and Jasper exchanged a loaded glance. Then Blackwell revealed, "We aren't allowed to say. It has to do with the creator and—"

"That Salemaestrus person, right?" she interrupted. "Sinclair told me about him."

Blackwell reared back in shock and even Jasper's gaze darkened.

"What, exactly, did he tell you about...that person?" Jasper asked carefully.

"He's the Prince of the Devils, running this place as a punishment for choosing the person he loved over his father," she recited from memory. "I'm assuming that's why falling in love is so taboo, then? Because that's what got him in hot water in the first place?"

"Precisely," Jasper confirmed. "And since Sinclair told you that, I'm allowed to say that it isn't just *taboo*. It's...disastrous. Your mother and father fell in love within Phantasma's walls and, subsequently, they were cursed."

"Cursed, *how?*" She leaned forward, on the edge of her seat now.

"Rumor has it that the curse made your mother—Tessie, right?—become more apathetic toward your father with every passing day, but your father became more dangerously obsessive with her at the same time. They both forfeited the competition, according to a couple of the Devils who were here at the time. Then about two years after your mother gave birth to you, when she was pregnant with a second child, she made a bargain with a Devil in New Orleans by the name of Andrea. Andrea's side of the bargain was to make your father forget the three of you existed so that your mother could leave him. But the curse that Phantasma had inflicted on your parents unfortunately also affected the bargain your mother made with Andrea. Over time, the curse eroded Andrea's magic and your father began to remember. Curses are corrosive little suckers like that."

Ophelia stood and began to pace as Blackwell added, "I wonder if the gouged-out name carved into the floor was your mother's. If he did that during his second stay here. Out of resentment, perhaps?"

"Did you ever notice anything odd about him?" Ophelia questioned. "I know I said I didn't want to ask you what he was like but was he...like me? Did he have..."

"Not that I could tell." Blackwell shook his head, instantly picking up that she was referring to the Shadow Voice and that she did not wish to mention it in front of Jasper. "There were no visibly obvious mannerisms or tics like yours at least. But outside of searching the manor for my tether and competing in the levels, he didn't leave his room. He summoned me only in the direst of situations, and hardly ever bothered to ask me to clean up the haunts in his room."

"And he never mentioned my mom?" she questioned further.

Blackwell winced. "He did mention he had a wife, once, and that he was here to win the Devil's Grant to get her back, but he made it seem like she had died, not..."

"Gotten the equivalent of a magical restraining order against him?" She laughed, the sound a bit high-strung. "This is... unbelievable. And on top of everything I am eternally tied to this place because of them. I can't stand it."

No, I hate it.

Her pacing had become frantic. She felt like adrenaline had been injected directly into her veins. Blackwell was growing more concerned by the second, while Jasper grew bored.

"This is all my mother's fault," she whispered. "This is all her *fault*. If she had told us the truth from the beginning, I wouldn't have to be here! If she hadn't somehow racked up debt and then left us with it, Genevieve would have never come, and we'd still be at Grimm Manor."

"Ophelia." Blackwell took a step toward her, hands raised in front of him as if she were a scared animal and he didn't wish to spook her further. "It's going to be okay."

"*How?*" she bit at him. "How is any of what you just heard okay? Especially when you and I are apparently just repeating history!"

Her mouth clamped shut in shock. She hadn't meant to say that last part. Hadn't meant to imply...

Jasper's interest was suddenly reignited. "Well, this just became much more entertaining."

Blackwell turned to the Devil and commanded, "Leave. *Now*."

"No, stay." Ophelia backed up as she looked between the two men, panic setting in. "I'll go."

She raced for the exit before Blackwell could argue, and though she knew he could stop her if he really wanted, he didn't. She threw open the door, and before she realized what she was stepping into, she was falling.

She had summoned the Whispering Gate again.

37

WHISPERING GATE

Ophelia wasn't sure if she'd ever get used to the feeling of freefalling. Or the whispers. She tried to grasp to the conversations as she fell through the hopeless abyss, but every hushed conversation slipped past too quickly.

Then she heard the voice.

The same loud voice she'd heard the first time she fell through this never-ending darkness. She tried to pull herself toward it as if she were swimming through the air.

Ophelia.

Ophelia's heart thundered and she spurred herself toward it again, or at least what she thought was forward.

Ophelia.

"Mother?" she whispered into the dark.

Ophelia!

"Momma!" she cried, swimming faster, unable to see a single thing in front of her and then—

—a single glimpse of light. A twinkle in the distance, calling to her. She pushed and pushed until the light grew closer, slowly taking the shape of person as she approached.

The shape of her mother.

Ophelia, my darling.

Tessie Grimm was a radiant vision of light. A sob racked Ophelia's body as she took in her mother's face, *her* face, for the first time since seeing the woman in a casket.

Ophie, you shouldn't be here for too long. This place is not for you.

"I didn't mean to come here," Ophelia promised. "I keep accidentally summoning it."

What have you gotten yourself into, child?

Ophelia swallowed. She didn't know how much time she would be able to stay here. Better to rip the bandage off quickly.

"Genevieve and I, we entered…Phantasma."

If Tessie Grimm wasn't already dead, Ophelia was pretty sure she'd have dropped right then and there.

What? Did the two of you lose your damn minds since I've been gone?

"Yeah. We kind of did. You *left* us."

Not voluntarily.

"I know." She swallowed. "But you lied voluntarily. Why didn't you ever tell me about Phantasma? Or our father?"

All the anger that had been burning inside Ophelia since she found her mother's corpse in their living room suddenly vanished now that she was face to face with the woman again. For the first time in so long, she felt like a child standing there, not angry but disappointed at the realization that parents are fallible too. All her bravado of wanting to confront her mother and scream and yell and blame her for everything that had happened dissipated the moment she realized that seeing her again was nothing short of a gift, and that gift should not be wasted.

Because it was the biggest regret of my life, and I wanted you to avoid all the pain that came with it. Things with your father—they ended terribly. And that was our own fault. We knew better and fell for each other anyway. I tried to make it work afterward. I had you and then Genevieve in hopes to make him happy, but Gabriel…he became a danger. And I became numb. Her mother looked regretful now. *I can't tell you what to do, Ophelia. And if there's one thing that's always been certain—you are absolutely my daughter.*

Another sob threatened to erupt from her. "Yes. I am."

But, please, for me, be careful.

"I…" Ophelia began, but she knew whatever she was about to say would be a lie. The truth was, she hadn't been careful. She had come to Phantasma despite her better judgment. Not to mention her relationship with Blackwell…

You received your magic, her mother inserted when she was quiet for a little too long. *I knew you could do it.*

It wasn't *I'm proud of you,* but it was as close as her mother would ever get. And besides, Ophelia was proud of herself. And finding more and more that mattered to her above anything else.

Ophelia swallowed. "Yes, I got my magic. And you would hate what I've done with it."

Why don't you tell me?

So, Ophelia did. She told her mother about how they learned of Grimm Manor's debt and her and Genevieve's fight and running away to Phantasma. She explained how she found their parents' names carved in the floor of the hidden room and what she'd been through in every trial. She confessed that she killed Eric. And then there was Blackwell.

Her mother was quiet as Ophelia spoke, face blank. And if Ophelia thought Tessie would have a lot to say about every little mistake she'd made, she was surprised.

First, I want you to know that you must carve your own path in life, Ophie. Our family legacy meant a lot to me, yes, but it's your turn to make your own legacy. Do not live your life according to what you think would have pleased me. I was too hard on you, I think. I thought I was making you strong, but I see now that I put too much pressure on you and it was too heavy. Death brings so much clarity.

Ophelia felt like she had been waiting twenty-three years to hear those words from her mother, and now that they had been spoken, something that had been broken inside of her for so long began to mend.

Second, and this one is important, stay the Hell away from that Phantom.

Ophelia shook her head. "He hasn't hurt me. I swear. In fact, I'm only alive because of him. I'm worried about Genevieve."

You have no idea what you're up against, Ophelia. Loving him will only ruin you. Do you understand me?

Ophelia was taken aback. Love? No...she couldn't possibly love Blackwell. He was a Ghost. And they had only known each other for a week. They were partners, lovers even, yes. But she wasn't *in* love.

Oh, my darling. I'm begging you to stay away from him.

Ophelia swallowed. From experience, she knew she couldn't promise her mother such a thing. As long as she and Blackwell were in proximity with each other, they seemed to crash together. The locket around her throat began to beat. She looked down at it.

"Mother? Where did our family get this locket?"

I'm not sure. All I know is that my mother passed it to me, as hers did to her, and so on for generations of Grimm women. You mustn't ever take it off.

"Why?"

Before her mother could answer, the light around her began to flicker.

"What's happening?" Ophelia asked.

It's time for me to go now. Good luck, Ophelia. Tell Genevieve I love her.

"I will. But we'll meet again someday," Ophelia vowed.

Her mother smiled.

Not too soon, though, my darling. Live.

38

NIGHTMARE

This time when she crashed through the floor, it wasn't as much of a surprise. Landing directly into Blackwell's arms, however, *was*. Debris rained down from the ceiling of the dining room—the exact same place she had crashed before—causing her to sneeze and splutter.

"Hold on," Blackwell said, cradling her to his chest before transporting them both away to her room.

"Did you know I would land in the same place?" she asked, stunned.

"I made an educated guess," he told her as he set her on her feet. "Are you alright?"

"Um…yes?" she breathed. "Maybe?"

"You summoned the Whispering Gate again," he stated.

"Yes."

"What did you find?" he asked.

"I found…my mother." Ophelia's hand flew to her mouth in disbelief as this fully sank in.

Blackwell's expression gave nothing away. "She must have been waiting for you."

Ophelia's breath hitched. "What do you mean?"

"When souls or Devils are on the Other Side, they summon the Whispering Gate to be able to communicate with each other across the different linear planes. Because you are a Necromancer—and a Specter—your soul has always been tied between life and death. I'm guessing that is what gives you access to the gate—as long as there's a strong enough pull from someone there who wants to speak with you."

"Does that mean I could see her again?" she asked, hopeful. "If I ever found a way back?"

He shook his head. "That, I don't know."

Now, Ophelia looked down at her hands, unsure how to approach what she was about to say next. "I told her everything. About Phantasma and my fight with Genevieve and about... us." She looked up at him now. "She was pretty adamant that we stay away from each other. I'm sure she fears the same fate for me that she and my father faced."

Blackwell was unfazed. As if he had been expecting this. "She's right."

Her heart dropped, and she stepped closer, lightly gripping the lapels of his overcoat. "I know I panicked after what I said in the drinking parlor. About repeating history. But I'm my own person. We won't have the same fate—"

"You're right, we won't," he said, tone solemn as he gripped her wrists and gently pried her hands from his coat. "When Jasper revealed what happened to your parents, when you said we were repeating history, I realized you were right in asking for space. There can be no 'we.' We've been flirting with danger a little too much. It's my turn to try and be the responsible one."

She narrowed her eyes. "After Jasper interrupted us, *you* are the one who said we'd be finishing what we started later."

He closed his eyes. "I changed my mind. This game is too dangerous to keep playing."

I changed my mind.

Those words cut through her like a blade.

Not even the dead want you. The Shadow Voice laughed.

"Think of us as"—he winced at what he was about to say—"business partners. If I wasn't as selfish as I am, I would tell you to leave Phantasma altogether, but I still need you to set me free."

"Business partners," she parroted, her tone numb.

"Yes." He swallowed. "I once warned you that beings in Phantasma wouldn't have good intentions or motives...we look out for ourselves first and foremost. I need to look out for myself before we run out of time and I fail this quest yet again."

"Excuse me for thinking that maybe all the times you were in my bed—my *body*—would make you regard me differently despite what you said then. We tried the space thing. It didn't work. Because we find each other, remember? That's what you said."

His eyes were missing their usual wicked spark as he stated, "I can't, angel. And you should understand that, because failing this quest would mean I have to take a decade of your life away. And I don't *want* to have to do that—I really don't—but I *will*. You need to remember that."

Her lip curled in utter disdain as her pride took the brunt of the blow his words just landed. "You're just as much of a bastard as Sinclair. The two of you hate each other, but you're no different. Selfish, egotistical. I've never once suggested that you needed to *care* for me—or that I cared for you any deeper than I would a friend. But I thought you respected me enough to at least refrain from reminding me—as if I were a naïve child—that I stand to lose ten years of my life to you. I promise I'm well aware of the stakes between us."

"A friend?" He lifted a brow. "Do you fuck all your friends like you've fucked me? But you're right—a child you are not. Naïve, however..."

"Go to fucking Hell," she spat.

His smile was tight. "Are we not already here, angel?"

"Don't ever, *ever*, call me that again," she ordered. "You want to be *business partners?* Fine. But we are going to keep this strictly professional. You can call me Miss Grimm from here on out."

"And you, Miss Grimm," he said, "can call me only when it's absolutely necessary to do so."

"Probably not even, then." She glared at him. "Feel free to go now."

Without another word, or even a semblance of regret, he vanished.

She curled up beneath her covers, desperate for the sweet nothing of unconsciousness. When she finally fell asleep, however, she didn't find peace.

The nightmare had always been the same.

Ophelia was standing in the large, open den of Grimm Manor. In front of her stood three faceless suitors while her mother and Genevieve stood off to the side. Looming behind her was the Shadow Voice, no longer a figment of her imagination but a smoky entity made of writhing, ebony-colored wisps. Shadowy tendrils were wrapped around her wrists and throat, like she was a macabre marionette, the Shadow Voice her puppeteer.

"Why would I want her?" the first suitor said. "She can't even control herself. And I'm not living with that thing in my house."

"Imagine having to share a bed with such a freak," the next one snickered. "And not the good kind."

"Too high maintenance," the last one agreed. "If she were normal, she wouldn't be so hard to look at, though, I suppose. If she broke free of that creature, I would take her into consideration..."

Her mother sighed in disappointment and exchanged a loaded look with her sister. "I guess she'll have to continue being our burden."

I don't want to be a burden, she tried to scream, but the Shadow Voice tightened its hold on her throat.

Hush, girl, it said. **We won't let them treat you like this.**

A knife suddenly appeared in her hand.

If they cannot live with both of us, they must perish.

"What? No!"

Kill them.

"No! I won't."

You don't have a choice, you belong to me. The tendrils around her wrist tightened and yanked her forward. **Make them pay.**

She approached the first suitor and watched in horror as the Shadow Voice manipulated her limbs and made her plunge the knife into his heart. Blood splattered across her face as the faceless person slumped to their knees.

The Shadow Voice cackled. **Next. Slit their throat.**

She reached up and dragged the sharp point of the blade across the second suitor's throat, blood pouring to the ground as they joined the first suitor on the floor. By the time she turned to the third suitor, they were cowering, pleading for their life. The Shadow Voice only became more amused.

Cut out this one's heart, the Shadow Voice demanded.

So, she did. She let the beating organ fall to the ground with a sickly splat.

Now, we take care of them. The Shadow Voice turned her toward her mother and sister.

This is when she dug her heels in. "No."

Yes, it hissed. **They think you're a burden. They don't want you around. Get rid of them.**

"No!" she screamed as her feet moved forward involuntarily. Her mother and sister, clung to each other in fear, looking at her as if she were a complete stranger. A monster.

She cried as she tried to resist the shadowy restraints lifting her *hand, preparing her weapon. As she brought it down, a shriek ripped from her throat and—*

She jolted awake. Chest heaving, the locket around her throat was hot to the touch, pulsing steadily. She glanced around to see what had awoken her from the nightmare, but there was nothing except the feeling of familiar static lingering in the air.

NIGHT SEVEN
OF PHANTASMA

39

SOMETHING FORBIDDEN

There was a hopeless feeling deep inside Ophelia's bones. After a restless night, she spent the entirety of the next morning tearing through every room she had access to in this wing of the manor. But there wasn't a single thing that she thought might be Blackwell's key.

She suspected that the object they were looking for was either in a part of Phantasma she could not reach, or lost forevermore.

Why else would no one have found it yet? she reasoned. *Why else would he not have found it yet?*

They had both known it from the start, but now that time was running out, it was really starting to sink in for Ophelia: she had made a very risky gamble, and she was going to lose. The only option she had left was to win the competition and ask for her debt to be forgiven. Which meant all of this was truly for naught. She and Genevieve would still lose Grimm Manor. They'd be exactly where they started—just with a little extra trauma.

She was so numb as she padded her way down the hall, back to her room, that when Sinclair appeared next to her, she barely acknowledged him.

"I see you're beginning to realize the gravity of your situation," Sinclair mocked. "Have you reached the point of reconsidering my offer yet?"

"No."

"Then perhaps I just need to wait you out a few more hours,

hmm? You'd really rather give up a decade to him than make one tiny little bargain with me?" Sinclair pressed. "If all of you mortals stopped giving him the years of your own lives to sustain him, maybe he'd fade away and be unable to do this to further victims."

Ophelia glanced at the Devil to her left with apathy. "I will not be taking on the responsibility of whether or not he makes deals with others in the future. He doesn't force anyone into a bargain, and he doesn't *want* everyone to keep failing."

She wasn't sure why she felt the burning need to defend Blackwell—she was still furious with him after all—but it made her blood boil that Sinclair had the audacity to say a single disparaging thing about her Phantom considering the Devil's own warped sense of morals.

Sinclair looked at her as if he thought she were pathetic. "You *do* care for him. Jasper said as much."

"Devils are shameless gossips," she muttered without acknowledging his statement.

"Mortals are pitiful romantics," he countered. "Falling in love no matter the cost."

"I didn't fall in *love*," she gritted out, a fire beginning to ignite in her belly. "I wish everyone would stop assuming things they know nothing about."

"It was just mindless pleasure, then? A *distraction?*" Sinclair's lips curled up in a taunting grin.

Her own lips curled with disdain. "How much did you watch us?"

"Enough." Sinclair slid in front of her, halting her steps. "Enough to know you're lying to yourself about your feelings as some sort of last ditch resort to spare yourself from the inevitable pain to come."

"I'm not," she insisted, but even she could hear the shaky

conviction in her voice. "It's been *seven days*,"—she swallowed—
"and he's been an absolute nuisance for most of them."

Sinclair laughed. "Except when he's making you scream his
name, right?"

Yes, she thought, her teeth grinding together. *Except when he's
making grand speeches about every little thing he admires about me, or
making the voice in my head shut up, or giving me the sort of unearthly
pleasure that makes me see stars.*

Sinclair reached out and dragged his index finger along her
clenched jaw and beneath her chin, tilting her face up to look
directly into his. "But if you insist it was just a distraction—
prove it. Let *me* distract you. I guarantee I can do it better."

"Never," she whispered.

He laughed. "Why? Because I'm a Devil?"

"Amongst other things."

"You aren't even a little curious?" The slit in the center of his
eyes widened, black swallowing his ruby-colored irises. "About
what I can give you that *he* can't?"

She swallowed. Truthfully, she *was* curious, but probably not
for the reasons he assumed.

And as if he saw that very thought in her eyes, he laughed.

"That's right," he purred. "Just say the word, sweetheart. If
you don't ask me to touch you, I won't."

She hardened her heart to what she was about to do. "Kiss
me. Touch me."

Wicked laughter rumbled in Sinclair's chest as he granted her
request, bringing her lips to his and sweeping his tongue over
hers with a confidence that made her feel utterly unprepared for
what she had asked for. He wasn't tender or gentle. His movements were sharp, his body hard, as he pressed her back into the
wall and roamed a hand down over her side, to her hip, to the
back of her knee, lifting her leg up to hook around him.

Though there was lust in their kiss, there was absolutely no heat. Her stomach did not flutter, her skin did not flush with anticipation. And though she could feel herself become wet between her legs, it was simply from the motions of the act itself, a biologically driven reaction. Not a passionate one.

His hand began to move between them, and he pulled back just enough to ask, "May I?"

"Yes," she answered. Clear. Short.

"You can command me to stop any time," he told her sincerely. "I do not ever take anything that isn't freely given—as is the nature of Devils and our bargains. Do you understand?"

A single nod.

"No," he told her. "I want to hear you verbalize it. Do you understand that you can tell me to stop, and I will?"

"Yes," she confirmed.

Without another word, he kissed her again and pulled up the side of her skirt to slip his hand beneath them, pushing two fingers inside of her when he reached her core. Curling them forward with a beckoning motion to hit that sensitive spot deep within her, he used the pad of his thumb to rub her clit at the same time. Her body barely reacted, the pleasure so much less intense than it had been with Blackwell.

Blackwell, who made her whimper and writhe with ecstasy, who made her blood boil and often had her ready to beg for more despite her vow to never do so.

With Sinclair, it felt like her senses had been dulled.

She broke the kiss, grimacing as she flattened her palms against the Devil's chest to push him away. He removed himself from her in an instant, dropping her leg and transporting himself several feet away.

"No. I can't, it's not right." She shook her head. "*You're* not right."

"Oh, it didn't look all that bad from here," a sultry, feminine voice said from the right.

Ophelia whipped her head to find Rayea leaning a hip against the wall, watching them. Sinclair gave the other Devil a languid smile in greeting.

"Then *you* have him," Ophelia spat as she straightened her skirts to leave.

"Been there, done that," Rayea remarked. "You're missing a good time. But I understand. Blackwell just has something about him, doesn't he? Those eyes, that mouth, that *tongue*—"

"I'm not going to let you get under my skin," Ophelia told her.

"Oh, sweetheart, you don't have to let me do anything." Rayea laughed. "I think I'm already there. I'll be sure to let Blackwell know you've moved on perfectly well next time I see him. Make sure I'm there to...comfort him."

With a wink, Rayea disappeared, leaving her alone with Sinclair once more.

"Have a good rest of your night, darling," Sinclair drawled.

Ophelia ran back to her room. She slammed the door shut behind her and slid down its frame to the floor as a deep sense of dread shattered through her. Something had taken root in her heart, something forbidden, without her realization. And now it was too intertwined with her very being to cut it out. Her heart had finally grown teeth of its own, and it was ready to tear itself to shreds if the time came.

LEVEL
SIX

40

DECEIT

Ophelia had a proper meal that night. Partly because her anxiousness had not allowed her to eat nearly enough during the past week of the competition, and partly because when she made it to the dining room, it was empty aside from Charlotte, who ignored her, per usual. She really hoped Charlotte survived, if only because the world needed more people who minded their own damn business and weren't afraid to speak up when needed.

By the time the newest Devil showed up to start the level, everyone else had trickled in to pick at the spread on the table as well. Not a single contestant in the room looked well-rested. The exhaustion was palpable, the bruises beneath everyone's eyes telling of their haunted, sleepless nights. Even Cade looked as if he had lost some of his fight. Though they all still gave the man a wide berth.

The Devil grinned at the seven of them with delight. She was the shortest Devil so far, her crown barely reaching Ophelia's shoulder. With voluminous, natural curls and deep brown complexion, her Devil's Mark stood out—a delicate, swirling, gold pattern that climbed and twisted over every inch of her skin. Like she had been tattooed by pure gold ink.

The Devil addressed them. "Welcome to level six, and congratulations for making it past the halfway point. My name is Phoebe."

Phoebe summoned the portal, and they went through the all-too-familiar song and dance of waiting for their clue.

A TRIAL OF SECRETS, WHERE BLOOD REVEALS THE PRICE,
TRUE OR FALSE, MAKE SURE YOUR CHOICE IS WISE.

A CRUSHING TRUTH, SEALED BY UNCERTAIN FATES,
FALSE TALES WON'T HELP, FOR YOUR BLOOD KNOWS THE STAKES.

Then the names were called. The routine would almost have been monotonous if not for the unknown terrors waiting on the other side. Cade, Leon, and *Baker*—the final contestant whose name she hadn't been able to remember—all went through. Luci flicked a glance to Ophelia in anticipation.

"Let's get this over with," Ophelia muttered when it was her turn.

As usual, it took a moment for the new setting to resolve around her, and she soon found herself seated at a round table, each of her wrists shackled to its top. Without hesitation, she used her Specter abilities to slip out of the cuffs, receiving a few muttered insults from others around the table, unhappy that she had such an advantage.

Before each of them was a set of buttons. Ophelia had two: one labeled *true*, the other *false*, as did Leon, Baker, and Cade. Luci, Charlotte, and Beau had three buttons. Luci's and Charlotte's were labeled *true*, *false*, and *skip*. Beau's, however, were labeled *true*, *false*, and *random*.

The levers from level four, Ophelia realized. Any advantages and disadvantages had carried over into this level, and she was eternally thankful that she had managed to neutralize her own levers before exiting that bloodbath. Cade had clearly managed to neutralize his own, too, after she'd exited.

The other details in front of them weren't as clear. The center of the table was inset with a pool of ominous black liquid and seven indented trenches jutted out from around the pool and stretched all the way to each person's right hand. Ophelia leaned forward to see that there was a small, needle-like spike at the end of the trench. A prick for their fingers.

A TRIAL OF SECRETS, WHERE BLOOD REVEALS THE PRICE...

"This is almost more ominous than the sea of lava," Leon whispered from where he sat directly on Ophelia's left. Baker was to her right and beyond that Charlotte, Cade, Luci, and finally, Beau.

A scraping noise echoed from the ceiling, and they all snapped their heads back to watch as seven square pillars of stone dropped down, one looming above each contestant, stopping about ten feet above their heads. Then Ophelia's dropped a foot lower than the rest.

Adrenaline shot through her veins, not knowing what to anticipate in this trial, and for a split second, she considered summoning Blackwell. She immediately extinguished that instinct, however. She could do this on her own—despite the fact that she had no doubt he was watching the show from the Other Side.

"What do we do?" Luci asked as the silence between them stretched on uncomfortably.

Ophelia looked back to the pillar above her. Lower than the rest. Did that mean...

"I go first, I think," she announced. She glanced back to the spike near her right hand.

Here goes nothing.

She pressed the pad of her thumb to the prick, swallowing the pinch of pain as it drew her blood, the drops streaming down the trench and rolling into the black pool of liquid. A cloudy swirl of crimson slithered through the pool before forming itself into letters atop the ebony surface.

She squinted as she read the words aloud. "Ophelia Grimm... kissed a Devil."

She paled as everyone gaped at her, scandalized. Everyone except Cade, who looked positively delighted.

"Look at her face," Cade sneered. "No doubt in my mind that Demon whore keeps Devils in her bed."

He didn't hesitate to press the *true* button in front of him, and it stayed flattened against the table. Beau went to follow his lead, but his *true* button refused to go down.

"What the Hell," he grunted, frustrated.

"You can only pick *random*," Luci pointed out.

"What the fuck?" he snarled.

"Someone sabotaged you," Charlotte said, not bothering to cover her amusement at the situation.

Beau bared his teeth at them as he reluctantly punched down the *random* button. They all watched in anticipation as the *true* button finally sank down. Beau sighed in relief.

The others hesitated to input their own answers, staring at Ophelia, trying to read her face. Luci bit her lip as her hand reached out to hover over her *false* button.

"*Don't,*" she rushed out before Luci could press it. "It's true."

Luci balked a bit. Charlotte, Baker, and Leon instantly pressed their *true* buttons, Luci the last to enter her answer.

"Told you," Cade boasted.

She gave him a vulgar gesture with her hand, but before he could respond, the pillar above her head groaned as it sank back into the ceiling to align itself with the others. Then it was Baker's pillar that lowered, indicating it was his turn, as the buttons reset themselves.

"Alright, simple enough," Leon declared. "If we all help

each other, we should be able to make it out without a problem. Agreed?"

They all nodded, including Cade, but Ophelia didn't trust him for a second. He gave her a feral grin as Baker offered up his blood next.

"Baker Broussard is colorblind," Baker read to them.

"Are you kidding me?" Ophelia grumbled, and at the same time Cade commented, "*Boring.*"

Baker furrowed his brow. "I'm not colorblind."

They all reached for their false buttons, but Leon exclaimed, "*Wait.* Baker—what color is Ophelia's dress?"

Ophelia looked down at herself. Her dress was very obviously red.

"Red," Baker answered.

"And what about Luci's?" Leon pressed on.

They all shifted their gazes to Luci, whose dress was a sunny yellow. Baker hesitated now.

"A light coral color," he finally answered.

"Are you stupid?" Cade glared at Baker.

"No, he's colorblind," Leon said. "I remember once, at dinner, you said something about how it was strange that there were pink apples here—except the apples in question were very much yellow. You're yellow-blue colorblind."

"How the Hell have you gone your whole life without realizing that?" Beau said.

Baker began, a gamut of emotions running over his face. "Before I came here, about two months ago, I had a bad accident. I fell two stories from a ladder and hit my head. The doctor said I was lucky I didn't die and that there could be long-lasting side effects. I didn't realize losing certain colors was one of them."

They all hit their true buttons—including Beau, whose suddenly worked.

Interesting, Ophelia noted.

The pillars above them reset. Charlotte was next. She pricked her finger and waited for the statement.

"Charlotte Williams is a..." she began.

"A *what?*" Beau asked, impatient.

Charlotte sputtered a bit. "A *twin?*"

"You mean you don't know?" Leon prompted.

"I don't have any siblings," Charlotte revealed.

"That you know of—that would be the twist, right?" Baker suggested. "I didn't realize I was colorblind until now."

Luci reached out and hit her skip button. Charlotte followed suit, which did not bode well for the rest of them.

"You've got to be kidding me," Cade growled. "How the fuck are we supposed to guess when you're unsure yourself?"

Ophelia took a deep breath and reached her hand over to her *true* button. Her locket warmed and she paused.

What if...

She moved her palm to hover over the *false* button. The locket went cold. She smiled as she pressed *true*.

Leon and Baker eyed her answer, the smile on her face, and decided to take the same leap of faith. After a moment, Cade begrudgingly copied, but Beau found that he once again could only press his *random* button.

"The disadvantage must alternate rounds," Leon pointed out to Beau.

Fortunately for Beau—or unfortunately, depending on which answer was actually correct—the random option once again picked *true*. Everyone's buttons reset—except for Luci's and Charlotte's *skip* buttons. It looked like their advantage was one and done.

Now it was Cade's turn, and he looked all too happy about

it. Ophelia shifted to the edge of her seat as she waited for his revelation.

"Cade Arceneaux killed his sister's husband," he read, his tone remaining even despite the slanderous statement.

Luci made a face, which Leon quickly locked in on.

"I suppose we should start by asking if her husband is dead?" Leon deferred to Luci. "Because I think we all know *he* is plenty capable of murder."

"Her husband died last year in a motorcar crash," Luci confirmed. "Cade and Lainie *were* both in the vehicle, but I know without a doubt that Lainie was driving."

"Correct," Cade corroborated. "Her husband was on the passenger side—the side that hit the tree. I was in the back. I had nothing to do with it." He smiled.

Ophelia narrowed her eyes.

"I don't believe him," Baker declared, hitting his *true* button.

Luci cringed at the hasty reaction, and Ophelia had a feeling they were going to finally find out the consequence of answering incorrectly.

"Me either," Charlotte muttered.

"I believe Luci," Leon insisted. "If she says she knows, without a doubt, then it's true."

"The asshole is probably hoping none of us believe him, so we all choose wrong," Ophelia added.

Baker paled a bit as he watched them all hit *false*. He tried to switch his answer, but it was too late. They glanced around at each other in anticipation, Cade's smile never budging, and for a long, tense, moment nothing happened at all.

Then the pillar above Baker slammed down to the ground, crushing him to smithereens and splattering blood across the room.

41

THE DEVASTATION

The scent of blood and vomit filled the room as Leon, Charlotte, Luci, and Beau retched in tandem at the gruesome tragedy that had unfolded before them. Ophelia's own stomach was churning at the feeling of Baker's blood smeared over her face. She used the skirt of her dress to wipe her skin clean while everyone else tried to compose themselves.

"No, no, no," Luci cried, whimpering. "This is a nightmare."

Charlotte began to yank at her chains, equally as desperate to leave. "Fucking *Hell.*"

Even Cade looked sobered, his posture painfully rigid as he gawked at the gut-stained pillar that was still atop of Baker's destroyed corpse. Ophelia hoped the heavy stone wouldn't move and reveal more of the gruesome sight beneath.

"Luci, it's your turn," Ophelia encouraged, trying to rally them forward so they didn't have to be here a second longer than necessary.

Luci was still gagging as she submitted her blood to the pool.

"Luci Veil is in love with Leon Summers." Luci went white with terror.

Ophelia winced for the poor girl. This level was devastating.

Leon cleared his throat. "That's false."

Luci still didn't speak, and Ophelia instantly knew the correct answer.

"That's...that's false, isn't it?" Leon pressed.

"It's true," Ophelia spoke for Luci. "Answer and let's move on."

Leon's expression turned pained. "Luci, *no*. It's against the rules to fall in love here. It's—"

"*Press your fucking button*," Cade commanded.

Leon pressed *true*. Luci began to cry.

This is utterly delightful. The Shadow Voice laughed, and Ophelia immediately shoved it back out of her mind.

Meanwhile, Beau had to choose *random* once again, and they all watched with bated breath. When his *false* button sank down, the shrieking began. Beau's was hysterical, his desperation a torture to listen to, and Ophelia plugged her ears as best she could.

Beau soiled himself as he begged and keened to be let out, trying to form the words to summon the Devil for a bargain—but he couldn't quite get them out and it was much too late. Ophelia closed her eyes as the stone came down and crushed him. And when she reopened them, even Cade—*Cade*—was sobbing in horror. The game skipped right to Leon's turn.

"Go." Ophelia nudged Leon. "Please, for Hell's sake, end this now."

Leon's hand shook as he pressed his thumb to the spike in front of him. When his message was revealed, he began to cry as well.

"Leon Summers is not in love with Luci Veil," he choked out.

They all hit *true*.

Never has anyone left a room faster than Ophelia when the exit appeared, everyone else clamoring to do the same as soon as their shackles released them.

The five of them piled back into the dining room.

Five, she thought. *Hell*.

A series of things happened all at once then. First, Cade fainted, dropping to the floor like a sack of potatoes. But none of them paid him any mind. No, they were all too focused on whatever was happening to Luci. She had begun to convulse. Her skin flushing red as she crashed forward into the still-set table, sending platters of food and crystal glasses clattering to the ground.

"What do we do?" Leon asked, panicked.

Ophelia shook her head, at a total loss. "It's Phantasma's curse. Whatever magic is affecting her...it's powerful."

Eventually, Luci's fit dissipated. None of them moved while she caught her breath, heaving as she tried to straighten herself up. Leon took a tentative step forward.

"Luci?" he whispered.

She looked at him with devastation. He stepped closer, reaching out to grab her hand—

—and howled in agony as soon as their skin made contact.

"No," Luci cried. "*No. No. No.* This can't be happening."

Ophelia froze and Charlotte slowly backed away from the scene.

Leon looked appalled as he said, "What have you done, Luci?"

That made Ophelia's blood boil.

"What has *she* done?" Ophelia demanded. "You're just as much to blame! Unless she fell in love with a brick wall, I'm sure you fed into this relationship just as much as she did!"

"We had a deal," Leon began. "We'd stop seeing each other as soon as we developed deeper feelings."

Ophelia flinched, then looked away. "It doesn't seem that it worked." And she knew all too well what that was like. "But it's done now."

"I want to go home," Luci sobbed. "I'm done. I'm *done*."

"Luci, *don't*," Leon pleaded. "We're so close. We're—"

"You don't love me," Luci whispered, and Ophelia's heart

ached at the devastation on the girl's face. "And I cannot bear being here a second longer. I, Lucinda Veil, surrender to Phantasma."

Within seconds, the Devil, Phoebe, appeared.

"Time to go," Phoebe stated as she took Luci by the shoulder.

Leon tried to grab Luci before she was transported away, but for the second time, her touch burned him, and he had to let her go. Leon plunged his hands into his hair, pulling the strands in distress. His knees hit the ground as Luci and the Devil blinked from the room.

Ophelia turned to see if Charlotte had stuck around, but she was nowhere to be seen and Cade was still unconscious on the floor.

How is this possibly my problem? she wondered as she placed a hand on the boy's shoulder.

"Listen—" she started, but he shook her hand off him.

"Just leave me alone," he told her, tone numb.

She hesitated, but when his body began to shake with his silent cries, she slipped out of the room without another word.

Ophelia wandered around the manor, aimlessly, until well into the witching hours. She knew tonight there would be no sleeping—at least, none that didn't involve nightmares—and so she distracted herself with more searching. At some point, Poe stumbled across her and decided to tag along, and Ophelia had to admit it was nice to have a companion while she worked on such a tedious task.

When she was certain she had checked nearly every nook and cranny, twice, she finally gave in and headed back to her room with Poe cradled in her arms. Arriving back in her room, she expected to find a haunt in progress, or at least the remnants of one that Blackwell hadn't been around to clean up. What she did not expect was Blackwell himself, waiting in her armchair, his body rigid with barely concealed fury.

"Oh," she said, dropping Poe to the ground in surprise. The feline landed nimbly on his feet, skittering back out of the room before she could shut the door.

"What are you doing here?" she asked, wary.

Blackwell stood, and somehow, she thought he took up more space than he usually did. Waving his hand in the air between them, the few tapered candles she had spread around the room ignited.

"You let him kiss you." He looked devastated.

For a moment, his words didn't compute in her brain. So much had happened in the last few hours that she had completely wiped from her mind the lapse of judgment she'd had with Sinclair.

"Do we really need to have this conversation?" she asked. "Which one of them told you?"

"Rayea got to me first. But, rest assured, Sinclair didn't pass up the opportunity to taunt me with all the salacious details." His green eyes darkened. "You let him *touch* you."

Now she was angry. "*And?* We're only *business partners*, remember? Who I do and don't let touch me is, therefore, none of your concern."

He closed the distance between them in two strides, bringing his hand up to rest against the door at her back. "As long as our oath is intact, *you* are my concern. When you put yourself in imminent danger, I'm forced to step in."

"I was not in imminent danger," she scoffed. "He told me he would stop as soon as I wanted him to—and he did."

"Which is the only reason he still exists," Blackwell snarled.

She gave a humorless laugh. "Oh, this is *rich*. You know, the hot and cold thing is really wearing thin. *You* made the decision to stop flirting with danger. I, however, made no such decision. I will do as I please."

"Not with him. He will never touch you again."

"And why not?" she exclaimed, chest heaving with her anger. "*You* won't be touching me ever again, so why can't someone else?"

The muscles in his cheeks contracted as he clenched his jaw, and she had a feeling if he were mortal, his teeth would have shattered. They stood there, staring at each other, the tension between them thick enough to cut with a knife.

"I can't stand it," he told her, his voice deepening as he fought for control of his emotions. "I can't fucking *stand* the thought of him—of anyone—pleasuring you except me. I'd rather cease to exist than know you've looked at anyone else the way you look at me when I'm touching you."

All the fight drained from her at the rawness laced in those words.

"Why?" she whispered. "*Why* are you doing this to me? This is *torture*, Blackwell. Worse than anything that Phantasma has put me through!"

"God fucking damn it, I don't *know*." His eyes fluttered closed as he searched for the words. "I know this is a dangerous path. I know I should have enough self-control to just stay the fuck away, but you are the only thing that's ever made me feel even a semblance of hope in this eternity of Hell. The dream I've been looking for—the one to wake me up. The thought of wasting another second when I will lose you forever in only three days has *ruined* me. You are the closest thing I will ever get to experiencing heaven, and I'm not ready to let it go."

"Blackwell," she pleaded. "I just watched Luci get cursed because she fell for someone in this godforsaken place. We *can't*.

This back and forth . . . we have to stop. I can't take it. It's tearing me apart."

"I know." He opened his eyes, and she almost sobbed at the devastation she saw in them. "I know. I'll go."

He made to step away from her, and she rushed forward to grasp the front of his shirt before he disappeared.

"I need you to know that you are the only person who has ever made me feel like I am capable of anything," she lamented. "The only person who has ever made me feel truly *seen*." She swallowed. "Sinclair's touch meant absolutely *nothing*. That's why I let it happen."

Her knees almost buckled at the look in his eyes. She wanted to beg the Devils, the Angels, the universe, to let her keep him for just a bit longer.

"But *your* touch?" Her voice broke now. "Your touch means fucking *everything*. And that's why we can't cross that line again."

He grasped her face in his hands.

"In a different life, in a fair one, I would've kept you until my eternal soul withered away to dust," he vowed to her.

Then he was gone.

NIGHT EIGHT OF
PHANTASMA

42

SORROW

Ophelia stayed in bed until the sorrow in her soul ebbed and the dinner bell chimed.

LEVEL SEVEN

43

VIOLENCE

Peeling herself from beneath the covers, Ophelia dressed for the trial ahead. Not just any trial—the one that would mark her official release from this sole wing of Phantasma and allow her to look for Genevieve.

It was the only thing that got her out of bed, truthfully.

When she made it to the dining room, Charlotte and Cade were already there, waiting in stone-cold silence. Leon, however, was nowhere to be seen.

"He forfeited," Charlotte answered her unspoken question.

Ophelia's brows rose. "Did you see it happen?"

Charlotte nodded. "Late last night I heard a scream in the corridor outside our rooms—his was two doors down from mine. When I went to see what was going on, he was being swarmed by a thousand crows. I'm pretty sure he lost an eye during the ordeal. I never realized how gruesome birds could be." Charlotte shrugged. "He forfeited in minutes. I think the crows may have been his greatest fear—the one he gave up entering."

"Birds? He was chased away by fucking *birds?*" Cade said. "That little pissant got Luci *cursed*, and he couldn't handle some fucking crows?"

"You can't always help what you fear," Charlotte reasoned. "I met my greatest fear the fourth day here. I nearly gave up then, too."

"Yet you're still here," Cade shot back. "I'm going to make that bastard's life miserable the moment I get out of here. He'll be lucky if I don't drown him in the river and leave his body for the gators."

Charlotte and Ophelia didn't respond. Charlotte because she most likely didn't want to hear any more from Cade, or in shock that the man was showing care for someone beyond himself for the first time. By the way he'd spoken to Luci, no one could have ever guessed he'd feel the need to defend her honor. But Ophelia was distracted by something else entirely. It had suddenly dawned on her that Phantasma hadn't thrown her greatest fear at her yet. A foreboding omen to say the least.

The three of them—the finale of their group—waited out the rest of dinner in silence. Ophelia was watching the clock, waiting for the Devil to appear, when Blackwell blinked in beside her in his ghostly form.

"Hey," she whispered to him, locket pulsing at his unexpected appearance.

Charlotte threw her a look of confusion, while Cade narrowed his eyes.

"Don't respond," Blackwell told her when he spotted the way Cade was watching her. "When you get into this level, make sure you summon me, alright?"

She dipped her chin in a subtle nod.

"Good girl," he murmured. "The way this level works—it's absolutely vital that I can be there to give you intel at the start."

Another nod from her and he vanished.

Two minutes later, the Devil arrived. Tall and slender, they had a medium-brown complexion and straight brown hair—and smooth skin where their eye sockets should be. Embedded in the backs of their hands were their eyeballs. The strangest Devil's Mark Ophelia had seen yet.

This Devil didn't bother with an introduction as they revealed the portal and their clue.

A CHOICE OF TWO TOKENS, A DECISION TO MAKE,
IF ALL ONLY TAKE ONE, NOTHING IS AT STAKE.

IF TWO CHOOSE ONE, AND THE THIRD TAKES ALL,
THE THIRD WILL WALK, THE OTHERS WILL BRAWL.

IF TWO CHOOSE ALL, AND THE THIRD TAKES ONE,
THE THIRD WILL BE FREE, THE OTHER TWO ARE DONE.

Cade was called through first. Then Charlotte. And finally Ophelia.

As promised, Ophelia didn't waste a second summoning Blackwell.

"Alright," Blackwell began without preamble, "I'm going to have to go back to the Other Side in order to see what they are choosing. Don't touch a single token until I return."

"Will I need to summon you again?" she wondered.

He shook his head. "Now that I've been here, I should be able to come at will, but if I'm not back in five minutes, call just in case."

She nodded and he blinked away.

The holding room she was in looked identical to the one she started in for level five. Only, instead of two handles in the small alcove carved into the wall, it was two round tokens made of obsidian. Their surfaces were embossed with what looked to be roses on either side, and though she had the urge to reach out and smooth her fingers over the textured surface, she resisted, heeding Blackwell's warning not to touch.

She kept track of the time in her head as she waited for Blackwell to return and had got to seven minutes and forty-two seconds when he popped back in.

"Alright, there's a dilemma," he told her. "Charlotte took one token—Cade took both."

Ophelia went through the lines of the clue they'd been given, carefully, in her head. Unlike the vagueness of the other trials, the clue for this level had been glaringly straight forward. An intentional warning. Or rather, a threat.

She swallowed. "So that means—"

"Pick your poison," he murmured. "Cade or—"

"Cade," she inserted immediately. "Charlotte can walk free. But he's not getting out of here."

Blackwell smirked. "Have I ever told you how much I adore a woman who isn't afraid to get her hands bloody?"

Ophelia ignored the way his words made her stomach flutter and took a deep breath as she grabbed both tokens, gauging the weight of them, of her decision, in her palms.

"You know how to use your magic," Blackwell told her. "Don't let him get close enough to touch you."

The walls around Ophelia shook and fell back one by one to reveal a circular arena with a six-foot stone wall surrounding it. On opposite sides of the arena were Charlotte and Cade. A door instantly appeared next to Charlotte, who swung her gaze to Ophelia in surprise.

"I knew he would take both," Ophelia said, holding up her own tokens in example.

Charlotte dipped her chin a respectful nod and said, "Good luck."

With that, she disappeared, and Cade and Ophelia were left alone.

The tokens in their hands dissolved into wisps of obsidian smoke. Cade began to stride toward Ophelia with purpose, interlocking his fingers and pushing them away from his body to crack the joints in his knuckles.

His malicious grin was all too confident as he announced, "I've been waiting for this moment."

"What moment is that?" she quipped back. "Your death? I'm sure the entirety of New Orleans has been waiting for this moment."

Cade bared his teeth as he continued to prowl across the arena. "I knew you were trouble the very first fucking day. You may bleed red, but you have dark magic in your bones. You summoned a Demon to torture me on your behalf. You skulk around talking to yourself and kissing Devils. You play at being as human as the rest of us, but we both know you aren't. Beneath the surface you're a fucking monster. I never liked that Luci ran around with your sister. Or that this city so readily invites your kind to live amongst us and encourages such witchcraft as what your mother did. It's evil. Unnatural. Your whole family has tainted blood."

Blackwell's expression had turned more murderous with every word Cade spoke, until the point that he was nearly shaking with his unconcealed rage. She knew that if it were in his power to rip the other man limb from limb, Cade would've been dead already.

"I should've killed him after he hit you," Blackwell seethed, tone dripping with regret. "Watching the light drain from his eyes would have been worth the risk of you hating me for doing such a thing."

"Is that why you spared him?" she questioned, shocked.

The intensity in Blackwell's eyes deepened, but he didn't confirm nor deny.

Cade simmered further. "Who the *fuck* are you talking to? What spells are you saying beneath your breath, Demon?"

Ophelia groaned. "For the last fucking time, I am *not* a Demon! And you clearly know nothing of paranormal beings, so stop speaking the names of those you are unfamiliar with! Demons reside in Hell! They cannot even leave Hell except for a single day a year! *I am a Necromancer.*" She smiled now, showing him her teeth. "And I wasn't reciting any spells, but if you'd like to see some magic, it'd be my pleasure."

Cade had gotten close enough, and it was time for her to show him exactly what he was up against. She summoned her magic to her fingertips, the blue sparks zapping out into the air as she poised her hands to strike. Cade came up short, watching her in disbelief as it slowly sank in what he'd gotten himself into.

"You really should have just taken one token," she told him with a smirk. And then she struck.

She aimed her magic at the center of his chest, a streamlined shot just like Blackwell had taught her. When the concentrated energy hit him, he stumbled back with a scream, the magic burning through his clothes and into his skin, but it wasn't enough to take him down—just enough to piss him off.

She aimed and fired twice more, the first strike hitting his right shoulder; he charged at her harder, the second shot missing when he feinted to the side. Ophelia began to walk backward, attempting to put more distance between them while he worked on closing it. She could feel Blackwell's energy somewhere behind her growing increasingly anxious.

"Go away," she told Blackwell. "I need to concentrate."

"No," he responded, firm.

"Don't be a nuisance." She turned to glare at him for a split second, before locking her eyes back onto Cade. "You're distracting me. I've got this."

For a moment, she didn't know if he was going to listen to her, but when she felt the static of his energy flicker out, she knew he had gone back to the Other Side to spectate. With her focus no longer split, she homed in on Cade dashing for her, waiting for her next hit. She gave it to him. One, two, three, in rapid succession. He dodged two but was slammed by the third, and she noticed it was beginning to wear him down. She could see the skin through the pocked holes she had created in his clothes, red and angry, bubbling with blisters from the burns of her magic.

"What's wrong?" she asked, tone dripping with innocence. "I thought you said this would be enjoyable for you?"

"Fuck. You. *Bitch*," he spat as his chest heaved and he pushed himself to trudge forward.

"I'm not even tired," she taunted. "For me this is the easiest trial we've had by far."

That got a rise out of him. He lunged forward, and she did nothing to stop him, waiting until he was in arm's reach and then, just before he crashed into her, she made herself invisible. He dove through her and landed on the ground with a pained thud, and Ophelia spun. Before he was able to push himself up, she threw herself atop him, straddling his hips as she pressed both her hands into his throat. There was a rage inside her she had never really felt before for another human being, but Cade had hardly acted human the entire time that they'd been here. There was a guilt, deep inside her, that told her she wouldn't come out of this unscathed—that taking a life would take a toll on who she was as a person. But the alternative was letting him win, and that was simply not something she could do.

She squeezed his throat until she blocked off his oxygen; he thrashed and bucked beneath her, trying to knock her off. She held tight, the muscles in her hands and biceps tightening with discomfort, unused to such strain. There was no time to summon any more of her magic to end it all then and there, however, because he managed to use his legs for just enough leverage to flip them over.

She grunted as her spine and the back of her head slammed into the cold, hard ground. Her vision went dark from the hit for an alarming moment, and when it faded back in, spots of light floated before her eyes.

"This feels familiar, doesn't it?" he said, seething, spittle from his mouth hitting her face.

Gross.

She wasted no time, turning invisible to slip out from beneath his hold. He roared in frustration at her ability to evade his attacks, grasping forward at whatever he could. Before she could fade all the way out, he managed to clutch her locket and snap it right off her neck. She rolled her invisible form to the side and got to her feet in one fluid motion. She returned herself to her solid state and braced herself to lunge for her necklace when something strange happened.

Her heart rate began to slow. The temperature in the room seemed to drop thirty degrees, and her head began to swim. Cade held up the locket with a triumphant smile.

Follow your heart. Apparently, that's exactly what she'd been doing this entire time. Emphasized by the way the organ inside her chest was about to stop entirely.

This needed to end now. The sooner it was over, the sooner she could find her sister. The sooner she was out of here for good.

She was too weak to attack at the moment, but she was grateful that Cade wasn't the kind of man to pull any punches. If she offered up bait, he would surely take it. So, she let her body drop to the ground, pretending to faint before she actually did. Within seconds, Cade took the opportunity to dive atop her. She almost rolled her eyes at how predictable he was. As soon as he was close enough, the locket still clasped in his grip, she struck. Clamoring to get her hand on the golden trinket, she managed to make the locket—and herself—invisible just long enough to fasten it back around her neck.

The heart in her chest began pounding once more.

As her strength returned, she made herself solid and threw a punch right into Cade's temple. Hard enough to make her knuckles throb but definitely nothing well-practiced. It worked well enough, though, and he slumped forward with a groan. Next, she crawled out from under him, lunging to her feet so she could slam her knee up directly into his face, smashing his nose and sending blood spraying over the ground as he screamed in agony. She didn't break for even a moment as she tackled him back to the ground, her palms becoming coated in the blood that was still gushing from his face.

Yes. Yes. Kill him, make it slow, gouge his eyes out and rip his flesh from his body, the Shadow Voice chattered, greedy for the violence as always.

"I'll make it quick," she promised to Cade sincerely. "A mercy you don't deserve after what you attempted to do to Edna. After the selfishness you displayed this entire competition."

No, not quick, agonizingly slow, the Shadow Voice hissed.

He tried to choke something out, but her thumbs were pressed into that sensitive indentation of his throat and only strained huffs of air escaped his lips. She loosened her grip just enough to let him have his last words, and they did not disappoint.

"You're going to burn in fucking Hell one day," he spat.

"And you're going to fade into obscurity now," she told him. "Soon enough, not a single soul will remember your name. You've made no lasting mark on this world. I know which fate I'd rather have between the two."

Something like devastation glistened in his dull brown eyes, but there was no more lingering as she slid her hands up over his face, gathered every bit of magic she had left on reserve, and blasted it into him. She nearly gagged at the sight, and smell, of his flesh melting away, as her magic seared through his skull.

The Shadow Voice cackled in delight as she hauled herself off Cade's lifeless body and stood on shaky legs. When she looked down at her hands, she found them covered in scarlet. But unlike with Eric, the shame and guilt was not immediate.

Ophelia found that she liked the blood on her hands just a little too much.

Yes, Necromancer, the Shadow Voice encouraged. *Embrace your calling, harbinger of death. Unleash your darkness on the world.*

44

ɪNTERTWINED

Ophelia's flesh pebbled as a strange vibration of energy ran through her, making her blood sing with power.

Cade's life force, she realized. She had stolen it, recharged herself with it.

A golden door appeared in the center of the room, and Ophelia wiped her stained hands on her dress before grabbing up her skirts and marching toward it, not bothering to glance back as she left Cade and his forgettable legacy behind.

As she made her way to the portal, to return to the manor, pride seeped into every inch of her marrow at the hard-won victory of making it to this point. But her high was quickly dampened as the dining room came into view around her.

Something was very wrong.

The change in ambiance was so visceral that her spine began to tingle at the shift in the air around her. Everything had become drenched in shadows, the food that was usually still out on the table in the dining room now nothing but dried-up fruit and the rotten carcasses of roasted birds. If she had once thought the Gothic opulence of the manor was something to behold, everything was now sharper, darker, too harsh for her to feel comfortable within the treacherous walls.

She frowned as she trudged through the archway of the dining room and into the corridor. It was pitch-black, not a single one of the sconces that lined the hall lit. The shadows around her seemed *alive*.

"Something wicked this way comes," an insidious voice crooned from down the hall.

She froze, her stomach a pit of fear. That hadn't been in her head.

"Hello, Ophelia," the Shadow Voice hissed as it stepped into view. It seemed to smile as it spoke, though it was only made of shadows and swirling tendrils of smoke.

"How did you get out?" She fought to contain the tremble in her voice.

"You let me out. When you gave in to my wicked desires."

It was the same as it always had appeared in her dreams, the embodiment of darkness, a manifestation of every sin in her mind. Almost human in its form, but there were no discernable features in its face, no eyes, just depthless black holes, and only a gash of razor-sharp teeth for its mouth.

"You mean—"

"You killed Cade with your bare hands, and now you have unleashed me on the world." Its raspy cackle sent a shiver through her body. "Oh, how I cannot wait to commit all of the sinful fantasies I have so longed to enact all these years."

She took a step back from the figure and it mirrored her movement. She halted and it did the same.

It laughed at the horror on her face. "Yes, you're starting to see. I am you and you are me. Our darkness is intertwined."

"No," she whispered. "We are not the same."

"Oh, but we are," it insisted. "Don't look so disappointed. This is what you've always wanted, yes? Me outside of your head?"

Her fists balled at her sides. "Not if it means you will be free to torture others like you have me."

"Are you saying you'd rather me back in your head?" it purred.

Her breath hitched at the question.

All her life, all she had wanted was peace. To be fixed. To not be a burden on those she loved most. But if being rid of the voice in her head meant she would never know peace in a different sort of way . . . was that worth it?

You don't need to fix yourself. You're not broken. But it's okay to get outside help if it gets too loud.

Blackwell's words came slamming back into her, and she realized how right they were. Every time the Shadow Voice urged her to do something insidious or viciously evil and she resisted . . . that was her choosing who she really was. And unleashing such a force on the world where she could no longer mitigate the consequences of the Voice's actions was a much larger burden than she was willing to live with if those were her only two options.

"Tick, tock," the Shadow Voice prompted.

"I'm not letting you go free," she declared, lifting her chin in defiance.

"Then come and get me," it snarled.

It plunged down the hallway and into the darkness, and Ophelia took off after it. Her skirts billowed behind her as she sprinted through the corridor and down two flights of stairs to the manor's first floor—a place she had not been allowed to step foot in since entering Phantasma. Her hair whipped across her face as she followed the same sharp turn the shadowy creature took as soon as they hit the bottom step, and ran out into the open space of the upper landing where the double, crescent-shaped stairwells led down to the front foyer. Milky moonlight drenched both the upper landing and foyer through the enormous Gothic windows, silhouetting the Shadow Voice as it continued to skitter through the night and down the left side of the crescent-shaped stairwell. She hurried after it, making her way down to the first floor, but as it plunged into the darkness beneath the overhanging landing, where the moonlight could no longer reach, Ophelia paused to yank down the brass candelabra from the post at the end of the banister at the end of the stairs, letting the dim light guide her into the unexplored parts of the manor.

At the very back of the foyer she found a U-shaped alcove with three sets of double doors. She held the candles before each of them in turn, trying to assess if any of them were slightly ajar. When she neared the set on the right, her locket's pulse began to thunder, and she didn't hesitate to yank the doors open and step through.

What she found was a room full of mirrors framed by lush, red velvet curtains. Each reflection of herself contained something different—one where she was screaming, one where she was crying, one where the smile on her face stretched unnaturally wide. A most terrifying vision.

Her dress was bloody and torn from her fight with Cade, and the firelight in her hand danced with hypnotizing fervor as she slowly turned to look at each version of herself.

"Come out, come out, wherever you are," she whispered.

Something moved swiftly from behind her, bursting out from one of the curtains and tackling her to the ground. The candelabra flew from her hand, bouncing noisily across the ground and skidding to a halt at the foot of one of the plush curtains. The flames ignited the fabric instantly, smoke filling the room as the fire licked its way up to the ceiling. Her focus, however, was on the Shadow Voice pinning her to the floor by her shoulders.

She struggled against its hold as its writhing, smoke-like hands elongated into something akin to talons.

"Ophelia Grimm," it rasped, dragging one of those sharp talons down the side of her cheek as the fire spread and the temperature in the room blazed dangerously close to suffocating. "You have always contained your own worst enemy."

She summoned her magic, using the spurt of power she'd received from Cade's death and blasting it through the tendrils of the Voice's shadows. As her magic ripped through the dark figure, its claws sank into her chest and ripped. She screamed in agony as her skin tore open, flayed away in jagged pieces. She tried to flip over and drag herself away from the creature as her blood swelled through the ruined fabric of her chemise and corset, but it pressed its weight down into her even harder and scrambled to keep her on her back. She tried to make herself invisible, but it wasn't working, and as the growing flames depleted the oxygen, she began to heave, smoke slowly seeping into her lungs.

She sent out another blast of her magic into the figure's core, and this time, it slashed open the sensitive skin of her belly, nearly gutting her in the process.

"Blackwell," she cried, desperate. "*Blackwell.*"

"He's not coming for you, sweetheart." The Shadow Voice laughed. "You're on your own."

"*Blackwell,*" she screamed until her throat was raw.

Over and over and over she called his name. But he did not come.

"When are you going to realize that the only person you can rely on is yourself?" the Voice spat. "When are you going to give up on the idea that he is your savior?"

She continued repeating Blackwell's name until it was all she knew, and the Shadow Voice grew angrier with each call of the Ghost's name on her lips.

"*Shut up,*" it hissed. "*Shut up!*"

The thing was, she didn't need Blackwell to always be her savior, but it was beginning to dawn on her that he had become her safe haven—someone who made the Shadow Voice go silent whenever he was around. And despite her injuries, and the fact that she was about to be incinerated, she didn't want him to come save *her* in this moment. She wanted him to come make sure the Shadow Voice didn't get away.

. . . it's okay to get outside help . . .

Yes. It was. She had been so alone for so long. Trapped in the confines of her own mind. She didn't see why she needed to be alone now, just to prove that she was the only person she could rely on. Because she knew that wasn't true.

"*He's not coming, you bitch,*" the Shadow Voice shrieked, and now Ophelia knew it wasn't just angry—it was frightened.

"He will always come to me," she whispered. "We find each other every time. And you cannot stand that, because it means I'm no longer alone with you."

The Shadow Voice screamed in fury as it poised itself to land its final blow, and she sucked in all the air she could manage to whisper Blackwell's name one last time.

And then everything went black.

45

Utterly Consumed

Something cold was pressed against Ophelia's cheek. As she blinked open her eyes, she found herself still lying in the mirrored room, but the flames and smoke were gone. As was the Shadow Voice.

And looking down on her as if his entire world had just shattered was Blackwell. His hand was cupping her cheek, the pad of his thumb brushing gentle, soothing strokes across her skin.

"Angel," he breathed, voice thick with relief as she came to. He gathered her up into his arms and crushed her into his chest, burying his face into her neck. "I thought I lost you. I thought..."

"What happened?" she whispered as she glanced around, noticing that her reflections in the mirrors were all uniform now.

"You..." He swallowed. "You hurt yourself. You clawed your chest and stomach to pieces. I was worried I didn't heal you in time." His eyes darkened. "I've never been so terrified to see so much blood."

"What? No...I didn't...the Shadow Voice..."

The Shadow Voice had attacked her. Its claws shredded her apart. The fire...

"What do you mean it was *here*—Wait. What fear did you give Phantasma as your payment to enter?" he asked. "Did it have anything to do with the voice?"

"Oh," she sobbed as the realization hit her. "Oh."

When tears began to stream down her cheeks, he swiped them away, letting her quietly process her thoughts.

"My biggest fear has always been accidentally harming myself because of it," she whispered. "I didn't mean to. I swear. It had felt so real—"

"Hey," he murmured, combing a comforting hand over her hair, the gesture rife with affection. "I know. It was an illusion. Phantasma is going to throw everything it has at you now that you're all almost to the end. But I'm here. I got to you."

She began to cry harder. "I didn't know if you'd be able to find me."

"Your injuries made it hard to hear you at first—our link from the blood bargain has been weakening," he admitted. "But I *felt* you calling. I've never had that sort of connection with any other contestant before. I told you before that nothing would ever stop me from getting to you if you needed me, and that will remain true forevermore. I would tear the universe apart at its seams if I must."

She wanted to roll her eyes at the drama of that statement, but, truthfully, her heart was swelling in her chest. She knew in every fiber of her being that he was telling her the truth.

He tilted her chin up to look her in the eyes. "Let me stay with you tonight. *Please.*"

She sniffed. "I always knew you'd be the one to beg first."

"I would stay on my knees all night if you wanted," he vowed, heat sparking in his eyes. "Just let me stay. Let me hold you."

There wasn't an instant of hesitation in her mind. "Take me back to my room and make me forget everything that just happened."

He groaned at the request, not wasting a second to transport her away and fulfill her request. Back in her room, he placed her down and she stepped from his arms.

She gestured to her dress. "Get rid of this."

He snapped his fingers and undressed her. He groaned at the sight, his eyes raking over every inch of her naked body, his face telling her that there were a million different things he wanted to do. But first, he had a promise to fulfill.

"Now, beg," she told him.

Shock flitted across his face, chased by fervent lust. He made a show of lowering himself to his knees before her, every movement slow, deliberate. He looked up at her face as he placed his fingertips at her right ankle and trailed them all the way up the side of her leg until he reached her knee, making her bend it up so he could hook her leg over his shoulder. He turned his face to place a kiss on her inner thigh, his gaze never breaking from hers.

"Please," he murmured against her skin.

She smirked down at him. "I'm sorry, I can't quite hear you."

"Wicked angel," he told her, his eyes blazing with want. "*Please.*"

"Please, what?" she asked, reaching down to plunge her hands into his hair, tugging gently with impatience.

"Let me taste you," he begged.

She tilted her head. "Is that all you want to do to me?"

"Not even close," he growled. "I'm going to devour your pussy and drink every sweet drop you give me. Then I'm going to fuck you until the only thing you can think or speak is my name. I'm going to make sure I bury myself so deep inside of you that neither of us will be able to tell where I end and you begin."

Warmth flushed over her body, and she felt herself become slick with arousal. A downward flick of his eyes, and she knew he'd noticed as well. He sucked in a sharp breath, and though she was the one naked, vulnerable, in this moment she was completely in charge and they both knew it.

"You get so fucking wet for me," he said, his voice becoming gruff as his own arousal grew. "I love how excited your body gets for me." His grip on the back of her thighs tightened. "I know you want my cock inside of you, angel. Be a good girl and say the word."

He was right, and though she wanted to have enough self-control to tease him longer, she simply didn't.

"Alright," she told him.

He groaned in relief as he leaned in and began to make good on his promises. And he did. He lapped at her swollen clit, her entrance, not missing a single drop that he milked from her body. The first orgasm hit her surprisingly quickly, and he hardly gave her enough time to catch her breath from it before he was working to wring out another one. Carefully, so carefully, he scraped his teeth against her tight bundle of nerves, making her hips buck forward and her legs begin to shake. He hummed in satisfaction as he held her steady.

"Blackwell," she whimpered, tightening her hands on the back of his head to keep herself stable. "I can't stand for much longer. It's too much."

He grinned against her as he blinked them into a different position. Her lying back on the bed, ass perched on the very edge so he could spread her legs wide and finish her off one more time with his mouth. When she came this time, she moaned his name.

"That's my good girl," he said as he prowled up her body, his mouth leaving a trail of kisses on its way to her breasts.

When he suckled one of the hard, rosy buds into his mouth, nipping gently, she thought she might perish from the pleasure of it. His hand came up to roll her other nipple between his fingers, pulling harder and harder until the pain became euphoric.

When he released her nipples, she tugged his face up to hers, meeting his lips in a haze-inducing kiss before lowering her hands to the buttons of his shirt and ripping them open. Threads popped and buttons went flying to the ground, and Blackwell huffed a laugh at her eagerness as she tore the shirt away from his body. She sighed in contentment as he moved his mouth to the underside of her jaw and over the sensitive part of her throat.

"I want your pants off," she told him. "Now."

A second later and they had disappeared. Oh, how she loved having a Ghost as a lover.

"Fuck me," she demanded.

"Yes, Miss Grimm," he drawled. "Your every wish is my command."

She made a noise of mock annoyance in the back of her throat, lightly tapping his shoulder with the back of her hand. "Don't start."

He gave her a wolfish smile. "*Don't* fuck you, then?"

She glowered and squirmed beneath him until she reached the hard length of his cock with her right hand and pressed it against her entrance herself. "Don't make me go back to making you beg. What is it you said before? You'd stay on your knees all night if I wanted? Maybe I'll change my mind and we can try that instead, hmm?"

He bit at her bottom lip with affection. "You're a menace."

"Only to you." She grinned, smug.

"And it'd better stay that way," he told her as he rocked his hips forward and gave her his entire length. He pulled out to the tip once more. "I never want another soul to touch you like this. Only me." He thrust back in. "I will fuck you until you tell me you can't remember a single other lover's name." Out. "Until you can't remember your own name." In. "Until nothing else exists but *this*." Out. "Us." In.

"There's only you," she swore as she writhed beneath him. Wanting more, more, more. He gave it to her. "Blackwell. Blackwell. *Blackwell*."

"In all the darkness, in all the loneliness, you have been my one source of light," he lamented as she began to come undone. "My soul will go to its grave with your name echoing in my mind."

His words made her crash over the edge, and he followed her moments later. As soon as they both recovered, he switched their position, him sitting back against the headboard and her straddling his lap. She slowly lowered herself on his still-hard length, thanking the heavens that he didn't need any downtime as he filled her completely once again.

He kissed her as his hands dropped to grip her waist, pumping her up and down his length in a steady rhythm as she pressed her chest into his, her nipples desperate for more friction. He seemed to realize what she needed, because he broke their kiss and leaned his mouth down to capture one of the rosy buds into his mouth as she arched up into him.

"Fuck," she panted as she picked up her pace. "Hell, that feels so *good*."

"That's right, angel," he murmured. "You're taking it so well."

"*Mmm*," she moaned. "Harder."

He squeezed her hips and guided her over him faster, hitting a spot deep inside her that was quickly becoming her favorite.

"*Harder*," she demanded, her breasts bouncing lightly with her effort now.

A grunt of pleasure came from his throat as he angled up his hips, his bent knees hitting her back, to drive into her until her eyes rolled to the back of her head with the bliss of it. She was utterly consumed. She wanted to stay here forever, wrapped around him. There was nothing in the world that could make her stop in this moment.

And then there was a knock on the door.

"Ophelia?" someone called. Someone familiar.

Genevieve Grimm.

46

MOTHER'S DAUGHTER

Genevieve pushed her way inside the door just as Blackwell clothed himself and Ophelia.

One look at their compromising position and Genevieve huffed. "You *would* follow me here and then end up having a more fun time than me."

Ophelia scrambled off Blackwell's lap. Her sister was clad in a dress she'd brought from home: pink chiffon that hugged her voluptuous curves sweetly. Ophelia's brain struggled to compute that Genevieve was really here, right in front of her, after all this time.

"Ophie? Would you like to make introductions?" Genevieve prompted sweetly.

"Vivi, this is Blackwell." Ophelia gestured to the Ghost who was watching them with intrigue. "Blackwell, this is my sister. Genevieve Grimm."

Genevieve held her hand out to him, and he bowed formally at the waist as he took it and pressed a chaste kiss to her knuckles.

Ophelia rolled her eyes. "Suck-up."

Blackwell grinned over at her as he straightened himself up.

"Tell me, Blackwell," Genevieve said in a saccharine tone. Warning bells immediately sounded off in Ophelia's head. "What are your intentions with my sister? Besides fucking her stupid, I mean."

Blackwell nearly choked at the bluntness of Genevieve's

words, but he quickly recovered with a laugh. "I think I should leave you both to have a conversation."

Ophelia's face dropped at his words, and she knew her sister had caught the disappointment immediately.

Blackwell leaned down to press a kiss to Ophelia's temple in reassurance. "I'm a call away. The two of you have a lot to catch up on and don't need me getting in the middle of it."

With that, he disappeared.

Ophelia and Genevieve stood, staring at each other for what felt like an hour before Genevieve finally sighed and broke the silence.

"You *would* follow me here even though I said I'd take care of things," she carped.

Ophelia gawked in disbelief. "Of *course*, I was going to follow you! You're my baby sister! What on earth were you *thinking* entering a place like this? You hate anything even remotely related to the paranormal, and yet you come *here?*"

"I was thinking that I'm perfectly capable of taking care of myself and wasn't going to sit by and watch you make yourself sick with worry about how we were going to get on without Momma." She took a deep breath. Then, "And I don't *hate* the paranormal, Ophie. What I hated was having it forced into every aspect of our lives growing up."

"Because making myself sick with worry for your well-being in this hellish place is much better?" Ophelia scoffed, ignoring that last bit of Genevieve's speech. That was a lot more than they had time to unpack right this second.

"I didn't think you would figure out where I was going," she muttered. Then, as if it just dawned on her, asked, "How *did* you know I came here?"

"I...might have found your diary." Ophelia looked down at her hands with guilt.

"You read my diary?" Genevieve half screeched. "I am going to *kill* you, Ophelia Grimm!"

Ophelia's fists balled at her sides. "I wouldn't have had to read it if you were just honest with me! You knew about our father, and you never told me, Genevieve. How could you keep such a thing from me? I thought we were closer than that, but all this time you've been living a completely different life."

Genevieve's face softened now, a look of regret in her eyes. "I didn't want to get your hopes up. Our father...he was so hard to track down. It took me a whole year of sneaking through Momma's records and hidden journals to determine who he was and where they'd met. And then when I found out it was this place..."

Ophelia swallowed and nodded. "After all of Mother's rules and warnings, this was the last place I thought our legacy would be tied to. And to find out about the curses..."

Genevieve's eyes widened. "You know about that part?"

"I know a lot more than you think," Ophelia affirmed.

Genevieve sighed. "Alright. Why don't we both start from the beginning?"

And they did.

The two of them were sitting, face to face, cross-legged atop Ophelia's comforter. Just like they used to when they were supposed to be asleep, and Genevieve would sneak into Ophelia's room to talk until they passed out well into the witching hours.

Now, instead of gossiping about which boy Genevieve kissed in the French Quarter, or which of their mother's customers definitely murdered the very relatives they were trying to summon, the two of them divulged every detail of their experience in the Devil's Manor.

Genevieve explained how she had been tracking Phantasma

ever since she figured out that their parents had met here, and the curse that had befallen them. She had intercepted several letters from a man named Gabriel White a couple years ago and kept tabs on his every move since. She'd last tracked him to New York—Phantasma's previous location before it had appeared in New Orleans.

Genevieve also explained how she'd accidentally found out they were in financial debt from a friend of a friend whose mother worked at New Orleans City Bank; when she confronted their mother about it, she was sworn to secrecy.

"She was afraid you were already under too much pressure," Genevieve admitted. "She was hoping to pay everything off in a few months. She even had me deliver some of the checks to the bank, so as not to tip you off since the two of you always went to town together. But then things got . . . worse."

"What things?" Ophelia pressed.

"No matter how many times I begged Mother to tell me why we were in debt, she wouldn't. Only that she had priorities that mattered more than the house. It was driving me mad not know-ing the full story. You know how I'm nosy—"

Ophelia snorted. An understatement.

"—and so I followed her."

"What do you mean, you followed her?"

"It was several months ago. You were sick with a head cold—remember?—and she said she was going into town to get you some healing herbs from that apothecary on Magazine Street she liked so much."

Ophelia *did* remember that head cold. She got one almost every year from New Orleans's erratic winter temperatures.

"Well, I knew something was going on when I found the exact herbs she was claiming she was out of stuffed in the back drawer of our medicine cabinet," Genevieve continued. "Not to mention she had been checking for the mail boy fifty times a day—there was no doubt in my mind she was receiving letters from our father again and didn't want us to accidentally get ahold of them. So, when she said she was going to the apothecary, I followed her."

"And where did she really go?"

Genevieve's tone grew more serious. "To meet a Devil."

"*What?*"

Genevieve nodded. "She was bringing some sort of rare items the Devil had requested in payment for their deal—the deal in which he erased our father's memory of us. But because of Phantasma's curse, the Devil couldn't fully eradicate Gabriel's memory of our mother. The last thing Gabriel wrote to her was that he was going back to win Phantasma and would ask to be reunited with her as his prize. We're in debt because she used most of the family's fortune to secure a second home in case we needed to leave at a moment's notice. One that would be much harder for him to locate."

"You mean we own a home that's not Grimm Manor?" Ophelia asked.

Genevieve nodded. "She made sure to have it warded by extremely powerful magic so our father wouldn't be able to pay a Witch or Seer to look for us anymore. The only problem is that she died before she was able to tell us about it and...I never found out where it's located."

Ophelia sighed deeply. Another wild goose chase.

"Now, how did *you* find out about our parents?" Genevieve pressed.

"Blackwell," Ophelia stated and then took a deep breath. She went through every point of almost every hour that she'd spent in Phantasma over the last week—leaving out a few of the more scandalous details here and there—and it felt good to get it all off her chest.

When she was finished, Genevieve gave a low whistle. "Mother would be having another heart attack if she knew you made a blood oath."

Ophelia winced and looked away.

Genevieve reared back. "You've spoken to her?"

"That part...there's this place called the Whispering Gate that I'm apparently able to summon if there's someone on the other side waiting to talk to me. She was."

Genevieve's eyes swelled with tears. "How was she? Was she okay?"

Ophelia nodded and grabbed her sister's hand, squeezing it with affection. "She wanted me to tell you she loves you. Very much."

Genevieve nodded, tucking a strand of her golden-brown hair behind her ear. "You'll have to explain more about that later. Right now, I want to know more about the Phantom and what the Hell you were doing when I found the two of you."

Ophelia flushed but only asked, "How did you even find me?"

"Oh!" Genevieve exclaimed. "A *Devil* told me that there was a Necromancer here whose face looked an awful lot like mine. Isn't that odd?"

"Very. Why would a Devil seek you out just to tell you that?"

"I *meant*," Genevieve corrected, "isn't it odd they noticed our resemblance? No one ever discerns that unless we're next to each other."

"Vivi." Ophelia sighed, exasperated. Of course that was what her sister was focusing on. "Go back to the Devil. What did they look like?"

"Hot," Genevieve smiled. "Dark hair, handsome face, an ass like you wouldn't—"

"Genevieve Grimm."

"He had creepy eyes, though," Genevieve continued. "Scarlet, with pupils like a cat's—"

Ophelia froze. Sinclair.

"What, exactly, was your conversation with him?" Ophelia demanded.

Genevieve gave Ophelia an odd look. "When I got out of that last level, he found me in the hallway. He told me that thing about us looking alike, and I knew right away you were here. He told me what room you were in, so I came to find you. What's going on? Do you know him or something?"

"Or something," Ophelia muttered before questioning, "How did you manage to get through all those levels? If I hadn't had Blackwell..."

Genevieve took a deep breath. "There's one more secret about me that I've never shared, Ophie."

Ophelia held her breath as she waited for her sister's explanation, but Genevieve didn't speak. No, she disappeared. Entirely.

Ophelia gasped. "You're a Specter, too."

Genevieve reappeared with a look of surprise. "A Specter? You mean—?"

Ophelia demonstrated her own ability, then explained, "We get it from our father, according to Blackwell."

"I still can't believe the Phantom you've been fucking actually met our father."

"Don't be crude." Ophelia blushed.

"Uh-oh, I know that face." Genevieve pointed at her, a look of fear in her eyes. "It's not just fucking. You have *feelings* for him?"

"I have an array of emotions for him," Ophelia muttered. "He can be quite the pain in the ass, I assure you."

Genevieve's grin was absolutely scandalized. "Oh, I bet he can be—"

"*Vivi!*" Ophelia scolded, playfully hitting her sister on the shoulder.

Genevieve tilted her head back and laughed. "I'm sorry, Ophie, I can't help but tease. I've never seen you like this! The juiciest thing you ever did was Elliott Trahan, and I've had more chemistry with a slice of bread pudding than you ever did with that stick-in-the-mud."

Ophelia grumbled good-naturedly before redirecting the conversation back to her original question. "So, you got through the levels by disappearing the entire time?"

Genevieve sobered. "More or less. You should've seen me during that true or false one. If I hadn't been able to unshackle myself, I absolutely would've been pummeled to mush. Turns out that I'm not too great at telling if people are lying."

"What about all the manor's haunts?" Ophelia asked.

Genevieve shrugged. "Easy to get out of those when you can walk through walls."

"You mean, you can control your powers that well?" Ophelia asked, slightly shocked.

Genevieve bit her lip. "Yes. I've been doing it since we were children. It's second nature to me now. It's how I always got away with things at home."

"I *knew* you were the one who stole that expensive bottle of liquor out of the cabinet during Mardi Gras all those years ago! No wonder Mother was so confused—you didn't need her key to do it."

"Well, she almost caught me that time," Genevieve muttered. "Actually, I'm pretty sure she figured it out, but she never even bothered to confront me about it. I guess it wasn't the right type of magic to make her notice me."

"Vivi…" Ophelia whispered. "Why didn't you ever tell me you could do such things?"

"Because…" Genevieve looked mournful. "I trust you, Ophie, truly, but when we were younger, I couldn't risk you slipping up and telling Momma. The way she sheltered you—I didn't want that. I was always afraid she'd find out I had magic and take away my freedom like she did yours. If only I'd known she probably wouldn't have cared at all."

"She didn't take away my freedom—"

"Yes," Genevieve interrupted. "She fucking did."

"I had a good childhood, Vivi. I just...had different responsibilities and expectations than you."

"You will never be able to fully understand how grateful I am that you are my big sister," Genevieve said. "If it had been anyone less selfless than you, I don't think we'd be as close. But I've always struggled to watch you put off your dreams and interests and...your whole life because of your sense of duty toward our family's legacy. I want you to be who *you* want to be, Ophie."

"*Are* we close?" Ophelia whispered. "There was this girl in my group...Luci."

Genevieve reared back. "Luci Veil?"

Ophelia nodded. "She told me you were friends. A whole group of you. I had never even heard their names before—it felt like you were living an entire life without me. Like you were leaving me behind."

Genevieve swallowed. "I never wanted to rub my social life in your face when it made you so sad. I wanted to tell you about my friends. I *will* tell you about them. I'll tell you everything, Ophie. You're the person I care most about in this world—you know that, don't you?"

Tears pricked the corner of Ophelia's eyes now. "Please don't ever drift away from me. I need you. It's us. Forever. Right?"

"Promise," Genevieve whispered as she leaned forward and wrapped Ophelia in a hug.

They stayed that way for what felt like hours, holding on to each other tightly as if to make sure that this was real, they were real and together, and it was alright now.

When Genevieve finally pulled back, she asked, "What happened to Luci?"

Ophelia winced. "She's alive."

Genevieve sighed in relief.

"She's also...cursed," Ophelia revealed before going into that entire story as well.

"Luci is one of the best people I've ever met," Genevieve said. "That's devastating."

"She was always nice. Her cousin, on the other hand..."

"Do you mean Cade?" Genevieve's eyes sparked with anger. "*Cade* was here? He's possibly one of the most egregiously awful people I've ever had the displeasure of meeting. And that was in passing."

"Good to see his reputation really does precede him." Ophelia nodded. "Especially considering I killed him."

"*What?*" Genevieve screeched.

"It was him or me in that last level, and I chose me."

Genevieve looked at Ophelia as if she were seeing her anew. "You've changed so much in so little time."

"I've never felt surer about who I am than I do now," Ophelia admitted. "I know that's strange. This is the last place I ever thought I'd find myself. But it's true."

"Well, it *is* the place of your origin," Genevieve joked. "Poetic, if you think about it. Or perhaps there's just something in the water here."

Ophelia gave a soft laugh. "Or that I'm just our mother's daughter."

Then Genevieve offered, "I'm proud of you, Ophie."

Ophelia could've sobbed right then. "I'm sorry for what I

said to you that day, in the alleyway. We had just said goodbye to Mother, and I was upset and stressed and I'm so sorry I drove you to come here."

"Oh, Ophelia." Genevieve shook her head. "I'm sorry if you ever thought for a second you drove me here. I was coming here either way. It had always been my plan. What you said that day... you weren't wrong. You've always cleaned up my messes, and I just wanted to do something for *you* for once."

A weight lifted off Ophelia's shoulders at her sister's words.

"Alright." Genevieve clapped her hands together before climbing off the bed. "Next item on the agenda—we have forty-eight hours to make sure you don't have to give up a decade of your life to a sexy Ghost. Where do we begin?"

Ophelia smiled. She'd found her hope again.

Night Nine of
Phantasma

47

COLLIDING

"We should come up with a team name," Genevieve suggested as they made it up to the sixth flight of the manor. They, being Ophelia, Genevieve, and a very amused Blackwell.

For the past three hours, they'd been going through as many floors and rooms of Phantasma as possible. They'd yet to run into any other contestants that might be left, and it was making Ophelia anxious. She wanted to size up her opponents before the next trial.

Genevieve, on the other hand, didn't seem to have a care in the world other than grilling Blackwell about any- and everything that popped into her mind.

What's it like being a ghost?

Do you ever worry your clothes are going to go out of style?

Or that you're egregiously behind on the latest technology?

Have you ever even seen a car?

How many people have you watched die in here?

How long is your—

Ophelia hadn't known where that last question was going, but she cut it off before Genevieve could even finish it. To Blackwell's credit, he took every question in stride. Even seemed to be enjoying Genevieve's antics as they wandered through the mansion. It made something deep within her ache. She ignored it, funneling all of her focus into their hunt.

All the corridors and hallways in the other wings looked

nearly identical to the one Ophelia had been trapped in all this time. Complete with elaborate dining rooms, libraries, and random broom closets. It didn't take long for them to realize that they *were* the same rooms, somehow just operating on different linear planes, all layered on top of the other in different pockets of the universe. It was enough to make Ophelia's head spin, quite frankly, but it made more sense why, of all the wings in the manor, Ophelia found her father's name carved into a place within hers. Which technically meant if other contestants had figured that out, they could've left messages for other groups to see. A detail that made Ophelia irate after all the worrying she'd done about Genevieve's whereabouts.

"I am open to team name suggestions," Blackwell humored Genevieve, his words cutting through Ophelia's thoughts and bringing her back into their ridiculous conversation.

"Let's see, what do we all have in common..." Genevieve trailed off, flitting down the hall ahead of them, to a new room. "We're all very attractive."

Blackwell's grin grew. "That *is* true."

Ophelia shot her sister a disparaging look. "Don't inflate his ego any more than it already is, I'm begging you."

"Which she does not like to do," Blackwell quipped. "She much prefers me in that position instead."

Ophelia elbowed him in the ribs as her cheeks flamed. He tilted his head back and laughed, and she had to fight the pain welling up in her chest at the sight. Because there they were, she and Genevieve reunited, Blackwell laughing with abandon, and all she could think about was how in two days she'd never get to have this experience again.

"What about—" Genevieve began as if neither of them had spoken, but was suddenly interrupted when something small and ghostly popped in by her feet. "Oh! Fluffy! You're back."

"*Fluffy?*" Ophelia and Blackwell questioned in sync.

Genevieve looked back at them. "What else was I supposed to call him?"

"His name is Poe." Blackwell smiled as he went over and scooped the cat up.

"No fair, you can pet him," Genevieve pouted.

"Don't worry, you're not missing much," Blackwell assured. "He's a dreadful scoundrel most of the time."

Poe launched himself out of Blackwell's embrace then, as if insulted.

Ophelia cleared her throat. "Alright, I think we need to call it a night. We've walked up and down at least ten flights of stairs and have searched every room with no luck. I am *exhausted*."

Genevieve snorted. "I'm sure you are after all that energy the two of you probably burned earlier."

Ophelia's face heated for the millionth time in the last hour, but Blackwell was grinning like a fiend.

He stepped up next to Ophelia, reaching over to brush a piece of hair out of her face and tuck it behind her ear as he told her, "I enjoy your sister immensely."

"I'm going to bed," Ophelia muttered as she playfully swatted his hand away and turned to stomp from the room. "I should have known the two of you would be an unbearable pair."

"Wait!" Genevieve rushed past Blackwell to keep up with Ophelia. "We're going to share a room from now on, right?"

Ophelia looked back over her shoulder at Blackwell, and they shared a loaded look.

It was he who said, "That's probably the best idea."

Of course, Ophelia didn't want to split up from Genevieve, but there was also a part of her, a very selfish part, that was devastated that the last time they were intimate together was the *last* time.

"I'll go get my things and meet you back at your room, Ophie," Genevieve said.

"Do you want us to go with you?" Ophelia offered, unsure if she wanted her sister to split up with them, but Genevieve waved off her concern.

"I'll be fine!" she assured as she rushed off.

Blackwell transported Ophelia back to her room a few seconds later.

"This is strange," Ophelia told him. "Like two worlds colliding."

"I'm glad you found her. Or rather, that she found us." Blackwell smiled, his arms circling her waist to bring her body closer to his. "Though, I wish she had found us at least five minutes later..."

Ophelia hummed in agreement and let him press a sweet, lingering kiss to her lips.

"I wish you could stay," she whispered.

"Me too." He sighed. "But maybe this will be easier."

She knew he was probably right, but it didn't stop the disappointment. He kissed her one last time before bidding her good night and vanishing, leaving her to change for bed and crawl beneath the covers while she waited for her sister.

Ophelia woke the next day with Genevieve's elbow in her back and all of her covers stolen to the other side of the bed.

"I did not miss *this*," she muttered before getting up and stretching.

She didn't remember Genevieve returning the night before—she must have fallen asleep—but now the entire floor was covered in *things*. One thing about Genevieve was that she was incapable of having a tidy room. Various articles of clothing and shoes and perfume bottles spilled from her two trunks, and

Ophelia was in disbelief at how much her sister was able to fit in just two bags.

There was a movement from the bed as Genevieve yawned and stretched.

"You brought more than one pair of shoes, Vivi?" Ophelia admonished. "You brought *perfume?*"

"You never know who you might meet," Genevieve grumbled at being judged so early in the morning. "Besides, I didn't bring any of the expensive ones."

"You are unbelievable." Ophelia shook her head. "Get dressed before I summon Blackwell. I want to get as much searching in as we can before tonight."

Genevieve hauled herself out of bed, and though it was deep into the afternoon because of the inverted sleeping schedule Phantasma had forced them all into, Genevieve still proved that she could never be a morning person. When they were both finally dressed, Ophelia called for Blackwell. It took several times before he finally heard her, which she had to quickly explain to Genevieve.

"See, this is why I hate magic," Genevieve muttered as they left Ophelia's room and headed down the corridor. "Too many fucking rules."

Blackwell popped in front of them a second later, a grave look on his face.

"What's wrong?" Ophelia asked.

"A few of the last contestants from the other groups are trying to hunt down people to kill before the next level," he informed them. "Only one person can attempt level nine, so this is usually about the time this sort of thing starts to happen."

Genevieve and Ophelia exchanged a look, and Ophelia knew what she needed to say next.

"Vivi…"

"No." Genevieve shook her head vigorously. "I'm not leaving after all of this."

"But if only one of us can get to level nine, why risk any more trials?" Ophelia reasoned.

"Then I'll forfeit before level nine," Genevieve countered. "But I'm *not* leaving you before."

"Well, if there were any time to forfeit, it would be before level eight," Blackwell inserted. "It's definitely the one with the most to lose since—"

"Oh, I'm sure they'd be fine," a deep, sinister voice interrupted, and Ophelia immediately tensed.

Sinclair appeared with a smug smile on his face, and Blackwell stiffened with barely concealed rage. This was not going to be good.

"It's *you!*" Genevieve exclaimed before swinging her gaze to Ophelia. "He's the one who told me where to find you, Ophie."

"Oh, *Ophie* and I go way back, I assure you," Sinclair said. "In fact, the last time we saw each other, my fingers were in her—"

"Finish that sentence and I'll fucking kill you," Blackwell threatened.

Ophelia was ashamed that all she could think of in this moment was that Blackwell had been right before—jealousy *was* a sexy color.

Genevieve, now realizing something much deeper was going on between the three of them, glanced around in shock.

Leaning into Ophelia with a proud grin, she whispered, "*Please* tell me they're fighting over you."

Ophelia threw a severe look at Genevieve that only made her sister's grin grow wider.

Sinclair tilted his head. "Be careful, Blackwell. One might

think your jealousy is dangerously linked to something very much forbidden."

"What happened between the three of you, Ophie?" Genevieve whispered conspiratorially.

"Didn't your sister dearest tell you?" Sinclair asked innocently. "Blackwell isn't the only one around here she kissed."

"He's the only one I *enjoyed* kissing," Ophelia retorted, and Blackwell's grin turned wicked.

"Meanwhile, no one has offered to kiss me once this entire competition," Genevieve pouted.

"I can change that," Sinclair offered.

"*No*," Blackwell and Ophelia exclaimed at the same time.

"I only came to make sure our dearest Grimm sisters found each other," Sinclair pressed on. "It would be such a shame if they were torn apart again just as they were reunited, don't you think, Blackwell?"

Ophelia narrowed her eyes at the Devil. "What's your angle?"

Sinclair laughed. "I suppose you'll have to figure that out for yourself."

With that, he disappeared.

"I've got to say, he's creepy, but in a deliciously hot sort of way, you know?" Genevieve said.

"I can't say that I do," Blackwell deadpanned.

"He and Blackwell are sworn enemies," Ophelia explained.

"And you kissed them *both*?" Genevieve laughed. "I would've never pegged you for such a drama queen, Ophie. Though, I sort of get it, the jealousy thing is even hotter than the men. Honestly, I've never been prouder."

"If Sinclair wants you two to stay together, I have no doubt that means it isn't a very good idea," Blackwell chimed in.

"Ugh. Just because one cryptic Devil says something, doesn't mean I should *forfeit*."

"He's right, though," Ophelia agreed. "Sinclair did not lead you to me with good intentions, I promise. He's self-serving first and foremost. And he has a vendetta against Blackwell."

Genevieve shook her head. "How can I leave you, Ophie? This entire endeavor was supposed to be *my* mission—not yours."

"You got me this far." Ophelia grabbed her sister's hand and squeezed. "I would have never been able to get through all of this if it wasn't you that I needed to get to. And you only came here for me in the first place, because I couldn't give up the idea of taking over Grimm Manor and Mother's business. But…"

Something in Genevieve's expression turned hopeful. "But what, Ophie?

Ophelia took a deep breath. "Things have changed. I've changed. I don't want the same things anymore."

"Then what do you want?" Genevieve pressed, reaching out to squeeze Ophelia's hand in encouragement.

It took everything in Ophelia to keep her eyes on her sister's face and not look at Blackwell, despite the weight of his gaze burning into her from where he stood.

"I'm still making my mind up about that," Ophelia finally answered. "But what I know for sure is that your mission here is complete Genevieve. You led me here. And it's saved me from a future that would have drowned me. And I have Blackwell to protect me until I can reach the end. Why risk another level that you don't need to?"

Genevieve was quiet for a long moment, gaze searching for something in Ophelia's eyes. Whatever she was looking for, she must have found.

"Fine," Genevieve whispered. "Can I at the very least stay with you until then?"

Ophelia's shoulders relaxed. She did it. She'd found Genevieve and convinced her to leave. Everything was as it should be.

"Alright, stay until dinner. And then we can say our farewells."

LEVEL
EIGHT

48

FRAUD

When it was time for the sisters to part ways, Ophelia could barely speak, afraid if she did, she would fall apart. They had spent the day searching the manor with Blackwell; Genevieve and the Phantom getting along better than Ophelia could have ever imagined. It helped that they both had an annoying sense of humor and the perfect subject to pick on—her. But the later it got, the less everyone felt like joking and now with the dinner bells chiming, the mood was solemn to say the least.

"You promise you'll be alright?" Genevieve asked.

Ophelia nodded. "I'm going to win this."

"I believe you," Genevieve said, then she shifted her eyes to Blackwell. "Take care of her, or you'll have two sworn enemies with a vendetta against you. Understand?"

Blackwell dipped his chin in acknowledgment. "It was nice to meet you, Genevieve Grimm."

Genevieve smiled. "I hope we meet again someday."

Blackwell shifted his gaze away, and Ophelia's stomach churned as she pulled her sister into a hug.

"I love you," she whispered in Genevieve's ear.

"I love you too," Genevieve whispered back. "Whatever you decide you want... make sure you protect your heart. Okay?"

Ophelia glanced toward Blackwell, wondering if he heard that, but if he had, he gave no indication of it. She nodded at her sister and stepped back.

"Oh, and Genevieve?" Ophelia prompted.

"Yes?"

"Clean your damned room when you get home."

Genevieve rolled her eyes before giving her sister a particularly vulgar gesture and picking up both her trunks. "Alright, you damned manor. I, Genevieve Grimm, surrender to Phantasma."

In no time a Devil was there—Zel—grabbing on to Genevieve's arm and transporting her away, to safety.

"It's almost over," Blackwell told her, wrapping an arm around her waist and reeling her into him. "Two more levels and you're free."

She nodded as she rested her forehead on his chest. Two more levels and she would be free. But he wouldn't.

For level eight, since there were no more isolated groups, Blackwell guided her to the foyer, where the remaining contestants had already begun to gather. Including herself and Charlotte, there were six of them total. Two of the others were men in their mid-thirties. One looked haggard as if he had only survived this far by the skin of his teeth. The other was surly, watchful eyes confident as he sized up the rest of them.

Charlotte gave Ophelia a nod of recognition while they waited for this trial's Devil to appear. The last person in the entire world she had expected was Sinclair.

The Devil slowly scanned the group, and when his eyes landed on her, without Genevieve, he grinned. Her stomach dropped.

"For those who don't know me," he began, "my name is Sinclair. Here's your clue."

The level's door appeared and there were only two words written on it this time.

CHOOSE WISELY.

Somehow those two words were more ominous than any of the other clues about fiery oceans and swinging saws.

"When I call your name," Sinclair crooned. "Step up."

Unsurprisingly, he saved her for last.

As she approached the door, Sin's smile turned positively feral. "I see your sister forfeited after all."

"Something tells me your newfound glee about that means you played me once again," she said.

"You really don't catch on quickly," he agreed. "Don't worry, though, I have a feeling you'll see her again *very* soon."

She didn't bother lingering any longer. She stepped through the portal and found herself entirely alone in a white-walled room.

"Hello?" she murmured, her voice echoing back at her in the empty space. Just before she could call for Blackwell, a familiar voice appeared behind her.

"*Ophie?*"

Ophelia spun around to find her sister looking dazed and confused.

"*Genevieve*. What the Hell—"

Before Ophelia could finish her sentence, however, someone else spoke her name.

Ophelia twisted around again and found...another Genevieve.

"That's not me," the first Genevieve said, a look of horror on her face.

"What the Hell is going on?" the second Genevieve questioned, alarmed.

Ophelia cursed. Of course. Sinclair's directions made sense now. She called for Blackwell, and when he finally arrived, alarmingly delayed, she waved her hand to the exact replicas of her sisters. They had been bickering for ten minutes straight over who was who.

"Any insight here?" she asked.

"This level is Fraud," he explained. "You have to identify which is the real Genevieve to win. But . . . there's something I've been needing to tell you."

She raised her brows. "Which *is?*"

"The stakes are much higher than losing Phantasma in this level."

"What does that mean?" she demanded.

He took a deep breath. "If you choose the wrong Genevieve, the magic will kill the real Genevieve outside of Phantasma. It's Phantasma's most powerful trick."

"*What?*" she cried.

"It's why I insisted she forfeit." He sighed. "If she had stayed, I knew the two of you would've ended up in here together, with the possibility of both of you dying."

"But she's the one at risk here, Blackwell! She's the one that will be dead out there if—wait."

Something was needling at the back of her mind. Something he had told her before—about her father losing his second attempt at Phantasma three days before it had come to New Orleans. Which was the same day her mother . . .

"Blackwell?" she choked out.

"Yes?" He stepped closer to her, eyes burning with concern at the sudden shift in her demeanor.

"How long does it take for Phantasma to move cities? How many days between each competition?" she asked.

"Less than forty-eight hours. Why?"

Which meant her father *had* lost around the day of the eighth level . . . *this* level. And the person her father loved most, the one who would have been used in this trial for him . . .

"I think I'm going to pass out," she whispered to him.

He was there in an instant, helping her to the ground as she began to hyperventilate. The two Genevieves stopped arguing long enough to rush over.

"What's wrong with her?" they asked at the same time, before glaring daggers at each other.

"Back off for a moment," Blackwell barked at them. "Give her some space."

He turned back to her and ran a soothing hand over her hair. She was struggling to gulp in enough air as she realized the magnitude of this trial.

"Ophelia. Breathe, angel. With me, okay?"

She nodded at him, and he began counting her breaths out for her.

When she finally regained control, she looked at him and said, "My father is the reason our mother died. It wasn't a heart attack. It was this level. He must have...he must have guessed incorrectly."

Blackwell froze. And she saw it, in his eyes, how he was running through the details, the timelines, and coming to the exact same conclusion. A sob ripped through her chest at the unspoken confirmation in his eyes. Something about him putting the pieces together as well, solidifying the reality of it, is what finally broke her.

"I'm so sorry, angel," he murmured as he wiped away her tears. "I'm so very fucking sorry. I had no idea, Ophelia. *I swear.* He had stopped summoning me to help him in the trials long before he got to this one. Sometimes, I wonder why he took my bargain in the first place. If there was anything I could do..."

"I don't understand what's happening," one of the Genevieves sniffed.

Ophelia took a deep breath and stood, Blackwell giving her

space to steady herself on her own feet. She took in the two Genevieves staring at her with concern. They both looked like impeccable replicas of her little sister. Golden brown hair, bright teal eyes beneath the same thick lashes as Ophelia's. Full eyebrows and even fuller lips. Every detail was there—down to each freckle painted across their rosy cheeks and the bridges of their noses, to their frilly pink gowns.

"I broke two ribs after falling down Grimm Manor's stairs when you were chasing me playing tag," Ophelia said, voice thick. "How old were we?"

"It was only one rib," they both said at the same time. Then the first doppelganger crossed her arms and said, "You were twelve. I was nine. And it was an *accident*."

Fuck. This was going to be difficult.

"You have to ask questions that aren't based on memories you have yourself," Blackwell told her. "The manor's magic can take what's in your mind and put it into the imposter's."

"What in the Hell does that mean? What could I possibly ask that I wouldn't already know the answer to—wait." An idea suddenly came to her, and Blackwell dipped his chin in an encouraging nod. "What about—how many people have you kissed?"

It was a question that Ophelia would have no exact answer for in her own mind, but whatever each version of Genevieve answered would be incredibly telling.

The doppelgangers were silent for a moment.

Then the first finally said, "I don't know *exactly*, if I'm honest. Too many drunk kisses at parties to remember every single one...but I'd estimate around thirty?"

"*Thirty?*" the second Genevieve scoffed. "That's insulting. It's only eleven."

They all turned to Ophelia, Blackwell observing her carefully, and she turned each of the answers over in her mind. She knew, without a doubt, that the first Genevieve was an imposter. Not because of the number, but because of the short glimpses she'd gotten into Genevieve's diary before she'd come to Phantasma. Genevieve had recorded even the most frivolous details of her life in its daily entries. What color she'd worn, what sort of birds she'd seen on her walks to and from the city, how many times Ophelia had rolled her eyes in a single morning...there was no way Genevieve would ever have to estimate such a thing as how many kisses she'd had.

The second Genevieve's answer, however, was a conundrum.

An exact number. But one that was highly implausible despite Ophelia only being able to remember a handful of names her sister had mentioned brief affairs with over the years. Not after Genevieve had admitted to keeping things from Ophelia as to not rub her social life in her sister's face. If Ophelia could count almost eleven in just her own memory, however, then that meant...

Ophelia reached up to grasp onto her locket with one hand and approached the first Genevieve. Nothing. As she expected. She turned to the second one. Again nothing.

She took a deep breath and then a leap of faith.

"Neither one of them are Genevieve," she declared.

At first, nothing happened, and she and Blackwell held their breaths. The two Genevieves glanced worriedly at each other as they waited for their own fates.

Then both of them dissolved into clouds of smoke.

"You did it," Blackwell declared, pride in his voice.

A portal appeared in the middle of the room then.

She strutted toward it with purpose. "Now, if you'll excuse me. I have a bone to pick with the Prince of the Devils."

49

HEARTS

One thing Blackwell had always been right about was that soft hearts did no one any good. They broke over and over again. They bled for those who didn't deserve it. So, when she finally got an audience with Phantasma's creator, her heart would not be soft. It would be hardened from all the heartbreak she had experienced in the last two weeks. And the heartbreak that had not yet come as her time with Blackwell dwindled to an end.

Unless she did something about it.

And if the Prince of the Devils refused to give her what she wanted?

Then she would show him her teeth.

LEVEL
NINE

50

TREACHERY

Ophelia stepped from the portal and emerged back into the foyer. She tore through the space with purpose, making her way to find a place with blank wall as she waited for Blackwell to reappear.

"Where are you going?" Sinclair demanded from his post next to the portal.

She paused, turning to bare her teeth at the Devil. "To finish this."

"What do you mean, *finish this?*" he said, seething.

"I suppose you'll have to wait and see, won't you?" She grinned.

A moment later, Blackwell blinked in at her side. "You're going to summon the door again." A statement.

"Yes," she confirmed. "I am."

Sinclair balked in disbelief. "That isn't possible. Only Salemaestrus can make it appear—when there's one last contestant standing."

Blackwell's smile was knowing. "She's done it before."

Sinclair sputtered. "*No.*"

Ophelia closed her eyes and recalled the scene of the door. It was right before she had met Blackwell, well, *officially* met Blackwell. It was at the end of the hallway in her group's wing, but she had a pretty good hunch that the location didn't matter. Only access to a blank canvas. She pictured how the doorway stretched up out of thin air, the enormous wrought-iron frame fitted with scarlet mosaics, the gilded handle.

Her locket began to heat around her neck, and when she opened her eyes, there it was. Sinclair gaped in awe at her for a moment before his expression gave way to fury.

"You do not understand what you are walking into, girl," he spat. "Listen to me—"

She laughed, cutting him off. "I suppose it's a good thing that's my problem and not yours, right?"

She strode to the door, Blackwell at her back, watching Sinclair to make sure the Devil didn't decide to charge at her. She grasped the handle and tugged, but the door didn't budge. She glanced back at Blackwell in question.

"You have to say the creator's name for it to unlock. It's why I couldn't help you open it before—I couldn't say his name unless you already knew it," he told her. "Usually, the final contestant receives it on the tenth day, but...it should still work."

"I'm warning you, girl," Sinclair said. "You will be sorry if you do this."

She paid the Devil no mind. Taking a deep breath, she turned to Blackwell and whispered, "Do you truly believe we can always find our ways back to each other? You've said before nothing would ever stop you from getting to me if I needed you. That you would tear the universe apart at its seams to keep that vow. Do you still mean that?"

He reached up to grasp her face in his hands. "With every ounce of my soul. When you go through that door, it will not be the last time I see you."

"You promise?" she whispered.

"I *swear*, angel," he vowed.

She nodded and called out, "*Salemaestrus.*"

The heavy metallic click of a lock came from the doorknob in front of her, and this time, when she pulled at the handle, the door swung open. There was nothing but darkness and the essence of power beyond the frame. Blackwell let her go, a pained expression on his face as he watched her step forward. A deep gust of wind sucked her inside and the door slammed shut behind her, severing her from Blackwell and the manor.

The gust of wind pulled and pulled at her body until she found herself approaching a single spot of light. When her feet hit the floor, she spun around in a circle, squinting to try and make out *something* in the shadowy abyss.

"Hello?" she called. "Salemaestrus! I'm here for my prize."

There was no answer. Only silence. Minutes went by, possibly hours, as she waited in the dark. And she was growing impatient. She wanted to do this alone. For herself. But she wondered what would happen if she summoned Blackwell. If there was a detail she was missing since she hadn't received a clue for this trial.

Just call him, she told herself. *It doesn't make you weak to ask for help. You're still going to be the victor.*

She called for Blackwell and waited. There was no response.

Maybe he can't be summoned in this level, she thought to herself.

But suddenly the energy shifted around her, power like she'd never felt before filling the space around her. Somewhere beyond the small glowing circle she was standing in, footsteps approached.

"Hello, angel," a deep velvet voice greeted her.

Blackwell stepped into the ring of light.

"Good, you heard me," she said with relief. "Do you know what I should do next?"

He was unnervingly silent. She narrowed her eyes. Something was different.

"Blackwell?" she whispered.

"Firstly, let me reintroduce myself." He dipped his head in a formal bow. "My name is Salemaestrus Erasmus Blackwell, Prince of the Devils. But you, angel, may call me Salem."

Five Centuries
Before
Phantasma

51

TETHERED

As Prince of the Devils, Salemaestrus thought he'd long ago experienced the darkest things Hell had to offer. He'd witnessed the gruesome purgatory pits countless times. Had watched souls within them tear each other limb from limb for centuries on end, in the hope of climbing out to a better afterlife. He'd been the harbinger of pain and death, himself, for many souls—mortal and immortal alike—over the last five centuries.

But the moment he realized she had been taken... That was an agony unlike he'd ever known.

It had been nearly a year since he'd vowed to her to never return to the heart of Hell, since he'd seen the rolling, infernal iris-covered hills of Nocturnia. Now he stood before the expansive gates of his father's palace, shoulders heavy with the weight of his broken vows. But there was nothing that would keep him from getting to her. Not even the promises between them.

The gates, made of onyx flames that licked all the way up into the tempestuous sky, parted for him almost instantly. Recognizing him. Blazing brighter as if to celebrate his return.

He stalked through the glittering, obsidian halls like a Hellhound following the scent of blood. But beneath the vicious fury shrouding him like a cloud of smoke, there was terror sinking into his bones. He could feel her here. Within these insidious walls, where she did not belong. Her heart was too soft for this place.

I'm coming, he swore. I'm coming for you.

A line of guards were posted outside of his father's throne room, waiting for him. It was nothing more than a show, of course. Not even an army would be able to stop his power. It was merely a point to be proven. That he was still the cruel, vicious Prince of the Devils his father raised him to be. That he could never be tamed.

A vicious snarl ripped from his throat as he unleashed a wave of dark magic over the unit of guards, splattering gore across the pristine, diamond floors, he thought that perhaps that was true. He could not be tamed. Would not be. Except by her.

He would be every bit of good she so desperately wanted to see in him as long as she was safe. But now... now he'd tear the world to shreds.

The double doors were still dripping with blood as he used his magic to blast them open. Beyond them, the enormous, black throne room was sweltering with heat from amethyst-and-ink-colored flames that covered its walls.

The King of the Devils was sitting atop his diamond throne, a crown of ebony flames resting atop his head. He smiled down from the dais at Salem. Purring atop the King's lap was his favorite little spy. The cat yawned lazily at the building tension rolling through the room as Salem approached his father.

At the bottom left of the dais steps, Salem spotted Sinclair, held captive between two Demon guards. It took everything for him not to charge the fucking bastard and rip him limb from limb. This was all Sinclair's fault, and he loathed the fact that he'd ever considered the other Devil a friend.

By the murderous look in Sinclair's scarlet eyes, that sentiment was returned.

Salem bared his teeth at the King as he approached the steps to the throne. "Where the fuck is she?"

His father laughed. "Is that how you greet your father after all this time?"

Salem seethed. "Don't fucking play with me. If you don't let her go, I will burn all of Nocturnia to the ground. And the rest Hell with it."

The smile never left his father's face. "Unfortunately, I do believe you would try such a thing. But there's one little detail you're missing, my Prince."

Salem narrowed his eyes as his father stood and transported down the stairs from his throne. The King stopped right in front of him, leaning in to whisper the most bone-chilling words he'd ever heard on his father's lips.

"I know your True Name."

Salem felt his blood run cold.

No.

It couldn't be.

He'd only ever given his True Name to one person...

"Ah, and therein lies the problem," the King said as he pulled back, with a smile still on his lips but only malice in his eyes. "You can play at being powerful all you want, Salemaestrus, but at the end of the day you gave all of your power away the moment you fell in love with a silly fucking mortal."

His father said the word mortal like it was a curse.

"But don't be too upset with her," his father continued. "After all, mortals are such fragile little things. Haven't I always warned you of that? It was only a matter of time until she succumbed to the torture. Though, I will say, I was mildly impressed she managed to last nearly three days before screaming your True Name for all to hear. Hoping you would come to rescue her."

Pain ripped through Salem at the idea of her being tortured, calling his name so desperately, only for him never to come. His vision went completely red as he lunged for his father, wrapping his hands around the man's throat.

"Why are you doing this?" he snarled. "She's done nothing to deserve it."

"She made you a fucking liability," his father hissed back as he ripped himself out of Salem's hold. "She made you a weakness to this entire kingdom. I warned you that you'd regret choosing her over your duty to Nocturnia."

"Then punish me," Salem demanded. "I'm the one who disobeyed you. Not her. Punish me."

The second the insidious smile began spreading over his father's face he regretted his words.

"Don't worry. That's exactly what I plan to do." The King snapped his fingers. "Bring her out."

The breath rushed from Salem's lungs as he watched two new guards appear from thin air a few feet away, a body hanging limp between them. He'd disemboweled his enemies, ripped out their hearts, and bled them dry for centuries without blinking. But this...he nearly vomited when he saw the state of her.

He pushed away the Demons that were holding her up, dropping to his knees on the floor as he cradled her body to his. He didn't care that his father would see the display as yet another weakness. He needed to touch her, to heal her. She was covered in so many bruises and lacerations that there was not a single square inch of unblemished skin on her body. Her dark brown hair was matted with blood. Her crystal-blue eyes were dull with pain. There was a nasty slice in her bottom lip, and she was—fucking Hell—she was missing her incisors.

"Angel," he whispered, his fingertips brushing over her face in soothing strokes as he worked to keep the terror out of his voice. He didn't need to make her panic. "I'm here, Angel. You're going to be alright. I'm going to fix it."

She swallowed, her watery eyes squinting up at him. "Salem... You're really here?" A sob erupted from her throat. "You came. You came for me. I told them you would."

The adoration that she still had shining for him in her gaze made him loathe himself. He didn't deserve it. He'd failed her.

He buried his face in her neck, petting a hand over the back of her head. "I told you, I'll always come. I'm sorry it wasn't sooner. I'm so fucking sorry."

She clung to him as hard as her remaining strength would allow as if she still didn't quite believe he was real. Devastating.

Too soon she was ripped from his arms. Magic slammed into his body, sending him flying back from her. He rolled back to his feet in an instant, but his father had already reached her.

Her back was flush to the King's chest, his arm wrapped around the front of her torso while his hand gripped her by the throat.

"Stop," Salem croaked. "What do you want from me? Do you want me to beg? I'll fucking beg."

"It's much too late for that," his father said.

"I'll return to Nocturnia," Salem vowed, staggering a step toward them. "For the rest of my eternal life if that's what you desire. Just don't harm her. Let her go back to her life."

"Don't move, Blackwell," his father's voice thundered through the room.

Salem froze in place. A magic hold flooded through his entire being at the invocation of his True Name.

The King smiled as he brought his lips next to Angel's ear. "Any last words, girl, for your beloved?"

A weight of hopelessness settled on Salem's shoulders as he was forced to watch Angel struggle to raise her head enough to meet his gaze. And the look of resignation in her blue eyes made him want to roar. He fought against the magic holding him, bucked and pushed until every muscle in his body was trembling with the effort. All to no avail.

"I love you, Salem," she whispered.

When his father's command wouldn't allow him to respond, the King laughed and ordered, "Speak, Blackwell."

"I love you," Salem choked out. "I'm sorry you ever met me. I'll never forgive myself."

"Please..." She swallowed with effort. "Please, don't forget me."

"Never."

"You promise?" she pleaded.

"I swear, Angel," he avowed.

Then the King of the Devils reached into her chest and tore out her heart.

Salem roared and the fire bordering the room burned brighter, slithering up the walls and stretching all the way to the ceiling above. His cry was so loud that even the beings in Heaven must have heard it.

The King snapped his fingers, the ones not wrapped around Angel's bleeding heart, and a Demon servant appeared. The King dropped the girl's corpse and heart to the servant's feet, and Salem cursed him for the grotesque display of apathy. "Dispose of her as we discussed."

The Demon gave a single nod before removing her limp, blood-covered body and disappearing.

"Approach me, Blackwell," the King ordered now.

"I will fucking end you," Salem swore as his feet involuntarily carried him toward the man. "I will not rest until I melt every inch of flesh from your bones and dig the forsaken heart from your own chest. I will feed it to your Hellhounds and then I will give them your soul to play with until it is ripped to shreds."

A cruel twinkle glinted in his father's eyes. "And how will you do that, son, when I banish you from here and tether you somewhere else?"

Salem snapped. "What the fuck are you talking about?"

"Did you think taking her away was your only punishment? That part was much too easy to be any fun," his father carped. "You wanted to betray me so you could play house with your precious little mortal, you wanted to let her wield your True Name? I've created a place where you will be able to experience both for however long I deem satisfactory."

Salem suddenly felt very tired. His father knew his True Name.

Every threat he wanted to aim at the man was empty. And now that Angel had been taken...he didn't have anything left to fight for anyway.

"Don't lose all hope so quickly," his father admonished. "I've left you a loophole."

Salem was too exhausted to ask what the loophole might be. No, not exhausted. Numb. Cold.

The King reached out and gripped his son's face with malice. "Salemaestrus Erasmus Blackwell, I am hereby sentencing you to my newest creation—Phantasma. A place of nightmares that you will rule with no memory of the traitorous little bastard you've become to me—and maybe you'll eventually learn how to deserve your title of Prince of the Devils. You will belong to Phantasma and myself evermore—unless you find the heart and a key to set you free," the King invoked.

"And if I do set myself free?" Salem wondered.

"You will receive a fair reward. What's your price?" The King smiled.

"I want every single soul who knows my True Name to forget it," Salem seethed.

The King laughed. "That won't bring her back. But you have a deal. If you manage to release yourself from Phantasma, I vow to forget your true name."

As the magic of his father's unbreakable vow settled over them, the King snapped his fingers and Salem watched as the other Demon guards he'd forgotten were still in the room shoved Sinclair forward.

"Sinclair. Please escort my son to your new home. Make sure you go over every little detail we discussed before the game begins, hmm?"

Sinclair dipped his head in a bow at the King's request before turning to Salem and making a sharp, beckoning gesture with his chin.

"Let's go, Blackwell," Sinclair ordered, utter hatred dripping off of every syllable.

Salemaestrus followed his former friend out of the throne room without another word. The only thought echoing in his mind her name. As it would until there was nothing left of him but dust.

Angel.

The King of the Devils watched his son disappear from the palace, waiting until he could no longer feel the Prince's essence within its walls.

"Poe," he requested to the empty room.

The cat appeared seconds later, a mewl ringing out of its mouth as it awaited orders.

"Follow them. Report back to me at the end of each game," he instructed.

The cat blinked out of the room once again as the King transported himself back to his throne. Settling back into its velvet cushions as he snapped his fingers. Four of his servants were immediately lined up in front of him, standing shoulder to shoulder at attention.

He tapped a foot on the ground, thoughtfully, as he tilted his head at one of the servants in particular. "Dahlia. Did you take care of the mortal as I requested?"

Dahlia, a young Demon with a gift for soul-singing stepped forward from the line. She reached into the pocket of her tailored trousers and pulled something out. A golden, heart-shaped locket.

"Yes, your Highness," Dahlia confirmed as she transferred the locket to the King's hand. "All that's left is to choose who will receive the mortal's soul, and when it shall be released."

"The soul needs to be reborn to someone who will not balk at a place such as Phantasma, but will have a healthy dose of apprehension in regards to it. We cannot make the game too easy for Salemaestrus after all."

"A paranormal mortal, perhaps?" Dahlia suggested and a spark of excitement went through the King.

"Precisely," the King confirmed. "Not a seer. They would have too much of an advantage. A being who will know the consequence of magic and will give the darling little curse I've placed on Phantasma heavy consideration before deciding to choose my son despite it."

Dahlia dipped her head in understanding. "And how long should I assure the necklace be worn before the soul is released and reborn?"

The King considered for a moment. "Let's give him five centuries. Make sure my magic has time to make him really forget her. Too much sooner and he might still be able to recognize her soul. Make sure whoever you compel to wear the necklace will never take it off until it is passed to the next host and so on."

"There is a Necromancer currently residing in the dungeon, your Highness. Hestia Grimm," one of the other servants chimed in. "The woman who was attempting to create an undead army. Her hatred for Devils and Hell may make her a viable candidate."

The King smiled as he tossed the locket back to Dahlia. "Perfect."

THE END OF
PHANTASMA

52

UNTETHERED

"I...don't get it," Ophelia said, hating how her voice began to shake.

My name is Salemaestrus Erasmus Blackwell, Prince of the Devils.

"I know," Blackwell said, a sad smile on his lips. "You've played a good game, though, angel. And now I can give you what you're owed." He began to circle her slowly. "Since you made it to the last level, I'll cut your payment to me for our blood bargain from ten years to five and you can otherwise walk away unscathed."

She frowned at him. "No, I get to choose what I use my Devil's Grant for."

He shook his head. "I'm afraid you entered this level too early to technically be the grand prize winner. The rules are that you have to be the last person in Phantasma, alive, to win the Devil's Grant, and there were still other contestants playing the game when you entered here. So, your choice is to take the reduced sentence or to be disqualified altogether."

She stared at him in disbelief. Of all the times she'd thought about the end of her journey in Phantasma, this had never been in even her wildest imaginings.

Salemaestrus Erasmus Blackwell. Prince of the Devils.

"So, what will it be?" He moved to stand right in front of her.

The Devil had a wicked mouth and a voice as smooth as bourbon.

"What is your decision?" he pressed as he trailed the tip of his index finger down one side of her throat, his lips mere centimeters from her racing pulse on the other.

"You tricked me," she whispered.

He laughed in response, his breath caressing her feverish skin.

He was so close that she could barely think.

Any coherent response to his question eluded her as another shot of adrenaline rushed through her veins, but the events leading up to this moment were burned into her mind with vivid clarity. She had done this to herself. She had been so *foolish*.

"But you don't have a Devil's Mark," she whispered. "And you were a *Phantom*."

He gestured to his silvery white hair. "I admit my Devil's Mark is particularly convenient for blending in as a Ghost."

"Are you *kidding* me?" she growled.

"Don't feel bad, angel, you aren't nearly the first person I've fooled. I've been at this for a very long time."

"*Why?*" she demanded.

"Sinclair told you a story of my past, did he not?"

"Yes."

"And what did he say?"

She swallowed. "He said that you fell in love and chose your lover over the King of the Devils—your father. As punishment, your lover was killed and now you must run Phantasma for the rest of your existence."

"All true," he confirmed. "Except my father did give me one mercy—a loophole. All I've needed was a heart and a hidden key and I would be untethered from this place. The only problem is that every time a new game begins, the memories of my true self are wiped away completely. The only time I am returned to my full self is when a contestant reaches this level until the start of each new game. My one reprieve. And even the memories I have as this version of myself have become murky with every passing century."

She gasped. "You mean the first time I met you..."

"You met the real me—*this* version of me." He nodded, then smiled. "What's left of me at least. You're the first person in centuries I was ever able to talk to outside of the competition and the manor. Who I was able to tell about the heart and the key. And it still did me no good. How could it, when my own memories worked against me? I hardly remember anything before I was tethered to this place. Except the rage for my father. That has remained."

Deep sorrow was laced beneath his words, and—despite the shock and betrayal of his true identity—her heart ached for him. What a miserable existence not to remember your own self.

"So, you choose a contestant each competition to help you find this mysterious key," she said. "What about the contestants you don't choose? Are they actually playing to win?"

He shrugged. "Sure they are. And if they do, they get their prize. But more often than not my chosen one makes it to the end. As you can clearly see. And those who lose their lives here simply fuel the manor's power."

"I don't understand why Sin talked about you as if you were two different people," she said. "Or why you were referred to as the creator if it was your father that made this place."

"Ah." He laughed. "That's because as part of the punishment he can tell people *about* me but never directly who I am within the competition. The two entities must be kept separate—the Devil and the Phantom. My father gave Sinclair his own loophole when he banished him here with me—as well as Poe, the little spy."

"Wait, even the *cat* was in on this?"

Blackwell snorted, before continuing, "The title of the creator is used for my alter ego's benefit since I become unaware of my true identity within the game. I suppose I *am* the creator, in a sense, considering Phantasma wouldn't even exist if it weren't a punishment for me. Sinclair's job is to make sure I don't break free. If he succeeds for long enough, he may be pardoned early, and some other fool who pissed off my father would have to take his place. A sort of insurance policy that I stayed as long as possible. My father is a spiteful man."

"I'm sure," she deadpanned.

He tilted his head thoughtfully now. "What I find most interesting, however, is how hard Sinclair tried to stop *you*. He's never worked so hard at it before."

She looked down at her hands. "I really thought . . . I thought I could save you. I thought I was getting close."

"Me too, angel."

Something about the way he said those words, the way he still called her *angel*, unraveled something within her.

"Was . . . was any of it real?" she whispered.

"As real as it could've been with only half my memories," he said, eyes shutting before she could see whatever emotion he was hiding in them.

"I know I should be furious at you, murderous even, but I . . ."

"Don't," he ordered. "Don't waste any of your emotions on me. This is where we must part ways, and feeling anything for me at all isn't worth it for you. It would be best if you just forgot me altogether."

"Everyone who falls in love within Phantasma is cursed . . . because falling in love is what got you into this in the first place," she stated, remembering the realization she'd had the first time she'd heard the story from Sinclair.

"My father has a sense of humor, don't you think?" He shook his head. "Yet he wondered why I chose someone over him."

"I'm sorry you lost them," she said sincerely, though the words made her ache inside. "Truly."

"It was a very long time ago," he told her. "I'm ashamed to say I can't even...I can't even remember them now. Sometimes, I get flashes of details, small hauntings from the past, but they're gone so quickly. Now they're just another thing time has taken from me. I'll never forgive my father for that."

"Blackwe—*Salem*," she corrected herself. She needed to separate the Phantom she knew and this Devil she was still unsure of. "I want you to know that it was all very real for me. It still is. I was going to ask to use my Devil's Grant to find and break your tether."

He froze in utter shock. "Ophelia."

"The bargain was that I had to find it before I left the grounds. So, it would have counted, right?"

He swallowed. "You would have done that for me?"

"*Of course*," she said. "You don't get it. I—"

"*No*." He lunged forward, clapping his hand over her mouth. His green eyes burned with new intensity as he ordered, "*Don't*."

She pushed his hand away and declared, "It's true, though." A single tear slid down her face. "And I know it's foolish, I know we've spent this entire time making sure we avoided this very thing. Does it really matter if I say it aloud or not? You've changed me." She took a deep breath, reaching up to hold on to the locket beating wildly around her neck for comfort. "Even the necklace has always seemed to know it. My heart is completely and utterly..."

She gaped at him in shock.

"*What?*" he asked.

"That's it," she realized.

"What's it?"

"What you've been searching for is...me. *This*." She yanked at the necklace until the chain snapped away and dangled the heart-shaped piece between them. The heart in her chest began to slow ever so slightly.

He looked at her as if she had gone a little bit mad, but there was also a spark of something like hope in his eyes, and that was what she was going to hold on to.

"Your father trapped you in a place where it's forbidden to fall in love or there's a dire consequence. You told me you needed a heart and a key . . . but what if that's not two separate clues? This necklace, it's enchanted, it beats with my own heart. In my fight with Cade, he ripped it off me and my heart, it . . ."

"It what?" Blackwell prompted.

"It nearly stopped."

Blackwell sucked in a breath before reaching forward and flattening his palm over her chest to feel her weakening heartbeat. "But what about the key portion?"

She shook her head. "That, I'm not sure. Maybe the key is inside of it? But no one has ever been able to get the damn thing open. But this has to be right, doesn't it? Sinclair taking such an intense interest in me . . . making you jealous . . . trying to drive any wedge he could between the two of us . . . my mother warning me to stay away from you . . . telling me to never, ever take the necklace off . . . always warning me away from Devils . . ."

Blackwell rocked back on his heels in shock, and that was all she needed as confirmation.

"Here." She took his hand and set the locket in his palm before curling his fingers over it. "My heart, it's yours."

"If you give this to me, you will die," he told her. "Do you understand that?"

"Yes," she whispered. "I could have died plenty of times in this manor. But I love—"

"*No. Listen to me,*" he implored as he recovered, moving to grasp her face in his hands, the warm metal of the necklace pressing against her cheek. "Your heart is one thing. Hearts can be fixed. But you will still be cursed. If I'm set free, I will be immune to the curse, my prize for beating my father, but *you* will still face the consequences for breaking Phantasma's cardinal rule. Even if Phantasma crumbles to dust."

She smiled sadly at him. "It's okay."

"Ophelia, *don't*—"

"I love you," she whispered. "I love you so much. You saved me. So many times, in so many ways, and it barely took you a week to change me so intrinsically. I may never be rid of my inner demons, but for this single sliver of time, whenever we were together, you made them *quiet*. I was able to hear *myself* for once. And I want you to know that I will gladly take on whatever this place is going to curse me with knowing you will finally get out of the Hell you've been trapped in for so long."

Tears flowed down her face as he shook his head at her confession, his expression marred by agony.

"*No*," he pleaded.

The pain hit her an instant later. Phantasma's cursed magic forcing itself through her system, making her knees buckle to the ground.

Loving him will only ruin you, her mother had warned her, but only now did Ophelia realized what she had really meant. She had meant that loving Blackwell would only affect *Ophelia*. Blackwell would walk away unscathed. She wondered if her mother had known about this all along. Or if Tessie Grimm had only learned of the scope of Phantasma's rules in the afterlife.

She doubled over as another shot of pain cut through her thoughts. And then Blackwell began to transform as well.

Her locket began to glow in his hand, a bright, icy blue. Grimm Blue. The locket lifted into the air, prying itself open and bursting with a light that enveloped the darkness around them completely. Blackwell roared as power and magic began to swirl around them from the necklace, flooding into his body. His full powers were returned to him. He was officially untethered from Phantasma. He was free.

"*No*," he snarled as soon as the light dissipated, and the locket fell to the ground with a pitiful clink. Her heart was now a slow faint thud in her chest. "He will not take you from me, too. Not again. Never again."

She cried out in misery as the curse continued ripping through her, her fingernails turning purple as her blood circulation slowed.

"Ophelia," he pleaded, scooping her necklace up from the ground, to clutch it safely back in his hand. "I can return a working heart to you as your payment for setting me free—but you have to verbally tell me you agree to that as your payment. The curse, though...that's another ordeal entirely."

She gritted her teeth against the pain as she forced herself to look at him, her next words coming out breathless. "The heart...yes...I agree to the heart...as my payment."

"This might hurt a little," he told her as his hands began to glow blue. He placed them both over her chest, and she felt the warmth of his magic move through her instantly. For a loaded moment, there was a heavy pressure within, an ache as something bloomed beneath her flesh. And then it was over, and she felt it.

A heartbeat. She took a deep breath of air, and Blackwell cupped her face in his hands, pressing his forehead down to hers in relief.

"Thank fucking Hell," he whispered.

She cleared her throat, her words still weak as she pressed, "Phantasma's curse..."

As soon as she mentioned Phantasma, an aftershock of pain rolled through her body.

He leaned back so he could look her directly in the eyes, soothing his hands over her face in comfort. "The only way I can break a curse of my father's that is this powerful is by making you a deal."

"If you..." He hesitated. "If you sign your soul over to me, I can eradicate the curse from it. I promise to return it to you, unblemished, after."

A sob racked through her chest. Signing over her soul to a Devil—no, the *Prince of the Devils*—was possibly the most inadvisable thing anyone could do. As much as she wanted to trust Blackwell's word to return it...she couldn't risk such a thing. If she perished without her soul, she would have no afterlife.

It's another trick, the Shadow Voice seethed. ***All of this is a trick to get your soul.***

"I can't," she cried, holding on to the lapels of his shirt. "Please, anything else. *Anything.* I'm begging, alright? *Please.*"

His gaze was full of remorse. "To break something like this, I need a significant amount of energy to balance out what's being destroyed. I would need a permanent tether."

Her breath hitched as the agony slowly began to subside, the curse beginning to settle deep in her marrow.

His green eyes held her gaze. "Phantasma was my permanent tether before. The souls that came through here supplied me with energy, and I supplied it back to the manor. Even with my full power returned, now that the ties between me and the manor are cut, Phantasma is falling apart. Which means that without bargains to sustain me, I'd have to return to the Other Side."

"Phantasma is *falling apart*?"

He nodded. "I can feel it. It's crumbling. The Devils will have to go elsewhere for business. The Apparitions will be released from the estate. Sinclair will have to return to my father for the remainder of his indebted sentence for failing to keep me tied here."

"If I agree to be your new tether," she began, her vision beginning to blur, "what would that entail?"

"Forever. With me."

"*And?*"

He smirked. "Is that not enticing enough for you?"

"Don't toy with me right now," she grunted. "What else?"

"Your soul would remain yours, but your energy and life span would not."

"Life span? You mean—?"

"If I lived for eternity, so would you," he confirmed. "I would be able to use your newly immortal lifeforce to fuel my magic and stay on this linear plane as long as I want without having to worry about constantly making bargains as other Devils do."

She took a deep breath. "Okay."

"Forever is a very long time," he warned. "Are you sure you know what you're agreeing to?"

"I know," she promised. "Especially considering I'm going to have to deal with your mouth for eternity. I don't take that lightly."

"Please," he drawled. "We both know how much you love my mouth."

She glowered. "I am already regretting this, honestly."

His face became serious once more. "Ophelia I...I am so fucking in love with you. I think I fell in love with you when you asked me how you could help me that first time we met. Prince of the Devils, and you wanted to save me. Maybe, somehow, I knew then that you could be the one to set me free. And I meant what I said that night, that you should hope we never met again, and I fucking hate that this is what it's coming down to. But...

every single second I've spent with you has reminded me what it's like to be *alive*. And I would trade every other soul in the world if it meant I would get to keep you forever."

A tear rolled down her face. He swallowed as he brushed it away.

"But..." he continued, "whatever the curse did to you—whatever unique side effect it has chosen to inflict—it would only affect you when it comes to being in proximity to *me*. You can still walk away, Ophelia. Go back to your life with your sister that you've always planned. You set me free of Phantasma, you don't owe me a decade of your life anymore. It will all be like this never happened."

"But it *did* happen," she told him. "And if I walk away now, the curse will make sure we'd lose each other forever."

He pressed his forehead against hers. "I worry you don't understand the burden of eternity. You don't need to tie yourself to me in worry that we'd lose each other. Now that I'm free, I will carry the memories of this time with you forevermore. The matter of my soul will always have your name etched into it. I may not have been able to remember my true identity within the manor, but I was still *me*. I know the truth of what I felt for you then and I know the truth of what I feel for you now." He took a deep breath. "And if you *do* choose to be my tether, I need you to know that does not mean you have to stay with me. You'd be free to live your eternal life however you want. Even if that means you decide you never want to see me again."

She took a shaky breath.

"Now or never, angel," he told her.

This was it. What everything since her mother's death had led to. Her choosing what sort of future she was going to have. What sort of legacy.

"What's your decision?"

EPILOGUE

Legacy

As Ophelia strolled through New Orleans, there was a sense of peace in the air around her. She was almost home, only twenty or so minutes out, and when she stopped in front of the restored cathedral, she remembered why that was.

Phantasma had crumbled to the ground and vanished without a trace. The cathedral had returned to its rightful place where the Devil's Manor once sat, no sign it had ever existed here at all. New Orleans after dark had become lighter in the past few weeks. Rumors that Devils no longer walked the streets had begun to circulate... something about the atmosphere having changed. People not as desperate to make inadvisable deals after the sun went down.

Ophelia had become more comfortable roaming the city by herself even past dusk. Had settled into the idea that she was powerful enough to look at the dark and could handle whatever might look back.

She quickened her pace up the road, hating to linger on things of the past when she had a much more exciting future. When she spotted the rose-covered gates of Grimm Manor, anticipation thrummed through her veins. She and Genevieve still had a lot to work out; they had been making an effort to untangle the delicate threads of tension from their childhood, but Ophelia had never been more confident of where she stood with her sister.

She's going to hate your surprise, the Shadow Voice rasped.

Ophelia ignored it, something that had become easier with every passing day. She had been working on putting together this surprise for nearly two months and absolutely nothing was going to ruin her mood about it.

She hurried up their long driveway, leaping up onto the porch to push their front door open, calling Genevieve's name as she stepped into the foyer.

"I have a surprise for you!" she announced.

She removed her walking jacket and slung it over the entry-way table, slipping her gift to Genevieve out of its front pocket as she padded her way through the house to the main den. Grimm Manor felt lighter than ever, which was partially down to the fact that it had been dusted top to bottom and the girls had taken it upon themselves to begin decluttering their mother's things, finally ready to lay Tessie Grimm's memory to rest. They had packed up all the sentimental bits and bobs into the attic space upstairs, of course, but a clean slate meant they could start making the place really their own. And Ophelia could decide which parts of her mother's practice she'd like to continue of her own volition and not because of any overwhelming guilt.

Since Phantasma had fallen, Ophelia had been carefully assessing what she wanted to do with her magic. She found that she'd developed a soft spot for other paranormal beings, ones such as herself, Genevieve, and Luci, who felt as if they had no choice but to thrust themselves into perilous situations when hard times struck. She wondered if there may be an untapped avenue of business to explore there instead of dealing with corpses and death day in and day out. To be a sort of safe haven to explore options of assistance in the paranormal realm before making an ill-advised deal with a being who had malicious intents.

The new Grimm legacy.

"Genevieve?" she called again as she checked the drinking parlor and the study.

When she made her way back to the living area, she slipped her shoes off and walked over to one of the large windows that lined the main wall. They had taken to tying the curtains back, letting in as much natural light as they could. A moment later, she heard footsteps behind her and smiled.

When she turned, she found Salem leaning in the doorway, the corners of his lips lifting in an exasperated smile as Poe purred away in his arms. The cat had apparently bonded to him enough over their centuries together in Phantasma that the little fiend decided to remain here instead of returning to Hell.

"Distracting your sister is not a task for the faint of heart," Salem commented, letting Poe drop to the ground and scamper off.

She laughed. "I know, why do you think I asked *you* to do it?"

He pushed away from the wall to walk over to her, wrapping his arms around her waist as he dipped his head to press an affectionate kiss against the side of her throat. "Welcome home."

She hummed in contentment. "Did the two of you make any progress on the locket research?"

As she mentioned the necklace, her hand automatically reached up between their bodies to touch the bauble clasped around her throat. It was cold to the touch, its heartbeat dormant since they used it to free Salem from Phantasma. It had made them all curious as to how her family received such a piece in the first place, but so far, they were unable to figure out how, of all families, the Grimm women came to possess such a crucial item from the King of the Devils himself. How serendipitous it was for it to fall into Ophelia's hands. And though it no longer held the magic it once did, it was still one of the most precious things she owned.

She tapped a finger against it now with affection. *One, two, three.*

"Just more dead ends," he answered. "Did you have any issues picking up the tickets?"

She shook her head as she held the envelope up for him to see. "They were waiting for me as promised. Thanks for arranging everything."

He tapped a finger beneath her chin, lifting her face up to his until their lips were almost touching.

"What's the point of having the full range of my power if not to spoil you? Convince the bank you paid off your house . . . take you on extravagant vacations . . . buy you all the pretty things you desire . . . I'm here to serve." He brushed a kiss onto her lips as she rolled her eyes.

"And by spoil *me* you mean send my sister off by herself so we can have more alone time, here, together?" she quipped.

It was his turn to roll his eyes. "We're joining her only a few weeks later, angel. And I'll need every second of that time to do all the things that I want to do to you. On every surface in this house."

Her pulse raced with excitement as she gave him a mock pout and asked, "You really need only a few weeks for what you have planned?"

He grinned like the Prince of the Devils he was and leaned down to press kisses along her jawline. His next words made her shiver.

"Actually, I'll need every second of the eternity you promised me to do what I have planned for you."

She flushed as he dipped her back in a heated kiss, making her head spin.

Someone cleared their throat from across the room.

"There are ten rooms in this house with locks on the doors if you're going to do this in the middle of the day," Genevieve told them.

"There you are!" Ophelia said as she disentangled herself from Salem's arms to rush over to Genevieve with the envelope. "We have a surprise for you!"

Genevieve lifted a brow as she lifted open the flap of the envelope and pulled out its contents. A surprised squeal pierced through the room, and when Ophelia glanced back at Salem, she saw that he looked quite pleased with the reaction.

"You mean it?" Genevieve implored.

Ophelia nodded enthusiastically.

Genevieve dashed out of the room. "I have to start planning what to pack!"

Ophelia laughed, and Salem came up to embrace her from behind.

"Now, where were we?" he murmured.

"I think you were about to try and ruin my soul and ravish my body."

"Ravish your body, yes. But I think there are a few things I'd rather ruin other than your soul..." He moved her toward the velvet settee, sitting down and pulling her atop him so she was straddling his lap. "This couch for starters."

He made a trail of kisses down her throat to her chest, right above the top of her corset line. Then he moved to brush his lips over her bare shoulders and arms, kissing each of the golden stars she had earned in Phantasma. Nine permanent reminders on her skin of what they'd done together.

"You're absolutely incorrigible," she hummed as she leaned her palms on his chest.

"You love it."

She turned her head to nip at his bottom lip. "Devil."

"Angel," he drawled.

She kissed him then, long and slow, reveling in the little piece of heaven she saved from the dark depths of Hell.

A Note from the Author on OCD

I like to say the idea of Phantasma came to me all at once, hitting me like a ton of bricks one cloudy afternoon in November 2021, but truly, my experience with obsessive-compulsive disorder has been building to this story for a very long time.

During the process of brainstorming the sort of adult romance I wanted to debut with, I was going through a period where my obsessive-compulsive tendencies were flaring up more than usual and the voices in my head were getting a little too bold. To my friends, these compulsions were alarming little anecdotes over lunch—'*that sounds like a horror movie*' one of them said (affectionately)—which is funny because, to me, someone who has lived with OCD my entire life, it was just another day of being unfazed by the increasingly creative scenarios my mind likes to conjure.

OCD has such a wide range of symptoms that it makes every person's experience with it different. Unfortunately, it has also become a commonly misused term conflated with the idea of being overly neat and clean, when in reality a lot of people with OCD have much darker symptoms. In my experience this has made explaining the real effects of OCD very hard as well as making it more difficult for people to regard the condition seriously. It's so important to me to convey, with the utmost sincerity, that I know people are not doing this to be malicious! Because of the misuse of the term, however, some of the ways this disorder is shown in this book may come off as exaggerated or dramatic—but the details of Ophelia's OCD are drawn directly from experiences that I, or someone I know who shares my condition, have had firsthand. And it's still only a fraction of the symptoms we live with daily.

Ophelia's story is a love letter to my journey of getting comfortable being in my own head (as well as my adoration for Gothic aesthetics and hot ghosts). And while her experience with OCD, *my* experience with OCD, might look a lot different from someone else's, I hope that the same message rings clear: struggling with your mental health does not make you unworthy of love. And I hope the people you surround yourself with are the sort of people who know that, too.

ACKNOWLEDGMENTS

Hello friends, both old and new, and welcome to this first venture of mine into the world of adult romance. I'm so grateful you're here. I started writing *Phantasma* in 2021 and never did I imagine all the things that would happen on the way to it being in your hands. Shortly after selling this book, I got really, really sick. I wrote *Phantasma* over a period of time when staying awake for more than three hours a day was a grueling challenge and I really worried for a while that I would never be able to get through. But Ophelia and Blackwell pulled me through their story and gave me a purpose when I desperately needed one.

To my partner, Iz, for being an absolute goddamn angel every fucking day of your life (this is an adult book so I can curse in my acknowledgment section now, right?). I think I speak for everyone who's ever known us together when I say I would not be a functioning human being if it wasn't for you. I swear I'll finally get that matching tattoo I was supposed to get six years ago to show my gratefulness for you getting me through 2023.

To my angel of an agent, Emily Forney, for believing in this story from the moment I pitched it to you. Knowing exactly the vibe I meant when I said grown-up Danny Phantom meets Gothic New Orleans. And for all the weight you carried during such a rough time for me, while always making me feel like a human when I worried I'm only good if I'm a creative machine. You're the best business partner I could have ever asked for. Always an icon.

To my editor, Jack Renninson, for really *getting* the soul of this book and for your excellent vision and guidance on this haunting adventure. I am so grateful you took a chance on this spooky, bloody romance and am endlessly thankful for the great care you took in working on these characters and believing this story could be something really cool.

To the rest of my team at Second Sky and Bookouture for being absolutely incredible every step of the way. Y'all made me feel so welcomed right away and I enjoyed working with you immensely. To my team at Grand Central and Forever, especially my editor, Sam, for giving this book such wonderful opportunities.

To all my friends who read the early versions of this book or let me gush to them about all my haunting ideas for it over and over again: Darci, Em, Andrea, Dee, Gabi, Raye, Elba, Becca, Night, and Cath. Thanks for always letting me talk too much.

To Dee, again, because you deserve all the thanks in the world for not only reading this very early on but for FaceTiming me for five hours straight while I went *point by point* through my outline to make sure I was doing Ophelia's story justice. You are my romantasy queen, the person I looked forward to reading this most, and I just utterly adore you.

To my sister-in-law, Lily, for reading a very early, messy draft of this book and being so excited for it. You're always the person I want to send my books to first. Isaac has given me so many things in this lifetime and the coolest big sister ever is one of my favorites.

To Dev and Loretta for beta reading this, giving me feedback and notes as well as all your excitement and enthusiasm. Truly so fortunate to have made you both as friends when I did and for all of our nerdy book talks and fangirling.

To my family. Although, none of you should actually be

reading these acknowledgments, because you listened to me when I said not to read this book right? *Right?* Because this is as tame as I'm ever going to be with my smut again. A warning to all.

To every bookstore, bookseller, reader, and librarian who has ever supported one of my books or my career—you make continuing my dreams possible every single day with your reviews, photos, recommendations, and support. Endlessly adore everyone who makes this community warm even when the industry and world can get a little too cold. Also, to all of my author friends, of which there are now too many of you to name, thank you for being such incredible people to work alongside and cheer on. Nothing makes me happier than seeing you all doing such amazing things.

To the cities of Lafayette and New Orleans for inspiring such magic. To the ghosts of my childhood for keeping me company.

To the real Ophelia—you are the goodest, fluffiest, prettiest girl in the whole world. Also to Delphine, Kai, and Gemini, of course, for all the cuddles. For everyone just catching on—I do in fact name my book characters after my dogs because they will never disappoint me, and I will never stop!

And finally, to those of you who also live with OCD—sometimes, our heads can be scary places to live, and I hope if you related to anything Ophelia goes through in this book with her own OCD, maybe you feel a little less alone. All my love.

ABOUT THE AUTHOR

Kaylie Smith (she/they) is a writer and lover of all things fantasy. They grew up in Louisiana where they frequently haunted bookstores and practiced her craft. After college she decided to pursue her lifelong dream of becoming an author, but when she isn't writing or reading, she can be found at home with her menagerie of animals, fussing over their houseplants, or annoying people about astrology.

You can learn more at:
KaylieSmithBooks.com
Instagram @KaylSMoon
TikTok @KaylSMoon
X @KaylSMoon